Isolation Island

A Johnny Moscato Novel

This book is a work of fiction. Any references to historical events, real people, or locales are used fictitiously. Names, characters, places and incidents are product of the author's imagination, and any resemblance to actual events, locales, or persons, living or dead, is entirely coincidental.

Copyright GR Managment Johnny Moscato © 2021

All rights reserved. No part of this book may be reproduced or transmitted in any form or by any means, electronic or mechanical, including photocopying, recording, or by any information storage and retrieval system, without permission in writing from the copyright owner.

Also from
Johnny Moscato:

The Project

Jimmy Darwin

The Project 2

No one has ever survived life.

The Rules

Isolation Island is a contest of survival and endurance. The remote island is located in the northern Pacific temperate zone with over sixty miles of coastline, an unforgiving climate, and formidable wildlife including black bears, wolves, moose, and wild boar.

Each contestant is dropped ashore alone, miles away from the others—no assistance, no production crew. The contestants must document their own journey with provided camera equipment. They must survive by themselves as long as they can and outlast everyone else. Last man or woman standing will win one million dollars.

Each contestant can bring twenty-five pounds of clothing and the following items:

1. Axe
2. Knife
3. Cooking pot and pan
4. Flint/ferro rod
5. 2 Tarps
6. Canteen
7. Sleeping bag
8. Flashlight/headlamp
9. Paracord/fishing line/twine
10. Fishing hooks
11. Weapon- choice of bow and arrows or slingshot.
12. Gill net

*In addition, each contestant is given an official Isolation Island first aid kit, basic hygiene kit, bear spray, and one emergency flare.

Unbeknownst to the contestants, bonus items are hidden around the island. Players will have to decipher a map or series of clues to find the buried treasure.

Contestants can tap out at any time by contacting the

production crew via the provided walkie-talkie. The contestants will have no contact with each other or the crew, otherwise. Contact with the crew, including a call for medical aid, will result in an automatic tap out.

The contestants will face many challenges including wild animals and the weather as autumn sets in, but perhaps the biggest challenge will be the days, weeks, or even months of isolation.

How long can a person survive in the wilderness on their own?

Ten contestants.
No time limit.
One million dollars.
One winner.
Who has the will and the skills to survive *Isolation Island*?

Chapter 1

Day 14

Routine Checkup

Producer Sharon Rose checked her makeup, bobbing around to catch her reflection in her compact. She wasn't working on the type of show that required a makeup artist. Isolation Island was meant to be rough and gritty and wild, but Sharon wasn't one of the contestants. She wouldn't leave her house to get the mail without makeup, the aura of professionalism and success a constant focus to the point of obsession.

A jolt from the Zodiac Medline bouncing over ocean waves knocked the compact out of her hand. Dr. Ben Rodney chivalrously lunged to pick it up for her, flashing a smile and a subtle bow of his head as he handed it to her. Page Hawkins, Sharon's personal assistant, rolled her eyes and shook her head, hidden behind her boss on a seat in the back of the boat, the *stern* to nautical enthusiasts, but Page was neither nautical nor enthusiastic. She was just trying to keep a phony smile on her face without losing her lunch.

Up front, cameraman Dyson Wolski shot B-footage of the Pacific Ocean and broad views of the island. Hutchinson Adalwolf, aka 'Hutch', a veteran of survival entertainment from both sides of the camera, was at the wheel of the Medline heading toward the shore where, fourteen days earlier, they had inserted contestant Derrick Bond.

Much to the surprise of the production crew, there had been no communication from any of the ten contestants since they were inserted individually around the island (locations selected at random). The fact that no one had tapped out in the first two weeks was a point of pride for the Producer. It was confirmation that she picked the right survivalists to participate in the challenge. As per the schedule, Day 14 called for the beginning of routine checkups for each contestant. The medical staff, consisting of Dr. Rodney and a backup doctor who remained on the Mothership—the production crew's floating home base—were charged with determining each contestant's physical condition and ability to continue the challenge. Survivalists can be a stubborn lot, unwilling to quit and often unable to recognize their own weaknesses. Dr. Rodney was there for the safety and protection of everyone involved with reality show in its first season of production.

The overcast sky had turned darker since they had left the Mothership, threatening to start dumping rain any minute. The cold, choppy Pacific seemed determined to smash the Medline against the rocky shore ahead. Hutch stayed calm and took his time, finessing his way through the maze of rocks and waves.

"Watch out for the rocks," Sharon shouted, stating the obvious with one hand mashing the top of her khaki sun hat to her head. The wide rim folded in the wind every time she turned her head, slapping her nauseated face. An annoyed frown punctuated every whack, but at least her makeup looked fantastic.

Hutch shook his head and returned a sarcastic, "Thanks a lot." He had tired of her two-cent additions to every situation by the middle of Day 1. She was technically in charge, but she knew nothing about survival and had yet to prove she knew anything about producing a television show. All she seemed to display is an expert ability to boss people around, an obsessive desire for control.

Hutch was not the type of man who relied on anyone but himself in difficult situations. He allowed himself to roll his eyes at the sight of Sharon's ridiculous hat for a quick moment captured by Dyson's ever-present camera, but wasted no time refocusing himself on the task at hand. One false move and the waves would take control of the boat. He throttled his way through, finding the perfect spot he had used to drop off contestant Derrick Bond on Day 1.

Sharon let a smile escape for a moment. She was quite proud of herself, taking false-credit for the selection of contestants. The fact that no one had tapped out in the first fourteen days was impressive, indeed—a testament to the selection process Hutch's predecessor, Nelson Greely, had actually developed. Nelson and Sharon had had a falling out days before they were due to ship out.

Hutch, always up for an adventure, had graciously stepped in, more than capable of filling Greely's shoes.

Hutch eased the Medline in for a soft landing, making it look much easier than it really was. Dyson jumped off first with his camera in order to get a shot of the rest of them getting off the boat.

Hutch jumped off and offered a hand to help Sharon which she refused. Her left foot failed to clear the side of the boat on the way off, hooking on the edge. She belly-flopped and face-planted in the gray sand. The shallow end of a wave petering out gave her a wash of cold saltwater and stole her hat. Hutch tried to help her up, but she shoved him away, somehow angry with his offers to lend a hand.

Sharon stood up, shook her wet arms, and engaged the ocean in its game of keep away with her hat. One wave pulled the hat away, lost force and receded. The next wave pushed the hat back toward shore, but away from her.

Dyson captured the silly spectacle, a childish grin peeking out from behind his camera.

Hutch shook his head and helped the rest of the passengers off the boat—Page, followed by two backpacks and Dr. Rodney. They watched Sharon for a moment. She was getting wetter and colder chasing her hat on the waves. Page lunged in and snatched it in one quick motion, her waterproof boots proving their worth.

"I would have gotten it myself," Sharon insisted, eyes darting from person to person, looking for any hint of a smile or snicker.

Dyson had turned away, pretending he saw nothing. He pointed his camera up to the gray sky, resting it on his shoulder with an oblivious look on his face, as if assessing lighting and his next shot.

Sharon grabbed the hat out of Page's hand and returned it to her head. "You better not have filmed that," she threatened with a finger pointed at Dyson's back as saltwater dripped down her face from the hat.

"Filmed what?" Dyson asked, continuing before Sharon could answer. "I'm going to go ahead so I can get a good shot of all of you walking through the woods on the way to Derrick's camp," he added.

The two women worked on wiping the sand off Sharon's navy

blue pants suit—a stubborn choice of attire, but she "had to look professional".

Hutch and Dr. Rodney sorted their backpacks.

"Sharon, you're drenched," Page pointed out. "Maybe you should change clothes."

Sharon replied, "I didn't bring a change of clothes. I'll be fine." She slung her waterlogged leather purse over her shoulder.

"I brought a change of clothes for you," Page said, reaching a hand into her oversized canvas bag.

Page was always prepared. She knew Sharon's clothes weren't practical for hiking through the forest. She had barely succeeded in convincing her boss to wear the black, waterproof hiking boots purchased by Page specifically for trips to Isolation Island.

"I'm fine," Sharon insisted. "Let's just get this done."

Sharon had alerted Derrick via radio the day before that they'd be coming to do a routine medical checkup—the only in-person human contact the competitors would have. The only other time anyone had verbal contact with the contestants was to gather the GPS coordinates for their camp locations. Each contestant was allowed to choose where to set up camp, provided it fell within their territory which was sizeable. They could also move their camp if they wanted. Their territories were large enough to ensure they wouldn't encroach on another contestant's territory without a lengthy hike and encountering barriers like rivers and impassable cliffs.

Hutch led the way to Derrick's camp and found it with ease less than half a mile from shore, right where Derrick had reported on Day 1. The only problem was Derrick wasn't there.

The camp was set up well. A simple lean-to shelter made with a blue tarp "leaning to" the trunk of a large fallen oak tree sprawled across a grassy channel. Hutch checked the shelter, hoping to find Derrick sleeping, but only found an empty "nest" made of leaves and pine needles under a black and gray sleeping bag laid out in the little cubby under the tree trunk.

The fire just outside the entrance to the shelter was nothing more than a pile of white ashes, growing wetter as the rain turned from a drizzle to a shower. A rumble of thunder growled a warning, expanding across the sky. A full-blown storm could be on its way.

Dyson spun slowly, filming the camp from within and then focused on close-ups of the shelter, fire pit, and various tools that had been left out in the now steady rain. An axe was lying in the grass. An empty pot turned on its side sat on the edge of the ashes from the burnt-out fire. Derrick's canteen was hanging by its strap from a broken branch jutting from the giant tree trunk that was part of his shelter.

Page pulled an umbrella out of her bag and opened it to shelter herself and Sharon. "Doc, get under this," she said, waving him over to where Sharon had sat down on the rings of a small log standing on end which Derrick must have been using as a stool.

"I'm okay. Thanks," Dr. Rodney replied, ignoring the rain in favor of looking into the surrounding forest. The rain clouds produced a dusk-like atmosphere, strange and ominous for mid-morning.

"Well? Where the hell is he?" Sharon asked.

Hutch was busy examining the state of the camp for any indication of where Derrick might have gone, but the weather held the biggest clue. "I don't know. He should be curled up in his shelter to stay dry."

"Maybe he went for firewood," Page guessed.

Hutch explained, "There's a pile of dry firewood in the corner of the shelter. I doubt he'd go out for firewood while it's raining."

"He probably went out before it started raining," Page reasoned.

"Derrrrriiiiick!" Dr. Rodney shouted into the woods. He tilted his baseball cap back on his head revealing the stubble making its way back from his last shave. He straightened his posture as if it would improve his hearing, extending to his full six foot four inches. He called out again and listened for a reply, but little could be heard over the sound of raindrops dancing on leaves.

Hutch pulled his radio off his belt and pressed the call button. "Derrick, come in. We're waiting for you at your camp." His voice echoed nearby.

Dyson pulled his attention off his camerawork and shared an alerted look with DocRod (as the good doctor was often referred to).

Hutch stuck his head into the shelter and pressed the talk button again. A fuzzy squelch of feedback gave away the position of Derrick's radio. Hutch found it covered by the flap of the sleeping bag, pulled it out and held it up for everyone else to see.

All the contestants had been lectured extensively on the importance of keeping their only means of communication with them at all times in case of emergency. Derrick shouldn't have left camp without it, not even to take a leak.

Dr. Rodney shared a concerned look with Hutch and with a sense of urgency in their voices, they took turns screaming his name in various directions, hoping one of their voices could carry to Derrick's ears.

There was no reply, save for the rain pelting everything in its path. They circled the camp's perimeter, shouting his name again and again receiving no reply.

Sharon showed no concern. She pulled off her left boot and turned it over to empty it. Two small pebbles fell out. Hutch stared at her with an aggravated look of disgust on his face.

"What?" she asked, noticing the searing daggers being shot in her direction.

"This is precisely why I insisted on having each contestant wear a GPS tracker," Hutch said in a tone intended to remind everyone.

Sharon and Hutch had argued over many safety issues on the journey to Isolation Island. In addition to the GPS built into the radio each contestant carried, Hutch advised embedding a GPS tracker in a necklace or bracelet to be worn at all times, but he had joined the project too late to accomplish all the safety precautions he would have normally overseen. Moreover, Sharon wasn't budging on the budget. It was readily apparent to Hutch why Nelson Greely, the previous technical advisor had quit.

"It's an island. He can't get lost. He'll come back," Sharon insisted. "He's not going to stay out in this rain forever."

"He could be injured," the doctor suggested.

"He could be dead," Hutch added. "If he had been equipped with a GPS tracker, we could locate him easily and…"

"He's fine," Sharon stood firm. "You're overreacting. Let's just wait here for a while. He *has to* come back." She examined the inside of her shoe, sticking a finger in to dislodge any other pebbles or debris. One last shake and a tap was enough to satisfy her. She put the shoe back on, almost falling off the narrow log in the process.

Dyson chimed in with his own observation. "There's some camera equipment missing. He must have taken it with him."

"But, not his canteen?" Hutch pointed out. "I'm going to look for him."

"And how do you think you're going to do that?" Sharon asked in a dubious tone.

"He's been here fourteen days. He's worn several paths—the one I picked up from shore and followed here, there's two more going in opposite directions, east and west, and there's probably another one branching off one of those, going north," Hutch explained, using karate-chop motions with his hands to point out the trails he could see.

Sharon removed her hat and ran her fingers through her jet-black hair trying to fluff the wetness away, seemingly more concerned with her appearance than the missing contestant. "No. I say we stay here and wait. He's going to come back soon. If you go walking off into the woods and Derrick comes back, we'll have to go looking for you."

"If he comes back, just call me. I've got my radio. I'm going," Hutch insisted, turning to follow the east trail without leaving time for another objection.

Sharon stood, knocking her head into the umbrella Page was still holding. "Let me remind you who's in charge here," Sharon said, trying to assert dominance. "*You* work for *me* and I'm ordering you to stay here and wait for Derrick to come back as he most definitely will."

Hutch turned and charged over as if he were out for blood. "When we're on this island, in the wild, *I'm* the one in charge. That's why you hired me. My job and my obligation is to these ten survivalists first and foremost. I'm not here to follow your orders. I'm here to support them, not you."

Disgust forced him to turn his head away. He looked to the sky to compose himself, the rain bouncing off his face not helping. "This is no joke," he continued, resetting his tone, but with each sentence that followed his aggravation built up again. "It's not a controlled environment. I know all you care about is your damn TV show, but you're not playing with actors on a set in Hollywood. These are real people out here in a dangerous environment. I'm not going to sit around and wait for a missing person to show up on his own. This is *not* your call."

Without further discussion or waiting for Sharon's approval, Hutch stormed off into the woods. Dyson hurried after him, camera ready on his shoulder.

The doctor followed, shouting, "Wait up."

Dyson stopped before he disappeared into the bush and waited for Dr. Rodney to catch up.

DocRod was insistent. "You wait here with the girls. I'll go with Hutch in case Derrick needs medical assistance."

Sharon frowned at the Doc's use of the word *girls* but didn't interject. She turned to Page with a bitter taste in her mouth. "What is it about the great outdoors that makes men decide they're in charge?" she asked rhetorically.

It was obvious Dyson wasn't happy to stay behind but he agreed. Stepping slowly backward, he filmed the doctor jogging away and being swallowed by the forest.

A last shout rang out. "Hutch, wait up. I'm coming with you," the doctor said.

Dyson relaxed his camera and turned toward Sharon, high stepping over some tall grass. "That'll be a nice segment," he reassured her through anxious breath. "If they find Derrick, that is."

*****

Hutch and Doc trudged along the trail worn by either Derrick, animals, or all the above. The abundance of ferns combined with large stones and boulders gave the forest a strange, prehistoric eeriness, like being pulled back in time.

There were signs of human activity everywhere—thin trees chopped to a blunt end, a small, untriggered deadfall trap, shoeprints in the process of washing away in the rain. There was no indication of a trail as recent as that morning but, on a worn path in the rain it was difficult to pick up the scent.

"Where do you think he went?" Doc asked, head on a swivel in search.

"Maybe the more important question is, why did he leave camp in the rain?" Hutch replied. He stopped short and held up a hand, indicating 'stop and shut up'.

"What?" Doc whispered, head ducked and darting around.

Hutch held a finger to his lips. "Shh." His eyes widened, head tilted, searching for a sound.

The snap of a twig crackled somewhere under the cover of fluctuating rain. It was starting to let up. Another snap came from the same direction, up an incline to their left, followed by an almost inaudible swooshing. Hutch turned his ear toward the noise.

Another twig snapped.

Hutch whipped his head around to get eyes on the area it came from. He ducked a bit to catch a glimpse of a dark patch that didn't belong to a tree or a bush. It moved out of view, behind the bush, heading in the opposite direction than they were walking. The brush voiced the indication of a large intruder walking at a casual pace.

Doc opened his mouth, but Hutch signaled for quiet again and then pointed uphill at a large black bear's butt waddling across an open break in the woods. It didn't look back at them or give any indication it was aware of their presence, but it carried something in its mouth.

The bear stopped and dropped its cargo, producing a thump on the ground. Hutch and Doc craned their necks to watch, careful not to make a sound. Neither could see what it was messing with.

The bear ducked its head out of sight, toward the ground, and raised back up against an unseen resistance producing the unmistakable sound of tearing cloth. A long, steady, heavy tear in one motion.

Hutch's heart sank. There was only one place a bear could get a hold of cloth. Technically, ten places, as there were ten contestants on Isolation Island. Either way, it added up to contact with a human and that's never a good sign.

Hutch and Doc threw identical looks at each other. The bear let go and ducked down again for a moment. Its face returned to view as it turned its head around, snout up, sniffing the air as if picking up an interesting scent.

Hutch and Doc remained frozen in place.

Hutch's heart sank again with the sight of the bear's snout, its light tan color a standard deviation from the black body. But, it was the red stains around the mouth that struck fear into both men.

The bear licked its chops, dipped its head and waddled away. Its prize not visible from Hutch's vantage point, but enough evidence for alarm. He listened for the animal's direction, concerned for both Derrick and everyone back at camp. The bear hopped off the path it had been on and traversed thicker terrain, uphill.

Hutch and Doc waited for the bear's noises to fade from earshot, making sure it was walking away from camp and then continued on their previously chosen path.

Was Derrick alive? In one piece? Neither man was willing to ask the questions out loud. Things were looking grim and it showed on their faces. Would they find him at all or would they need DNA tests to identify his meager remains?

Hutch tried to stay positive, but the realist in him prepared for a gruesome scene. He veered in the direction the bear had come from, mind wandering, rehearsing worst case scenarios and emergency protocols.

Doc didn't say a word. He wasn't a survivalist, but common sense dictated a list of horrible things that could have taken Derrick out of the competition or taken his life.

DocRod was an experienced medic, but animal attacks weren't exactly a common occurrence in his hometown of Baltimore. What would a bear attack victim look like? The risk of exsanguination—severe blood loss from multiple wounds—would be the main concern, but he wasn't equipped to perform a transfusion. The best he could hope for was stopping the bleeding before his patient bled out.

A giant crow, its feathers black as coal, fluttered about in the distance, chased by a smaller crow from limb to limb of a towering oak tree. The smaller squawked a complaint as it lunged at the larger bird. Cawing filled the air with the flyover of a long chain of crows racing each other. They seemed to be drawn to a common direction.

The two fighting birds carried on as Hutch and Doc approached. Hutch was more interested in where the other crows were headed. The fighting crows shrieked at each other, flying low above the men. The larger bird dropped the item the two had been squabbling over. It hurled toward the ground like a tiny comet—a debris-covered ball trailed by a fleshy tail. It bounced off Hutch's hat and flopped down onto his foot. The object, a human eye with its optic nerve still attached stared up at him, literally.

Hutch let out a reflexive gasp and jerked his foot, flinging the eyeball in the air. It landed on the path, taking a short roll before the fighting crows swooped down, each grabbing an end. The larger crow pulled the eyeball, the smaller pulled the optic nerve and a gruesome tug-of-war ensued until the 'rope' tore. The large crow swallowed the eye in one simultaneous fling and gulp down its gullet. The other crow launched into flight with its consolation prize.

"Did that just happen?" Doc asked, a shaky, nauseated quiver to his voice despite his medical experience with detached body parts.

Hutch looked over his shoulder. "That *was* a human eye. Right?"

"It sure looked human," Doc verified.

Things were looking bleaker for Derrick. Hutch suggested they follow the crows to find the eyeball's owner. They left the beaten path, traversing through the thick vegetation, their feet slipping on the loose, wet leaves carpeting the ground as they pulled themselves uphill. They were on course to intersect the bear's route. The rain picked up again, shifting angles with every gust of wind.

The bear's route took them around a bend with a towering rock wall. Rainwater rushed off in little, scattered waterfalls, splashing down on another worn game trail. They followed the new trail in the direction the crows had been flying. The rain suddenly began to slow to a drizzle as if being turned down by a spigot.

The trail leveled out and widened to a clearing under a tree with low, long reaching limbs which provided a natural umbrella. Hutch stopped short. He had found the crows' destination. They were fluttering in groups on the ground, fighting over scraps.

Dr. Rodney stopped next to Hutch, looked up and then lunged forward, arms flailing, shooing the birds away. "Get out of here," he shouted, running in a circle to clear the area under the tree.

He was careful not to fall into one of the many holes dug in the ground near the tree. He counted at least five holes of varying depths, but his eyes were drawn back up the tree.

Above Dr. Rodney, a torso with shredded limbs hung from a low-lying branch. The legs had been chewed off at the knees, pant legs and all. The eyeless head slumped over a noose made from the standard-issue cordage allotted to each contestant. Chunks of flesh were missing from the eyeless face.

The only recognizable part of his body was the tattoo on his one remaining forearm—an eagle sitting atop a faded red, white, and blue globe with a banner bearing the acronym USMC—United States Marine Corps.

They had found Derrick Bond.

Hutch looked up at the body, inching forward as he searched for clues that might explain how Derrick came to be hanging there. There was only one obvious conclusion.

Doc was the first to say it out loud. "He killed himself?" A mixture of sadness and confusion overcame his face.

Hutch maintained his poker face. "The bears didn't tie him up there, that's for sure."

"Why would he kill himself in the middle of the competition, the night before a routine medical check? It doesn't make any sense," Doc thought out loud.

Hutch had no answers. He pulled his radio out and pressed the talk button "Sharon. Come in."

After a moment of squelch, a reply came. "This is Page. Over."

Hutch took a deep breath and looked at the hanging man again before replying. How would he break the news? What would it mean for the game? Did the game even matter anymore? A man was dead.

Hutch pressed the talk button again and simply stated, "We found Derrick Bond."

DERRICK BOND

Day 1

9:04am

Age: 29
Occupation: ex-Marine
Home: Texas
Status: Single

"Woooooooooooo!!" former Marine Sargent Derrick Bond howled, celebrating the moment his boots were on the ground of Isolation Island's sandy shore. The Zodiac Medline that dropped him off could be seen pulling away in the distance as the stocky, 5'9" bulldog filmed his first moments of the game. He was all smiles and full of energy. "Pumped up," as he described it for the camera he was using to film himself.

After two tours in arid Afghanistan, the wet, chilly northern Pacific island was a welcomed change. Just knowing a body of water was close by soothed his mind. He never wanted to go back to the desert again. He had lost too many friends there.

"Let the games begin," he declared, his wide, flat-nosed profile filling half the camera shot as he walked up the shore. His boots squeaked with every slip on the slimy greenish gray stones blocking his way to the tree line. He lost his balance sending the camera shot into a whirling blur for a moment before catching himself.

"Whoa. That was close. The last thing you want out here is an injury," he lectured. "I'm going to have to be extra careful. These rocks are slippery." He wiped his hand on the dark green USMC shirt he was wearing under his forest camouflage coat and then rubbed his nose. "High tide is coming in. I better get my gear off the beach."

He turned around and panned the camera right to left for a view of the vast, desolate ocean. The Medline was gone from view and with it his last contact with humanity for weeks or months, however long he could endure. None of the contestants knew what the others were doing or how long they'd last. They wouldn't be notified when people tapped out of the competition or any other progress.

Derrick took another minute to absorb the sight. It wasn't easy to get so far from civilization. The vastness of the ocean on one side, a dark, imposing forest on the other beckoning and threatening at the same time.

"Wow. Listen to that." He paused to capture the calm through the camera's microphone. "It's eerily quiet out here, even with the sound of the ocean. It's weird. The sound of waves is usually soothing, but here…it's like the Pacific is quietly waiting for a chance to swallow you up. Creepy."

A look of worry filled his eyes as they glassed over. The novelty of the contest had worn off in an instant. He sighed and swallowed hard. Reality hit him like a ton of bricks. This was no joke. He had to survive on this deserted island on his own. No food rations. No shelter, but what he could build. No electricity. No internet. No supermarkets. No human contact.

He turned the camera back to a close up of his face. "I better get started," he said, the words eaten by the silence. His equipment was more than one person could carry. He cleared it off the sandy part of the beach first.

Next, he had to explore and pick a place to set up camp. He put his backpack on and kept the camera rolling as he hiked through the woods, looking for the perfect spot or, at least, something to get him through the night. There were limited hours of daylight and he couldn't afford to waste them wandering around. Decisiveness was key in the wild. If you take too long making a decision, it could kill you.

"My survival strategy for this game is gonna be all out," he explained to the camera. "I'm a big, muscular guy and I need to use that to my advantage, but it could be a disadvantage. I'm gonna need to eat as much as possible to fuel these muscles. It ain't gonna be easy, but that's what I'm gonna do. If I can't find enough food, I'm done, no matter what else happens. So, I'm gonna hunt, fish, set traps, whatever I gotta do to get food."

He was already breathing heavy from the exertion of hauling

his equipment. He stopped for a moment to look around.

"I can't live off of plants out here. I'm gonna need fish, meat—protein. Some guys prefer to conserve energy, doing as little as possible to get by, but that ain't me. I'm going all in on eating and working hard. If I don't succeed on the food front, I'll just have to tap out. I'm not gonna cry about it. I didn't come out here to lose, but I didn't come out here to sit around and slowly starve, either. Hard work and a positive attitude. That's what it takes to survive in the wilderness."

He continued on until he came to a clearing and the trunk of a large, downed oak tree. It was strewn across a natural, bowl-like depression in the ground.

"I like this. This tree ain't going nowhere," he said with a hearty slap of the trunk. "I can incorporate this into my shelter," he added, ducking to look under the tree. It formed a small tunnel, large enough for a four-foot person to walk under. Derrick's gears started turning.

"I can stuff up the other side of this hole with branches and leaves and use the tarp to create a lean-to shelter on this side. It's good enough for a temporary shelter, but I think I can convert it into something more permanent."

He paused to assess the rest of the area. It was perfect. An unobstructed, flat area fanned out from the downed tree, creating a funnel effect with a small hill on the left and another on the right.

Derrick presented the area to the camera, then turned it on himself. "It's perfect," he said with a close-up of half his face. His warm breath fogged the lens for a moment. "This is where I'll be calling home for the next few months."

He turned the camera off and returned to shore to collect the rest of his supplies.

10:45am

Derrick returned excited after his fourth and final trip to shore. He hurried to the camera with a large, glass bottle in his hand. He turned the camera on and began to film.

With a close-up of his face, he said, "Look what I found."

He turned the camera on his prize. The tinted green bottle was corked to protect a rolled up piece of paper inside.

"On my last trip to get my stuff off the beach," he explained, fumbling the camera as he sat himself down in the grass where his shelter would soon be built. "It suddenly dawned on me to take a different path, so that I could explore a little more."

He set the camera down, pointing up from the ground. He held the bottle up and jiggled it on display.

"That's how I found this little beauty. It was hanging from a tree. I got the little rope it was hanging from, too. The rules say we can use anything we find on Isolation Island, so...bonus."

He pulled a tangled mess of twine from his jacket pocket and showed it to the camera.

"This bottle will be useful for carrying water. I can pretend it's champagne. I can even boil water in it, if need be. But, what's most exciting, is *this*."

He held the bottle up again to point out the scroll inside, jiggling it around to make a rattling noise.

"There's a message inside," the enthusiastic survivalist announced, pulling the cork out with a ceremonious pop. He shook the bottle around trying to get the paper out the narrow neck.

"I wonder what it could be. A treasure map? An SOS message from some castaway stranded on an island far, far away?"

The rolled up piece of paper slid out the neck of the bottle. Derrick untied the twine that held the message closed and unrolled the scroll. He flattened it out on his lap.

"I was right the first time. It's a treasure map," he said, looking the paper up and down before lifting it to show the camera.

The parchment, deliberately weathered for effect, showed a series of symbols. An arrow pointing to the top of the page was marked with the letter N for north. There was a rocky shore indicated by a group of black boulders bordering wavy lines indicative of water, probably meant to represent Derrick's insertion point. He recalled seeing the large boulders near the sandy part of shore. A long, winding line represented a creek or river stretching from the edge of the paper down to the west of the rocky shore.

There were different types of trees—generic trees with a trunk topped by broccoli crowns, crudely drrawn pine trees, and trunks with branches without anything to represent leaves. One tree stood out above all the others. Its branches were low, reaching out in all directions. Its trunk had a distinctive oval hole toward the bottom. Under this unique tree a short dotted line led to an X. Ten misshapen ovals, like footprints led from the tree's trunk to the X.

"Okay, this is pretty simple. I have to find this fancy tree with all the branches spreading out," Derrick explained for the camera. "It shouldn't be that hard. I'm sure I'll recognize it when I see it."

He turned the parchment on its side, tilting his head as if a slanted perspective would help. Using his index finger, he traced the "river" back and forth, describing it for the camera.

Another symbol caught his eye—the black silhouette of a bear high above the treasure tree. To the east of the river, a distinctive line wound between two groupings of trees. The silhouette of a boar indicated it was most likely a game trail.

Derrick turned the map back to have North pointing up and nodded his head, looking it over one more time.

"When they were telling us the rules, before we came out here," Derrick recollected out loud. "The producer told us we could use anything we found on the island and she made a point to say, 'even buried treasure.' I thought she was joking, but that must be what this map is for. Maybe there's some buried treasure that can help us on our journey on Isolation Island. Or maybe it's money." He squinted one eye shut and switched to a pirate's raspy accent. "Or maybe thar be a chest full-a gold buried by sailors long, long ago. Yarr." He straightened out his face for a second but it contorted into a bright smile and sheer excitement which appeared to be beyond his control or desire to restrain.

The map was useful, not only for finding the treasure. It told Derrick which direction to go to find water. It would save him a lot of time and guesswork.

He imagined a scenario in his head where he ventured off in the wrong direction looking for water and injured himself.

"This is as good as gold," he told the camera, grateful he found the map. He gave the parchment a kiss for good luck and rolled it back up.

The camouflage-clad Marine stood up, dusted himself off and put the scroll in his coat pocket.

"First thing's first," he said. "I need to get settled in and build a temporary shelter before I go running off on a treasure hunt. But, it's something to look forward to," he added, wiggling his eyebrows for the camera. "Something to look forward to can be a very valuable thing out here."

The desolation seemed to swallow him back up for a moment, intruding on his excitement. He broke the spell by getting to work on unpacking his supplies and starting his shelter.

STEPHANIE HAMILTON

Day 1

11:27am

Age: 29
Occupation: Artist
Home: Colorado
Status: Single

Stephanie Hamilton hopped off the Zodiac Medline, dropping onto one of the few rock-free beaches on Isolation Island—a short strip of dense, dark gray sand about fifteen feet from the tree line. Her equipment had already been unloaded, waiting to be hauled to the new home of her choosing. The crew had set up one of her cameras on a tripod to capture the beginning of her bid for the million dollar prize. She kissed her gloved hand and waved goodbye to the crew as the boat backed away.

Turning to the camera she let out a quick sigh and said, "Well, here we go." She was quite adorable bundled up like a first-grader on a snow day. Temperatures on Isolation Island were expected to average in the 40s and 50s for the first month, then plummet as old man winter prepared to took over. If the contestants lasted long enough, they'd eventually have to deal with subzero windchill and an undocumented amount of snow. The uninhabited island was so remote, there wasn't a lot of information available on record.

Stephanie gazed into the seemingly impenetrable forest, thick with spruce, cedar, oak and a wide variety of other trees—an impressive assortment. Isolation Island was quite diverse, given how remote it was. The nearest sign of civilization was over a thousand miles away.

Stephanie threw her backpack over her shoulders and took the camera with her to scope out a good spot to set up camp. She used the time to get used to talking to the camera and introducing herself to the millions of viewers she hoped would one day follow her adventure on television and the internet.

"So, let me introduce myself. My name is Stephanie Hamilton. I'm an artist and free spirit currently floating around Colorado when I'm not on deserted islands. People ask me why I want to do this. Most people can't imagine going twenty-four hours without electricity and the internet." She flashed a heartwarming smile with a hint of nervous tension, but there was more written on her face suggesting she was in her element. She welcomed the excitement of the unknown and the known challenges ahead of her.

"Isolation Island, for me, is all about adventure," she explained as she climbed a steep hill leading away from shore. "It's a chance to test my survival skills. I'm pretty confident that I can, not only survive out here, but thrive. I love the wilderness, obviously. I love being surrounded by green life rather than gray concrete. Mother Nature is the most talented artist and I just can't get enough of admiring her work. Every day is a new work of art."

She lost her balance for a moment, her backpack almost pulling her down backwards. She flailed her arms for leverage until she regained her footing. "Whoa," she said for the benefit of the camera. "That was close. It's slippery out here." She let out a steamy breath and continued more carefully.

"Starting today, this is my new home," she went on, panning the camera across the woods. "I *live* here now. That's the way I'm looking at it. Homesickness is what will do you in out here. I can't be homesick if this is my home. And, who knows, maybe I'll stay here even after the competition is over," she added, punctuated by a giddy laugh. "Let's see." She tilted her head and gave the camera a reserved smile that said, *anything is possible.*

The hike inland was taxing. There were no worn paths. Downed trees covered in slippery moss blocked her desired route. She caught it all on video. Uneven ground, prickly bushes, a million rocks that could turn her ankle and send her out of the game and a canopy full of birds wondering what this creature was doing here.

"The first thing you have to have in your mind at all times is to be careful. You've got to repeat that over and over in your head."

"Be careful..."

"Be careful."

"As hunger and dehydration set in, along with the inevitable sleep deprivation, your mind starts to deteriorate. You're not as sharp as you would be normally and the chances of making careless mistakes skyrocket. An injury out here means your game is over. Any injury could be life threatening. Even a small cut could get infected and send you home."

She paused to look into the camera for emphasis. "And, poof—there goes your chance at a million dollars."

A faint but distinct howl, long and drawn out, froze her, just as she was about to get going again. She held her breath to listen. A second howl answered, a bit louder, but still far away.

"Kind of early in the day to hear wolves," she whispered to the camera, listening for more. Another faint howl came from the opposite direction.

She looked directly into the camera, her face filling the frame. "This is as wild as it gets."

She pulled her beige, knitted hat down to her eyebrows, then pulled it back up into a more comfortable position by yanking it by one of the two teddy bear ears she had added herself. Her little button nose twitched.

"I need to find a good spot to set up camp and get a fire started. Fire is a human's best friend out here..." She paused to consider modifying her statement and added, "as long as you keep it under control." She rubbed the tip of her nose with the shirt sleeve sticking out beyond the cuff of her coat sleeve.

"And...we keep moving forward," she said for self-encouragement before carrying on.

The terrain leveled out, allowing her to pick up her pace. There was still a lot of equipment to move waiting for her at the beach. Not far from the beach, (she wanted to be close as the ocean was a potential source of food) she found a natural grassy clearing on a good, level piece of ground. She set up the camera to take a wide shot and placed herself in the middle, arms stretched out to her sides.

"I think this is my new home," she declared, proudly. Looking around as if performing the act of assessing the area for the benefit of the camera, she added, "I can work with this. This is good." She laid her hands on her hips, elbows pointing out as she surveyed the area some more. A final nod of confirmation punctuated her decision.

"Shelter, fire, water, food," she listed like a survival mantra, counting the elements out with her gloved fingers. "I have to get all my stuff up here and get to work."

12:49pm

Stephanie returned to her chosen plot of land with the last load of equipment, dropping it on the ground in front of the tripod. She pressed record to start a new clip.

"So…I've got all my gear," she said, breathing deep, heavy breaths. She kept her back to the camera, hiding her slim frame behind her bulky, dark blue parka as she moved away, assessing the area again.

"I'm thinking I'll build a debris shelter right here," she said, waving her hands around a clear, flat, grassy area centered for the camera.

She turned to position herself on the virtual front porch of her hypothetical dwelling. Looking down at an imaginary object, she cupped her hands into parenthesis looking back and forth at her hands and behind her. "I'll put my campfire there," she decided.

Turning her head around to point behind her, she added, "I definitely want a fireplace inside the shelter. It's going to get cold, especially at night. So, I want to have two fires. One inside and one outside. That's a lot of firewood, but I'll probably only have one going at a time."

She slid over to where she planned to have the back wall of her debris shelter and mimed a building action. "I'll make the back wall a nice, stone fireplace. Then, build some insulated side walls. I can use pine branches and whatever debris I can find."

She twisted at the waist and spun, describing the shelter in her head and physically placing the invisible parts where they belong. "It'll be a modified debris shelter. I'll make the front wall out of logs. Frame in a doorway. And, eventually make a door. This could work. That'll be my long-term shelter and I can add to it whenever I want."

The excited survivalist rubbed her hands together in

anticipation. "But, first, I need a temporary shelter to live in during the construction phase," she explained and set to work unfolding a tarp.

She repositioned the camera to film a fixed position off to the left of where her permanent shelter would ultimately be built. The camera watched as Stephanie came and went, bringing long, thin sections of tree back one at a time. She used these to form a teepee-like structure and wrapped her tarp around it. It was a long process she wanted to get done before dark.

"Ta-da," she sang when she was done, striking a pose like a Price Is Right model.

She proceeded to describe her creation in a gameshow announcer voice while she waved her hands about like Vanna White punctuating a turned letter.

"Here we have the latest in survival architecture. This simple wikiup shelter seats up to six people comfortably, eight people uncomfortably, and sleeps four people if you stack them right."

She opened the door flap and motioned inside, pointing to her laid out sleeping bag.

"Wall to wall pine bedding combines comfort and practicality for the ultimate in sleep technology, complete with dirty sleeping bag and a handy can of bear spray nearby."

"You'll be the envy of all the other wild animals in the jungle," she concluded with a bright, over-exaggerated smile, batting her eyes.

She stood back and took a more serious look at her work, back to the camera. "It'll do for now," she confirmed and turned to give the camera a gloved thumbs-up.

Overheated from exertion, she took off her coat, revealing navy blue overalls. A long-sleeved thermal shirt with a floral pattern on gray background peeked out from under the overalls.

A breeze blew a strand of long strawberry blonde hair which had found its way out from under her hat. It tickled her face, landing across the bridge of her nose. She tucked it back under her hat, rolled up her sleeves and marched out of the camera's view.

A few minutes later, she returned with an armful of stones. She would use them to circle in a section inside the wikiup to form a fire pit, but not before several more trips to find stones.

When she was done hauling and arranging, she picked up the

camera and brought it inside for a closer view. The stones formed a circle with one side built higher than the other to act as a heat reflector. It was all centered under the opening in the tarp at the peak of the structure so that smoke could vent out.

"Not bad for a day's work," she said, proudly. "Day 1 goals complete. Maybe I can do some exploring before I lose daylight. Maybe find a water source."

SEATON ROGERS

Day 1

12:09pm

Age: 33
Occupation: Screenwriter
Home: Utah
Status: Single

"I really love the outdoors," Seaton Rogers began, kicking off his adventure with his first video clip.

He stood in an awkward pose, stiff and deliberate, his shoulders raised, his hands clenched in fists at his sides. The rim of his forest-camouflaged trapper's hat was pulled a little too low, causing him to tilt his head back to better see through his black-framed glasses. Layers of clothes concealed his lankiness.

I really love the outdoors? he thought, but the words had already escaped and been recorded. An involuntary frown stopped him.

"Cut," he said to an imaginary director or perhaps the future editor. His sourpuss expression captured as the camera continued to do its thing.

"That's stupid. Of course I love the outdoors," he said, pushing his hat a little further up his head so he could see. His glasses got a helping finger to raise them, as well. "I wouldn't be out here if I didn't like the outdoors. Why would anybody who hates the outdoors chose to live outside for an indefinite amount of time? That was a really dumb thing to say. I don't want my very first clip to start off like that. What a first impression?" he rattled off in a hurried, tone as he paced back and forth.

"Okay," he said, stopping and replicating his previous awkward pose, sans the hat in his eyes. He looked like the Big Bad Wolf in the middle of a huff—shoulders raised and squared, chest thrust outward, stomach sucked in—and he was clearly self-conscious about what to do with his arms. They just hung there, frozen with tight little fists, as if he were holding onto two broom handles for dear life.

"Okay, take two, I guess," he said, but the camera had been rolling the entire time.

"My name is Seaton Rogers," he formally introduced—more awkward than formal, adding a stiff little bow. "But, you can call me Sea."

He pursed his lips, head trembling as if he were trying to stop it from shaking but failed miserably. It boiled to an outburst. "Cut," he shouted, frustrated.

"But, you can call me Sea," he said, mocking his own voice with a slow, doofus tone, breaking into a fit of pacing again. "That's stupid. There's no one here to call me anything. Why did I say that? Stupid, stupid." He stopped short of slapping his forehead with two consecutive swings.

A new idea hit him. He stopped pacing and charged the camera to turn it off. Lining up a view to a boulder on the shore, he zoomed in to a frame that would catch him head to toe while sitting on the boulder. He pressed record again and climbed the rock.

His legs dangled off while in the seated position. He swung them nervously, hoping it would pass for playful or, at least, relaxed. He folded his hands and rested them on his lap.

Clearing his throat, he said, louder than necessary, "My name is Seaton Rogers. I'm thirty-three years-old. I'm a Screenwriter and I live in Utah."

Then—silence. He forced a smile, eyebrows knitted. He stayed frozen in position as if waiting for mom to snap a picture he didn't want to take, his mind a blank for possibly the first time in his life.

"Cut," he ordered again, hopping off the rock.

Looking down as if considering each step carefully, he tried to shake the scenes he had recorded out of his head, but only moving on could do that or, at least, pause them in his mind. He turned off the camera and folded up the tripod, mumbling something about the filming part of the challenge before a clearer thought prevailed.

"I'm filming a show I'm never going to watch because I can't stand seeing myself on camera. Good idea," he said, carrying his equipment across the rocks, toward the tree line.

He stopped short, reminding himself to take in the moment. He was here. He was doing it.

This is it.

He turned to look at the ocean, the shore line, left and right.

I've been waiting for this for a long time.

A deep, cleansing breath relaxed him.

I'm all alone.

The mere thought brought a genuine, uncontrollable smile to his face—an introvert's dream had come true.

There's no one here to bother me.

No one to argue with.

No one getting in my way.

Just peace and quiet.

His smile refused to fade and he walked off into the woods with it lighting up his face, the struggles over filming pushed out of his mind. A new thought took over:

Who needs a million dollars when you have an island all to yourself?

He imagined being the last contestant remaining and winning the competition without having to see another person for the next few months.

JILLIAN HILL

Day 1

1:15pm

Age: 45
Occupation: Homemaker
Home: Kentucky
Status: Married, 6 children

"Fer me, the hardest part of this here challenge is gonna be bein' 'way from my family—my husband, we got us six kids, nine little gran-kids," Jill Hill explained with a gravelly, high-pitched southern twang. The camera was set upon a tripod ten yards away, watching as she fashioned an A-frame for the front wall of her temporary shelter.

The spot she had chosen was within view of the bay that started on the east side of Isolation Island and stretched inland, near the middle of the island. The positioning of her camp gave her a panoramic view from the top of a rocky cliff. The price was having to climb a steep hill every time she returned from a trip to the shore, but she was willing to make the tradeoff. It was a relatively safe spot. No reason for animals to venture out on the rounded plateau she had claimed for herself but, if they did, she was virtually cornered.

"People ax me how come I wanna come out here like 'is." Her voice swelled with pride, emphasizing the answer. "I tell 'em it's cuz I wanna show my kids and my gran-kids they can do anything if they believe in theyself. And I want 'em to be proud of me. And I want 'em to know they Gammy's a badass. I can make a fire. I can make a shelter. I can ketch fish," she rambled on while she topped her structure with a tarp creating a long, narrow, wood-reinforced tent.

"That'll do it," she declared with the last end of the tarp secured with paracord.

"This'll do fer now. It's a good base. I can add to it little by little, day by day and turn it into somethin' more permanent. The thing about survival is, ya gotta work hard. Nobody ain't gettin' nowhere if'n they ain't workin' hard. Blood, sweat, 'n tears. Ya reap what ya sow. God helps them that helps theyself," she added as if trying to start a collection of cliché's on video. She was a survivalist after all, not a filmmaker. Like most of the contestants, she was uncomfortable in front of the camera initially.

The snap of a twig behind her made her whip her head around. It came from beyond the tree line. All she could see from where she was standing was green mixed with an occasional gray trunk. The forest seemed distant—a different world, apart from her clear, treeless piece of property. She craned her neck and took a few steps to the side, silent as she listened and looked for any sign of movement.

"That sure did sound like a foot steppin' on a twig," she whispered to the camera. "And not a small foot neither."

She took a silent step closer, giving whatever it was time to make another move. "If I'm lucky, it's something I can eat. If I ain't lucky, it's something that wants to eat me."

After several minutes of silence, she dismissed the noise and got to work arranging stones for a fire pit as she narrated her progress.

"There's plenty of these here rocks down by the bay. I can make a nice fireplace with 'em. Hard part's haulin' em up here. But, like I says, I ain't 'fraid a hard work."

She used the stones she already had to make a square near the opening of her shelter but ran out while building up a heat-reflecting wall. She stood up and approached the camera.

"I'll be back," she said before turning it off.

The sun came out of hiding and brightened up the day in an instant. Jill looked up to see clear sky as if she had been transported to a different island. The temperature had been rising steadily all morning. It was over fifty degrees and with the physical exertion, she was beginning to perspire. She took her bright orange parka off and hung it on the tiny nub of a cut off branch left on the tall, thin support log that split the front A-frame. She kept her orange, insulated bib pants on, but unbuttoned the bib, letting it flop forward, exposing her cream, knit sweater. Her hair fell to her shoulder when she took off her hat. A mixture of blonde and gray flashed as she fluffed with her fingers, knocking a pink hairband lose. With a bow, she threw her hair forward and whipped it back as she straightened in a quick jerking motion. She had snatched the hairband off the ground in the process and used it to tie her hair back.

She put her empty backpack on and took a small camera mounted on a selfie stick with her to go look for more stones to finish her fireplace. The beach was the easiest place to find them and had the widest selection. It wasn't far away but the steep terrain provided a workout she wasn't afraid of undertaking.

She recorded herself while she walked, first explaining her mission to get more stones. "Once I get a fire going, I can set out to find some drinkin' water. Gonna have to boil any water I find out here. Dirty water will make ya sick," she explained as she trekked downhill through the forest.

"Me and my husband been married twenty-five years. We always took the kids out huntin' with us. It's a family activity in the Hill household." A proud grin graced her face, made all the more rugged by the deep lines around her eyes and mouth.

"I been takin' care of kids fer all my adult life. Had my first baby when I was sixteen. So, I never done much more than raisin' kids," she explained, lamenting the lack of wild teenage years most people are afforded to grow and find themselves.

She had never had time to party, to be irresponsible, to do anything but what her parents expected of her, which was be the model of the archaic female gender role—stay home, cook, clean, spit out plenty of children and obey your husband. It was part of her family's religion that dictated women should be subservient to men and she had been raised to be proud of filling the role.

Jill Hill was devoutly religious, but she had a desire to break the mold when it came to defining what a woman should be. She had spent most of her life following what the bible said a woman should do. Coming to Isolation Island was retribution for the years she had sacrificed for her children, her husband, her family and her faith, keeping her survival instincts bottled up and suppressing her desire for adventure.

This was, quite literally, her *wild time*, but it was much more than that. She wanted to prove to everyone in her life, that she was more than a good mother, more than an obedient housewife, more than a servant—she was a survivor, she was strong, she was a badass.

"This is the first time in my life that I been away from my kids. I been away from my husband plenty of times, but never away from my kids. My youngest is ten now and she ain't used to bein' without Mommy around."

She nearly wiped out, tripping over a log blocking her route to the beach, but she caught herself. The camera went berserk for a moment, then still with a close up of a deep blue eye with a thick eyelid and a web of crow's feet.

"Lesson one—if ya fall down, pick yourself back up. I been drillin' that into my kids my whole life. Never give up. Nobody's gonna give ya squat fer free. Ya gotta keep fightin' fer everything." Her voice got noticeably more southern-country when she recited the mantras she swore by to help her through life.

She made it to the edge of shore, where the forest ended with a blunt, eroded cliff. It was only around four feet down to the rocky beach, exposed by low tide but, she took it the hard way. She slipped and slid down the steep embankment on her ass. Landing on the rocks, she pitched forward, banging up her forearms and elbows trying to break her fall. Her radio, the only means of communication with the production crew came flying out of her pocket and crashed against a rock before bouncing into the shallow puddle of seawater which had escaped the tide.

She never lost grip of the selfie-stick, picking herself up as she had always done her entire life. A few scrapes and cuts painted blood-red lines down her arms, but she was more concerned with the radio that was now fully submersed in sea water. She almost fell again, slipping on slime-coated stones on her way to snatch the radio out of the water. She held it at arm's length looking at it and gave it a few drying shakes for good measure.

"I sure as shoot hope this thing's waterproof," she told the camera, almost expecting a reply.

The radio was in one piece but there was no way to test it short of calling the Mothership. Unfortunately, calling the Mothership meant an automatic tap out. She wasn't willing to risk a test call. Instead, she used her shirt to wipe the radio down, turned it on to find a full, normal screen.

"Looks like it ain't broke. They done told us not to communicate on the radio less I'm tappin' out."

She examined the screen—battery indicator full, GPS coordinates seemed legitimate, three reception bars, despite the hairline crack in the screen which was now evident.

"This here's my lifeline, but with a little luck, I ain't gonna need it. I ain't never tappin' out, but it'd be nice to know it works if'n I I get injured and need help."

Jill wiped the blood from her arms, revealing a few minor cuts and scrapes. She could patch them up herself with the first aid kit each contestant was issued. Deciding it could wait, she set to the task of picking stones suitable for the fireplace and placing them in her backpack, careful not to overload it. She was at the cul-de-sac of the narrow bay. The wind didn't blow in quite as hard as the shore exposed to the endless Pacific did and the calmer water meant better fishing.

As she filled her pack, her back to the water, across the bay, a half-mile away, a grayish-white wolf stood at attention. He waved his snout in the air, trying to pick up Jill's scent for information only an animal would find useful. He kept his eyes on the foreign figure of the woman as she stood, sidestepped and crouched repeatedly, picking up rocks and shoving them in her pack—strange behavior.

Another wolf padded out of the forest and stood by the first. Watching. Assessing. Was this new creature to the island a predator to avoid or prey to be stalked?

Jill zipped up her backpack. She could have fit more stones in, but there were two limiting factors—the backpack's weight limit and her own ability to haul them while hiking through the sketchy forest. She couldn't spend all her energy at once and a great deal had already been burnt moving her equipment, finding a place to camp and building a shelter. The last thing she needed was the view she got when she turned around for a last look at the bay.

"Uh oh," she whispered calmly when she saw the wolves, now three standing side by side across the bay watching her.

She turned the camera to film the trio. Their faces looked innocent and even friendly as they were not far removed from man's best friend; the cuddly fur babies Jill had always had and loved. There wasn't a time in her life that she didn't have at least one dog. In her adult life, she was accustomed to having three or four at a time back on her ranch in Kentucky. But, she wasn't fooled by the innocent puppy-dog eyes staring at her.

"Looks like I got company. Now, I love me some dogs and them's some beautiful animals, but I ain't no fool. They ain't dogs. They wild wolves and I ain't no master. When they look at me, they lookin' at food."

She watched them as they watched her, all of them still for a long time. Finally, two of the wolves turned back into the forest. The last one dipped his head to sniff the ground.

Jill spun the camera back around to film herself. "I ain't fixin' to be nobody's food out here," she swore, open palm held in the air.

She backed away slowly and found an easy spot to climb off shore, back into the forest.

"All ya can do is pray to god and hope god protects you," she explained as she made her way back to camp. "The good lord works in mysterious ways."

EZRA GREER

Day 1

2:02pm

Age: 51
Occupation: Truck Driver
Home: Alaska
Status: Widower, 3 children

"What have I gotten myself into?" Ezra Greer asked himself out loud for the benefit of the camera. He looked up and down the shoreline from his insertion point. The Zodiac Medline that ferried him to his new home was long gone, but he was too overwhelmed by the view and desolation to move. It was both beautiful and terrifying at the same time. Clear blue sky. Calm ocean waves. It was almost hypnotizing.

The paralysis was temporary, just long enough for reality to set in and his mind to refocus on the challenge ahead.

"You know, you sign up for something like this and you go in with a positive attitude and confidence, thinking you're going to take the challenge head on and tear it up. But, when you get out here and see the wet, gloomy forest, the empty ocean out there, and you feel the chill, it's…" He paused, searching for the right word to describe the feeling and finally came up with, "sobering."

He pulled his pea-green cuffed knit hat down over his ears and let out a deliberate, sighing exhale. His short graying beard had been pre-grown deliberately to provide a little extra warmth and a gritty, survivalist look.

"This is real now. This is my new reality. I'm here for as long as I can withstand with no one else to rely on."

The forest looked menacing. Knowing there was no civilization to be found anywhere on the island made it all the more empty. Knowing it was full of hungry, territorial animals made it all the more intimidating.

"It's scary," he said, twisting his head up and down shore. "It really is, but I'm not afraid. I know I've got the skills to make it out here."

He paused to absorb the silence, not sure if he believed his own words. "But, you have to acknowledge that it's a scary situation..." he added, choppy with his speech, as if improvising. "...so that you don't get...overconfident. You can't feel too comfortable out here or else you run the risk of letting your guard down."

He turned to the camera to emphasize his thought. "And that's when you're liable to make a mistake; to get careless and put yourself in a bad position."

He turned to look toward the edge of the looming forest.

"You don't want to get into a bad position out here. It's," he trailed off, never to complete the thought.

He gathered his things and began the quest for a suitable place to settle in. Pointing the camera down at his feet, he captured each footstep as it squished into the wet leaves and grass. The ground was like a wet sponge, audibly saturated.

"Waterproof boots are a must out here. There's moisture everywhere. You get wet just walking through all this thick bush. Everything that touches you is wet," he explained, carving his way inland.

"My first order of business is finding a good area to build a temporary shelter. I'm going with a quick set up, throw up my tarp and work on getting a fire started. The temperature is going to drop significantly at night and I don't want to get caught out."

"Now, I'm on an island in the Pacific and you might think *Pacific island* means warm, sunny, tropical, palm trees and coconuts, but this isn't Hawaii. This isn't the South Pacific. We're closer to Siberia and Alaska. The climate here is more like Canada. It's cold, wet, and windy. There's a reason this island is uninhabited. Let's just say no one would choose this as a vacation spot..."

A nearby rustling stopped him. He craned his neck to see, but the thick vegetation exposed nothing. The rustling continued, then stopped abruptly for just a moment. The void was filled with the sound of a large stone thumping the ground as if it had been flipped over.

Ezra clutched the canister of bear spray holstered on his hip. The rustling resumed. He couldn't tell if it was coming or going.

"Hey bear," he said, deep and sharp, assuming it must be a bear. What else could flip a stone that sounded that heavy?

The rustling stopped with the sound of his voice. He ducked to see under some branches uphill. About fifty yards away, a large furry face rose into view—a black bear. Ezra pulled the bear spray out and held it ready.

"Holy shit," he whispered. "That's a huge bear. To be honest, I didn't believe there'd be bears on this island which is out in the middle of nowhere surrounded by miles of ocean, but there's the proof. Things just got a bit more real."

Ezra backed away as the bear watched. The expressionless fuzzy face looked almost inviting, like a big, cuddly teddy bear. He knew the bear would attack if challenged. He inched away slowly, trying to be as non-threatening as possible.

"If you encounter a bear in the forest, leave it alone. Don't make eye contact," he whispered to the camera. "Always have bear spray ready, should the bear come too close. By too close, I mean within the spray's reach. That means about twelve feet or less."

The bear sniffed the air, dropped down and then popped back up again for another whiff.

"You don't want to use the spray too soon and not hit him," Ezra continued. "If a bear is coming your way, back away slowly, don't turn and run. Back away slowly, with your spray ready, holding it with two hands," he instructed. "Make sure the safety clip is off and talk at a medium volume as you back away. Most close bear encounters end right there. The sound of your voice is usually enough to scare it away, but if the bear persists, if it continues to come at you, give him a short burst of spray. With decent aim, just a couple seconds of spray should blind the animal and make it hard for it to breathe and you can make your escape. These spray cans usually only have six to eight seconds of spray in them. So, don't use it all at once and keep it ready in case you need to give it another zap. Studies show bear spray is more effective than a gun in most encounters. So, even hunters carrying guns should have bear spray handy."

His lecture concluded, he turned the camera to his smiling face.

"That's a little tip from your Uncle Ezzie," he quipped with a wink.

The bear dropped back to all fours, disappearing from sight, but Ezra could hear the large beast as it brushed through the forest away from him. It was a welcomed sound, but his heart was pounding, nonetheless.

"Wow. It's amazing how your body reacts. The bear wasn't even that close, but I can feel my heart jumping in my chest, adrenaline surging. Fight or flight. You have to be ready to act at the drop of a hat. A bear like that probably weighs over four hundred pounds. Tear you apart."

Ezra turned and continued in the same direction, away from the bear, looking back over his shoulder every few steps.

"Needless to say, one of the biggest threats out here is animals like that. They've probably never seen humans before. At least, not enough to be afraid of humans. There are no cities for them to be afraid of, no loud machines to scare them off. I'm six-foot-two, two hundred thirty pounds but, by myself, I probably look like a potential meal more than a threat. It's like someone my size seeing a five-year-old. No match."

As if the reality of the situation had suddenly hit him, he picked up his pace along the worn path to put some space between the bear and himself.

"I'm not going to want to build my shelter anywhere near an active bear trail," he explained. "If this is where his daily rounds takes him, I want to be far away from here."

Ezra Greer veered off the animal trail and continued to explore.

Chapter 2

Day 14

Don't Leave Me Hanging

Sharon had insisted on hiking to the site where Derrick Bond's body hung, bringing Dyson and Page with her. The mutilated corpse was too much for Page. Who would have thought death by hanging could look so gruesome? Perhaps, under normal circumstances it would be easier to stomach but, in the wild, humans are treated like every other animal. Death means an easy meal and it's first come, first served.

Dyson lifted the camera to his shoulder to start filming.

Sharon put a hand over the lens and pushed the camera down. "What the hell are you doing?" she asked, outraged.

"I'm filming. Don't we need recorded evidence of what happened here?" he asked, looking to DocRod and Hutch for validation. His intentions seemed sincere.

Hutch intervened. "He's right. This is basically a crime scene."

Sharon rushed over to Hutch, always in a hurry to disagree without thinking things through. "What crime? He killed himself. It's no one else's fault. It's tragic but it's not a crime."

Hutch replied, "You don't know that. It *looks* like he killed himself but, unless you have a bunch of CSIs on the crew, we need to document the scene as best we can. What if someone else did this to him? What do you plan on telling his family when they ask what happened?"

Sharon had no answer for that. She was more concerned with her reputation. Of all the survival shows on TV, no contestant had ever died, much less committed suicide. She was on the verge of panic. There'd be a full investigation exposing her shoddy management and creative accounting. What would become of her career? There would be lawsuits, scandal. Derrick's family was bound to sue and the producer would be at the top of the list of those held responsible.

Dyson resumed filming, but Sharon still wasn't ready to let that happen. She jumped in front of the camera, blocking the view.

"Wait," she ordered. "Let's just…wait." She was trying to cook up a scheme, a cover-up, some way out. "Let's just think this through," she said, suddenly calm, trying to make it rub off on the rest of the crew.

Dr. Rodney continued what he had been doing the entire time—examining the scene, the holes in the ground, the hanging corpse. He noticed Derrick's camera equipment was missing. "We're going to need the stretcher to carry him back to the boat," he informed the woman in charge, his eyes focused on Derrick's neck.

"Wait. This isn't our fault," Sharon started again. Everyone seemed to notice the use of the word 'our' she was using deliberately in attempt to make it seem like they were all in it together.

In reality, Sharon was the one who set everything up. The one who insisted on cutting corners. The one who bent over backwards keeping costs down at the expense of safety. Even if it had nothing to do with a contestant committing suicide, it wouldn't look good.

"He sounded fine last night," she insisted. "Nobody could have seen this coming." She was referring to the quick call she had made the night before via radio informing Derrick the crew would be coming to conduct a routine medical check. The call was hardly long enough to assess a person's mental status. Because the main challenge of the competition was the isolation, no conversation was allowed beyond simple instructions and emergency communications.

"Are you sure it was him?" Hutch asked her.

"What do you mean?" she asked in return.

Hutch made the same face he had made every time Sharon's annoying habit of asking *what do you mean?* popped up. He let it go this time but his patience was waning. "I don't know. It's just…you talked to him last night. That would mean he hasn't been hanging here for even a full day. He looks pretty ripe. What do *you* think, Doc?"

Dr. Rodney was on his toes, taking a closer look at the body. Although he was a doctor, his main area of expertise was helping injured, living people in the ER, not autopsies in the wild with no instruments or labs to run tests.

"I think he looks like he's been up here for longer because the animals got to him. But, he's got injuries that can't be attributed to the hanging. Looks like he was struck on the back of the head with a blunt object. Hard to tell. I'll know more when we get him down."

"Struck by what?" Sharon asked.

"The question might be, by who?" the good doctor proposed.

"Are you saying another person did this to him?"

"I doubt he hit himself in the back of the head and, judging by the size of the wound, I don't think he would have been able to hang himself," Doc assessed.

Hutch asked Sharon, "What did he say, exactly, yesterday?"

"I told him we were coming for a routine checkup. He said, 'ok' and then I verified that his camp was in the same location he reported previously. He said, 'yes' and that was it. I told him we'd see him tomorrow. He didn't reply."

"And what time was that?" Dr. Rodney asked.

Sharon turned to Page for the answer, but she was still turned away with repulsion. "Page?" Sharon prompted.

Page, still rattled, replied without turning around. "Around 5pm."

"Okay," Hutch said, mulling over the information out loud. "So, it wasn't really night yet, but still, he hasn't been dead for even twenty-four hours if he was indeed the person you spoke to on the radio."

"What does it mean?" Page asked shrugging her shoulders and turning halfway around.

"I have no idea," Hutch answered. "I just like to have the facts straight in my head."

"There's at least two distinct sets of footprints," Doc pointed out, searching the ground for clues.

Indeed, there were. One set had come from a hiking boot's sole. The other looked like the bottom of a set of waterproof rubber boots. The area was mostly grass but the holes in the ground and the dirt extracted from those holes provided a sample of footprints partially faded by the rain.

"He must have spent a lot of time here. I'd say he was here

multiple times, obviously to dig for something," Hutch surmised.

Page finally took in the full view. The holes in the ground made sense to her. "He was probably looking for one of the treasure chests," she explained. She pointed at finger at Hutch as she took slow deliberate paces toward the hanging tree. "Your predecessor, Nelson Greely buried the treasure chests about a week before the contest began. I can check the records when we get back to the Mothership. I've got the location of every chest documented. I'll bet that's what he was digging for."

Dyson had been filming the entire time. He got many shots of the body from every angle, the holes dug around the tree, the grassy areas—everything he thought might be of importance. When he was done, he set the camera on the ground and looked up at the corpse. "Are we ready to get him down?" he asked, rubbing his hands together to prepare himself for touching a dead body, something he had never done before.

Hutch held Dyson back. "I'll get the body down. You and Doc go get the stretcher from the boat so we can carry him back."

"Wait," Sharon insisted, again. "His body has already been mutilated. There's no point in bringing him back in this condition. We tell his family he was attacked by wild animals. We can spare them the pain of knowing he committed suicide. There's no reason…"

Hutch cut her short. "You mean, spare you the lawsuit. How is telling his family he was eaten by wild animals any better than suicide. We're taking him home. We're telling the truth. End of story," he said in a stern, raised voice meant for everyone to hear.

He didn't bother explaining why it was the right thing to do. She knew why. She wasn't going to get her way this time. All she could do was fold her arms and send him a searing glare. He ignored it and started climbing the tree.

Dr. Rodney motioned to Dyson. "Let's go," he said, avoiding eye contact with anyone. Downhill, he could see the ocean through the trees in tiny traces. The shore was closer than it was to Derrick's camp so DocRod chose a worn trail he hoped would lead directly to the ocean rather than taking the longer route via camp. Hutch noted their choice of direction as he scaled the tree, but didn't object.

It was easy to get to the limb Derrick was hanging from, but getting out on the limb was more difficult. The limb itself was thick and sturdy, but walking out on it would have required quite a balancing act while wet and slippery. Hutch chose to crawl out on his belly perhaps the same way Derrick did.

He studied the rope, the tree limb and another limb—lower and to the left. He narrated the deed according to the evidence before him. "He probably stood on that lower branch and fashioned the rope around this thicker, higher limb. It's easy to reach. Then he put the noose around his neck and…" The ending caught in his throat. "At least it was quick and painless. I hope."

He pulled his survival knife from its sheath and gave the limb a whack, slicing through the cordage in one swing.

The body hit the ground with a moist thud. The rain had trickled out but he felt a large plop hit his hat. He looked up with a squinted eye. A line of crows perched on a higher limb looked down at him, not afraid to take credit for the bombing. He cursed them under his breath and shimmied his way backward. Dangling from the lowest point of the branch, he dropped down to the ground. His feet skidded in the mud but he kept his balance.

Page backed away, wanting nothing to do with the corpse. Sharon inched closer as Hutch crouched over the body to check his pockets.

He pulled out a piece of parchment that had been folded up. It was the treasure map that led him to this spot. Other than that, his pockets were empty.

Hutch turned the body over to examine it. He found the gash on the back of the head DocRod had mentioned and turned it toward Sharon so she could see.

Sharon held herself, arms folded, trembling from the cold or nervousness. "I see it. Maybe one of the other contestants killed him and stole the treasure chest," she surmised.

"Anything is possible," Hutch admitted. "He could have injured himself. Maybe a Widowmaker clipped him." Looking around, he pointed out three possible culprits in the vicinity—large, dead trees and branches that could break and fall at any moment, crushing and killing anyone in their way. "But, why would he hang himself afterward? And, if he was injured, how did he manage it?"

"So, all that's left is the possibility another contestant is responsible. Maybe someone is trying to eliminate the competition," Sharon tried again, grasping at straws to shift the blame onto someone else.

A blood-curdling shriek echoed through the woods, cutting through the calm, startling Hutch and causing Page to almost jump out of her skin. It was followed by a steady stream of painful screams.

A second voice hollered over the screeching. "Huuuutch! Heeeelp!" Dr. Rodney cried out from afar.

Wasting no time, Hutch sprinted down the trail in the direction of the commotion.

DERRICK BOND

Day 1

6:19pm

Age: 29
Occupation: ex-Marine
Home: Texas
Status: Single

Derrick Bond pressed record on his hand-held camera, holding it close to his face so that he filled the frame.

"They call me Bond...*Derrick* Bond," he said, performing his most debonair expression. It came off a bit more constipated than dashing. He laughed, knowing he wasn't pulling it off. He moved the camera to arm's length, revealing his shelter in the background. A fire crackled just outside the opening.

"I've often been tempted to change my first name to something like Eggbert, just so I can say, 'They call me Bond...*Eggbert* Bond.'" He laughed again. "It's hard to be intimidating when your name is Eggbert," he explained, humored all over again by the notion.

He presented his camp to the camera. There wasn't much to it. He hadn't walled in the shelter yet, but it would do for the first night.

"As you can see," he told the camera. "I've got a nice fire going and I built a tripod."

The tripod wasn't for the camera. That was supplied to him. The tripod he was talking about was for the fire, consisting of three straight branches stripped of bark. He had tied them together at the top with paracord and spread the bottoms out to stand above the fire. Another piece of paracord hung from the center of the triangle, a covered, black pot dangled at the end tickled by wisps of flames.

"And what do we have cooking in here?" Derrick asked,

lifting the lid and aiming the camera inside. He jiggled the pot with a few taps of his hand to animate the contents.

"It's just water," he explained. "Not very exciting, normally. But, out here, water is worth more than gold. I'm excited to have come across a creek with sparkling fresh water while I was looking for materials to build with. I had planned on looking for water tomorrow, but I'm excited to have something to drink tonight."

He put the lid back on the pot to let it boil.

"I like to let any questionable water boil for about ten minutes. I once drank untreated water and I don't want to go through that hell again. There are all kinds of nasty things lurking in untreated water. Even if it looks clean, it doesn't mean a thing. The invisible microbes living in the water will knock you on your ass and right out of the competition."

Derrick showed off his temporary shelter and explained how he would keep working on it to turn it into a more permanent dwelling. At the top of his list of things to do was constructing an elevated bed to get himself off the ground. He discussed the location and materials in depth with gusto and enthusiasm.

He had nothing but time, as all the contestants did, but there were things that needed to be done that had deadlines attached to them. In an endurance competition such as Isolation Island, finding enough food to sustain yourself without wasting away was imperative and you have to acquire food before you run out of energy.

At the end of the camp tour, what little there was to see, Derrick set up the camera on the *camera's* tripod and rushed out of frame.

"Aaaand..." he teased. "One more feature..."

Hunched over, he rolled a two-foot section of log into view, stood it up and slapped the top.

"Instant seating," he boasted. "And, this is just the beginning. I really like doing things in stages. I can use this stump to sit on now, but eventually it will become the base for the throne I'm going to build. Nothing beats having a chair with a back so you can really sit back comfortably," he explained, turning back and forth between the camera and the log.

He sat down and stretched his arms out slowly, demonstrating the 'sit-ability' and comfort of his new chair.

Swaying side to side, he pounded his fists on his knees, chanting in his best Borat impersonation, "King in the castle, king in the castle."

He laughed at his own performance. Talking to a camera was difficult for Derrick, but he was getting used to it and even started to enjoy it. A laugh track might have helped or a director to yell cut, but he was left to his own devices. He bluntly transitioned to a new train of thought.

"I figured I'd work hard today while I have the energy. I've got no delusions about this competition. It's going to be tough. I've got more energy today than I'm going to have the rest of the time I'm out here. If I can get myself set up before I run out, it's going to make life much easier for those days when I just can't lift a finger."

The former Marine adjusted his hat and leaned forward with his elbows on his legs. He seemed to be making decisions in his head, forgetting the camera was rolling.

After three minutes of silence, he snapped back to the real world. "That's what I'm gonna do," he said as if the camera were privy to the thoughts in his head. He pulled the treasure map out of his pocket and unfolded it to have another look.

"This is what I'm going to do tomorrow," he explained, holding up the map for a second. "I might as well go for the treasure while I've got the energy. If I have to dig for it, it's not going to be easy, but there could be some very useful rewards. It doesn't make much sense to me to continue working on camp when there could be something in the treasure that could make my life much easier."

He took another moment to think about the idea in silence, then nodded his head.

"That's what I'm gonna do," he confirmed.

9:48pm

"My girlfriend dumped me about a month ago," a somber Derrick confessed to the camera.

The sun had been gone for almost three hours, but he still

wasn't asleep. He was hunkered down in his shelter, laying tucked into his sleeping bag and quite cozy with the warmth from the fire wafting in. He propped himself up on one elbow for a more personal interaction with the camera, his headlamp illuminating a circular beam around the shelter with every move of his head.

"I was going to surprise her with the news that I was selected to be on Isolation Island, but when she found out that I applied without telling her, we got into a big argument and we broke up," he lamented. "Rather, *she* dumped *me*. Not my choice," he added.

He cocked his head and froze, eyes lifted to the side. Something small was rustling leaves not far away. He listened for any indication of what animal it might be and if it was coming closer, but the sound ended as abruptly as it started.

"Funny that she would break up with me before the contest. I mean, I could come home a millionaire. But, that just proves something I felt all along. She never had any faith in me. I can't be with someone like that. Maybe she did me a favor."

The camera caught a flash of his glassy, teared-up eyes before he turned his head away. A bit choked up, he continued, "We met on my twenty-first birthday. In a way, I matured into a man with her, but I can't help feeling being with her was a waste of time. You try to build a relationship, a life with someone, for years...then...it's just over."

He squeezed a single tear from his closed eyes with his free hand and took a cleansing breath.

"I don't want to think about that right now. But, maybe Isolation Island is exactly what I need. I can't make any stupid, drunken phone calls to her. I can't try to win her back. Maybe I can get my head together and get through this. It might even make this competition easier, knowing she's not waiting for me to come home. I don't have to think about where she is, who she's with, or what she's doing."

Derrick nodded a confirmation of his musings. He really believed the time alone would help. Being out in the woods, surviving alone could be a great growing experience; a time to reflect on the past, look forward to the future and develop a new appreciation for life. It could also be a harrowing experience that breaks a person and sends them into a spiral of depression and despair. Only time would tell which side Derrick Bond would land on.

"I think, overall, Day 1 went well. I got everything done that I wanted. I'm surprised at how much I got done, actually. I haven't been eaten by bears or wolves yet. Let's see how the night goes. I'll have to wake up every few hours to tend to the fire, but let's see if I can sleep on this mess."

He adjusted himself, tossing and turning to settle into a comfortable position. It wasn't easy. His sleeping bag didn't provide much cushioning and it didn't take long to realize the bedding of pine needles and leaves was inadequate.

"I'm going to have to make some improvements to my bed. I go crazy when I don't get a sufficient amount of sleep. Lack of food, dehydration, combined with lack of sleep is a recipe for disaster out here. Add the cold and rain and it's a recipe for death."

It wasn't the cheeriest thought to end the day with. Derrick didn't want the final clip from Day 1 to end on a negative note, but he had difficulty bringing himself back up. The camera waited through several minutes of silence for his closing statement.

Finally, he said, "Tomorrow, I begin the hunt for treasure. Treasure will make everything better."

A glimmer of excitement and enthusiasm brought a smile to his face and, with that, he waved goodbye to the camera, said goodnight, and turned it off.

KIMMIE ARDEN

Day 1

6:21pm

Age: 36
Occupation: Nurse
Home: New York
Status: Married, 2 children

At 5'4" Kimmie Arden was no giant, but she had a workhorse mentality. Her strategy was, "keep yourself busy, keep yourself fed, keep yourself alive." And, above all, "be prepared."

She had long, natural red hair which she kept pulled back and clipped at the base of her neck, leaving wisps of hair framing her face even while wearing a hat. She wore an open, oatmeal-gray sweater she had knitted herself specifically for this occasion. Under it, her family peeked out, frozen in a group pose at their recent Fourth of July party, an annual family reunion. She had the picture printed on her t-shirt to keep her company. The way she leaned into her husband was endearing, not even tall enough to reach his shoulders as he towered over her. Her two sons, one on each side of Mommy and Daddy brandishing grins with missing front baby teeth. Two sets of Grandmas and Grandpas sat in front of a wall of uncles and aunts, brothers and sisters and cousins. They were a happy family and Kimmie was determined to win the million dollars for them.

She had spent the beginning of Day 1 the same way everyone else did—looking for a place to set up camp and building a shelter, but she skipped the temporary shelter. Instead, she opted to construct a more permanent debris shelter. She had cut and hammered narrow wooden posts into the ground and used them to frame in and weave walls made of branches with leaves.

Once completed, the shelter would be tall enough for her to stand up inside comfortably, topped with a green tarp steepled in the middle with log support beams. She made good progress quickly with this type of shelter. It would be a sturdy, well insulated structure. She planned to add to it day by day.

The front wall was just a tarp, but it was only temporary. She planned to build a stone hearth and swinging door on Day 2 to complete the structure. A simple fire pit sufficed for Day 1.

She had been so swept up in building her shelter, she hadn't said much to the camera as it captured mostly silent images of her progress throughout the day. She didn't even bring the camera with her when she left to gather material for building and firewood or when she came across the babbling brook that would become her fresh water source. By the end of the day, she decided to sit down and acquaint herself with the camera.

"My name is Kimmie Arden," she formally introduced herself standing in front of the camera, smoke rising from the fire behind her. "I'm from Albany, New York. Um, I'm married. I, uh…have two sons, Jake and Devon. And…I'm, uh…a registered nurse."

She mimed an awkward, skirt-less curtsy, signaling the introduction was over. Her relationship with the camera would have to develop with time. Talking to an inanimate object was a new experience for her. A long moment of silence ensued as she tried to think of something to say.

"I'm going fishing," she blurted out. "I've got maybe an hour of daylight left, I think. But, I'm dying to see if I can catch any fish out here."

She began gathering her fishing equipment. Primitive as it was, at least, she had metal hooks and real fishing line. A long, thin, straight stick she had found while gathering firewood would serve as the fishing pole. She tied one end of the fishing line to the tip, fashioned a dry wood chip to it to serve as a bobber, and tied on an empty hook.

Dangling the hook for the camera to capture, she said, "Now, I just need some bait. I'll see if I can find something on the way to shore."

Walking through the forest was no stroll in the park. In many places, it was thick with vegetation which needed to be hacked through. Animal trails—beaten paths forged by creatures taking the path of least resistance—made the going easier, but they didn't always provide the most direct route to the desired destination.

Kimmie carved her way through the forest, stomping out a new path to shore. Along the way, she stopped to turn over large rocks, hoping to score some fishing bait. After a few failures, she hit the jackpot. Flipping a smaller, flat stone over revealed two earthworms that began to panic as soon as their cover was lifted.

"Bingo, bango," she said, a curious expression she had a habit of using.

She scooped up both worms before they could escape into the soil. The one she didn't impale on the hook went into her jacket pocket. A quick zip locked it in to be used later.

"If things get really bad, I'll be eating the worms myself," she told the camera, patting her pocket before continuing to shore to find a good fishing spot. The going got tougher—having to be careful not to lose the worm she had on the hook, having to be careful not to stick herself with the hook or get it snagged on a leaf or branch.

Kimmie cursed herself for jumping the gun. She should have waited and put the worm on the hook when she was ready to put her line in the water. It was little things like this which drove her crazy. She scolded herself with whispers of insults meant to get her head in the game.

Upon reaching the shore, she found a spot near a tree which had fallen into the ocean, its uprooted end still trapped on land. She set up the tripod to get a wide shot of the area she planned to fish from, atop a small boulder which would give her a better casting point.

"My husband and I take our kids fishing all the time on Lake Champlain. But, we have real fishing poles and reels and bobbers and plenty of bait," she told the camera as she balanced herself on the boulder and tossed the line in the water.

She turned with a smile provoked by thoughts of her family and added, "Plus, we bring sandwiches. I know it's only Day 1 but I'm already hungry. Traveling here was enough to work up an appetite. I'd love to get a fish and fry him up. It'd be a great mental boost, too. Any confirmation that you can make it out here is a boost."

She pulled her line into a new position, closer to the tree trunk, hoping some fish would be there enjoying the cover. Her improvised bobber floated well enough to keep the hook from sinking to the bottom.

"Confidence is important. I'm generally a confident person, but I've been married for twelve years and my husband and I do everything together. We're one of those couples that truly enjoy each other's company. We're pretty inseparable."

A hit on her line stopped her short.

"Something's nibbling," she said, excited.

She gave it a test tug but felt nothing on the hook. Pulling it out of the water, she made sure the bait was still there and then tossed it back in.

Returning to her story, she said, "So...we do everything together, me and my husband and the kids. I don't get any time to myself. And, although I'm confident with my husband around—he's more than capable of being out here, too—I really wanted to come out here to see if I could do it by myself. It's nice to have a big strong man to help you, don't get me wrong. But, I think every person, I'm not just talking from a woman's point of view, I think every person has in them a desire to learn what they're capable of; a desire to prove themselves."

Kimmie was getting a bit more comfortable with the camera but an annoying thought reminded her she was basically talking to no one and she clammed up.

Another hit on her line provoked a yelp. This time, whatever was on the other end tried to pull Kimmie right off the boulder. She yanked the pole, making sure the fish was hooked well and raised it to her shoulder. The line ran back and forth in the water. She could see the fish close to the surface and pulled the line with her hand, hoisting her catch out of the water, onto the boulder. It flopped around, trying to get loose.

Kimmie grabbed the fish and held it down before it could escape. With fish in hand, she hopped back to shore without getting her feet wet and hurried over to the camera to celebrate.

"Woo hoo!" she exclaimed holding the fish horizontally in frame. "Yes! Look at that."

It was indeed an excellent catch, at least 18 inches in length and close to three pounds. It was black on top and gray on the bottom, separated by a shiny silver streak.

"I have no idea what kind of fish this is, but I'm going to call it Dinner," she bragged. "Honey, I love you," the successful fisher said, addressing her husband through the camera. "But, this one was all Kimmie."

She took it off the hook with ease, happy to avoid pulling the fish's insides apart. Kneeling on shore, the fish out of view of the camera, she cut the head off and gutted it.

"I would keep the guts for bait but I don't want to bring it back to camp. It'll only attract hungry animals," she explained above the sloshing sounds of dismemberment. "In fact, I plan to make a prep kitchen down here so I can clean and gut whatever I get and toss the excess into the ocean. That way, I can chum the water, too. I don't want dead fish parts or animal parts around my camp."

She lifted the finished product to show the camera.

"Now, let's get this guy back to camp and cook him up. Kimmie is eating on Day 1!"

8:15pm

"I enjoy going out into the woods knowing I could survive without a supermarket, without stores, without online shopping or outside help," Kimmie explained to the camera as she sat hunched over the fire, frying pan in hand.

She had taken the time to whittle a spoon which she would use to eat with after she was done flipping and pushing the fish around in the pan. Some non-stick cooking spray would have been nice.

"Our society has robbed us of what's natural. I read a lot of dystopian novels and people think it's never going to happen—society will never collapse. But it will. It has to. Maybe not within my lifetime, but maybe within my kids' lifetime or my grandkids' lifetime. I don't have grandkids yet, but you know what I mean."

She flipped the two fillets she had scaled, the skin still intact so she could reap the benefits of the beneficial fish oils.

"Humans as a species have survived for so long, not because of electricity, cars, and computers—that's all relatively new—but, because we were able to live off the land, avoid predators, and hunt and grow our own food," Kimmie preached, laying out her views on life and human society.

"I think it's a travesty that the majority of the population can't even build a fire, even with a lighter. Fire—possibly the most important human tools of all time and essential for survival. When my kids are old enough, probably ten years-old, I'm going to teach them how to make a friction fire, how to handle fire, and how to respect fire. They should be teaching basic survival skills in schools. It's more than a novelty. It puts you in touch with nature. It's good for the mind. I'll bet it can even prevent depression," she went on.

"We should surround ourselves with grass and trees and water, not concrete, electronics, and Starbucks. We live in this busy, drive-thru society," she lamented, shaking her head.

"Sometimes I wish I could just take my family off the grid and live in the woods. Unfortunately, the only places you can really do that are in cold climates, like Alaska. I hate the cold. I couldn't deal with long winters. As it is, Albany is not my cup of tea, weather-wise."

Kimmie pulled the pan out of the fire, off the two tall rocks she used as a grill, and showed the cooked fish to the camera. With only the fire to light the shot, it was difficult to see the finished product well.

"Now, we eat," she declared as if the camera would get a portion.

She shoveled a big chunk into her mouth using the wooden spoon. A look of sheer ecstasy overcame her. "Mmm…that is good. Wow," she said, eyes rolling back in her head as she chewed slowly. "It's funny how food always tastes better when you're outside. Even better when you're deep in the forest by yourself with no civilization for a thousand miles."

She enjoyed every bite of her first catch. It was more than a meal. It was a triumph—an early win. It was validation, encouragement, and reward all together. It was worth more than a Thanksgiving Day feast.

"If I can keep catching fish, I'll be alright. I'll see how it goes. Maybe I'll build a smoke house. Smoking fish and meat preserves it and it tastes great. Let's see how it goes. I'll fish some more tomorrow, maybe make some deadfall traps. I can make a fish trap and a bird trap, too." The thought of the adventure ahead of her brought a smile to her face. "I can't wait. It'll be fun."

Tucker Jordan

Day 1

7:07pm

Age: 28
Occupation: Yoga Instructor
Home: Vermont
Status: Single

"This has been a good day," Tucker Jordan told the camera in his soft-spoken kind-hearted voice as he crouched in a garland pose, hands flattened together in front of him in a praying gesture.

Tucker was a gentle survivalist who prided himself on his love for the planet, peaceful nature, and spirituality. The first thing he did when he arrived was find a spot he 'vibed with' and performed some yoga poses he thought would help him bond with his environment. The environment remained indifferent, but Tucker conjured up some 'positive energy' that made him feel welcomed. He told the camera he could feel it connecting with his soul.

After over two hours of his yoga and 'bonding' ritual, he finally got to work hauling his equipment, building a temporary shelter and starting a fire. It ate up the entire day. He had to hurry to finish before losing daylight, but he managed to erect a suitable "tent" using a big brown tarp strewn up with cordage between two trees.

Now, it was too late to start looking for water, but he still had a generous ration in his canteen, as all the contestants were allotted to begin with. He took a few healthy gulps and screwed the top back on.

"I really like this spot," he told the camera, looking around, soaking up the view.

From his vantage point, he could see through a bit of forest before it fell away down the hill. Over the treetops in the distance, the Pacific Ocean was disappearing into darkness as the sun set to the west.

Tucker took a deep, cleansing breath and let it out slow and steady. "There's a lot of positive energy here. I can feel it. It's no coincidence. It's telling me I'm going to win this competition. I can feel it in my heart and soul. You have to believe your heart when it's talking. You have to listen to your soul. It knows what you need."

A tear escaped from the corner of his eye. "I can do it. The key is to blend with nature. You can't come out here and be an intrusion. I want to harmonize with the planet. That's what long-term survival is all about."

The camera watched as he stood motionless through the end of his monologue. "I didn't come here to destroy everything and cater it to my whim. I'm going to make a home here. I'm going to thrive," he finished.

The temperature had dropped significantly over the past hour, the sun descending in the sky, but Tucker remained without his outer layer of clothes so that he could perform his nightly yoga ritual. He pulled the green and brown striped toque off his head, exposing his long, light brown hair pulled into a man-bun. Blond streaks highlighted his hair in contrast to his golden tan skin—a product of working at a beach resort the past two years. He tossed his hat in the shelter and set up the camera on a tripod to capture his yoga routine.

He focused a great deal of time on a Lord of the Fishes pose, explaining in docile tones how he hoped it would grant him success on the fishing expedition he hoped to embark on the next day.

A full hour of unusable footage followed—more yoga poses, the mention of positive energy twenty or thirty times and long periods of controlled breathing. Not exactly the action-packed TV the producer was hoping for.

2:01am

Tucker sprung up from a dead sleep in the middle of the night. Propped up on his arms he froze sitting up, listening. It was pitch black inside the shelter. Haunting sounds bombarded him from every direction. Wolves howled to each other from afar. The sound of a branch cracking nearby startled him. He felt around in the dark until he found the camera. He used the night vision feature to help find his headlamp. It was right where he had left it, next to his sleeping bag.

More strange sounds—something climbing around in a nearby tree. It was heavy—rocking and rattling limbs.

Tucker put his headlamp on and crawled out of his shelter, camera first. Even with the light, there was nothing to be seen. The camp was the same as when he had fallen asleep, except the fire was dying out. He got to his feet and scanned the edge of the woods with his headlamp and camera.

Another burst of shaking branches behind him spun him around. He followed the sound to the edge of camp, reluctant to go wandering into the woods in the middle of the night. The lack of moonlight on the overcast evening added to his concerns.

The shaking branches progressed for a moment then stopped abruptly with the sound of something hitting the ground. Tucker's eyes widened, the sudden silence perplexing. His mind replayed the sounds he had heard over and over, trying to identify them.

Would a bear be climbing trees in the middle of the night?
Why has it stopped moving?
Are there predatory cats on this island?

Tucker backed up, eyes peeled. He ducked back into his shelter to get the bear spray—a small shred of security. Although he would have preferred to hear whatever had caused the noise moving away until it faded into the night, he was satisfied by a long period of silence. Ten to fifteen minutes passed without another close sound.

"That was weird," he whispered to the camera. "But, whatever it was, I don't think it's a threat. It would have attacked by now."

He listened for another ten minutes but a strange silence had taken over the forest. He put some more wood on the fire, stoked it back to life and went back to sleep inside his shelter.

WES WOOD

Day 1

8:38pm

Age: 57
Occupation: Farmer
Home: Mississippi
Status: Married, 8 children

Wes Wood had half his log cabin built by the end of Day 1. He kept working even after it got dark. It wasn't tall enough to kneel in yet but, covered with a tarp, it would suffice for one night. He could crawl in and stay warm and dry in his sleeping bag and low ceiling.

"Not bad fer a day's work," he told the camera with his heavy southern accent. The camera had been in the same position all day—atop a tripod twelve feet from the construction site.

Wes had chosen a flat, clear spot only five minutes away from shore, but it was high and dry and surrounded by tall trees to shield him from the Pacific winds. Camerawork was not high on his list of priorities. A work, work, work mentality had guided him his entire life and it was no different on Isolation Island. It was the backbone of his survival strategy. He hadn't taken a break all day, unless relieving himself on a tree could be counted as a break.

He had been mostly quiet throughout the day, mumbling to himself from time to time as he chopped down logs, hauled them and fitted them together to make a sturdy twelve by twelve foundation that would grow into a full cabin eventually. He had already begun to integrate a hearth into the wall opposite his sleeping area. Even working flat out without any breaks, it would take a few days to build, but it would make for an excellent long-term shelter.

"Tomorr'a Ima finish up the walls," Wes explained to the camera, his teeth causing a slight whistle on the S in *walls*. "Gonna build me a bed. Make a door."

He spit on the ground. With his bare hand, he wiped whatever didn't make it past his overgrown gray beard. Looking into the camera, only one eye seemed to be on target, the other pale gray eye was slightly askew leaving you to wonder what he was actually looking at.

"I ain't never been outside-a Miss'ssippi. Born and raised. I ain't never had no use fer travel. When I's a younger man, I'd go out in the woods huntin' 'n a-trappin' to help feed the family. I can survive anywhere y'all wanna put me. I know there's bears and wolves out here. They ain't scare me one bit. But, I hear they got moose up here, somehow. Ya gotta watch out fer moose. They big and ugly and they'll kill you fer no reason at all."

He wasn't entirely correct. Although moose attack more people than bears, the attacks rarely result in a fatality. However, with no hospital in the forest on a deserted island, any injury is potentially fatal.

"I ain't here fer no adventure. I ain't here fer no spiritual growth or no hogwash like that. I ain't here fer nothin' 'ceptin the million dollars prize," Wes told the camera, shifting gears. He gathered his tools in the dark, using his headlamp.

"I never worked with no bow and arrow before. Give me a shotgun or a rifle any day. But we's workin' primitive out here and I ain't no fool. I can guarantee I'll bag me a moose if'n I sees one. God done put animals here fer us to use and, by golly, that's what I'm gonna do. There ain't no mercy out in the wild."

He paused, shining the headlamp down on the ground in circles all around him. Unsure of where his bouncing thoughts were headed next, he chose to turn the camera off.

"That's enough fer today," he mumbled as he approached the STOP button.

2:33am

Wes Wood turned on his headlamp. He had fallen asleep wearing it on his head in the confines of his unfinished log cabin. He was awoken by the sound of snorts and grunts just outside his shelter. He turned the camera on, using its night vision capabilities to look out the open entrance. All he could see was the first layer of trees at the edge of camp, tinted green on the camera's screen.

Another grunt came from behind him on the other side of the wall. Something with large nostrils was sniffing around. Its footsteps were heavy, but slow as it investigated the new foreign structure that had popped up earlier that day.

"Lordy, here we go," Wes whispered to the camera. "There's somethin' out there."

He held his breath and listened again. More grunts and snorts combined with a dragging foot or hoof circled the outside of the cabin. He slipped out of his sleeping bag, prepared to run for his life, but he'd have to crawl out of the cabin first, putting himself in a dangerous position. He opted to stay put for the time being.

"Hey bear," Wes tried, hoping whatever it was would be scared away by the sound of his voice.

It was answered by a quick, confrontational grunt blowing through flaring nostrils. Groping around, Wes located his canister of bear spray and pulled off the safety clip. He aimed it at the incomplete doorway, ready to strike at first sight.

"Hey bear," he warned again.

A hoof knocked at the side of the cabin.

Wes dropped the camera, clutching the bear spray with both hands. He spun his headlamp around trying to locate his bow and arrows. It was in the corner, right where he had left it. There wasn't enough room to shoot with a bow so, he crawled over and pulled an arrow out, giving it a little shake as if testing it's potential to use as a handheld weapon. A short spear was better than nothing. He readied himself in a precarious position, laying on the ground because there wasn't enough room to stand. He cursed himself for working longer to finish the cabin.

"I don't know what the heck that is. It could be a bear…or a wild boar…or a moose," he guessed out loud, the camera capturing his words as it filmed the blank tarp ceiling.

A strong wild scent wafted in. Wes sniffed at it, thinking the smell might help him identify the animal. It could have been any of the animals he had listed. He was an expert when it came to cattle, hogs and chickens—farm animals—but he had no experience with the wild animals of the Great North.

Whatever was lurking had had enough. Wes could hear it receding into the woods with slow, dragging steps. Determined to identify the intruder, the stubborn farmer crawled out the doorway on his elbows and knees, carrying the camera in one hand and the bear spray in the other.

Getting to his feet, he scanned his camp. Nothing had been disturbed, but there wasn't much that could have gotten disturbed. He checked the ground for footprints, but the grassy area surrendered few clues. He braved his way around in the dark, checking the outside of the cabin as he circled around back. A grunt from within the forest brought him to the edge of camp to investigate.

Shining his headlamp into the woods, he scanned left to right. The light only penetrated about twenty feet, casting shadows that complicated visibility. Through the shadows a large hump appeared. Wes focused on it with the camera. It was an enormous lumpy rump. A short tail flicked to life. A grunt from the other end produced a puff of steam.

"It's a moose," Wes whispered, astonished his prediction had come true.

The animal heard him and whipped around. Giant antlers and flaring nostrils filled the camera screen. Wes fumbled the camera, almost dropping it as he looked up. Even at the distance of twenty feet the animal was menacing, standing almost seven feet tall and huffing a warning as it dragged a front hoof on the ground, threatening to charge.

Wes froze, hoping the shining light of the headlamp would confuse the animal. It didn't work. The moose charged, sending Wes running for his life back across his camp, into the woods. The camera only captured darkness and branches whipping by as Wes ran with it in his hand.

The moose followed, weaving through the trees, zigzagging, frantic to trample the intruder.

The camera caught the audio as Wes ran for his life.

"Fuuuuuuuuuck!"

Heavy hooves stomped the ground like a full stampede.

Wes thought about turning around and trying to use the bear spray, but the moose was too close. He'd be trampled as soon as he turned around.

Testing the moose's agility, Wes circled around trees, making his way back towards camp. The moose refused to let up, changing direction with clumsy pauses, allowing Wes to put some space between them.

At almost sixty years-old, Wes knew he couldn't run forever. He summoned the strength for one last sprint back to his cabin, gambling his life on the possibility of finding safety inside. The moose regained ground in the clearing, ducking its head to lunge at the fleeing man as it caught up.

"Oh help me Jesus!" he cried out as he dove into the cabin through the short doorway, disappearing from sight, confusing the charging beast.

It changed course, veering around the half-walls of the cabin, coming to an abrupt halt on the other side.

Inside the cabin, Wes tossed the camera onto his sleeping bag, grabbed his bow, readied an arrow, and laid on his side, pointing it ready to fire at the doorway. He knew an arrow to the head wouldn't do much damage to an animal with a skull like a moose but he was desperate and hoping to hit an eye.

The moose looked around the back of the cabin for its rival for a moment, then turned its attention to a boar trying to sneak by in the woods undetected. The moose charged after the boar and the two animals disappeared into the darkness of the forest.

Wes sat frozen in his defensive pose, heart pounding like a jackhammer trying to escape through his throat.

"Oh mercy. Holy flippin' crap," he repeated between long, heaving breaths.

It took almost ten minutes of swearing for him to regather himself and come up with a more articulate expression.

"That was crazy. That was…da-gum crazy. Too close for comfort."

After a long period of silence, he picked up the camera and turned it on his face.

"First night here, first moose attack. I done survived it by the grace of god. This here's the real deal, y'all. No joke. I coulda been killed."

The lucky man physically shook the experience off, loosening his body from the grips of peril. Above all, he didn't want to look overly weak or scared in front of the camera. He took a deep breath and let it out slowly, grounding himself.

He looked directly into the camera, close up. "That was crazy, but I look on the bright side. That moose is a lot of meat waiting to feed a hunter like me. I'm gonna work on that tomorrow," he vowed before turning off the camera and settling back down for the rest of the night. He had to wait for his heartbeat to return to a normal rate and even then the threat of another close call made it difficult to fall asleep.

Chapter 3

Day 14

High Stakes

Dr. Rodney and Dyson were halfway down the trail to the shore on their way to the Medline to retrieve a stretcher to facilitate moving Derrick's body, or whatever was left of his body. The two didn't speak a word until Dyson turned his camera on and resumed shooting.

"What are you doing?" Dr. Rodney asked.

"Um…I'm doing my job," Dyson replied.

"I think we're done shooting. I'm going to recommend pulling all the contestants and going home. A man killed himself. The show's over," DocRod explained, more than a hint of hostility in his voice.

"I'm going to keep shooting until the plug is officially pulled if you don't mind," Dyson said. "I passed up some good job offers for this gig."

"It's over," Dr. Rodney insisted.

"We can turn it into a documentary or something—what really happened to Derrick Bond on the mysterious Isolation Island? Are the producers to blame? Controversy, scandal, and the tragic death of an American hero. That's the kind of stuff that sells."

"Forget it," Dr. Rodney growled, putting his hand over the camera lens, pushing it away.

"Come on. Let me get a shot of you walking through the woods. One shot. Just give me a head start. I'll shout when I want you to start walking," Dyson directed, hurrying down the trail without waiting for confirmation.

"I said no," the doctor shouted after him.

Dyson turned around, camera rolling, and walked backwards capturing whatever footage he could. Dr. Rodney followed, reaching at the camera every few steps, but it was just beyond reach as Dyson hustled to stay one step ahead.

Frustration boiling over, DocRod shouted, "Dyson! I'm going to shove that camera up your ass if you don't stop."

Dyson grinned, continuing to back up, refusing to stop.

Just as Dr. Rodney was about to charge the camera, Dyson took one step too many. The ground collapsed under his back foot. Gravity sucked him in backwards. He let out a scream, interrupted almost as soon as it started.

Dyson gasped and screamed in pain. Sharpened wooden stakes pierced through his body—two through his abdomen, one through his chest, several through his arms and legs. He was now impaled in a trapping pit, five-feet deep, with three-foot wooden stakes meant to immobilize and kill any animal unfortunate enough to fall in. The trap had been camouflaged, covered with leaves and debris laid over a framework of sticks. Perhaps he would have noticed it had he been watching where he was going.

Dyson's eyes bugged out of his head, staring straight up at the sky. He took a labored breath in and screamed another blood-curdling cry. Blood gushed from multiple wounds, spraying in the air and landing in his mouth and eyes. He raised a trembling hand, attempting to clear his mouth and nose so he could breathe unimpeded.

Dr. Rodney rushed to Dyson's aid but there was little he could do with six or seven dirty stakes sticking through the victim's body and blood spurting everywhere. Severed arteries, torn muscle, pierced internal organs—there were too many wounds to deal with. He tried anyway, jumping into the pit to try to stop some of the bleeding.

It didn't take long for Dyson's screams to stop. Dr. Rodney took over, crying out for Hutch's help. The good doctor tried to lift the impaled man off the stakes, but it was no use. His hands slipped on the greasy blood as he tugged, sending him down to one knee, his right eye landing an inch away from the sharp end of the stake sticking through Dyson's chest. There was nothing left to do but yell for help and try to comfort the dying man. Dr. Rodney held his hand and Dyson squeezed with his last ounce of life.

They didn't know each other well, but when Dyson's hand went limp, Dr. Rodney let out a cry of frustration and began sobbing. Dyson Wolski died with his camera still clutched in his other hand, a ghastly expression of shock frozen on his face.

Covered in Dyson's blood, Dr. Rodney tried to pull himself out of the trapping pit. Dirt caked on the blood as he slipped back in, again almost impaling himself. He decided to wait in the pit until Hutch showed up and resumed screaming for help to mark his location. It was a precarious position—trapped in a pit, covered in blood in the wild where any predator could pick up the scent and find an easy meal. The wait for help seemed to take forever. Hutch answered the doctor's pleas for help, assuring he was on his way, but the damage was done. They now had two dead bodies to deal with.

Hutch came sprinting down the trail, clutching his hunting knife in one hand. He stopped at the edge of the pit. No need to ask what happened, he expressed his frustration over what was obvious. "Fuck. Fuuuuuuck!" he yelped. "Are you okay?"

"I'm uninjured," Dr. Rodney assured him. "This…this isn't my blood."

Hutch turned to take a pacing lap to vent, hands on his hips, head turned to the sky. How had everything come undone so quickly? Two deaths on his watch was unacceptable.

Sharon and Page came rushing behind him. Sharon stopped short, staring at Dyson with dead eyes and a somber expression as if she wasn't surprised at all.

Page shrieked in simultaneous shock and grief, falling to her knees at the sight of the second dead body she had seen in a single day. "Wha…how…what happened?" she managed to articulate.

No one answered.

"What *is* this?" Page tried again, still in shock, her hands trembling.

Hutch offered a helping hand to Dr. Rodney, heaving him out of the pit safely in one motion.

"It's a trap," Hutch explained for Page's benefit. "Derrick must have made it in hopes of trapping food. We need to be extra careful walking around out here. There could be traps anywhere."

They all looked at each other, hoping someone would know what to do next.

"You need to get washed up," Hutch told Dr. Rodney. "You can't be walking around the woods smelling like a fresh kill."

There was nothing more they could do for Dyson except get the stretcher from the boat, extract him from the trap, and bring him home to his family for a proper burial. Expressions of disbelief and horror only served to waste time before they finally headed toward shore together.

FLOYD BENSON

Day 2

2:22pm

Age: 26
Occupation: Pizza Delivery
Home: Florida
Status: Single, 2 children

When Floyd Benson arrived on Day 1, he said to the camera, "The key to this game is energy conservation." He was living up to his declared strategy, conserving as much energy as possible on Day 2.

That's not to say he did nothing. He set up a simple debris shelter—a small dome made of wood, leaves, branches, even a little mud, all topped by a blue tarp for added protection from the elements. A framed insert made of branches and leaves served as a door, fitting snuggly into the entrance.

Instead of an indoor fire pit, he opted to use a series of large stones to heat his humble dwelling. The stones would warm up in the outdoor fire pit until Floyd was ready to go to sleep. His last task of each night would be transferring the heated stones into his shelter to keep him cozy at night. It was part of his energy conservation strategy—he hoped to sleep through the night instead of waking up over and over to tend to the fire.

Floyd's first night was rough and cold. He found the stones didn't retain enough heat to keep him warm through the entire night. He addressed the problem on Day 2 while the camera rolled and he lounged outside his shelter.

"Last night got pretty damn cold," he reported, fidgeting with his gloves. He never looked directly at the camera, choosing to pretend it wasn't there to make him feel more comfortable.

"My heating system doesn't quite last a full night. What I'm going to try tonight is basically the same thing, but with a second set of stones in the fire outside while I sleep. Then I'll wake up halfway through the night and hopefully have the second set of hot stones to bring in and get me to morning."

He thought about his idea for a moment, staring straight at the ground. After a long period of silent deliberation, he admitted. "I might have to rework the whole thing. It's only going to get colder as winter approaches."

He shook his head, deciding to think about it later. The current method could work for the time being.

"So, this is it, pretty much," he declared with a throw of his hand. "This is what survival looks like for me. It's slow and it's boring most of the time, but it's all about existing. That's my goal—to just exist here, longer than anyone else. Nothing glamorous. Nothing fancy. I'm not building a big log cabin and furniture, nothing like that. I'm just going to wait it out while the other contestants break their backs exhausting themselves with silly, unnecessary projects."

Floyd rarely moved while he spoke. Even his lips seemed too lazy to assist his speech. He would have made a good ventriloquist.

"I was homeless for a couple years and this is how I got by—conserving energy. My homeless friends called me Floyd the Sloth. I didn't take offense to that. I took it as a compliment. I love sloths. They're so stubborn and committed to conserving energy to a point that it's funny. They can be crawling across a street, holding up traffic. It's like, 'Hey, move it sloth!' but the sloth just keeps moving at his own pace, like…"

Floyd acted out the scene in super-slow motion as if the top half of his body was crawling across the ground, being pulled along by long, lanky arms.

"Hurry up sloth, you're going to get run over by a car!" Floyd said, playing all the characters in his little skit.

"And the sloth's like, no, no. Gotta conserve my energy. It's very important."

The improv ended with Floyd laughing at his own performance.

"Or, maybe, in their own minds, sloths think they're in, like, super-ninja-stealth mode."

He mimed the sloth's crawling motion again.

"And the sloth's like, 'They'll never even know I was here.'"

After another quick laugh, he stood up for the first time in hours and approached the camera.

"Time to start looking for water," he said and turned off the camera. He had finished his starting water ration early that morning.

4:53pm

"I know I'm not playing the game with the most exciting strategy," Floyd told the camera, standing still for a close-up of his face.

"But..." he continued, turning the camera around to reveal a wide lazy flowing river. "Look what I found," he bragged.

"Freshwater for drinking. And, a potential source of food."

He directed the camera up and downstream from his perch—the stumpy end of a fallen tree jutting out over the water.

"This is about as exciting as it gets," Floyd maintained. "I don't expect I'll get a lot of airtime when the show hits TV screens, but I'm not here to be on TV. I'm here to outlast everyone else. I'm here to win a million dollars. A million bucks could last me a long time. I can start my own business and pay other people to do all the work. This here is what my American Dream looks like and it begins with this river. It's is an amazing find. I don't know if anyone else is going to have a resource like this. This is a game changer. I'll come back tomorrow with some fishing line and sit here all day until I catch something to eat. I can set up a gill net, too."

He turned the camera back on himself and gave a single thumbs up, along with a quiet, conservative, "Woo hoo."

7:47pm

"I chose this spot to build my camp, specifically for this feature here," Floyd explained, walking the camera over to a long, branchless log that lay on the ground, stretching from the forest into the clearing.

He sat down on the log and captured on camera his proximity to the fire. "Instant seating. No work required." He tapped his index finger on his temple. "Work smarter, not harder."

He shifted his weight, settling in for a long sit as he waited for the water he collected from the river to boil.

"The biggest pain in the ass with water is not just that you have to boil it, but you have to wait until it cools down enough to drink. All the while you're sitting thirsty."

He lifted the lid to check on the water's progress. No sign of boiling, he returned the lid and sighed.

"There's not much else to do out here but wait. Wait for your water to boil. Wait for it to cool. Wait for a fish to bite. Wait for the other contestants to tap out."

Over five minutes of silence passed as he sat like a statue on the log. He even blinked slowly and infrequently as if it burned too many calories to justify the effort.

Finally, he jerked out of his trance and told the camera, "I'm getting pretty hungry. Now that I found the river, I'll set up my gill net tomorrow. Basically, stretch it across part of the river and wait for something to get tangled up in it. Boom…dinner. Minimal effort."

ZOEY PRICE

Day 2

3:08pm

Age: 24
Occupation: Dance Instructor
Home: Montana
Status: Single

The tenth (and final) contestant was Zoey Price—a slim, 5'7" vegetarian with blonde, braided pigtails and an optimistic glint in her eyes that could just as easily be interpreted as a vacant stare. She wore a light-pink onesie snow suit with darker-pink stars on all four cuffs and white water-proof boots. Her white hat had a triangular nose with black whiskers and long, floppy bunny-ear flaps that dangled braided lengths of yarn capped by white poms.

Zoey wasn't first on the list of accepted contestants or even tenth. She had landed on the list of alternates to begin with, but one of the original ten chosen had backed out due to a death in the family. One person's misfortune had led to Zoey's big break.

After insertion on Day 1, Hutch had bet DocRod fifty bucks Zoey would be the one to tap out first, giving her one night at best before "reality slaps her in the face." He was expecting a tap out by sundown on Day 2. That time was approaching, but Zoey hadn't even considered tapping out, yet.

Her first day was difficult, but she was resilient and optimistic. Damp wood made it impossible to get a fire started. The territory she had been assigned jutted out to the north, catching more rain and moisture than other parts of the island. She had built a small debris shelter—a tiny igloo made of sticks, covered with leaves. It was just big enough to crawl into and store her supplies. It was only temporary, but she was proud of it and hoped the low-profile design would help keep warmth in.

After four hours trying to start a fire, she had realized she'd be sleeping without it on her first night on Isolation Island. She had gathered more leaves and piled them up on her debris shelter for added insulation, but it was a cold first night. The shelter sufficed to keep her from freezing, but she had shivered all night, burning calories she'd find hard to replenish in the wild without resorting to meat.

On Day 2, things were looking up. The sun had come out, the wood had dried enough to burn and Zoey began work on a larger, long-term shelter modeled after her little debris shelter. The new debris shelter would be much bigger, with room for an indoor fire and tall enough to stand in.

By three o'clock the structure was tall enough to crawl in. She gave the half-finished circular walls a tarp roof and moved on to other tasks. Water and food were making their way to the top of the list of priorities.

"Sticking to a vegetarian lifestyle out here is going to be a challenge, for sure," she explained to the camera as she set out in search of food. "But, I want to prove to people that you don't have to eat meat. You don't have to kill animals to survive."

Zoey blazed a new trail through the forest, making slow progress until she came across another clearing, similar to the one she had chosen for her camp. There was one big exception—this newly discovered clearing was overrun with dandelions in various stages of growth—a gold mine for a vegetarian survivalist.

Zoey let out a gasp of wonder, capturing her find on camera. "Score! Look at that. Dandelions. That is food for Zoey. Every part of the dandelion is edible. I can make tea, eat it raw, cook up the leaves in a pan like spinach, or add it to other greens for a salad. This is a great find."

She fell to her knees, pulling up dandelion leaves and shoving them in her mouth. After two handfuls, she reconsidered as she chewed.

"I'm really hungry but, now that I think about, I should probably take these back to camp and clean them first. Animals pee and poop everywhere."

She continued her harvest, shoving dandelion leaves in her side pockets, explaining, "The benefits of being a herbivore is your food can't run away. Your food doesn't try to bite you back. You don't need bait. You don't end up with guts everywhere attracting predators."

She grinned ear to ear, proud of herself for her denial of how difficult the challenge would become the more time passed and winter approached. A tiny flash of red in the woods caught her eye, exposed by a breeze, then disappearing behind a leaf. It brought her to her feet.

"Oh my god. No way," she exclaimed, rising slowly and repeating phrases of disbelief several times on her way to the edge of the clearing. She lifted the rough, textured, oval green leaves to the side, exposing a cluster of little red raspberries. She showed them to the camera.

"Oh baby! Look at that. Raspberries. I can't believe it. And, somehow, the animals haven't gotten to them yet. Bonus!"

She followed the line of berries that peppered their way across a wide area of bushes. Some were purple, some were red, others were green, not fully developed. She held the camera under her arm while she picked every ripened berry she could find and shoved them into her pockets. Once the raspberries were all plucked, she moved on, pulling off a generous portion of leaves from the plants.

"I can add the raspberry leaves to the dandelion leaves and make a nice tea to warm me up at night," she explained to the camera, the shot obstructed by her coat.

Her excitement was bubbling over. With her pockets full, she practically skipped back to camp, stopping one last time at another patch of greens. She focused the camera on some narrow leaves fanned out with a long, skinny stalk of tiny flowers in the middle.

"I knew it. I knew I'd be able to survive here," Zoey bragged. "More food for Zoey. I can totally win this thing. It's in the stars."

She set the camera down in the grass and began plucking leaves again while she explained, "Most people think astrology is bogus but that's just because they don't understand it. The stars can guide you, you just have to know how to read them." She flashed a confident smile the camera couldn't see. "With the help of the stars, I *will* succeed."

She showed off her new catch for future viewers to see. "These are plantain...weeds," she said, reluctant to use the word *weeds* to describe her food. "They grow all over the place and they're edible. Umm...I don't really know a lot about them, but I know you can eat them and most people consider them to be unwanted weeds messing up their lawns." She gave the camera an uncertain smile and moved on.

When she got back to camp, she laid out her harvest in a cast iron pan. Starting with the raspberries, she ate with great delight for the first time on Isolation Island.

"Mmm…this is great, really great. This is energy." She popped another raspberry in her mouth, eating them one at a time, chewing and savoring for as long as possible.

"The survival gods have smiled upon me," she claimed. "If I can get in touch with the spirits of Isolation Island, it could give me a great advantage," she added, voicing her thoughts in a display of her eclectic beliefs which seemed like a custom-made collection of various myths and superstition.

She spent the rest of the day explaining the rituals she could use to tap into the island's 'spiritual realm'. She was dead serious. It was too early for delusions induced by hunger or thirst to explain away her strange beliefs. Her excessive reliance on spirituality was something she had brought from home to the island. She had spent countless hours consulting the stars and spirits in an attempt to gain an advantage in her everyday life and now she hoped it would help her in the competition.

STEPHANIE HAMILTON

Day 2

3:10pm

Age: 29
Occupation: Artist
Home: Colorado
Status: Single

"Look at this," Stephanie said, squatting at the edge of the clearing she had chosen to build her camp. She used a handheld camera to capture images of plantain weeds growing in random spots. She swept the camera steadily over the tops like an aerial view from a tiny helicopter. "Free food," she declared.

"You've probably all seen these weeds growing in your yard or the park, pretty much everywhere. What you might not know is that these leaves are edible. This boring little plant is called *plantain* or *White Man's Foot* and it might not look like much, but if you know what you're doing, they're very useful as food and medicine."

She plucked a small leaf and popped it in her mouth for the camera to see. She chewed liked a llama, her large green eyes pointing up, searching her brain for data.

"They're a little bitter," she explained as she chewed. She tilted her head back and forth in a gesture of uncertainty. "They're not bad. They taste like salad. The younger ones are less bitter. You want to avoid the older, stringier ones, but I can add them to a fish soup for some added nutrition. Definitely want to wash them first." She picked a few more.

"As the story goes, white men brought plantain weed from Europe to North America. They left of trail of plantain weeds everywhere they went. Supposedly, Native Americans were able to track the white men's movements by following this trail like footprints. That's why the Native Americans called it *White Man's*

Foot."

She smiled a goofy smile into the camera lens. "I don't know how true that is, but it makes a neat story."

She began harvesting the younger leaves, pulling them out in fistfuls with one hand.

"I'm not a big believer of what we call *history*. To me, history is just a perpetual game of *Operator*. In fact, the game *Operator* is all the proof I need to know that history is fabricated. Maybe sometimes, part of it is true, but too many times we find out the truth had fallen through the cracks long before it got to us. People add their own commentary and conjecture every time the story is retold. You can't trust that. Add to that the fact that history is told by the winners and it's anybody's guess what really happened in the past. I prefer to focus on the present and the future. Those are the things I can affect."

She stood up, tossed a few plantain leaves in her mouth and chewed with a nonchalant expression. "But, I digest," she said, proud of her corny pun without showing the camera.

"Plantain leaves also have antiseptic and anesthetic properties. You can crush up the leaves and put them right on a sting or a bite. I can make tea with it if I want. It's good for a whole bunch of things. Good stuff. All natural."

7:11pm

"I think I'd rather be stranded and isolated on a nice, warm tropical island. Well, not stranded. I can't imagine being *stranded*," Stephanie told the camera, kneeling by the fire inside her wikiup. She had caught another fish and was cooking it up with the greens she had collected.

The weather on Day 2 had been as good as it gets on Isolation Island—sunny and dry—but a storm could always roll in at any moment without warning.

"Even here on this remote island, I know I can leave any time I want," she continued, flipping her fish fillets over. "That bit of knowledge does something to you. On one hand, it's a great comfort. On the other hand, you have to be a lot more disciplined.

When the weather goes bad and you're freezing, stuck in your shelter all day, and you're hungry and you're thirsty, and all you want is to be back home with your loved ones, with a roof over your head that's not leaking—it may be comforting to know you're one phone call away from leaving, but it also makes it hard to keep your finger off the call button."

She took the frying pan off the fire using a wide strip of bark as an oven mitt and showed the finished fish to the camera. A small portion of shriveled plantain leaves stuck to the bottom of the pan.

"Mmm…protein. And, a side of veggies. That's what I call a wilderness meal."

The happy camper set the pan down on a flat rock outside the fire pit circle. A pot of boiled water was cooling nearby. She lifted the lid to reveal the concoction she had brewed with plantain leaves.

"I also made some tea," she said. The greenish tint to the water in the black pot wasn't picked up by the camera. "It might be a little weak, but at least it'll have some flavor to it."

She emerged from the wikiup to eat outside, enjoying her food as the sun went down and laid to rest another peaceful day.

"I need to build a chair and a bed, so I'm off the ground," she decided out loud as she sat on the grass.

Her permanent shelter was taking shape behind her. Half the structure was finished with thin, vertical logs hammered into the ground to make the side walls. She planned to construct the back wall out of piled stone to incorporate a fire place. A tarp would serve as the roof, of course.

Before going to bed that night, she added more wood to the fire inside her wikiup explaining, "I don't want the fire to be too big. Can't let it get out of control. Although I could rebuild my shelter if it were to catch fire, my tools are irreplaceable and, so am I."

WES WOOD

Day 2

3:22pm

Age: 57
Occupation: Farmer
Home: Mississippi
Status: Divorced, 8 children

Wes Wood held the radio in his hand with his finger hovering over the call button as he sat on a boulder on the same shoreline he had been dropped off on just one day earlier. He bowed his head away from the all-seeing camera, one leg bouncing on a nervous foot.

"I ain't here to get eaten by no animals," he explained as he had for hours on Day 2.

The run in with the moose had rattled him more than he had been willing to admit the previous night. After some time to think about it, he imagined being eaten, not by the moose which could have killed him, but by hungry scavengers taking advantage of the moose's efforts.

"This is some serious shit here. There ain't no one around to help me if I get attacked by a bear or them damn wolves or another damn moose. I ain't slept more than two hours. Every time I falled asleep, I started hearin' some dang critter sniffin' 'round my shelter."

He held the radio with two hands, lifting it up as if it would give him better reception, then resting it back on his lap again. He shook his head over and over, rocking back and forth.

"Screw this shit," he said, lifting the radio up again. "I miss my family and I ain't no good to them if I come back dead."

His thumb hovered over the call button. With a deep breath, he pulled his thumb back to give it a running start. The thumb froze in that pose. The air sighed out of his lungs as he collapsed from his straight-backed decisiveness, dropping his elbows onto his knees as he hunched over, uncertain again.

"I don't wanna be the first one to tap out," he said. "Maybe I'm not the first, but I don't wanna tap out this early. I still got work to do on this here island."

The proud Mississippi farmer regathered himself, embarrassed by his moment of weakness in front of the camera and stood up. It had actually been more than a moment of weakness. He had spent the entire day debating with himself, trying to put on a brave face, but flashbacks from the first night seeped into his head more and more as he tried to keep busy. With the flashbacks came the increased heartrate and fear associated with a near-death experience.

There was no cowardice in tapping out. He had had a dangerous run in with the largest wild animal on the island and survived unscathed. One could consider that lucky rather than a bad omen. It was a harsh Day 1 and, like all the contestants, he knew it would only get more difficult as the days passed, but none of these survivalists had come all this way just to quit.

Wes built up his courage, reminding himself how he'd look on camera if he were to give up so early. It gave him a new level of determination. He receded into the woods, returning to the project he had been working on (on and off) all day—getting his log cabin finished.

DERRICK BOND

Day 2

5:21pm

Age: 29
Occupation: ex-Marine
Home: Texas
Status: Single

"I quit my job to come out here and play this game. I drove a delivery truck for a parcel service. I'm not supposed to say which company," Derrick said as he trekked through the forest with a camera strapped to his desert camo ranger's hat. It captured his progress from the void between the hat and one of the folded-up sides.

"I put all my stuff in storage. I don't have a place to live back home so, I truly have nothing to return to." He let out a nervous laugh amid the heavy breathing brought on by exertion. He had spent the entire day exploring, hoping to come across the Treasure Tree, but the going was slow as he learned the forest got thicker the farther he ventured. The river had been easy to find using the map, but Derrick chose to do a grid search for the Treasure Tree and it was eating up a lot of time. He knew the general direction to search, but the crude map was hardly to scale.

"The longer I stay out here the more money I save on rent," he said, as if suddenly realizing it. He flashed an uneasy smile the camera couldn't capture as it filmed from atop his cranium. It only captured the wilderness surrounding him, the branches brushing by.

There was no sign of any tree that even remotely looked like the wide, low limbed Treasure Tree. The forest began to look like the same frame of a cartoon being played over and over—pine trees, oak trees, thorny bushes, ferns, ferns, ferns. Pine trees, oak trees, thorny bushes, ferns, ferns, ferns...

Derrick reminded himself that he only needed to follow the game trail to the tree, but there were several game trails in real life and only one depicted on the map, if it was indeed a game trail. He took out the map and unrolled it for another look.

"This map has no scale on it," he complained to the camera. "I don't know if two inches is a mile or five miles or ten feet." He threw his hand, shaking his head. "This tree could be an hour's walk or two hours or half a day."

He looked back at the trail he had carved through the forest, knowing he'd have to start making his way back to camp soon. No one wants to be walking around in the woods at night, but worse—he wasn't sure he could find his camp without any trouble after a full day of roaming.

"I'm gonna try to follow the game trails back to camp," he explained doubling back on his own path. "As soon as I pick up a game trail, I'm taking it. It's too much work cutting my own tunnels to nowhere." He had burned an exponentially higher amount of calories taking the path of most resistance.

"Hopefully, I'll be back at camp before the sun goes down," he said before turning the camera off. Saving the battery in case he got stuck in the woods and needed the camera's light and night vision after dark made sense to him even though he had a flashlight. Can't be too careful. He had little more to say on the record anyway.

9:44pm

"Damn it," Derrick hollered through the darkness. He was answered by the distant howling of wolves.

"None of this looks familiar," he huffed, camera turned back on in the growing desperation that he might be capturing his last night on Earth.

"I think I'm lost," he finally admitted, his voice cracking with despair. His steamy breath floated away, off the edge of the camera's view after every sequence of words. "If I die of exposure out here, hopefully someone will find this video and know what happened to me."

He was only half-joking, but there were two parts to the joke. Dying of exposure could come if he didn't find his camp or, if he *did* find his camp, he could die of exposure in the coming days because he had wasted an entire day wandering the forest without gaining any advantage in the form of treasure or food.

"This damn island is haunted or something. Listen," he whispered, pausing to avoid making noise.

Turning his head to slowly pan the forest behind him, the camera picked up the unmistakable sound of something walking through dry leaves in the distance.

"I swear it sounds like something walking on two feet," he whispered, even softer, searching the dark forest. The camera followed his head, jerking and whipping around as the sound got closer, but there was nothing within visibility by camera or naked eye.

"What the hell *is* that?" he asked, his whisper breaking up.

The sound stopped abruptly and Derrick was at a standoff, waiting for the noise to resume or for a different noise that might help him identify what was following him. He visually mapped his escape route, should the follower give pursuit, whatever it was. Unfortunately, the flashlight didn't let him see far.

The standoff went on for what Derrick estimated to be fifteen minutes. His legs were beginning to tremble, frozen in the same spot, back twisting in the other direction to continue looking behind him every few seconds.

"This is bullshit," he finally whispered to the camera. "There was definitely something following me and now, nothing. It sounded way too big to be a bird or small mammal. How could it just stop making noise? It couldn't have flown away."

Derrick swallowed hard, gave one last scan of the forest with his flashlight and resumed moving forward, almost tiptoeing on the animal trail. Looking down at the clear path he eased his mind, reminding himself he was bound to come across animals walking near an *animal* trail.

The sound didn't return. In fact, the forest became still and quiet with only Derrick's own movements as they seemed to be amplified against the silence. There was not a breeze to rustle a leaf. Even the wolves had ceased their long distance conversation.

Derrick walked without a word for as long as he could bear,

the camera only capturing his footsteps and breathing. The encounter with the unidentified walker had taken a backseat to his original problem.

"I can't believe this," he finally said. "I'm lost in the fucking woods at night. I could be out here the rest of my damn life." After a long, uncertain trek through the woods in the dark, he was on the verge of coming undone.

Just as the words had left his mouth, a new sound caught his ear. He held his breath. Could it be? Yes, it was—the crashing of ocean waves. It couldn't be far.

"Do you hear that?" he asked the camera, pausing to capture the glorious audio. "If I can get to shore, I can find my insertion point and find my camp from there."

The comment turned to a lecture about different methods for finding your way when you get lost—things he had learned in the Marines. His own advice worked. He followed the sound of the ocean to the shore, the shore to his insertion point, and his insertion point to camp. In less than an hour, he was back at his beloved shelter, letting out a burst of vulgarity-riddled celebration, going as far as to drop to his knees and kiss the ground.

Before settling in for the night, he had one last comment for the camera. "I'm gonna find that treasure tomorrow," he promised like it was a fact.

Chapter 4

Day 14

New Horizons

No one was sure whether Page's tears were due to fear or mourning but, they continued the entire way to shore. She fell short of using the old cliché, "This isn't what I signed up for." It didn't need to be verbalized. None of them had signed up for *this*. With Doc leading the way and Hutch bringing up the rear, they poured out of the forest, onto the beach, single file and deflated. Doc stopped short.

With her eyes glued to the ground, examining it for booby traps, Sharon almost walked into his back. Page almost crashed into Sharon's back, her vision blurred by tears.

Hutch popped out from behind them all and took a few deliberate steps toward the ocean. "What the hell is that?" he asked himself and everyone else, eyes fixed on the ocean.

They fanned out, examining the horizon. A plume of smoke billowed at the edge, like a tornado touching down somewhere beyond sight.

With nothing but bad news to report from land, Hutch had purposely avoided contacting the Mothership, but now he pulled the radio out and switched to the correct channel. "This is Hutch," he said. "Is everything okay? I see smoke on the horizon. Over."

They all waited, gathered around the radio, watching the smoke continue to billow and get darker. There was no reply.

"Come in Mothership. This is Hutch. Do you read me? Over," he tried again.

The radio sounded a single crackle, but returned no reply.

Doc intervened. "That doesn't look good, Hutch. We better check it out. Where's the Medline?"

Hutch led them up the shore, toward their landing spot, trying and retrying to get in touch with the Mothership along the way.

"Why aren't they answering?" Sharon huffed, trying to keep

up with the long strides of Hutch and Doc.

Hutch wanted to tell her to figure it out herself, but instead he stated what he thought was obvious. "Maybe they *can't* answer."

Page let out a worried moan, straggling behind them, unable to contribute anything constructive.

"Okay. There's no reason to panic," Doc said, trying to sound calm and unconcerned.

They took turns trying the radio, watching the smoke on the horizon as they hurried across the beach. Stretches of rockiness slowed them down from time to time. Suddenly, Hutch stopped short, looking up and down at the gray sand, the tree line, and the ocean.

"What? What's wrong? Why are we stopping?" Sharon demanded.

Hutch turned to look in the direction from which they came, answering Sharon's question with the gesture and confused look on his face.

"Oh, no. No, no, no. Don't tell me you're lost," Sharon growled, threatening to boil over and start throwing blame.

Hutch continued looking up and down the shoreline, replying to Sharon with one word. "Worse."

"Worse? What could be worse? How can we be lost on the beach?" she demanded. With only two directions to go, it was a legitimate question.

Hutch looked at her sideways, lips folded in. He was an inch away from going off on her but calmed himself, keeping his tone as professional as he was able to fake. "We're not lost. I know exactly where we are," he informed her, failing to disguise how annoyed he was with her.

"That's good…right?" Page asked, searching everyone's face for a hint.

Only Doc seemed to be figuring out what Hutch had already realized. The doctor covered his eyes, rubbing them with his fingers as if he was trying to wake himself from a bad dream.

"No, that's not good, Page," Hutch answered. He kicked his foot into the sand, creating a divot to mark the spot. A few feet to his right, there was a similar divot in the sand. He pointed to a strip of ocean in front of it. "That's where Sharon fell. That's where she lost her hat." He pointed out the general areas he was talking about. "That's where we entered the forest," he added, pointing into the woods.

Page's expression changed from confusion back to horror, finally realizing what Hutch was hinting at. She shook her head and grabbed two fists full of his coat, pulling him in toward her. "No. It can't be," she said in a panic.

Hutch didn't resist. He simply stated the truth. "Yes. I'm afraid so. This is where we left the boat."

DERRICK BOND

Day 3

2:11pm

Age: 29
Occupation: ex-Marine
Home: Texas
Status: Single

"I haven't eaten in three days. I spent yesterday getting lost in the forest with nothing to show for it. I burned up half the day today looking for that damn treasure," Derrick told the camera, a questionable desperation in his voice. He wasn't the best actor. His facial expressions looked more like he had to go to the bathroom than his intended look of defeat. The close-up of his face, looking straight up his nose wasn't helping. Half the frame was big, black, bottomless nostrils with one nose hair reaching out, taking center stage.

"But," he said, turning the camera around to reveal his ruse. "It was all worth it," he almost shouted, his tone livening to excitement as he captured the view from his vantage point.

There before him, the glorious Treasure Tree could not be mistaken. He approached it, camera held out for a steady shot. He added a soundtrack with his voice—a triumphant mixture of 'dums' and 'das' swelling in intensity as he got closer to the tree he had been dreaming about.

"It's the Treasure Tree," he announced and followed up with several rounds of a breathy simulated crowd cheering.

Circling halfway around the tree, he stopped, noticing an indentation in the ground. He aimed the camera down, kneading the ground with his feet.

"Oh, this is too easy," he said, dancing around like Snoopy in slow motion, feeling with his feet. "I can feel the difference in the ground," he claimed.

He settled on one spot, bouncing on his right foot. "The dirt is hard here." He shifted to his left foot two feet away and bounced again. "And, here, it's soft. It has a little give. You can tell someone had dug a hole here recently. The ground hasn't settled and hardened yet. And…"

He lined himself up against the tree and counted his steps to the soft spot. "…It's exactly ten paces from the tree, like the map suggests. This has to be it."

He tested the ground again, fanning out to determine the size of the area.

"It's around six by six feet," he concluded. "That's potential for *a lot* of treasure."

Turning the camera back on himself, he lamented, "Too bad they didn't give me a shovel," referring to Sharon and the show's crew.

To the contestants, Sharon was the face of the show. She insisted on being the only one to have contact with the contestants so she could maintain strict control. There were contracts in place, official rules to be followed and a number of legal consequences if any were breached. Isolation Island was more than a place. It was more than a contest or a TV show. It was a business and Sharon treated it *only* as a business.

Derrick dropped to his knees and tried digging with his hands. He was right—the soil was soft and loose. It wasn't easy and it would take a long time, but he continued digging with his bare hands all afternoon, hoping the treasure wasn't buried too deep.

5:30pm

Derrick sat with his back against the side of the hole, his hands dirty and swollen from digging. He had managed to make a crater three feet deep, less than five feet in diameter. Piles of dirt and rock surrounded the rim. Articles of clothing were strewn everywhere, lying wherever they were tossed as Derrick labored and worked up a sweat.

"How deep did they bury this stupid thing?" the exhausted Marine grumbled. He had been working for hours on an empty tank, driven by the overzealous high of finding the Treasure Tree. He had burned a lot of calories without replenishing them.

"I can't keep doing this. I need to focus on getting food or I'll be worthless," he explained to the camera which he had positioned looking down into the pit from a tripod to monitor his progress.

"But…I have to be close to the treasure and it, whatever it is, could give me a huge advantage," he reconsidered. "It might even be food."

He wiped the sweat off his forehead with the back of his dirty hand, creating a broad streak of mud. The fact that he was essentially sitting in a trench didn't escape his imagination which triggered memories of Iraq and Afghanistan.

The last time he had sat in a ditch he dug with his bare hands was in Afghanistan when an IED claimed the lives of three of his fellow Marines and left him stranded in the desert by himself. He walked for miles to put some distance between him and the explosion before digging his own trench in the sand and waiting over eight hours in the searing heat for a rescue chopper to arrive. It was an eternity to wait, knowing the enemy could have arrived at any moment to investigate the explosion. The ordeal could have been worse, but it left an emotional scar, nonetheless.

His Isolation Island trench had dirt walls, instead of sand, but sitting in any hole in the ground was enough to trigger bad memories. He hauled himself out before any flashbacks could begin playing in his head.

"I need a better way to dig," he said, dusting himself off with his swollen hands. He held them at length, flipping them over to examine both sides. Tiny cuts and scrapes announced themselves as if triggered by sight, aggravated by grains of soil.

He put his hands on his hips with a sigh, keeling over a bit, shaking his head. "I need food. I can't do any kind of digging without food."

The camera was still pointed at the ditch as Derrick mumbled a plan he intended the future audience to hear. The lack of food was starting to have an effect on him. His blood pressure was dropping, causing dizziness every time he stood up. Hypoglycemia was making his tired hands tremble and lethargy was slowing him down to a snail's pace. The growing fog clouding his thoughts slowed him down even more and caused rapid fluctuations in mood.

Abandoning the search for treasure for the rest of the day didn't mean his work was over. He still had to gather the camera equipment and the rest of his things and hike back to camp. On the plus side, he had a direct route between the Treasure Tree and camp memorized to avoid getting lost again.

SEATON ROGERS

Day 3

3:22pm

Age: 33
Occupation: Screenwriter
Home: Utah
Status: Single

"Winner, winner, fishy dinner," Seaton Rogers sang, celebrating his latest catch as he pulled it from the ocean. He swung it onto land, excited to show the camera perched on the tripod nearby.

"And it's that easy," he bragged.

He had every right to brag. In the almost three days he had been on Isolation Island, he had already built a kick-ass yurt, several animal and fish traps, and caught an almost unfair amount of fish with hooks and a gill net he had strung across the nearby river.

The king salmon he pulled from the ocean was a dull silver fish almost twenty inches long. It flopped around on the rocky shore as Seaton attempted to pin it down. He flattened it out, holding the body down with his knee and cut its head off with his knife. The tail curled upward with one last impulse before it settled down.

Seaton lifted the body, weighing it in his hand up and down.

"Wow. That's probably eight pounds of meat. Looks like some kind of salmon," he said, looking into the camera. It was closer to six pounds, including the guts. Seaton wasn't an expert fisherman by any means and, coming from Utah, he had almost no knowledge of Northern Pacific fish. It didn't really matter. He'd eat anything he pulled from the ocean.

He nodded his satisfaction. "Awesome. I'll use the head to make fish soup and, if you ever find yourself having to survive alone in the woods, don't forget to eat the fish's eyes. They're rich in vitamin C. I'm going to have to build a smoke house to start preserving all the food I've been catching," he explained as he gutted and cleaned the fish right there on shore.

He piled the innards on a piece of bark he called his bait purse. He had been collecting entrails and folding them in the bark to carry and use as bait in his various other traps. It was an effective strategy. He had been eating consistently, much to his surprise, but he knew not to get overconfident. The food could run out at any moment and he had only been on Isolation Island for three days.

It was too early for anyone to get cocky, but Seaton allowed himself a healthy level of confidence. He was never one to suffer from an inflated ego. His entire life he had tended to swing in the other direction—not necessarily negative but grounded. His friends and family would describe him as having a good head on his shoulders without really understanding what was going on in that head most of the time.

When he was done cutting and cleaning, he had enough fish for a few meals and enough bait for several traps.

"The best part of being out here, for me, is the alone time," he explained to the camera as he took a new route back to camp with his catch. He intended to check his traps on the way.

"I love the alone time. It's just…pure freedom. There's no one telling me what to do. No one to argue with. I make all the decisions out here. I'm a democracy of one. You can't get that anywhere else. I decide when I want to wake up. I decide when to go to sleep. I decide when I want to work and when I want to relax. I do whatever I want, however I want without anyone telling me I'm doing it wrong. And there's no one here to complain about it. I really love it. I might just have to stay out here forever."

He walked past a bird trap that hadn't been triggered. It was a simple pyramid-shaped cage he had built with sticks and fishing line. The pyramid was propped up on another stick that was tied to a small bit of fish guts meant to lure a bird in. If a bird pecked at the bait, it would dislodge the brace, the pyramid would fall and the bird would be trapped. Simple and effective, but nothing had taken the bait yet. A second bird trap in another location had yielded one small grouse on Day 2. It had been a small meal, but protein was protein.

Seaton moved on toward another trap—a deadfall. It was located, of course, on a game trail. On his way to pick up the game trail, he came across a glass bottle hanging from a tree.

"Well, well, well. What do we have here?" he jested for the camera's benefit. "Glass bottles don't grow on trees. Let's see what's inside."

He untied the bottle, planning to get the rest of the rope down after checking what's inside. The cork came out with a celebratory pop. He showed it to the camera, flipping it on each side as if future viewers might not be familiar with corks.

"That'll make an excellent bobber for my fishing line," he said and put the cork in his pocket for safe keeping.

"There's a scroll inside," he said as if it wasn't showing up on camera. "I wonder what it could be."

He shifted to a poorly performed English accent.

"Mysterious scribblings? A secret code?"

He pulled the note out and unrolled it. His eyes lit up.

"No. Poems," he said with a silly grin.

He held the open scroll up for the camera, turning left and right as if showing it to a group of people. "Poems everybody," he added, concluding his tribute to his favorite band, laughing at his own performance. Flattening the scroll out on his lap, he read the poem out loud.

IF IT'S TREASURE YOU DESIRE, DO NOT DESPAIR,

JUST CLIMB TO THE TOP AND YOU'LL FIND IT THERE,

WHERE THE FIRST SIGN OF SHORE COMES INTO SIGHT,

TAKE TEN HEALTHY PACES AND DIG ON YOUR RIGHT,

THE HELP YOU NEED CAN BE FOUND ON THE SHORE,

WHEN THE ROCKS AND THE ROOTS CAN BE SEEN A

LITTLE MORE

"Treasure! Awesome," he exclaimed as if things couldn't get much better. "Climb to the top and you'll find it there," he read out loud again. "I think I know what it means. There's a cliff overlooking the ocean. I've been wondering about it because the ocean comes right up to the base of the cliff, but I think if I go during low tide there will be some beach exposed. Maybe that's what 'when the rocks and the roots can be seen a little more' means."

He read the entire clue back to himself, his lips moving without a sound. "I'm not sure what I'm looking for, but I'll hike down to the bottom of the cliff tomorrow at low tide and see what I can see."

He showed the scroll to the camera again, bragging, "I'll be searching for treasure tomorrow. This is just a huge bonus. I hate to say it out loud, but things really couldn't have started off much better for me. I was afraid I'd be struggling out here, but I couldn't have asked for a better start. Not only is this a potential bonus, but it's something to do. I can explore some more along the way and who knows what else I'll find."

He kissed the scroll for good luck, rolled it up and put it in his pocket before retrieving the length of rope the bottle had dangled from.

"I can use this, too," he said. "Every little thing you find out here is a little bit of treasure. You can find a use for almost any scrap of manmade garbage. On one hand, it's sad to find plastic bottles and junk in such a pristine wilderness. On the other hand, it can make your life easier or even save your life if you've got nothing else. Like the plastic bottle I found on shore yesterday."

Seaton was referring to a single-serving water bottle he had collected from shore on Day 2. He had used it to demonstrate to the future audience how to make a minnow/bait trap. He cut the spout-end off with his knife, making a funnel which he inverted and inserted into the bottom end, wedging it into place.

He had captured the short work on camera, explaining, "Bait fish, minnows, whatever, swim in but they can't find their way out. Easy peasy."

The glass bottle and clues to the treasure were far from garbage. The extra supplies buried by the crew could be the key to winning the competition and Seaton knew it. The temptation to immediately embark on a treasure-hunting mission buzzed in his ears, but he knew it wasn't a good idea to go traipsing around the forest in the dark. He let his mind run wild imagining what the treasure could be while he continued checking his traps on the way back to camp.

5:55pm

Seaton found all his traps were empty, but he had pounds of fish that could last him a few days if necessary, so it was no cause for concern. In fact, he was better off. Harvesting too much food too quickly could be wasteful.

His camp was coming along nicely. The yurt was built on a platform made from logs. There was a stone fireplace in the middle. A hole in the tarp roof vented the smoke. He had a raised bed and plans to make more furniture.

It was too late to set out in search of the treasure. Instead, he put the finishing touches on a chair he had started building the night before.

Seaton was a bit of an insomniac, not an "early to bed, early to rise" type of person. When the sun went down, he continued working on projects inside the yurt by the light of the fire and his headlamp. He planned his days and nights out so that he could get the maximum amount of work done efficiently. Getting set up in style was a priority for him and he was happy to be ahead of schedule.

With all his goals for Day 3 met and exceeded, Seaton tested out his new chair. He set it near the outdoor fire so he could relax while cooking the fish he had caught. Half of it. The other half would be smoked over the indoor fire overnight.

ZOEY PRICE

Day 3

5:13pm

Age: 24
Occupation: Dance Instructor
Home: Montana
Status: Single

Zoey Price put the finishing touches on her rock sculpture near the river. She thought it would be a good idea to add her own landmarks to her territory. At least, that's what she told the camera. In reality, she was too tired and weak to hike back to camp after venturing out for water. She had been sitting on the ground playing with river rocks, making three little towers she called *The Triplets*.

With her energy fading and her supply of greens dwindling, the river began tempting her stomach with promises of food.

Does fish really qualify as meat? She began to rationalize and flex her beliefs to see how much they meant to her. Was she willing to starve for them? Was she willing to tap out; to surrender her once in a lifetime chance at winning a million dollars?

Building a simple rock garden/sculpture soothed her, giving her time to let her mood swing back and forth. Eventually, they swung back to everything she had stood for before arriving on Isolation Island. She left The Triplets near the river and brought a pot of water home for processing.

6:15pm

"I am *so* hungry," Zoey complained to the camera she had set up on a tripod facing the front of her completed debris shelter. She had used two tarps to make the roof and protect the sides. A gap between the tarps on the roof allowed smoke from the indoor fire to escape.

She dumped an armful of wood onto the fire inside and came back out with her stash of leaves in a purse she had made from the bark of a birch tree. There were no raspberries left so late in the season and she hadn't found any new sources of food. The vegetarian lifestyle was severely limiting her options.

She sat on a length of log she had strewn across what she called her front porch. The plantain and dandelion leaves tasted worse with each bite, but she wasn't giving up on her vegetarian ways just yet and she refused to let her situation get her down. Deep down, she knew it was going to be a challenge to outlast the meat-eaters while only eating leaves and berries (if she was lucky enough to find more berries). However, she wasn't willing to admit it to the camera.

"The good thing about not eating meat out in the wild is you don't run the risk of attracting predators," she explained, fishing for positive points to mention. "You don't stink of fish. You don't have to protect your food from other animals the way you would if you shot a moose or a deer."

She did her best to keep her face from cringing with each leaf she shoved in her mouth. Her body was craving more.

"I hope I can find some new food sources. Mushrooms would be nice." The thought brought a smile to her face. The smile triggered a burst of optimism.

"I'm sure I'll find more food sources. I'm a strong believer in nature. Nature will provide. The survival gods will smile upon me and help me through my spiritual journey on Isolation Island. So many factors are at play. I can feel the influence of the stars, Mother Nature, and the island gods. I wish I had my tarot cards with me. Maybe I'll make a set. I can use strips of bark."

Zoey babbled on about nature, spirituality, astrology, and how her psychic had told her she was going to win the competition, but "winning" the competition might not exactly mean she'd last the longest. The psychic explained how there could be a spiritual reward much greater than any cash reward could ever provide.

While she contemplated what her psychic meant, Zoey stared off into the distance, not noticing the growing plume of smoke behind her. It became thicker and darker, billowing out the roof vent and the sides of her debris shelter. The wind blew it away from her as she sat oblivious just outside the growing fire.

Flames shot out the sides of the shelter, engulfing the dry leaves and sticks that made up the walls. The heat on her back and loud crackling slapped her in the head. She sprung up and just before she turned around, a gust of wind blew the thick smoke in her face, blinding her for a moment before panic set in.

"Oh my god, oh my god, no!"

She fluttered her hands, dancing with the burning shelter, trying to find a way in to save anything she could. She lunged in the doorway, staying low, but the smoke and heat turned her away. A glimpse inside told her it was too late. The bedding and sleeping bag weren't visible. The tarp roof was melting and the walls were sending flames twenty feet in the air. All she could do was back away from the heat and smoke and watch as three days of work burned before her eyes.

She looked at the camera as if asking for help, but there was no one watching, of course. Reminding herself she was all alone, she dropped to her knees and cried. The death of her shelter wasn't the biggest reason for the tears. The shelter could be rebuilt, but all her supplies were also going up in flames.

A sudden realization struck her heart. She felt around the outside of her pockets with her hands. They felt empty. She stood up and spun, searching the whole area. Ducking her head into her old temporary shelter, she validated her inkling that nothing was left inside. The temporary debris shelter was far enough away to escape harm and it gave her a glimmer of hope knowing she'd have someplace to sleep that night, but there were no supplies save for the lone tarp she hadn't gotten around to removing from the roof and the axe she had left in its sheath outside. One more panicked glance around camp turned up nothing, not even the one thing she needed most.

"Oh my god," she said through sobbing breaths, the worst news of all sinking in. "The radio. I left the radio in there."

JILLIAN HILL

Day 3

6:17pm

Age: 45
Occupation: Homemaker
Home: Kentucky
Status: Married, 6 children

"So, I come up here to do some explorin' and I'm only 'bout twenny minutes from camp, but look what I done found," Jill said making her face fill the camera, orchestrating a big reveal.

She turned the camera around for a wide shot of a freshwater lake. Its dark water stretched as far as the eye could see to the left and to the right, but it was only around one hundred twenty yards across to the other side. The shoreline was heavily wooded, but trails carved by thirsty animals were evident on both sides.

"Check it out, y'all. How many of the others got a lake to themselves? I'm gonna try me some fishin' at this here waterin' hole tomorrow," she said, panning the camera left to right to show off her find.

Jill wasn't great with a camera—a little too fast and shaky. She tended to keep her eyes glued to the camera's little display screen trying to get the perfect shot. Whispers in her head reminded her that she was here to make a show and she wouldn't get much air time if her camera work was shoddy.

She started over, recorded another take, sweeping the camera left to right. Out of the corner of her eye, she caught a glimpse of a figure in the woods across the lake. It looked like pieces of a human peeking out behind the branches and leaves. She turned her attention, studying it with her eyes as she continued panning the camera to the right.

"What the hell is that?" she asked, giving up on the camerawork. She squinted, favoring her good eye.

It didn't help. It was already dusk, the figure was far away, and she had old eyes. She tried locating the questionable figure with the camera. Maybe she could zoom in on it. But, she couldn't find it. It was either gone or hadn't existed in the first place. Perhaps it was just a deceiving collection of leaves and bushes shaped like a person. Nonetheless, it sent a shiver up her spine.

"Maybe it was just one of the other contestants," she thought out loud for the camera's sake, continuing to search with it.

"Maybe I ain't the only one that has access to this here lake. That'd prolly be unfair. Still, they told us we ain't gonna have contact with the other players."

She turned the camera on herself and shrugged her shoulders.

"It was prolly nothin'. I best be getting' back to camp 'fore it gits dark."

11:27pm

"It's only Day 3 and I already miss my lil ones. I miss my husband. I miss my nice warm house," Jill said with the camera filming her face from a few inches away on the floor of her shelter.

Her head was bundled up for warmth so that only her eyes and nose were exposed between her hat and the sleeping bag. After lying there for hours, unable to fall asleep, she turned the camera on for simulated companionship.

"I'm a little creeped out by what I saw at the lake. Err...what I think I saw. There shouldn't be no people 'round here. I wonder if I should report it on the radio, just to be on the safe side," she thought out loud.

The fire crackled just outside the entrance of her shelter, the tall stone heat reflector directing the warmth in. Her feet needed it the most. The temperature had dropped under forty degrees after the sun went down.

"I bet my kids would like it out here. Huntin' every day. Cookin' over a fire every night."

She blinked in slow motion until her eyes drooped closed for the night. Her words began to float on fluffy clouds pulling her toward dreamland. "It's so peaceful 'n quiet out here. Fire goin'.

No one round fer miles."

Her mind drifted away on thoughts from her past, hopes for her future and plans for the present. She reached out, eyes still closed, feeling around for the camera. She located it, picked it up and turned it off with a press of the POWER button.

Within minutes she was snoring away, cozy in her sleeping bag, dreaming of chicken-fried steak and mashed potatoes, eggs and sausage and grits, fried chicken and biscuits and more fried chicken and more biscuits and gravy—thick delicious gravy. After three days without eating, her mind was telling her it was time to find some food.

Chapter 5

Day 14

No Time to Panic

"What do you mean, this is where we left the boat?" Sharon asked.

It made Hutch's blood boil. There was that stupid question again. The one he despised well before meeting Sharon. *What do you mean?* She seemed to use it to respond to everything he said. *What do you mean, I'm putting the contestants in danger? What do you mean, we should be checking in with them every day? What do you mean, the island hasn't been mapped out properly? What do you mean, the radios are inadequate?*

He clenched his fists tight and tried not to lose his temper. Not that Hutch was a short-tempered person. He was a good combination of laid back and professional. Sharon just had a way of pushing his worst buttons. Perhaps not on purpose. She was just the kind of person Hutch had always despised—incompetent, stubborn, and controlling—a horrible combination.

"What do you think I mean?" Hutch fired back, his voice jumping straight to hostile. He pointed at the sand. "These are our footprints. This is where the boat was anchored and right there is where you fell flat on your face in the water."

"Where you anchored the boat? Are you sure you anchored it?" Sharon bit back. "If you had anchored it, it would still be here, wouldn't it?"

"Don't take that tone with me. I know what I'm doing. I anchored it just fine. I'm positive," Hutch swore, looking out over the ocean, expecting to see the Medline floating around on its own somewhere.

"So what then? You're saying someone stole it?" Sharon persisted.

Hutch examined the footprints. They were partially washed away by the tide, making them hard to identify, but he was sure he recognized the landing spot. Smoke was still billowing on the edge of the horizon and they had no way to investigate. Hutch tried the radio again but received no reply.

"Isn't there some emergency frequency you can try?" Page asked on the edge of more tears.

Hutch ignored her. There was nothing more they could do short of swimming back to the Mothership through miles of frigid ocean. He cursed himself for being in the situation to begin with; for accepting the job at the last minute; for trusting Sharon had brought the appropriate supplies. As mad as he was at Sharon, he was also mad at himself. He had always prided himself on his ability to be prepared for anything and everything that could go wrong in a survival situation. Now, he was stranded on an island in the Pacific with no support, no boat, two dead bodies, and at the mercy of Sharon's incompetence.

He gave Sharon a foul look. "Well?" he asked her. "What do we do now, Boss? Didn't you and Greely make plans in case things went sideways out here?"

"No, I didn't plan for the possibility that we'd lose contact with the Mothership and you'd lose the boat at the same time," Sharon growled, not afraid to stand up to Hutch. "Who the hell could have planned for this? Two dead bodies, the goddamn Mothership is probably on fire and you lost the fucking boat."

"I didn't lose the boat," Hutch insisted.

"Then where is it? Either it floated away on its own because you didn't secure it or somebody stole it," Sharon raised her voice another notch.

The latter implication caught everyone's attention—somebody stole it. Who would do such a thing? If someone *did* steal the boat, did they take it to sabotage the Mothership?

Page covered her mouth with one hand, muffling a gasp. Sharon's face tightened up and turned away.

Doc washed his hands and face with ocean water and stood up again, his clothes still soaked with Dyson's blood. "We need to make a fire," he said. He wasn't the only wet one. The rain had dampened everyone's clothes.

Hutch just nodded, looking out over the ocean. They were now thrust into the game themselves in a way. It was now Day 1 for them—shelter, fire, water, food. They needed to get working on the basics before they lost daylight.

Dr. Rodney took off his bloody coat and shirt and crouched at the edge of the water to clean them. His muscular biceps flexed as he submersed his shirt, twisting it to wring it out. A crimson cloud poured out and dispersed as new waves came in to pull the blood out to sea. He used the semi-clean shirt as a washcloth to sponge the blood off his coat.

Sharon walked off, up the coast. Page normally followed like a paid puppy dog, but not this time.

"Where are you going?" Hutch called out.

Without turning around, Sharon answered, "I'm going to that rocky outcrop to see if the boat is on the other side," referring to a long, dark peninsula jutting out into the ocean a half mile up the coast. Waves crashed against the black boulders, threatening to pull anyone in if they weren't careful.

Hutch couldn't let her go alone. "Wait up, I'll come with you," he shouted, but she kept charging ahead, determined. He turned to Doc and Page before chasing after her. "You two wait here. Get those clothes clean and start collecting firewood. We'll be right back."

Sharon slowed when the beach got rockier, allowing Hutch to catch up to her but not on purpose. She looked like she had been crying, a telltale sniffle she wasn't able to disguise remained.

"What are you not telling me?" Hutch asked.

"What do you mean, what am I not telling you?" she replied.

Hutch grumbled. It was going to be a long ordeal if she intended to ask what he meant every time he asked a question or made a statement. He already knew that. Talking to her was like pulling teeth, but Hutch was determined to extract every single one if he had to, no matter how painful.

"Who would want to steal our boat? Who would want to sabotage the Mothership?" Hutch asked, as specific as possible.

"I never said someone sabotaged the Mothership," Sharon answered.

"You implied it. If someone stole our boat, it stands to reason they were responsible for the smoke on the horizon," Hutch hypothesized.

"You don't know that smoke is from the Mothership," Sharon insisted, purposely evasive.

"What else could it be? Why else would they not be answering our calls?"

Sharon slipped on a wet stone, lunging forward. Hutch caught her with one hand before any part of her body touched the ground and yanked her back to her feet.

"Be careful," he reprimanded.

"I'm fine. Let go of me," she snapped back.

He didn't let her go. He held her there to keep her attention. "Look," Hutch said, holding her arm. "I know you want to be in charge and boss everyone around, but you need to lose the attitude right now. We're in a fucked up position right now and it's because you have no idea what you're doing. It's no wonder Nelson Greely quit. You're impossible. You're totally unprepared for this project. You've got no safety measures in place. You've put everyone in danger with your incompetence. Not just the contestants, but the crew as well, and me and yourself. So, congratulations big boss woman."

Sharon dug her nails into Hutch's hand and pulled to release her arm from his grip. "Incompetent?" she growled. "I'm the incompetent one?" She pointed a finger in his face. "You're the one who lost the boat. You're supposed to be the survival expert here. So, spare me the commentary and just do your job."

Hutch slapped her finger out of his face. "You were in over your head with this project before it even got started. What do you know about producing a survival show?"

"It's reality TV," she claimed, attempting to charge off but hindered by the slippery rocks. The last thing she wanted was to injure an ankle and have to limp around at the mercy of others. "I've worked on plenty of reality shows," she said over her shoulder.

Hutch shook his head and followed. "This isn't the same thing. It's not a house full of idiots arguing with each other. This is serious business. People can die out here. You've already got two casualties on your hands and who knows how many more on that smoking ship out th..." He pointed to the horizon, but the smoke was gone, disappearing in the haze rolling in.

The abrupt end to his sentence made Sharon stop, turn, and take notice. Empty ocean stared back at her. They looked at each other, their expressions fallen from confrontational to concerned.

"There," Sharon said. "They must have put the fire out. Everything's going to be fine."

Hutch furrowed his brow. "Or the ship burned up and sank," he suggested. "Or it's still on fire, but drifted away too far for us to see. We can sit here guessing all day, but it won't do us any good arguing over the unknown." He tried the radio several more times as they made their way to the rocky outcrop, but received no reply.

The dark, slippery boulders were difficult to climb. Sharon fell off the first one she scaled, landing in Hutch's arms before her ass hit the ground. The romantic position was thwarted by their angry eyes. He stood her back up immediately with a frustrated sigh.

"Why don't you wait here?" Hutch suggested. "I'll go ahead and see what I can see."

"I can do it," she insisted.

"I'm not carrying you around if you twist your ankle. There's no reason for you to come with me," he barked. "Just...do me a favor and wait here."

"Fine," she said, giving in. "Make it snappy big man." Her voice was full of resentment, but he let it slide without a comment.

When he approached the top of the peninsula, Hutch found the climb more difficult than he had expected. His age was catching up with him after an almost sixty-year chase. He paused, looking for the next foothold and to catch his breath. "It better be there," he repeated to himself over and over as he continued, not sure if he'd lose his mind if he didn't see the missing boat on the other side.

He crested the top of the rock pile and got to his feet. The other side didn't offer anything dramatically different. It was a long stretch of rocky shore and ocean, only the waves seemed a bit angrier. There was no boat or any sign of human activity. A narrow stream ran into the ocean a little ways up the shore but, other than thick forest inland, there wasn't anything else to see.

Hutch climbed back down and returned to Sharon, who he found sitting on a large stone, shivering. Her clothes were still damp, the temperature was dropping, and the wind whipping off the ocean cut right through her. He offered her a hand to help her up, but she was too stubborn to accept it, standing up without assistance.

"You need to change clothes before you freeze to death. Let's get back to Derrick's camp and get a fire going. Come on," Hutch said in a non-negotiable tone.

"I take it you didn't find the boat," Sharon guessed, her voice devoid of emotion.

"Nothing but empty ocean and rocky shore," he informed her.

Dr. Rodney and Page weren't thrilled with the news either. Not only had they found nothing, the excursion had eaten away a chunk of precious daylight. They took the firewood Page and Doc had collected and hiked back to Derrick's camp. Getting a fire started would have been difficult with all the damp firewood they collected, but Hutch planned to use Derrick's stash of wood to get the fire started and use the fire to dry the new, wet wood.

Although he had a ferrorod, Hutch chose to use the cigarette lighter he had on him to start the fire.

"What about the bodies?" Dr. Rodney asked, laying out his clothes to dry. While Hutch was getting the fire started, Doc had used some sticks and cordage to make a drying rack. He stripped down to his underwear and hung his clothes on the rack near the fire, drying himself as well. Unfortunately, there wasn't much more he could accomplish while being tethered to the fire.

Sharon emerged from Derrick's shelter, changed into the dry set of clothes Page had brought along. "We can't really do anything with the bodies without the boat," she replied, as if Doc had asked for her opinion.

He ignored her and repeated the question directly, "Hutch? The bodies?"

"We need to bury them," Hutch answered before ducking into the shelter. He emerged a few moments later with a bundle of clothes. "Page, you need to get out of those damp clothes. You and Doc can cover up with Derrick's clothes for now." He spread the clothes out on his arms so they could pick through the selection.

Page chose a heavy gray sweater that was about ten sizes too big and a pair of pants that were about twenty sizes too big, but the clothes were dry and there was even a nice, thick pair of socks that looked like they hadn't been worn at all. She took off her coat and hung it on the drying rack. Her shirt was harder to remove. It was so tight and damp, it stuck to her skin. She struggled to peel it off. Doc was about to step up to help her, but she wiggled her way out, threw the shirt on the rack and pulled her pants off.

Page's bare skin made the men's heads turn. Her perfect body had been hidden under baggy clothes since they had met her. The men's gentlemanly instincts kicked in and they turned their heads to face each other.

Doc cleared his throat. "Bury them you say?"

"Yes, yes, bury them," Hutch replied, trying to remain professional and focused. "We should bury them. There's nothing else we can do. They'll get eaten by scavengers and attract predators to this area, putting us in danger, as well."

They tried to ignore Page as she walked around in her purple bra and panties, hanging her damp clothes to dry, but it wasn't easy and she wasn't shy.

Sharon wasn't impressed with the display. "How are you going to dig a hole deep enough to bury them?" she asked, keeping the men on point.

Hutch answered without delay. "There are holes already dug where we found Derrick's body. All we have to do is lay them down and cover them up." The impersonal nature of such a burial gave him pause. It was far from an ideal situation. "We can always come back and dig them up again. Bring them home for a proper burial," he added, the idea of exhumation not helping anyone feel better.

Page put Derrick's sweater on. It was long enough to be a dress on her, landing just above her knees, but it was too cold to leave her legs exposed. She pulled on a pair of Derrick's army green cargo pants, buttoned and zipped them up, but they dropped to the ground as soon as she let go.

Hutch dipped into Derrick's supplies and cut a length of paracord she could use as a belt. He let her tie it on by herself. Doc, on the other hand, was too tall for Derrick's clothes. They fit him like a preteen after a growing spurt.

"If we're doing this burial, we have to get going now. It'll be dark soon," Hutch said to Doc. He grabbed one of the tarps folded up and stored under the giant tree trunk that served as the main beam in Derrick's shelter.

Doc finished dressing and they prepared for the hike, grabbing the flashlight and headlamp in case they got caught out in the dark. Although Hutch had come prepared for the wilderness, almost all his supplies had been left on the Zodiac. He never could have anticipated the boat disappearing. Still, he kicked himself for leaving items like the guns on the boat without supervision. He took Derrick's bow and arrow for a small shred of protection.

"Whoa, wait," Sharon said. "You're going to leave us here by ourselves?"

"You're not by yourselves," Hutch pointed out. "You have each other. What's the problem?"

Sharon put on a brave poker-face. "No problem," she conceded, calming her frantic voice. "Maybe you could bring back some food."

Hutch just chuckled as he and Doc walked away. They'd be lucky to get back before dark if all they did was carry Dyson to the pits and cover the bodies. Acquiring food would have to wait until tomorrow.

Halfway up the trail, Doc blurted out, "Maybe one of the contestants took the boat. It's the only thing that makes sense." He had been racking his brain since they realized the boat was missing.

Hutch had considered the possibility as well. "You might be right. And it wouldn't even be against the rules, technically, because they're allowed to use anything they find," he reasoned to lighten the mood. "Wouldn't that be something?"

"I don't know," Doc said, reconsidering. "The contestants are too far away from each other for one of them to have wandered this far. And, what? They just happened to find our boat on the random day chosen for a wellness checkup?"

"I wasn't suggesting it was an accident or a coincidence," Hutch replied and they both chewed on the idea in silence as they hiked through the forest under dwindling daylight.

ZOEY PRICE

Day 4

6:48am

Age: 24
Occupation: Dance Instructor
Home: Montana
Status: Single

"I didn't see this coming at all," Zoey lamented, standing over the ashes that used to be her shelter. The fire had burned fast and died out over the sleepless night. All her psychics and astrology had failed her. The 'island gods' were nowhere to be found. The only bit of luck in her favor was the fact she hadn't set the entire forest on fire.

Unidentifiable hardened puddles of melted plastic peeked out from under white ashes peppered with the black, charred remains of metal. Somewhere in the powdered graveyard was the melted radio, the single item that could get her out of her predicament but nothing was salvageable. The only thing that avoided the blaze was the tarp on her temporary shelter, the axe which she had left stuck in a log outside the shelter, two cameras, and the tripod.

"I can't believe this," she sniffled in front of the camera. "I am so screwed. I've lost everything. I don't even know what to do. Someone will have to come along eventually, for a medical check or something, but without any tools, I don't know how I'll survive until then. I don't even know how long that might be."

She kicked a pile of ashes with her toe, hoping to magically uncover something useful. "My sleeping bag is gone. All the extra clothes. My raingear."

She continued listing items lost to the fire like a eulogy, but there were more important things to focus on. There were tough questions to start asking and decisions to be made. As reality began to set in, the questions followed. No answers. Only questions, sparking a tirade of criticism. She wasn't in the least bit concerned that the camera was rolling.

"This is crazy. All they told us was to keep our radio on us at all times. They didn't say anything about what to do if we lose the radio or the radio breaks. They're so damn secretive about everything. I get that part of the challenge is being alone, but they could at least check up on us from time to time to make sure we're still alive."

The log she had used as her front porch chair had burned up in the fire. She plopped down on the grass outside her temporary shelter and sobbed. Frustrated screams amid the blubbering carried through the forest, but there was no one there to hear her distress calls.

As tears ran down her face, they reminded her how precious water was and how she couldn't afford to waste another drop feeling sorry for herself. She dried up and pulled herself together.

"I guess I have to start making some decisions. Should I stay or should I go? I can stay here and wait for someone to show up or start walking until I find another contestant."

She didn't provide an answer. She wasn't ready to make the decision yet. "I should have ran into the fire to save the radio," she lamented.

Then, it finally hit her. "Oh my god. The ferrorod. The ferrorod is gone, too. How am I going to make a fire?" She held the sides of her head as if trying to prevent an explosion. "I should have saved some embers. I had a giant fire burning all night and I didn't save any embers. Stupid!"

She searched through the ashes with a long stick, digging around every little trickle of smoke, but the digging made the smoke disappear. The fire had burned itself out. When she realized there was nothing useable left behind, she dropped to her knees and wept with her hands hiding her face from the camera.

3:15pm

Zoey Price debated with herself all day—should she stay or leave? She had wandered around, trapped in uncertainty as she collected dandelion leaves to eat and searched for more berries. There were none to be had, but she collected other useful items along the way—a straight, narrow stick, perfect for a drill for fire-making and a curved stick about a foot long which could be used as a bow to spin the drill. All she had to do was sacrifice a length of shoelace.

Down by the sea, she collected a few empty clam shells and a piece of driftwood she determined would make a good hearth board. On the way back to camp, she chewed on the dandelion leaves she had collected, dragging herself slowly along a beaten animal trail.

The sight of her camp and the pile of ashes she was considering calling home for the next few months made her heart sink again. The reality of the situation set in anew every time she looked at it. Moping over to the temporary shelter, she dropped the materials she had collected on the ground and set up a camera on the tripod.

She pointed the camera at the ground and framed in her fire making materials—various sticks and twigs, the hearth board—and added a pile of pine bark shavings she pulled from her jacket pocket.

"I still haven't decided if I'm going to stay put and wait for help to arrive or go out on my own to find help," she explained to the camera. "What I *have* decided is to let fate decide. I've gathered everything I need to make a fire. If I can make a fire, I'll stay. If I can't, I have to leave. Without fire, my days are numbered no matter what I do, but I'd rather die walking than sitting still."

She knelt down in the grass and arranged the materials in order. The components to make a bow and drill kit first, then the pine bark shavings, then the various sticks and wood to build the fire.

"I've got no flint or ferrorod, so I'm going to have to make a friction fire. It's not going to be easy, but it's my only hope. I'm going to make a bow and drill kit. I've done it before."

With the axe, she prepped the hearth board by chiseling it flat on top and bottom. Scratching her knobby nose with one hand, she flipped the board over with the other assessing her progress and deemed it good enough.

"This is going to be my hearth board," she explained to teach the future audience and to keep her mind focused on the task at hand rather than the rapids of Shit's Creek that were trying to pull her down.

With the sharp corner of the axe, she bored a shallow hole in the middle of the hearth board and notched out a V from the edge of the board.

"My drill will spin in this hole, creating friction and heat," she instructed, holding the board up for the camera to capture. "This notch will let air get to it and allow an ember to form."

Picking up the straight stick to show the camera, she said, "This is my drill. Nice and straight. Not too thick, not too thin. I'm going to strip the bark…just because. I'm not really sure if it's necessary but it's the way I was taught."

She stripped the bark and cut both ends blunt. Leaning to the side, she pulled one foot out from under her and untied her boot.

"I've got this." She stopped untying to hold up the curved stick, stuttering to come up with the proper words to describe it. "This…um…curvy stick. This is going to be the bow."

Pulling the lace out of her boot, she continued to narrate her actions. "I'll tie my shoelace to each end, not too tight…and…now the drill stick goes in."

She held the drill against the shoelace and twisted so that the lace wrapped around the drill, tightening the lace. Pulling one of the clam shells from her pocket, she held it up with two fingers for the camera to see, then put it in the palm of her left hand. One end of the drill fit into the shell, the other into the hole on the hearth board.

"This will make it easier to spin. If you don't have a shell, you can use a rock or a bottle cap or whatever you can find, but you need something to hold the drill steady while allowing it to spin. And, there you have it. We work the bow back and forth, the drill spins and hopefully we can make an ember. I've got pine bark ready. I'll drop the ember on the pine bark and blow on it to get a flame."

Zoey hesitated to follow her own instructions knowing she had placed her fate in the outcome. She looked at the camera and took a deep breath, placing one foot on the hearth board to keep it steady.

"Well, hear it goes. If I can't make fire…"

She nodded as she went through the steps of making a fire over again in her head, making sure she didn't forget a crucial component.

"I *will* make fire. Positive attitude. I'm going to do this," she reassured herself and started working the bow back and forth.

7:25pm

Dusk had fallen and after almost four straight hours of trying, Zoey still had no fire. The hearth board she was using had several holes and notches worn away without success. Her hands were tired, swollen and slowing with each attempt. Bloodshot eyes told the tale of her failure and the tears that came and went each time she tapped herself out and picked herself up again for another try. But all the positive thoughts and prayers she whispered didn't help. The survival gods seemed to be ignoring her all together. Another failure. Her last ounce of strength was spent throwing the bow at the camera for a narrow miss. She was too tired to weep again.

Too tired to even cry again, she looked up at the sky and the stars that were beginning to show themselves, the stars she had put so much faith in. It was clear to her they had already spoken.

"Well…I guess I'm leaving camp tomorrow to search for help," she said.

TUCKER JORDAN

Day 4

9:42am

Age: 28
Occupation: Yoga Instructor
Home: Vermont
Status: Single

Tucker Jordan's camp was improving at a slower pace than the rest of the contestants, with the exception of Floyd Benson, although, Floyd's slow progress was by design. Tucker's progress was hindered by his compulsion to eat up several hours a day with yoga routines. He had a million reasons to perform each pose and used up many hours of video footage explaining the pose and the purpose to the camera at great length. So much so, that it looked more like a yoga instruction video than a survival show.

At the end of his two-hour morning routine, he sat down outside his still unfinished hut. Building materials were strewn around his camp, waiting to be added to the thick walls made from layers of branches woven together between vertical logs spaced out around the perimeter.

"This isn't just a survival competition. The thing that takes a toll on you more than anything is the isolation—no human contact. We're social animals. We need other humans. That's just a fact of nature," Tucker claimed while enjoying some dandelion tea he had brewing during his morning routine.

"Doing my yoga every morning and every night makes me feel in touch with my people back home. I can feel their energy and I know they can feel the energy I'm broadcasting out to them. It's all positive and it's all good. I can let them know I miss them and I can feel the love coming back to me. It eases the loneliness a little."

He took another sip from the big black pot. A piece of

dandelion leaf stuck to his front teeth. He worked it off with his tongue and swallowed it.

"This is a mental game just as much as it is physical. You have to keep your mind occupied. You have to keep your mind healthy and nourished. And, it's all up to you. There's no one here to lean on."

He took a last sip of tea and emptied the rest into his canteen. The shining sun and clear sky promised a pleasant day ahead. Tucker turned off the camera and gathered supplies for a fishing trip.

12:41pm

Tucker turned on the camera strapped to his toque as he approached his destination.

"So...I wanted to hike back up here today to show you what I found yesterday," he explained. "The battery on my camera had died while I was exploring and I didn't bring a backup with me so, I wasn't able to record it yesterday. But, here it is."

He stopped to get a stable shot. Through the woods up ahead the reflection of the sun sparkled and flickered off the ripples of a freshwater lake.

"Isn't it great? I wasn't expecting this at all," he said, walking the camera nearer for a closer look.

He stopped short of the edge of the lake, pointing the camera down at a half-eaten fish lying on a rock. Its body had been torn to bits, the head and tail still intact. Flies buzzed around eager to feed.

"Shit," Tucker said. "Whatever was eating this can't be too far away. It looks pretty fresh. Probably a bear. I hope I didn't disturb him. He might not be too happy with me."

He scanned the woods behind him and scrutinized the shore across the lake but didn't see any animals. Still, he didn't want to get between a wild animal and its food. He cut a few chunks off the fish to use as bait and moved on along the narrow, grassy shore on the edge of the lake, looking for a spot to try his hand at fishing. A path had been worn in the grass, no doubt by thirsty animals.

Tucker hadn't eaten much of anything, short of dandelion and plantain leaves. Not because he was opposed to eating meat. He hadn't had any luck fishing in the creek where he got his drinking water or the ocean.

His fishing pole was nothing more than a stick with fishing line attached. He tossed the baited hook in the lake and waited, head on a swivel watching out for predators. A steady wind blew the line back toward shore and rustled the leaves in the forest, covering up the sound of footsteps behind him.

He pulled the line out as the wind subsided and cast it back in. The stillness uncovered the sound of feet or paws brushing through the dead leaves that littered the forest floor. Whatever it was, it was close. Tucker whipped his head around, almost dropping his pole in the water. The camera's view scrambled as he turned back and forth searching for the origin of the noise. It stopped for a moment, then shuffled on slowly.

Tucker couldn't see anything but trees and brush and vines hanging and climbing in every direction. His visibility was limited to under twenty feet in the thickness of the forest surrounding the lake. Somewhere beyond that visibility something was moving, perhaps stalking him. He pulled his line out of the water and held his breath, listening for clues. It seemed to be moving closer, to his right, so he high-stepped to his left, trying to make as little noise as possible. His movement sped up his stalker.

"Oh god, oh god," Tucker whimpered.

He dropped his pole and entered fight or flight mode, instinctively choosing flight. Without even seeing what creature was coming, he sprinted down the path on the edge of the water, trying to decide between turning inland or jumping in and swimming across.

It was a nice day, but the temperature hadn't even cracked sixty degrees and the water was even colder. Swimming wasn't an option, it was a last resort with the threat of hypothermia. He ran to the half-eaten fish and turned into the forest from there, back the way he had come, hoping whatever was after him would settle for some free fish scraps instead.

Tucker kept running, panting out profanities to himself that the camera picked up as they whipped through the woods together. Branches slapped him in the face, scratching him up as he fled, but it didn't slow him down. Nor did the fact that he had no idea which way he was going anymore.

Finally, he dared to slow down enough to check behind him. The forest looked empty and still. With all evidence convincing him he had managed to escape, he came to a stop to catch his breath. His heart kept pounding and his eyes kept searching but, by all accounts, he was alone again.

"That was intense," he said through heaving breaths.

He was desperate for food but, not desperate enough to take his chances by the lake again while some anonymous beast stalked him. He'd have to settle for hunting crayfish at the creek where he obtained his drinking water.

EZRA GREER

Day 4

11:12am

Age: 51
Occupation: Truck Driver
Home: Alaska
Status: Widower, 3 children

Ezra Greer had come a long way in the first four days. He cataloged every aspect with his video equipment, going into great detail, explaining every step of the construction of his shelter; every aspect of the traps he set in hopes of acquiring food; every aspect of survival that crossed his mind. It was shaping up to be a complete survival training guide.

There seemed to be no end to his expertise. Every time he explained what he was working on, he also explained several other ways it could be done and a wide array of alternatives to his choices. He was knowledgeable and efficient and seemed to love every minute of it.

Ezra's log cabin was something to behold. Spacious inside by survival standards, with a built-in, stone fireplace. It was nestled in the corner of a small clearing, the forest its backyard. The front door was made of skinny white birch logs fashioned together vertically and fixed on a spear that served as a type of hinge. He had left a small, square peephole near the top to be used to look out for predators. A large, brown tarp kept the rain out, serving as a peaked roof over the entire structure.

The cabin even had its own front patio made of flat stones he had hauled from various locations and laid on the ground he had leveled out.

Ezra was also doing well in the food department. He returned to camp before noon on Day 4 with a rabbit he had found caught up in a snare trap he had set on a game trail. He had enjoyed a variety of food early in the competition—fish, grouse, crayfish, plantain leaves, limpets, and mussels. A stash of acorns had accumulated in his larder as a last resort should he experience any difficulty finding more palatable alternatives. Acorns needed to be processed by leaching out the bitter tannins and, even then, they had a tendency to taste horrible. It wasn't worth the effort while he continued to have luck hunting, but they remained in his stash for the upcoming winter months.

Ezra approached the camera he had set up on its tripod facing his quaint little cabin, turned it on and backed into frame to show off his latest acquisitions. He held up the gutted rabbit in one hand and a message in a bottle in the other.

"Look what I found," he said, loud and proud. The smile on his face suggested he had already looked at the scroll rattling around in the big glass bottle. The cork had already made its way into his pocket.

He unrolled the scroll to reveal a map. X marked the spot where treasure could be found on a patch of land between the fork in the river he had been getting his drinking water from.

"Right there," he said, pointing to the X on the map. "There's treasure to be found. And, this contest just got a whole lot more interesting."

He had not discovered the fork in the river thus far during his exploration, but it looked easy to find. Crossing the river to get to the treasure was a different story. Ezra imagined there had to be a way across that wouldn't be too risky. He trusted the producers of the show, even though the one he trusted most—Corbin Rossi—had quit, leaving all the major decisions in Sharon's incapable hands. More than his trust in the producers, Ezra trusted his own abilities. He wouldn't take any unnecessary risks.

The map was simple, without many details, but one that stood out was a symbol that looked like a shovel. It wasn't far from the fork in the river and it was set near the silhouette of a pine tree.

"I'm assuming I can find a shovel on the way to the fork in the river which must mean the treasure is buried," Ezra reasoned. "I think I've got time to, at least, scope it all out today. I'm going to get right on it," he added before turning the camera off.

2:30pm

"It's already been harder than I thought it would be out here, but I could get used to it," Ezra explained to the camera mounted on his head as he trekked through the forest in search of the shovel on the map. His assessment was surprising given how successful he had been. He had been making it look easy.

"Coming in, I was worried about making fire because it was so damp, but it's not impossible as long it stays dry. My shelter is coming along nicely. I've got a nice stash of dry wood inside. I'll keep adding necessities to my camp and maybe even a few luxuries if I get around to it."

His humble nature seemed to prevent him from thinking he was doing better than the other contestants, but he was excelling.

"People asked me why I'd want to come out here and rough it like this. To me, it's better than living in this suicidal society we've developed. Some people prefer the term unsustainable, but I call it suicidal. Every aspect of our society is killing us; it's killing the planet. We're causing a mass extinction to take place and our names will be on the endangered species list eventually."

"Every aspect of our society is broken and beyond repair," he lectured. "It's beyond repair because of human nature and it's sad because we know exactly *how* it's all broken but nothing can be done to fix it. That's why I do this. That's why I'm into survival and self-reliance. You can't count on society to do anything but collapse. When it does, I'll be ready."

Ezra arrived at the river—right where he knew it was. He had been down river multiple times, but there was no sign of a fork. Theorizing the fork must be up river, he walked the riverbank against the current.

The river was wide and slow in some spots, narrow, rocky, and rushing in others. Ezra didn't have to walk far to find the pine tree depicted on the map. There were lots of pine trees, but the one he was looking for was easy to distinguish from the rest—it had a long, metal shovel hanging from a low-lying limb. He was able to cut it down while standing on his toes, but he still had to find the spot to dig.

"There she is," he declared with a laugh. "And I was worried it'd be hard to find a specific pine tree in a pine tree forest."

He looked the tree up and down. "That rope could come in handy, too," he said, referring to the long rope the shovel had been hanging from. "But, I'm not a fan of tree climbing unless it's absolutely necessary. I'm not very good at it and I don't like to take unnecessary risks when I'm by myself in the middle of the wilderness. If I get injured, it's game over. Not worth the risk."

He abandoned the idea of retrieving the rope and started walking again, reassuring himself, "If I really need the rope for something, I know where it is. I can always come retrieve it, but I think I can live without it. With limited supplies every little shred available seems like a big deal." He still seemed hesitant and unsure, but he moved on.

"Step one is complete," he said, arriving at the edge of the water, again. "I got the shovel, but I don't see a fork in the river. I'm assuming I'm supposed to be able to see it, somehow," he added, scrutinizing the other side of the river.

"Judging by how easy it was to find the shovel, I can't imagine finding the fork is going to be too hard. Then again, maybe it'll be extra hard, since finding the shovel was a cakewalk," he hypothesized, making his way upriver again. "Or maybe crossing the river is going to be the real challenge. Who knows?"

He didn't have to walk much further and there was no guesswork involved when he came to the fork in the river. A long, flat, clear, grassy peninsula cut the river in two. Ezra could see both branches. The one on the other side of the peninsula disappeared around a bend that took it into the forest. The peninsula itself looked like it had been mowed and manicured.

"Well, this has got to be it," Ezra said panning the camera on his head back and forth. "Only problem is…I don't see a way across."

The river was flat and wide with a slow, easy roll on Ezra's side of the fork. He broke a long branch off a nearby downed tree and used it to test the depth of the river. It plunged down to his hand without touching the bottom. He rolled up his sleeve and submersed his arm up to his elbow, but still didn't hit bottom. That settled it—it was too deep to walk across.

"I didn't see any good places to cross anywhere on the way

here," he explained. "And there's no way I'm swimming or walking across. The water's just too damn cold and too deep. I'm going to have to build a boat or a raft of some kind. If I build a boat, I can use it for fishing, as well."

He looked over at the peninsula again. The river that forked off on the other side moved faster and rougher. He wondered if he could go farther upriver and cross before the fork, then find a way to cross to the peninsula from that side. Walking another hundred yards upriver, he didn't find a spot to cross. In fact, the river was wider and devoid of any rocks with no sign of being any different farther upriver.

"There's nowhere to cross, but I see a perfect spot to launch my boat from, right there," Ezra said, pointing a finger at a flat clearing that eased into the calm, flowing water. "I can paddle my way to the peninsula, no problem."

He looked the area over again and came to a definitive conclusion. "I have to get working on a boat. That's the only way to go, keeping in mind I'm going to have treasure to bring back with me. There's no telling what it might be."

With one last look around, he put his hands on his hips and reconsidered. "Then again, the treasure could be an inflatable boat," he said, laughing at the irony. "Who knows? That's the tricky part about surviving in the wild. Sometimes, there's no way to know what the right decision is. You just have to make a decision, follow through, and hope for the best."

WES WOOD

Day 4

3:00pm

Age: 57
Occupation: Farmer
Home: Mississippi
Status: Divorced, 8 children

"Just like that, I got me my own boat," Wes Wood bragged, ready to board his vessel.

He stood in the calm, knee-high water on the edge of the bay, testing the short, narrow boat he had spent the past two days working on. It was nothing more than a frame made of wood and covered with a tarp, but it floated without him in it. The next step was to see if it would bear his weight without sinking.

The camera set on the tripod on shore witnessed the test. Wes put one leg in, trying to keep the craft steady. It was unstable in the relatively still water of the bay. He pulled his other leg in and sat on the center brace that served as a seat. Holding the sides of the boat, he rocked it back and forth as far as he dared, testing the limits.

"Not bad," he shouted to the camera. "It ain't that stable but I ain't sinking. I think I need to make me one of them outriggers. I can't be flippin' over in the ocean with this thing. These waters is cold."

He also needed to make an oar. After the successful test, he could make the oar, add the outrigger for stability, and then go fishing around the bay. Not that the fishing was bad from shore, he caught a couple, but he was anticipating it wouldn't last forever. The boat would give him more options. Although, it also came with the risk of ending up in the icy ocean water should something go wrong.

Wes pulled the boat back on shore, up past the tree line so the changing tides couldn't play with it. "Pretty soon, I'll be able to go anywheres I want. Maybe I'll visit some of the other contestants and sabotage their camps," he said, casting his voice for the camera to pick up.

"Nah, that'd be against the rules," he reconsidered as the camera continued to film the shore.

"I wonder how the others is doin'. I seen they got some women entered in this here competition. I seen 'em on the ship on the way out here. I guess that's alright with me. I ain't against it. Ain't none of them gonna win, so it just makes my job easier," he said with good, old-fashioned misogynistic certainty, choosing to forget the fact that he himself was a heartbeat away from tapping out on Day 2.

"Women needs men to survive and men needs women to multiply. That's just the way the good lord made it. I ain't gonna argue with god. These days, everybody got a problem with it, but they can't fight nature. Jesus ain't died on the cross fer nothin'," he explained as if his closeminded opinion was law.

He unwrapped the tarp from the boat and folded it up. The plan was to get back to camp, stopping to set some traps along the way. Back at camp, he'd work on his shelter. He packed up the camera equipment and was on his way.

Switching to a camera mounted on his hat, he picked up right where he had left off.

"If y'all ask me, them women shouldn't be out here. I ain't afraid to say it. They takin' a spot away from a man to provide fer his family. I ain't saying nothin' else about it," he claimed and then proceeded to eat up another hour of camera time repeating himself and defending "the way he was brung up," on his way back to camp.

FLOYD BENSON

Day 4

3:06pm

Age: 26
Occupation: Pizza Delivery
Home: Florida
Status: Single, 2 children

"If I win the million dollars, I'm gonna buy me a motorcycle, maybe even marry my girlfriend and get us a nice big house," Floyd Benson dreamt out loud for future viewers. "We'll have to see about those last parts but definitely the motorcycle. I've got all sorts of time to sit around here and figure out which motorcycle I want."

He sprawled out on two long logs he had rolled together so he could rest outside his shelter without being on the ground. He called it the woodsman's hammock.

"You don't get extra points for tiring yourself out. You don't get extra points for building elaborate structures and useless furniture. It may not be the most exciting way to win this game, but I'm sticking to my conservation strategy," he explained, only lifting a finger to plug one nostril so he could blow a booger out. His strategy may have been boring, but his repeated attempts to explain his strategy was even worse.

"This is a trial of endurance. I'll be able to outlast the others that are working themselves sick because, at some point, they're going to run out of energy. They'll tire themselves out and be able to do less and less. Then, boredom will get a hold of them and they'll have to tap out," Floyd explained as if he had it all figured out.

"I can deal with the boredom, the hours upon hours of doing nothing. The one thing that's starting to get to me already is I miss my kids. I miss my girlfriend. When your strategy is to conserve your energy, you have lots of time alone with your thoughts and I keep thinking about my kids. They're three and five—at that age where everything is still new to them. I feel like I'm missing out on that."

Floyd's voice cracked without warning. He closed his eyes to fight off tears.

"I haven't been the most attentive father," he confessed, quivering through slow, choppy thoughts. "They're so new to this world. I have to start being there for them to teach them what's what. I want to be there for them. It's ironic that I finally realize that now, when I physically can't be there for them until this contest is over."

He took a deep breath, wiping the few tears that escaped his closed eyes, and shook the emotion away.

"I'm going to make it up to them when I get home. I'm going to win this for them and I'll be able to spend more time with them," he vowed.

Rather than risk the camera capturing another emotional outburst, he turned it off and resumed doing absolutely nothing.

4:33pm

In the four days Floyd Benson had been on Isolation Island, the camera rarely captured him doing anything except lying down, so his venture away from camp to explore the shoreline was a big event. He collected mussels and limpets along the way. It was more like a casual stroll down the beach than an exploration expedition. He hadn't planned on seeing much more than ocean waves and rocky shores.

To his surprise, he found a stretch of sandy beach. The sand was gray and compacted, but it was flat and devoid of any rocks he could turn an ankle on. It was easy going, right up his alley. His feet sunk into the sand slightly, leaving boot prints in his wake.

A flock of seabirds congregated well offshore. Floyd stopped to watch as they circled and dove into the ocean. With each dive, a flurry of fish jumped out of the water, flashing their shiny silver bodies. Nature was doing its thing, oblivious to Floyd and his plight.

He turned the camera on the feeding frenzy and zoomed in for a better look. "Check that out. That is wild. A flock of birds feeding on a school of fish," he narrated. "Man, I wish I could get out there. That'd be some good fishing. I could catch some birds too."

He looked around the beach behind him as if hoping to find a fishing boat. "Damn. That's too far out. I can't get out there."

All he could do is watch and capture nature as it went on with its daily business. He focused on a bird that dove in and came back up with a fish flopping around in its beak. The bird zipped away with its prize. Three more birds gave chase, hoping to steal the fish or catch it if it fell. They all landed on the beach and a battle ensued. The biggest bird was nearly twice the size of the others and managed to chase away the smaller ones. It grabbed the fish and flipped it into its mouth and down its gullet in one graceful motion.

Floyd enjoyed the show and kept filming as the fish and the birds drifted into deeper water. It was getting harder to film, the birds becoming dots in the sky.

"Wow. That was pretty wild. Just another day in the life of nature, but us humans don't get to see much of…"

"Holy shit!" Floyd yelped, jumping back a step, trying to keep the camera steady.

A great white shark breached, thrusting into the air with its mouth open. The birds scattered but the shark was too quick. It clamped its jaws together taking a mouthful of fish and birds and plunging back into the ocean with a mighty splash.

Floyd's mouth fell open while he watched. "Uh…I…um…" He couldn't get any words out, caught between making a comment and holding his breath in anticipation of another breach.

It didn't come.

Finally, Floyd said, "I guess I won't be going fishing out there. That's for damn sure."

The spectacle had dispersed. The birds flew their separate ways. The shark didn't appear again.

Floyd stared at the ocean, wondering what was going on below the surface. "I didn't even know sharks come this far north. That was big enough to be a great white."

He turned the camera on himself, taking a close-up of the top half of his face. "That was the most incredible thing I've ever seen in my life."

Chapter 6

Day 14

Communication Breakdown

Doc and Hutch found Derrick's body right where they had left it. The only problem was a pack of wolves had also found it. There were only three gray wolves, but they were fully grown—close to one hundred fifty pounds each. They feasted on Derrick's meat, his bones cracking in their powerful jaws, sending a shiver up the spine of any humans within earshot.

Doc and Hutch watched from up the game trail, frozen in indecision as the wolves settled in and took their time enjoying their free meal. Hutch pulled an arrow out and pulled it back in the bow, aiming at the closest wolf which was standing with its side facing the men. Doc cringed as Hutch took aim, neither of them sure it was a good idea. The wolf lifted its head, licking its bloody chops as it looked around.

Hutch held his aim glimpsing the mismatched eyes of his target. It had one gray eye and one brown, giving it a sinister look. The seasoned survivalist knew attacking a pack of wolves was risky business. The prospect of bringing some meat back to camp was tempting. Scaring the wolves away long enough to bury what was left of Derrick, then dragging Dyson up to the site and burying him, as well, before the wolves returned was too far-fetched. Hutch lowered the bow, releasing the tension carefully. He had other people's lives on the line and he wasn't willing to put them at risk.

Turning to Doc, Hutch received a nod of approval, confirming he had made the right choice by not shooting. Neither of them were comfortable with letting the animals devour Derrick, but they didn't have much choice. Hutch pointed with his chin back in the direction from which they had come. They crept away silently, back toward camp.

When they got to a safe distance away, Doc finally spoke. "You made the right call back there," he reassured.

"I know it," Hutch replied. "But, it doesn't make it any easier."

"We have to focus on the wellbeing of the living at this point. Unnecessary risks are..." He thought for a moment. "...un...necessary," he completed with a shrug and a shake of his head.

They cut a new path toward Dyson. Doc resumed trying to make contact with the Mothership without success. "Can we call anyone else on these radios?" he asked.

"Like who?"

"I don't know. Anybody. A passing ship, 911. There has to be some kind of maritime rescue..." he grasped at straws, deflated by his inability to imagine who could be available to rescue them.

Hutch shook his head. "I'm afraid not. We should have satellite phones, but Sharon chose to go with Fisher Price walkie-talkies instead."

Dyson's body was just as they had left it. Seabirds and crows were first on the scene to begin the feast, but they were easily scared away. Hutch and Doc pulled the spikes out of the ground around the dead body to avoid injuring themselves. With a joint effort, they pulled Dyson off the remaining spikes and laid him down.

Doc looked down at the young corpse, then up at Hutch. "Should we say something?" he asked, uneasy.

"Like what?"

Doc stuttered, trying to come up with something profound or comforting. Coming up short, he went with, "Rest in peace, Dyson Warren."

"Dyson Wolski," Hutch corrected.

"Crap. Sorry."

"That's okay. Let's get on with it. We're losing light."

Using the wooden spikes, they chiseled away at the sides of the ditch, burying Dyson right on the spot he met his demise. They left him under a mound of dirt framed by the ditch. They hoped it would protect him from scavengers while remaining easy to find again once they were able to get off the island.

*****

Page tended to the fire and drying clothes at Derrick's camp while Sharon used her radio to try to contact the nearest contestant.

"Floyd? This is Sharon. Come in," she tried and waited, sitting on a log near the fire for a response.

There wasn't any.

"Contestant Floyd Benson," Sharon tried again, as if she'd have more luck with a more formal approach. "This is Producer Sharon Rose. Do you read me? Come in."

Again, there was no reply.

Sharon stood up, her hand wielding the radio, threatening to throw it into the fire. "Do these fucking radios even work," she huffed. Her gesture was a bluff. She wasn't stupid enough to chuck the radio into the fire even if she was running out of reasons not to. She sat back down, her hands cupped around the sides of her face, obstructing Page's view.

Page watched silently. She knew better than to stick her nose into one of Sharon's tantrums. Telling Sharon to calm down had an enraging effect on her. Telling her everything would be all right would also precipitate a reaming out along with a list of why things were not going to be all right. It was best to either be quiet or offer to take over the offending task.

Page chose the latter. "I'll keep trying, Sharon," she said, holding a hand out to receive the radio.

Sharon handed it over as Doc and Hutch returned to camp. "That was quick," she said.

"What's *she* doing?" Hutch asked, pointing his chin at Page as he pulled his backpack off.

"She's trying to get in touch with Floyd Benson. He's the closest contestant," Sharon explained.

"Trying?" Hutch asked.

"He's not replying," Page answered, stepping away from the conversation to keep trying the radio.

Hutch shot Doc an are-you-thinking-what-I'm-thinking look. Doc returned a blank stare that said, "huh?"

"Maybe Floyd took the boat," Hutch guessed.

"Why do you insist it had to be one of the contestants that took the boat?" Sharon huffed.

"Well, I'm pretty sure it wasn't a bear," Hutch snapped. "Who else is on this island? Only the contestants. Right?"

Sharon didn't answer with words, but the face she made spoke volumes. What it was saying wasn't quite clear, but there was something there. She turned her head away to mute her facial expressions, but it was too late.

"Only the contestants, *right*?" Hutch repeated with more emphasis.

He looked to Doc for assurance, but only received an uncertain expression. Doc mouthed, "I don't know," as he shrugged his shoulders.

"This isn't a game anymore, Sharon. If I find out you're hiding something, I swear I will leave you here to fend for yourself," Hutch threatened.

Sharon pursed her lips with her eyes closed, trying to shut out the world. "Yes," she hissed. "Only the contestants."

"Then who else could have taken the bo…"

The radio crackled, interrupting. "Yes, hello. I can hear you," a voice came through.

Hutch hurried over and snatched the radio out of Page's hand before she could reply. He whispered, "Sorry," for the rude gesture, then pressed the talk button. "Floyd? Are you okay?"

"This is Ezra Greer," the voice on the other end replied.

Hutch gave Page a confused look.

She answered the silent question with an explanation. "I couldn't get a hold of Floyd so I tried the next closest contestant. I just wanted to see if I could make contact with anyone."

"Good thinking," Hutch approved before replying to Ezra. "This is Hutch, Ezra. Just checking in. Is everything okay?"

Ezra replied in as few words as he could, careful not to get sucked into a conversation that might violate the rules of the game. "Yes."

Hutch waited for an elaboration, but Ezra wasn't biting.

"You've had no problems thus far?" Hutch prodded.

"Nope," Ezra replied.

"Have you seen anything out of the ordinary?"

"Nope."

Hutch looked to Sharon, not sure what to say next. Sharon got up and pulled the radio out of Hutch's hand.

"That's enough," she insisted, taking over the call. "This is Sharon, Ezra. Keep up the good work. We'll check in on you again in a few days. Over and out." She turned to Hutch fuming once again. "There's no reason to alarm the other contestants," she spat.

Hutch took it to mean she was still hoping to salvage a TV show out of the declining situation. He pulled the radio out of Sharon's hand and gave it to Page. "Make contact with all the contestants and make sure everyone is okay," he ordered.

Page accepted the radio, but looked to Sharon for ultimate approval. Sharon gave her a nod and Page went into the shelter to make the calls without Hutch and Sharon fighting over it.

"So, how did you manage to bury the bodies so quickly?" Sharon asked Hutch and Doc.

Hutch waved the question away with his hand and tended to the fire, leaving Doc to answer. "We didn't."

"What do you mean, you didn't?" Sharon asked, eliciting a groan from Hutch.

"There wasn't much left of Derrick," Doc elaborated. "There was a pack of wolves working on him. It was too dangerous to do anything about it. We were only able to bury Dyson."

Sharon folded her arms and strolled by Hutch, giving him a judgmental look and a disapproving humph.

"What do we do now?" Doc asked, not directed at anyone in particular.

Hutch answered, "Floyd Benson is the closest contestant and he's not answering. We need to check on him. We set out tomorrow at first daylight."

Sharon was visually displeased with Hutch's decision or the fact that he was taking control or both, but she didn't have a better plan. "So, I guess we're sleeping here tonight," she said, as if there were any doubt. "Are we all going to fit in the shelter?"

Hutch replied. "I think so, if we clear out the firewood. It'll be tight, but we're going to want to be close to each other for body heat anyway."

"How long do you think it'll take to get to Floyd's camp?" Doc asked.

"Depends on how rough the terrain is," Hutch replied, unwilling to take a guess. There were too many unknown factors. They had the GPS coordinates for Floyd's camp, but the map of the island, made by Nelson Greely, wasn't extremely detailed. "If we follow the shoreline and it's unobstructed we might be able to make it by nightfall tomorrow, but it might be better to set up camp along the way and stretch it out to the next day. At least, we have Derrick's supplies."

Page emerged from the shelter to report her progress. "Everyone that replied said they were doing well, but I didn't get an immediate response from three more contestants."

The group exchanged worried glances. *Three* more?

"Who?" Hutch asked.

"Tucker Jordan, Jill Hill, and Zoey Price."

JILLIAN HILL

Day 4

4:13pm

Age: 45
Occupation: Homemaker
Home: Kentucky
Status: Married, 6 children

"You gotta thank god fer every day you got on this Earth," Jill Hill said, keeping herself busy, as usual, and spouting clichés, as usual.

She spent Day 4 exploring the area around the lake and the lake itself. It was a lucrative trip. She caught two trout and a handful of crayfish, or, as she called them, "crawdads". Rather than bringing the food back to camp to process and cook, she decided to have a picnic by the lake.

"You gotta thank god fer the little things in life," she continued, giving the pot she had brought a shake. Six crayfish were boiling, their shells beginning to turn red, indicating they were almost done.

"It's the little things that make life. Can't take it fer granted just cuz things get rough, like bein' out here. When the goin' gets tough, sometimes you just gotta set yourself down and remember—god'll never give us more than we can handle. Sometimes, life ain't easy. We all know it, but god'll test you to show you—you can do it. That's why I'm out here—to show that I can do it. I done heard the call from god and this is me answering the call—fer me and fer my family."

The camera watched and recorded from atop the tripod several yards away. Jill and her fire were centered in frame on a clear grassy shore with the dark, still lake in the background.

A noise coming from somewhere behind the camera caught her attention. It was the first time something spooked her.

"Somethin' ain't quite right in this forest," she told the camera in a just-between-you-and-me voice. "I feel like I'm being watched or stalked or I don't know what," she elaborated, straightening up to look behind her. She scanned the forest all around, as far as she could see.

It was another dry day, but the forest was dim with overcast skies giving everything a grayish tint, causing it to seem later than it really was.

"It's kinda creepy being the only one out here," she whispered, barely loud enough for the camera to pick up.

Behind her, not thirty yards away, a bear eased into the lake and swam quietly across. Its black fur blended in with the dark water, only its head sticking out and a stream of ripples behind betraying its location.

Jill didn't see the bear at all until it heaved its body ashore. The splash and dripping made her whip her head around.

"Oh my god," she exclaimed, almost falling backward as she turned just in time to see the dripping backend of the bear disappearing into the woods.

"I hope he ain't plannin' on comin' this way," she said, looking back at the camera as if hoping for guidance. "Dang it. I'll bet these fish guts is smellin' pretty good to him right about now."

Jill rummaged through her backpack to get her bear spray. Contestants were instructed to keep it readily available at all times but, somehow, it had made its way to the bottom of her pack like keys in a purse. She pulled it out, gave it a shake, and set it on the ground next to her. With her bare hands, she scooped up the scraps of fish and bones she had carelessly left on the grass and tossed them into the lake. Hungry fish were happy to dispose of it properly. The water swirled as the brief feeding frenzy ensued. She squatted at the edge of the water to rinse her hands off.

With her dripping hands held out to her sides, she walked back to the fire, reprimanding herself. "I gotta be more smarter than that. I'm starting to get comfortable here and that's a no-no."

She sprang to attention, scrutinizing another sound in the woods behind the camera again. There was no shortage of strange sounds on Isolation Island. Squirrels, birds, deer, bears, wolves—they all had places to go and things to do.

Spooked, she whispered to the camera, "Maybe comfortable

ain't the right word. What's the word I'm looking fer…"

She mumbled um and uh a few hundred times, unable to think of the word. Even scratching her head didn't work, but she tried it anyway. The word she was looking for was complacent. Every good survivalist knows disaster could be right around the corner. Getting too confident because you managed to make it through another day without dying could easily lead to one of those disasters.

Jill gave up on trying to remember the word and chose to say, "I gotta stay on my toes," and left it at that. She had lasted almost four full days, but there was a much longer road ahead if she wanted to get to the million dollars.

SEATON ROGERS

Day 4

4:20pm

Age: 33
Occupation: Screenwriter
Home: Utah
Status: Single

Seaton Rogers walked along an exposed, rocky shore, his eyes following the obstacles on the ground. The camera waved around as he searched for the area mentioned in the treasure clues.

"I'm from Utah, but I'm not, I repeat, I am NOT a Mormon," he explained, keeping the camera entertained. "That's the first question I get when I tell people I'm from Utah. For the record, I don't follow any religion, in case anyone is wondering."

He was far from camp, in an area he wouldn't have ventured to had it not been for the clues. The poem suggested he would find assistance in obtaining the treasure around this shore, specifically during low tide. The mussels clinging to the exposed rocks were a bonus treasure all their own. Seaton collected the narrow black shells full of protein with minimal effort.

"I'm against all the fairy tales people tell themselves to make reality more palatable. You won't ever see me praying for good luck. I don't have any delusions about life on this planet," Seaton continued, laying out his outlook on life.

"You won't see me talking to dead animals, thanking them for feeding me," he explained, putting his hands together and bowing as if pretending to pray. "I know a lot of survivalists think it's a necessity and it's disrespectful to NOT thank the animal."

His presentation was peppered with changing voices he performed to simulate various characters.

"As if the animal can hear them and is thinking, 'Oh, you were hungry? Okay, go ahead and eat me then," he said, nonchalantly.

"I was kind of upset that you killed me, but I didn't know you were hungry. Plus, it was so nice of you to thank me...'" He smiled and batted his eyes with the intention of looking like a doe-eyed deer.

"The hunters that thank the animal just want to make themselves feel better for killing something. It's stupid. If anything, it's disrespectful to say thank you to something you just killed. Imagine someone murdered you..."

He paused and decided to change the course of his thoughts as he plucked two more mussels from their home. "...or a crocodile just bit your head off and then said a little prayer thanking you for the nutrition you provided so that it could survive a few days longer.

He acted out the feeding process graphically as he continued, "Then it tears giant chunks of your flesh off your dead body and comments to his friend about how amazing you taste. 'Boy, was I hungry. This guy is so tender and juicy,' chomp, chomp."

Seaton seemed incapable of stopping his rant or, perhaps, he thought it was entertaining. He certainly entertained himself and, alone in the wilderness, that alone was worth something.

"And humans are even worse," he went on. "Animals will just kill you and eat you, but humans dismember the corpse neatly like a freaking serial killer,"

He delivered the lines more like a standup comedy routine than a serious issue. It was obvious he was making it up as he went along.

"We'll kill a turkey, cut off its head, pluck its feathers out, pull out its guts and shove half a loaf of bread up its ass before sticking it in the oven to roast for hours. Then we all gather 'round and thank god for the whole sick ritual because *that's showing respect*."

Seaton was trapped somewhere between the comedy and tragedy of it all. He shook his head in disgust with a smirk saluting how ridiculous it was to think about. There was no suggestion that he was above it all or any different. It was just a personal quirk of his which surfaced often enough to make him unpopular among people who listened to him long enough.

"What kind of respect is that? And, don't even get me started on the wishbone ritual. Talk about disrespectful. Imagine if that crocodile grabbed your leg and his friend grabbed the other leg.

Make a wish, grrrulululu,"

His crocodile voice sounded more like a drunken George Burns, causing him to burst out laughing at himself. "That was the most pathetic crocodile impersonation of all time," he admitted.

His laughter subsided when he realized where he was. Directly inland from where he was standing, rose the highest point around his territory. He backed up to get a better view of how tall the cliff was. There was no way to scale it. He'd have to find access from the sides. He pointed the camera at the cliff. It looked to be well over two hundred feet tall.

"JUST CLIMB TO THE TOP AND YOU'LL FIND IT THERE," he recited from the clue. "That looks unclimbable. But, I suppose there's *got* to be a safer way to get up there. I can't imagine they'd make me climb the face of a dangerous cliff with no equipment. If I can find another way to the top, I'll go. If not, no amount of treasure is worth risking my life."

The base of the cliff was obstructed by forest, but the cliff was narrow, like a pillar, and green grass could be seen on the edge at the top. Seaton had an idea of how to get there, but today's mission was to find the assistance the clues eluded to. He refocused his effort toward that goal.

"WHERE THE ROCKS AND THE ROOTS CAN BE SEEN A LITTLE MORE," he recited from memory. He had the scroll in his pocket, but he was confident he remembered it correctly.

He found a spot that fit the description to a T. A four-foot tall section of eroded land on the edge of the forest was exposed by the low tide. A tangle of roots, rocks and dirt hung on for dear life. Among the roots, Seaton spotted a piece of opaque plastic jutting out a few inches. He hurried over, camera in hand.

"That's got to be it," he declared, almost tripping over rocks in his excitement to investigate.

The bag was thick as a tarp. He could feel an item inside and it felt like the handle of a shovel. He pulled the long, narrow bag out of the dirt. It gave quite a bit of resistance. Using all one hundred sixty pounds of his weight, he pulled the bag out, falling backward when it surrendered.

The elated survivor untied the end of the bag like a kid on Christmas and pulled out the present—a long, wooden-handled shovel he could use, not only for digging up treasure but for anything else he could think of. The bag was immediately allocated to hold the mussels which he had been collecting at a conservative rate because of the lack of space to carry them.

"There's prize number one," Seaton said, holding up the shovel to show the camera. "This is an advantage, even if I don't find the treasure. I can dig a well to store live fish until I'm ready to eat them. I can sharpen the edges and use it as a secondary cutting tool. I can dig a pit trap. There's lots that I can do with a shovel like this. It's a great find."

He held up the long, narrow plastic bag.

"I'm going to spend the rest of the day filling this bad boy up with mussels to take back to camp," he claimed, but he was exaggerating. The bag would have held about a hundred pounds of mussels if filled to capacity. He gathered as many as he thought he could eat in one sitting and called it a day.

DERRICK BOND

Day 4

5:01pm

Age: 29
Occupation: ex-Marine
Home: Texas
Status: Single

Derrick Bond sat in the second of two deep ditches he had dug searching for the treasure promised on the map. The first hole was over five feet deep and had produced nothing. He tried digging a second hole three feet away from the first. Now, he was almost five feet deep again and there was still no sign of the treasure.

The first hole had been more promising. The dirt was looser and there were fewer rocks—signs someone had been digging there before Derrick. He chalked it up to diversion—whoever had buried the treasure had dug a decoy hole, he thought. Regardless of the reasons, he had wasted a lot of time and energy and had nothing to show for it.

Covered in dirt and exhausted, he climbed out of the ditch, disappearing from the camera's view for a moment. He had left it running, focused on the back end of the ditch where he had been digging, hoping to capture the moment he found the treasure. Dragging his feet over to the tripod, he let out a sigh of defeat.

"Another day wasted. Unless they buried this thing six or seven feet deep, I'm digging in the wrong spot. It's…depressing, to say the least."

He wiped his forehead with the back of his dirty hand. With a few twisting motions, he stretched and cracked his aching back. His shoulders slumped like his arms were about to fall off. The bright, optimistic glow in his deep brown eyes, which had been there on Insertion Day and surfaced from time to time despite adversity, was gone.

"I need food. I can't keep expending all this energy with nothing to show for it." The weakness in his voice confirmed the assessment. It barely picked up on video.

He looked back down the second hole, hoping he had missed some obvious sign that the treasure was there—the corner of a wooden chest, a hint of plastic, a barrel, a shoebox, anything. Dirt and rocks stared back at him. He had grown sick of the sight.

"I'm going fishing with what little daylight I have left. I can check my deadfall traps on the way back to camp. Maybe I'll get lucky."

Changing locations wasn't an easy task. He had to pack up all his equipment and take it with him. He couldn't leave it out, exposed to the elements and the constant threat of rain which persisted on Isolation Island. The defeated soldier turned off the camera and broke down the tripod. He wouldn't dare leave behind the axe he used for digging, but the tarp he used to pull the dirt out of the hole was set up with a paracord system that was time consuming to dismantle. Lengths of paracord were connected to the tarp and ran up and over one of the low-lying limbs of the Treasure Tree so that he could pull dirt out of the ditch. He'd used the axe to chop up the ground and scoop it onto the tarp. It wasn't the ideal way to dig, but he had overlooked the clues pointing to the shovel's location. It also made the axe dull and difficult to chop wood with, so he had to spend a lot of time after sundown sharpening it with stone.

7:10pm

After another unsuccessful fishing trip to the salty, frigid waters of the North Pacific, Derrick dragged his butt back to camp, mentally defeated and physically exhausted. Constant failure was taking its toll on him. His feet grew heavier with every step. He didn't have the heart to keep his head up. Having the camera recording was the only thing that kept a shred of life in him. It was the closest thing he had to someone to talk to. He held the camera in his hand, letting it swing with blurry visions as he talked through his troubles.

"I've never failed so much in my life. I've always been kind of good at pretty much everything, but this place is just impossible. I'm cold. I'm thirsty. I'm hungry. I feel lightheaded and dizzy every time I stand up. I'm just…spent, you know? I don't know how much longer I can take it. The fish aren't biting. I'm going to have to spend the whole day hunting tomorrow. Food is my top priority right now. I have to eat. Everything else has to wait. Screw the treasure."

Screw the treasure. The mere thought of giving in would have made him shudder if he hadn't been so tired. The 'never say die' attitude was ingrained in him, part of his stubbornness which he preferred to call perseverance. In the real world, it usually paid off, but one poor decision on Isolation Island could lead to disaster. Abandoning the search for treasure may be the correct decision, but it still bothered him.

A glimmer of hope stuck out from underneath a rock. Derrick gasped and focused the camera on a tiny tail belonging to a creature that had walked into one of his deadfall traps.

"Oh mamma," he exclaimed, the sight bringing him back to life in an instant.

He could tell by the size of the tail it wasn't a huge kill or even a medium-sized kill, but a few bites of protein was better than nothing at this point. With one hand, he lifted the rock which crushed the animal to death and caught it on video with the other hand. A flattened scrap of gray fur with four little mouse feet spread eagle was exactly what Derrick was expecting and Mother Nature did not let him down. It wasn't a meal fit for a king, but it was protein. In the wilderness, you take what you can get.

Derrick picked up his prize by its tail and dangled it in front of the camera. Its body spun, displaying how thin the four-inch carcass was.

"There it is," Derrick said. "I'm eating tonight. I know it looks pathetic and disgusting but, at this point, I'd eat a skunk if I could find one and kill it."

He skinned and gutted the mouse on camera, using bits of the tiny internal organs as bait to reset the trap.

"Now, I don't recommend eating mice. If I wasn't in such a dire situation, I wouldn't take the risk. They can carry diseases, like hantavirus, but it's a chance I just have to take. I've used up a lot of my energy reserve digging for treasure," he explained to future viewers.

He held up the processed mouse carcass to show the camera. It was thin, with purplish, almost transparent meat.

"It ain't much," Derrick admitted. "Not even a mouthful, really. I'd be lucky if I got a gram of protein out of it, but it's meat. It's something. And I'd rather have something than nothing."

The mouse would do next to nothing for him nutritionally, but it gave him something just as important—confidence and a little hope. They were two commodities which had dwindled away and eluded him, but it only took one tiny mouse to breathe new life into him.

When he got back to camp, he brought his fire back up to par and roasted the mouse meat in front of the camera. When it was done, he sat on his log 'chair' and picked small strips of meat off the mouse with his teeth. There wasn't much left after cooking it. He chewed with a questionable grin on his face.

"After not eating for four days, any meat is going to taste like filet mignon, or so you'd think. But, somehow, mouse still just tastes like crap."

He looked at the charred carcass impaled on the roasting stick, searching for a more palatable bite.

"But," he concluded, tearing the next bite off, "beggars can't be choosers." He hoped it was the last mouse he'd ever have to eat.

KIMMIE ARDEN

Day 4

6:15pm

Age: 36
Occupation: Nurse
Home: New York
Status: Married, 2 children

It was only Day 4 of the survival competition, but mood swings could set in early—par for the course. No one really knows what to expect from themselves as hunger, sleep deprivation, dehydration, and isolation threaten to take them out of the game. The highs and lows of life are amplified in the wild. Above all, with excess time to think, the competitors were bound to do some deep soul searching.

Kimmie Arden was no exception. Even with camp life starting off on the right foot, she sunk into despair as early as Day 4. It wasn't because of hunger. She had caught enough fish to sustain her. But, the life back home she had put on pause was waiting for her to return.

She sat by the fire with her head in her hands and a distant stare. The camera watched for over twenty minutes of silence and stillness.

Her mouth finally came to life, but the distant stare continued. "As a nurse, most people expect me to say how rewarding the job is or how much I like helping people. But…to be honest, it sucks," she said, monotone and emotionless. "It really, really sucks. I tell people how much it sucks all the time. I hate the job. I hate having to go to a hospital every day. I hate every minute of it."

The admission seemed to pull her out of her head, back to the temporary reality which didn't seem so difficult compared to the thought of having to go back to work when she gets home.

"Nurses are overworked, underpaid, underappreciated, and downright abused," she continued. "I think part of the problem is that it's been a traditionally female vocation. Society's tendency to take advantage of women just naturally transferred to the nursing profession. We're worked to death, asked to do more and more and work longer hours and cover extra shifts because they refuse to hire enough people to handle the workload."

Her voice sped up with frustration and anger, her hands animated as if strangling an invisible supervisor.

"And, then, if you mess up because you're overworked, you could kill someone, but no one seems to care until it happens and then they want to crucify you. It's like that through most of the medical industry and everyone in the medical industry knows it, but it just keeps getting worse and worse. The madness never stops. I blame it all on money and profits, but there's more to it than that. New doctors are still subjected to long, sleepless shifts as if it were a right-of-passage rather than dangerous negligence."

To add to her frustration a mosquito zig-zagged around her face, past her ears so she could hear it buzzzzing. She swatted her own ear out of reflex and quite hard, but the bug was back buzzing around her eyes again. After another swing and a miss, she gave up, trying to ignore it.

"I'd like to say I'm out here to make my family proud or for some deep philosophical enlightenment, but really I just want to win the million dollars so I can quit my job. It's really killing me. My health is deteriorating, at only thirty-six years-old. My family never gets to see me because I work all kinds of crazy hours. My kids are growing up on their own without their mother around. My husband and I have our own set of problems and I don't see any end in sight."

She locked her jaw shut when her voice began to quiver. Tears filled her eyes.

"I know money doesn't solve everything," she said, sniffling. "But, a million dollars sure would help right about now. It'll give me a break."

She wiped the tears from her eyes, producing a fake laugh for the camera.

"That's what I need right now—a break. Even *this* is a break for me," she said, gesturing to her surroundings with her hands.

"I'd literally rather be out here in the wild, fending for myself with wild animals around every corner, than be at work. I want to go back because I miss my family, but I can't go back to that job."

She sniffled some more and wiped more tears away, thinking through her dilemma, the weight of four worlds on her shoulders—her kids', her husband's, and her own.

"I can't go back to that job," she repeated. "I don't know what I'm going to do, but I can't go back. I absolutely have to win this competition."

The thought of winning brought a childish grin to her face, transforming her into the Kimmie that arrived on Day 1.

"If I win the million dollars, I'm going to buy some investment properties in Mexico or Belize. I can just rent them out and take the family to visit whenever we want. My husband and I used to dream about doing that before we had kids."

The glimmer of optimism ran away from her face as quickly as it came. The contrast between then and now weighed heavy on her. It was the same old story—a young, newlywed couple with big plans for the future found time had a habit of slipping away faster than they had thought possible. Deflated, her shoulders slumped and she stared back into the fire.

"Somehow, life gets in the way of dreams. It's sad and it's often a slow process that creeps up on you without realizing it, but the daily grind can get a hold of you, suck you in, and never let you go. Your whole life can just pass right by before you know it."

It was a realization people often found at the bottom of a bottle, but she didn't even have a beer to take the edge off. She lifted her head and looked directly into the camera.

"I'm not letting that happen anymore," she vowed, on the record.

STEPHANIE HAMILTON

Day 4

6:24pm

Age: 29
Occupation: Artist
Home: Colorado
Status: Single

    Stephanie Hamilton was on her way back from catching a fish and gathering a handful of raspberries. With the intention of expanding her horizons, she had chosen a new route back to camp and it paid off. Hidden in the hollow of a half-dead oak tree, the neck of a glass bottle peeked out. She hurried over. The idea of a fully intact glass bottle was enough to get her excited, but the scroll inside promised much more than she had anticipated. She sat on a rock and unrolled it on her lap. Some contestants got a visual map, others, like Stephanie got written clues.
    She read the clues aloud with the camera focused on the lettering:

ANYONE CAN SURVIVE, BUT IT'S YOU WHO WILL THRIVE IF YOU HAVE THE RIGHT TOOLS BY YOUR SIDE.

OVER BY THE FALLS, WHERE THE WOODEN SNAKE CRAWLS, YOU MIGHT WANT TO CLIMB THE WALLS

BUT MANY HAVE REGRETTED WHEN PREMATURELY THEY JUMPED

IF YOU DON'T LOOK CAREFULLY YOU COULD END UP STUMPED.

Stephanie raised her hands in the air, along with the camera and scroll. "Woooo! It's a treasure hunt!" she celebrated.

She dropped her arms and reread the scroll, her lips moving but silent.

"Okay," she said, still looking the scroll over. "OVER BY THE FALLS. There must be a waterfall somewhere, which could be a treasure all by itself. First thing tomorrow, I'll follow the stream where I get my water until I find a waterfall."

She read the other part that grabbed her attention out loud again. "WHERE THE WOODEN SNAKE CRAWLS. Hmm. I don't know what that means, but maybe it'll make sense when I find the waterfall."

She stuffed the rolled up scroll back into the bottle and returned to camp full of excitement for the new adventure.

Her camp was neat and organized. The shelter looked almost like a permanent structure and turned out just as she had described on Day 1. Only the front door needed to be finished, but she had been using the tarp from her temporary shelter in the meantime. The temporary shelter wouldn't go to waste either. It would be turned into a smokehouse for preserving fish and meat. She would need it soon. The fishing was excellent on her part of the island and her bird traps caught two skinny grouse. She planned to step up her hunting and fishing when the smokehouse was finished.

The outdoor fire pit had a tripod build over it with a boiling pot suspended. She had whittled a spoon to cook and eat with and work had begun on a chair with a back to make her more comfortable. Every night, after the sun went down, she worked on the smaller projects inside by firelight. A stonewall fireplace made up the back wall of the shelter, providing plenty of heat throughout the night, as well.

If the contest had been based on speed of progress and execution, Stephanie would have been in the lead. But, the test of endurance was the ultimate challenge of Isolation Island. How long she could last was yet to be seen.

Chapter 7

Day 15

Morning Dew

What was left of the production crew—Sharon, Page, Doc, and Hutch—had a miserable night in Derrick's cramped shelter. It was never intended to sleep four people, let alone two men over six feet tall.

Hutch was the first to wake just before the sun came up, but he couldn't get out of the shelter without disturbing the others. He was tucked away in the far corner away from the entrance and furthest from the fire. Next was Page, then Sharon. Doc was closest to the entrance and the fire, not because he needed the most warmth, but because he had to sleep with his legs sticking out the entrance.

Hutch lifted his head, checking to see if his sleeping companions were awake. He could hear Doc snoring away. For a moment, Hutch's mind drifted to contemplating whether or not snoring had an evolutionary purpose. Perhaps it kept predators away. Even if it only kept scavengers away, it served a good purpose. His head floated without a care in that moment of the morning just after waking, before all the pressures of life had a chance to sink back into the brain.

He rubbed his eyes and brought himself back to reality. The reminder of the two dead men and the possible loss of more gave his heart a jolt. It wasn't fear. It was motivation—the ultimate morning wakeup call. It was time to get moving.

"Page," Hutch whispered, nudging her shoulder. "Wake up."

Page turned over without opening her eyes.

"Page," he barked louder, hoping it would wake everyone at the same time.

Six weary eyes opened at once, heads twisting back and forth wondering where they were and what that objectionable noise was.

Doc snapped to attention after a moment. He sat up, propping himself up with his arms behind him. "What's wrong?" he asked.

"We've got to get going," Hutch reminded his sleepy companions.

Doc tried to rub some life into his face with his hand. Sharon and Page began to drift back to sleep. Hutch clapped his hands, startling the bunch.

"Come on, people. It's time to wake up," he bellowed.

Sharon grumbled, "I'm not ready to wake up," turning from her back to her side.

They had the sleeping bag unzipped to maximize coverage. Doc pulled it off everyone at the same time and shimmied his way out the door.

Sharon huffed, covering herself back up. Page eased over her and crawled out. Hutch was less delicate. He climbed over Sharon, knocking each limb into her side on purpose on his way out. She growled and used the sleeping bag as a tortilla to wrap herself like a burrito.

Daylight hadn't quite arrived yet. The fire outside the shelter was still going but dying down. There was no point in building it back up. Hutch just wanted to pack up everything they could carry and set out for Floyd Benson's camp as soon as possible. They paused around the fire to warm their bones for a moment.

Hutch turned to Page. "I swear I will leave her here if she's not awake by the time we're ready to go," he warned.

"I'll make sure she's up," Page promised, rubbing her hands together for warmth.

It was growing lighter by the minute. A layer of dew coated the entire camp, transferring to clothes and skin with every touch. Hutch began collecting Derrick's supplies, packing them into his own backpack. Doc followed suit while Page stayed out of the way trying to contact the Mothership and the missing contestants on the radio. There was still no reply.

Hutch snatched the sleeping bag off Sharon so he could roll it up. Sharon cursed him, but it didn't faze him. Without any verbal warning, he took down the tarp roof of the shelter, sending drops of dew raining down on Sharon. It finally got her moving. She sprung up and out of the way, shaking the water off.

"Asshole," she growled.

Hutch just looked at her with a blank stare as he continued

doing what needed to be done. Page came to Sharon's rescue with a hand towel she pulled from her bag and helped dry any exposed skin. There wasn't much. The outfit Page had packed for Sharon, which she had worn through the night was warm and water resistant.

Hutch packed the tarp away and returned to the campfire. "Pardon me, ladies," he said. It had the opposite effect of what he had intended. It drew attention to him as he unzipped his pants standing over the last dying flames of the fire. A stream of urine rained down, causing an audible sizzle as it extinguished the fire.

"Nice. That's really classy," Sharon criticized.

Hutch zipped up and turned around. "The last thing we need is to start a forest fire, Your Highness."

"So, that means you have to pee it out? Pour some water on it," Sharon disputed.

"Great idea. Should I use your water ration? I'm sure as hell not pouring mine out," Hutch challenged.

Hutch did one last sweep of the camp, checking every crack and crevice with one purpose in mind. When he came up empty-handed again, he asked the question that had been creeping in and out of everyone's mind. "What the hell happened to his camera equipment?"

With everything else in Derrick's camp in their backpacks, everyone grabbed their own canteen and followed Hutch, setting out in search of Floyd Benson's camp. From consulting his map, Hutch knew there was a creek between the two camps and deduced it was the same creek he had seen emptying into the ocean on the other side of the rocky outcrop on shore. He led the group north, hoping to cross the creek before making their way to the shoreline to the west.

WES WOOD

Day 5

9:13am

Age: 57
Occupation: Farmer
Home: Mississippi
Status: Divorced, 8 children

Dressed in his finest waterproof forest camo from head to toe, Wes Wood set out from camp with the intention of finishing his boat and launching it before noon. He had all the tools he needed as well as fishing gear and traps, but with no watch he'd have to estimate noon.

"Trappin' animals ain't workin' out so good fer me 'round camp," he explained to the camera mounted on his hat as he made his way along a game trail. "And, here's why."

He arrived at one of his snare traps. It had been sprung, but there was no animal caught in it.

"I got me this dang fox 'round my camp," Wes said. "He been stealin' bait out all my traps. Look-it." He pointed with the hiking stick he had recently made. It was a sharpened spear on one end, almost four feet long. It had a cross carved into the top "handle" as well as four vertical hash marks with a diagonal line through them, indicating the five days he had been on Isolation Island.

The fox had only left its paw prints behind. It had figured out a way to spring the trap and take the bait without getting caught. This was the case with almost all the traps Wes had been setting. Every day he'd check the traps and every day he had been outfoxed by what he imagined to be the same fox over and over.

"I gotta find somewhere else to set up some traps," he decided, continuing along the trail that would take him to the edge of the bay and his boat.

3:09pm

Wes Wood's boat was an eyesore, but it floated and with the outrigger attached it was much more stable, giving him the confidence to venture out and explore the bay area. The outrigger was a piece of driftwood shaped like an elephant's tusk. Attaching it to the boat with two more lengths of wood and cordage made removing it a tedious chore he would not mess around with. The tarp that covered the frame of the boat was now a permanent fixture. The boat would have to be useful enough to justify the sacrifice.

Wes's camp was situated in a corner of the island where the bay meets the open ocean. A rocky outcrop protected his boat launching point from the choppy waves of the Pacific. Choosing to take the boat for a test run in calm waters, he paddled deeper into the bay. First, he stopped at a few choice spots to fish where dead trees had fallen. All he managed to catch was one small fish he decided to use for bait.

Paddling deeper into the bay, he came across the first sign he had seen in five days that a human was nearby. A small column of smoke rose from the forest's canopy on the other side of the bay, deep in the woods up steep hill.

He turned on his camera and pointed it at the smoke. "Must be one of the other contestants," he surmised.

"They done told us we ain't supposed to have no contact with the other contestants," he reminded himself out loud for the camera's sake. "But, they ain't said we can't sabotage them," he rationalized with excitement in his voice and a mischievous smile wrinkling his face more than usual.

The idea sparked a newfound energy within him. "Hooo-weeee," he bellowed, using the adrenaline surge to paddle harder and faster as he imagined the many ways he could gain an advantage by bringing other contestants down.

He thought he had found a loophole in the rules, but he knew what he was planning could be considered cheating. Rather than risk a ruling, he stopped paddling, letting the boat drift on its own while he destroyed the evidence of his intentions.

He rewound the video clip he had just recorded to before he

filmed the smoke. Pointing the camera at the floor of the boat, he pressed record to cover the incriminating video clip. With the boat's tarp covering the camera's lens, Wes resumed paddling while he serenaded future viewers, singing an out of tune version of his favorite country song. The sound of water clapping against the paddle kept time as he made sure to make the performance long enough to cover up any mention of sabotage or contact with another contestant.

After the song, he double-checked the video. The evidence was gone. As far as anyone would know, it had never happened. He put the lens cover back on the camera for added security, turned it off, and left it by his feet at the bottom of the boat.

ZOEY PRICE

Day 5

9:50am

Age: 24
Occupation: Dance Instructor
Home: Montana
Status: Single

Zoey Price pressed record on one of her two remaining cameras and held it up in front of her face for a close-up. "So…it's Day 5. My shelter has burned down. All my equipment burned up, except for a couple cameras, a tarp, and an axe," she summarized. "It's unfortunate, tragic even, but it's all part of my journey."

Despite her brave words, her eyes teared up. She struggled to hold back the tears and keep her voice from quivering. Taking a deep breath, she reset herself, trying to think of something positive.

"I was born on February 28th which makes me a Pisces. A Pisces never gives up. We follow our hearts. We're guided by our feelings and intuition. So, I'm going to trust my intuition and my gut feelings," she explained.

"Last night was a beautiful, clear night and the sky lit up with stars. I'd never seen so many stars in my life and it really hit me, how lucky I am to have this experience. Yes, it's going to be difficult, but I have to follow the path laid out for me. The stars revealed themselves to me and showed me the direction I must go to save myself."

She was dead serious, but her expression fluctuated between wild-eyed and teary eyes, flashes of enthusiasm and despair. She looked to be either on the verge of uncontrollable laughter or breaking down into a crying fit from one moment to the next.

"The stars and my intuition are telling me to go east. So, that's what I'm going to do. I'll follow the shoreline as long as I can and hope that I run into another player. The problem I'm having with that idea is...I know my game is over. Making contact with another contestant is against the rules. I'm okay with that, but if I find another player and make contact, that player might be pulled from the game, too, for having contact with another player—me."

She looked down at her feet as if reconsidering the decision to leave. Shaking her head, she added, "I hope I don't get another player disqualified. I hope the producers will understand it was an emergency. And, that's all I can do."

Her voice became more stable and resolute. "I can't stay here and wait when I have no idea how long I'd have to wait."

She ran the camera around her camp one last time, her sniffles picked up by the microphone made for a dramatic conclusion to her camp life.

"Goodbye camp."

At ten o'clock in the morning on Day 5, Zoey Price left her burned out camp in search of assistance.

4:28pm

When you don't know how far you need to go, the journey is always longer. Zoey knew finding another contestant wasn't going to be easy. They were spread out across the island specifically to prevent them from having contact with each other. At some point, she'd need to cross a body of water or climb a rock wall to find assistance, but there was no telling how long the journey would take to get to the obstacles.

By late afternoon on Day 5, Zoey was making her way up the beach, but she was slowing down. The sky had become overcast, threatening rain. It was time to start making decisions. The biggest question on her mind was where she would spend the night. She had the tarp from her temporary shelter, along with the paracord which had held it in place. It was enough to string up a tent to keep her dry, but it wouldn't keep her safe or warm.

As the wind picked up and the temperature dropped, she knew the rain was coming. Getting off the beach and setting up a shelter was a priority. She'd only have one more chance to make a fire before the rain made it impossible, but something kept her on the beach a little longer. Up ahead, the shore was cluttered with driftwood and other debris discarded by the ocean. There were bits of faded color among the debris.

Zoey rushed over when she realized what she was seeing—plastic and tin with the faded logos of products from all over the world. She captured it on camera.

"Oh my god. Look what I just found," she said, making sure the camera got a shot of each item.

The first was perhaps the most useful—a plastic water bottle with its cap on. It was tattered, scratched, and empty, but it could be used to carry water and, if she had the know-how, she could even use it as a vessel to boil water in. As a bonus, the bottle had three more twins nearby. They were all empty. One lacked a cap and another had a small hole in the bottom, but they were all useable.

The next item she was excited about was a dented soda can. The logo was too faded to read, but labels didn't matter. "If I can find water, I can carry some with me. If I can make a fire, I can use the can or even the bottles to boil water," she said, her voice suddenly quivering to a halt.

Crouched on the beach among the driftwood, Zoey wrapped her arms around her knees with a bottle in one hand and the camera in the other, weeping intermittent tears of sorrow and joy.

She buried her head, muffling her voice. "This is...I mean, I can't believe this...I know its only garbage, but this garbage could save my life," she said, her emotions heavier than warranted.

A realization halted her tears and caused her to lift her head. "Imagine that. Garbage saving my life. I've always been against the use of disposable plastic bottles and such."

Wiping the tears from her eyes she decided, "I's *still* against it, but it's really weird to see how valuable it can be under certain circumstances."

She stood up and tossed her newfound treasures into a pile.

"I'm going to take these bottles and cans home with me and recycle them," she vowed.

The other bits of treasure on shore that day were tangled and mangled—a small piece of fishing net, a mess of tangled fishing line, and a shoe that looked like it had been chewed on by a dog before being set adrift in the Pacific Ocean.

She crammed one of the bottles into the faded, blue sneaker. The others she stuffed into the makeshift backpack she had made using the tarp.

With all the distractions, she hadn't noticed the end of the beach up ahead. She looked up to see a sheer, dark cliff protruding from the forest, extending to the sea. Waves crashing violently at the base made it impassable by sea and there was no way she could climb the beast, but she imagined another contestant on the other side—rescue, salvation.

"I've got to find a way around that cliff," she told the camera, pointing it at the obstacle.

A distant rumble of thunder called out a warning. Zoey turned off the camera and hurried along the beach, hoping the cliff might provide a natural shelter or, at least, a wall she could use for a lean-to. There was nothing of the kind on shore. Either way, the tide was liable to rise and flood her out. She followed the base of the cliff inland, the terrain becoming steeper at first, but then there was a drop-off down to a dry basin. It was more than she had hoped for. The base of the cliff had been eroded away, creating a cave big enough to set up camp in without having to use the tarp to stay dry.

Zoey rushed down the hill, sliding down the first half and almost tumbling down the last third on her way to explore the cave. She switched to stealth mode, approaching with caution in case another creature already called the cave home.

The cave was empty. There were no footprints to indicate any recent animal activity. It was big enough so that she could build a fire under the overhanging stone cliff. She slid off the loops on her shoulders to lower the tarp from her back. It fell to the ground, her drill and bow kit spilling out as she considered if there were any dangers in using the cave as a shelter.

Another rumble of thunder, this time closer, made the decision to spend the night much easier. Zoey dumped the rest of her things in the cave and scrambled to gather firewood before the storm caught up to her. There was no time to search for water to boil, but if she could get a fire started, she'd at least be warm tonight and if the rain arrived, she'd have safe, drinkable water delivered.

With the impending rainfall in mind, she harvested some wide, flat leaves from a beech tree. They would serve as funnels to gather rainwater in the plastic bottles.

The first drops of rain fell as she returned with a load of firewood, kindling, and leaves. The sky darkened another shade or two by the time she got back with what would have to be her final load of firewood. She started settling in to her new home. The rain came pouring down all at once as if had been waiting for her to take cover. She was safe and dry inside the cave, but the temperature was dropping rapidly.

Her hands were still swollen from her previous attempt to make fire with the bow and drill, but desperation blocked out the pain. She worked the contraption again, frantic to get results. After ten minutes, a glorious little stream of smoke rose up from under the drill. She sped up, determined to make it work this time.

The smoke became steady and she pulled the drill from the hearth board. To her delight, a red, glowing ember appeared, intensifying and growing as she blew on it and dumped it onto a pile of dry bark shavings and pine needles where it disappeared.

"Dammit," she spat but, unwilling to give up, she got down on her hands and knees and kept blowing. A trace of red was still alive. A darkening cloud of smoke rose slowly as she took another breath and encouraged it to grow. Another lungful exhaled at a calm, steady rate brought a flame to life in an instant and it grew, eating up the pine needles and bark shavings.

"Yes! Keep going. Don't go out," she cheered and encouraged as she built a teepee of small sticks and twigs over the flame. It didn't take long to grow into a healthy fire that could last her all night. She screeched a celebration and kept piling wood until it warmed the entire cave.

"I can't believe I made a friction fire all by myself," she said, forgetting the camera wasn't filming. "And I can't burn the cave down," she joked, applauding achievement before realizing she was only talking to herself.

STEPHANIE HAMILTON

Day 5

12:05pm

Age: 29
Occupation: Artist
Home: Colorado
Status: Single

Stephanie Hamilton had followed the narrow river, her freshwater source, upstream all morning, but there was no sign of a waterfall. The long journey was made easier by using the animal trail which ran parallel to the river. As many contestants did, she treated the camera as a friend to talk to and pass time during long walks and other monotonous tasks.

"If I win the million dollars, I'm going to buy a huge piece of land in Honduras, someplace away from other people with some beach frontage, and build a house. I want to create a self-sustaining compound. It'll have a huge garden," she effused, the camera mounted on her head capturing the sights and sounds of nature along the way.

"I'll have a chicken coop for eggs, a pond for fish and ducks," she continued dreaming out loud. "I can have all kinds of fruit trees in Honduras. I've always wanted to live somewhere I can grow tropical fruit trees—mangos, guava, papayas."

The mere mention of food made her mouth water and her stomach beg, but she continued, nonetheless.

"And, kiwi. I'd love to grow my own kiwi. Basically, I want my home to be a place I never have to leave. That's been my goal my entire life. My family used to go to the beach for every vacation and I'd always dream about staying there. Like, why not live in the place you like to vacation? Then, every day would be like a vacation."

She sounded like a little kid talking about what she wants to be when she grows up, but her innocent rambling about her hopes and dreams was endearing.

"Of course, most people think it's unhealthy to stay at home all the time, but I'd love it. I don't leave the house much now. I guess people imagine how *they* would feel if they never left the house and project that feeling onto others. I kind of understand—if I was sitting at home, depressed and disheveled because I never leave the house, that *would* be unhealthy. But, I'm happy as a pig in shit when I'm at home. I love not having to leave. Leaving is a chore. Interacting with other humans is taxing. It drains me. If I have to do it often, I absolutely hate it. I can do it, every once in a while, and I even enjoy it from time to time, but leaving the house *every day*, talking to people *every day*—that would drive me crazy. *That* is not healthy to me."

She was turning the camera from a friend to a therapist, something all the contestants did from time to time.

"Part of the problem I have with people is everyone is always telling you what to do and how to do it, even if they don't practice what they preach. I'd never presume to tell other people that their choice to go out and mingle with people is unhealthy to them. Part of me *does* think people would be better off if we all stayed at home and minded our own business, but that's a different story. Plus, it wouldn't be good for the economy. But, my point is, I don't tell other people what to do and they shouldn't tell me what to do."

The river and the animal trail seemed to go on forever, as did Stephanie's rambling, but it helped pass the time.

3:25pm

"...and an art studio overlooking the ocean. That'd be the greatest..."

After hours of walking and describing her dream home in great detail, Stephanie stopped short and turned her head to listen. She had been fooled into thinking she was nearing a waterfall a few times along the trip, but it was only the sound of rapid portions of the river. This time, however, it was the real thing. Hearing it, she could tell the difference. The water crashed down hard and steady and louder than the rapids.

"That's got to be the waterfall," she insisted and took off, double time up the trail.

Through the tops of the trees she caught glimpses of a cliff that took shape more and more until she came out in a clearing next to the river. A tall, narrow cascade of water rained down from atop the cliff, some of it turning to mist before splashing into the deep plunge pool below. The sight was so mesmerizing she almost forgot why she was there. As exciting the thought of finding the treasure was, she continued to enjoy watching and filming the waterfall for a moment before remembering to scan the area for clues. She had the rest of her stay on Isolation Island to enjoy the waterfall.

"OVER BY THE FALLS WHERE THE WOODEN SNAKE CRAWLS." She recited the clue from memory, scouring the environment with the camera.

"WHERE THE WOODEN SNAKE CRAWLS," she repeated, wandering as she searched for a tree or a branch that might resemble a snake. Nothing jumped out at her, so she widened the search, away from the falls.

Not far away, she found a vine wrapped around a tree, circling its trunk like a snake slithering up. She backed away, looking up the tree for any indication of treasure or another clue, but there was nothing. It was just a tree and the vine looked more like a vine than a snake. Nothing else jumped out at her. It was all generic forest. She returned to the falls.

"It has to be somewhere around here," she insisted, looking up and down. Then, her attention turned to the clearing on the other side of the river. "Or, it might be over there," she deduced.

Behind the waterfall, a rock ledge above the waterline would give her a path to the other side. She climbed up and surveyed the path. There was one problem—the waterfall had concealed a long gap in the rock ledge. She'd have to take a running jump across and hope to land without falling short or slipping into the plunge pool below.

She backed up, readying herself for a sprint and a long jump she wasn't sure she could make. "I'm going to have to jump it," she said, but the word *jump* made her pause.

"Wait," she said, "MANY HAVE REGRETTED WHEN PREMATURELY THEY *JUMPED*"

She looked down into the plunge pool, the cold water splashing up at her.

"Maybe it's not on the other side."

She looked up. The rock wall was wet, slippery and mossy. She reminded herself, "YOU *MIGHT* WANT TO CLIMB THE WALLS."

"This isn't it," she surmised and climbed down off the ledge.

"IF YOU DON'T LOOK CAREFULLY, YOU COULD END UP STUMPED," she recited. "I've got to find a stump and the wooden snake."

There were four stumps in the vicinity belonging to four fallen trees. One fallen tree was in the river, the bottom of its trunk jutting out. The others had fallen away from the river. She checked around the closest stump. There was no sign of treasure or another clue or anything extraordinary.

Thunder crackled and rolled across the sky, urging her to give up and take shelter. She looked up at the darkening sky. The top of the cliff pulled her eyes away. A squiggly branch protruded over the top.

"Is that the wooden snake?" she asked the camera, backing up to get a better look.

As she stepped backward slowly, her foot caught on an exposed root and sent her down on her butt. She rolled over and picked herself up, cursing her clumsiness. Dusting herself off, she noticed the root she had tripped over. It zigzagged above ground, like a snake, ending at the stump of the tree which had fallen into the river.

"Oh, holy crap," she exclaimed, seeing an additional and crucial detail she had overlooked. "I can't believe I didn't notice this right away."

She turned the camera on the tree stump. It had a massive circumference but, unlike the other stumps—severed and jagged—the wooden snake's stump had been clean cut by a chainsaw.

"Duh. Someone cut this stump," Stephanie said, showing the difference between the natural stumps and the machined "treasure" stump. "Okay, this has to be it," she deduced, "but where's the treasure? Inside?"

She examined the stump closer. It was tall enough to house a chest or some sort of treasure. The tree trunk protruding from the river was jagged, occurring from a natural break. This pleased her. The tree had not been chopped down just for her treasure. The stump had been modified by machinery.

But, where *was* this treasure?

The ground around the stump looked too densely packed to dig and it certainly hadn't been dug up recently. Her eyes followed the outer ring of the stump. It wasn't a growth ring. Someone had cut a ring just inside the bark. She tried to pry her nails into the separation, but the joint was too tight.

"This must open, like the lid of a trashcan…somehow," she said, furrowing her eyebrows, trying again.

It didn't budge.

"I should have brought the axe. I can try chopping my way into it."

As if the sky was clearing its throat, another rumble of thunder reminded her time was not currently on her side.

"Damn it. I should have brought the axe, but I didn't want to carry it all day long hiking through the woods looking for this thing."

She looked up at the sky again. It was darker and more menacing. The treasure wasn't worth getting wet and cold for. At least, not now. She was doing well on all fronts. There was no need to take an unnecessary risk. As it was, she barely had enough time to get back to camp before dark.

"Okay, now I know where the waterfall is. I can take a faster route back to camp and come back tomorrow with the axe. This was not a wasted day. This was a successful journey. This is good," she said with a genuine smile, "I wonder what kind of treasure is in there."

Another crash of thunder hurried her along. Her curiosity would have to wait.

"I better get out of here."

SEATON ROGERS

Day 5

3:33pm

Age: 33
Occupation: Screenwriter
Home: Utah
Status: Single

From atop the highest point in his territory, Seaton Rogers had an excellent view of the thunderstorm over the ocean in the distance. He predicted, if it stayed on the same path he was observing, it would miss him and his corner of the island. On camera, he caught the blur of rain and spectacular veins of lightning streaking down over the ocean.

"Someone is going to get rained on," he speculated. He had no idea where the other contestants were located, but he imagined they were spread out across the entire island.

The storm distracted him from his reason for making the long hike to this vantage point, but provided some entertainment while he rested. He sat on a small boulder enjoying the view of the ocean and storm a little while longer, taking in the moment as it was offered.

"There's something about seeing a storm over the ocean from afar. You're not part of it. It's not threatening you. It's just nature doing its thing. Nature doesn't intend to threaten you. Nature is just nature. It's not angry. It's not purposely violent. It's just the elements of our planet interacting. It's beautiful."

Seaton snapped himself out of Mother Nature's spell and stood up, shovel in hand. "Time to get to work. I've climbed to the top. Now, I have to see…" He paused, unrolling the scroll to consult the clues again.

"…WHERE THE FIRST SIGN OF SHORE COMES INTO SIGHT," he read aloud.

"I'm just wondering," he said, looking around, "which shore this might be referring to. To see my own shore, I'd have to be close to the edge of the plateau I'm on here."

The plateau was a small clearing that sat atop a lonely, out of place cliff which looked like it had been shredded by the sea over hundreds of years. Seaton crept to the edge.

"This is the only spot I can see my own shore. But the next part of the clue says to take ten paces. TEN HEALTHY PACES, to be exact. If I took ten healthy paces from here, I'd fall to my death," he explained to the camera.

He walked backwards, retracing the steps that brought him to the edge, his eyes glued to a distant shore jutting out from somewhere he couldn't see. It was just there, to the left, miles away. He kept backing up until the ground made the peninsula disappear.

"Oh! This has got to be it," he said, testing the theory by moving back forward.

The peninsula reappeared. He moved backward again to make sure no other bits of shore could be seen anywhere, then, moved back to the spot where the first sign of the peninsula appeared. Taking one step to the left made it disappear again. He reset himself and took a step to the right. It disappeared again.

"This has to be it. Now to figure out what ten *healthy* paces are."

He looked over the entire scroll again, hoping the exact wording would provide another hint. Shaking his head, he read the final step to finding the treasure aloud. "TAKE TEN HEALTHY PACES AND DIG ON YOUR RIGHT. What the hell is a healthy pace?"

He rolled the scroll up and took ten long strides forward.

"I guess there's one way to find out," he said, looking at the ground to his right. It didn't look like it had been disturbed recently, but neither did any of the ground in the vicinity.

He pushed the shovel into the ground with his foot. The resistance and density of the soil wasn't encouraging, but he lifted the layer of grass up and dumped it behind him, marking the spot.

The tedious part of every task the contestants had to endure was the filming. Although he would have loved to dig as fast as he could to get to the treasure, Seaton had to stop filming and set up the camera on its tripod to record the event. He zoomed out, framing in the area and tilted the camera back a bit to capture a little more light. Battery power check—60%. Everything looked good. He pressed record and resumed digging. About two feet down, he stopped. He had been bringing up a lot of rocks and the digging overall was difficult.

"I don't think this is the right spot," he said, a bit dejected and out of breath.

Resetting himself to 'WHERE THE FIRST SIGN OF SHORE COMES INTO SIGHT,' he took a deep breath and examined the ground ahead of him.

"Ten healthy paces," he repeated. "What's a healthy pace?" he asked himself again. "If my pace is healthy, it's normal. An UN-healthy pace would mean shorter strides. So, maybe I just need to take ten normal paces."

His second attempt brought him several feet short of the first hole he had dug. He plunged the shovel into the ground on his right. It was also covered with grass, but the soil was softer. He looked up and smiled at the camera even though he was out of frame.

"I think this is it," he said with enthusiasm. A rumble of thunder from the other side of the island seemed to provide a dramatic confirmation. He had to reposition the camera again before he could find out for sure.

The looser ground made the digging easier and faster and within a few minutes the shovel stopped short, producing a telltale knock. Seaton looked up at the camera and shook a victorious fist in the air. Thumping the shovel down a few more times, his ears confirmed a large wooden object below.

"Sounds like a treasure chest to me," he told the camera.

He dug and scraped a small section clean to expose a flat, wooden plank—the top of a crate. The letters S-L-A-N-D stared up at him. He recognized it as part of the Isolation Island TV show logo.

"There it is," he bragged, smiling ear to ear.

It would take almost an hour to unearth the whole crate enough to pull it out of the ditch. He yanked it out by one of the two rope handles on either side, landing on his backside with the final heave.

Seaton's excitement was limited by his energy level, having spent most of it digging, but he wasn't ready to rest just yet. He crawled over to the latch on the front of the box and released it. The top swung open on a hinge, revealing the coveted treasure of Isolation Island. Seaton's face lit up like a child on Christmas morning.

"No way," he exclaimed, reaching in with both hands.

He pulled out a hammer and a box of nails to show the camera.

"Look at all this stuff."

He pulled out each item to show the camera as he narrated.

"A hand saw. A set of good sharp knives. More fishing hooks, thank goodness. A net. More fishing line and paracord. This is great."

He piled the items on the ground next to the box as he dug deeper.

"Food!" he shouted, his eyes tearing up as he read the labels on the cans. "Beans, fruit, potatoes, mushrooms."

A bag of rice followed. "Carbs, sweet carbs," he commented, cuddling the bag against his cheek.

His face lit up another notch when he saw what was next. "No way…salt and pepper." The watertight container the salt and pepper shakers came in could come in handy as well. "I don't normally like pepper on my food but I've really been craving salt. At this point, I'd even welcome having some pepper to spice things up a little, but I'd definitely trade it for some garlic."

He pillaged on with great delight, a new surge of energy propelling him. "Toilet paper!" he shrieked like a little girl, pulling three rolls out and hugging them with gusto.

"What's this?" he asked, producing a shiny metal coffee can with no label. "I can't be," he insisted with disbelief, fumbling to get the lid off in his excitement.

Under the lid, he found a foil, tamper-evident cover. Wasting no time, he tore it off, the rich aroma of coffee hitting him in the face instantly.

He let his tongue hang out, making a drooling Homer Simpson face as he let out a moan of ecstasy. "Mmmm…coffee," he said, turning dead serious suddenly. The look on his face made it seem like the find was a matter of life or death.

Holding the can up to his nose again, he inhaled long and deep like he was huffing paint. "Oh yeah. That's the stuff." His eyes rolled back.

With his head spinning and before he could wonder how he was going to make the coffee, he found a coffee pot turned on its side near the bottom of the treasure box. He cradled it like a baby in his arms. "Okay, I can stay here forever now," he joked, nodding his approval at the camera.

Leaning in to see what else was at the bottom of the box, he furrowed his brow.

"Another fishing net?" he wondered aloud, taking the item out for a better look. It was too thick to be a fishing net and it was wrapped tight in itself in a football shape. A metal ring on one end gave him the hint he needed. He jumped up and spun around, dancing with the bundle.

"It's a hammock," he celebrated.

The happy camper took a victory lap around the back of the camera before returning to see the last of his treasure. The bottom of the box was lined with a folded, maroon blanket. He lifted it to make sure there was nothing hidden underneath.

"Wow," he said to the camera, sitting on the ground next to his bounty. "This is more than I could have ever hoped for. All these items will be put to good use. All these items will not only make my life easier, but make this an overall more pleasant experience."

He looked at the pile and the box it came in with a suddenly perplexed look. "Hm. Now I have to figure out how I'm going to get all this sh...shtuff back to camp," he said, catching himself before letting out a word that would have needed to be bleeped out.

FLOYD BENSON

Day 5

6:25pm

Age: 26
Occupation: Pizza Delivery
Home: Florida
Status: Single, 2 children

Floyd Benson turned on his camera when he got back to camp.

"So, I just got back to camp. I went to get water and now some of my stuff is gone. The axe is gone," he explained, filming an empty log standing on end. "I left it sticking into this…um…block of wood…er…this…log. It's where I always leave it. Some of my clothes are gone, too. I left them drying near the fire."

Floyd scanned the entire camp, proving the items he was looking for weren't there.

"I don't know if an animal dragged my clothes off into the woods or what, but what kind of animal would take the axe?" he asked the camera.

He checked in his shelter to see if the axe was there or if anything else was missing. There was definitely something else missing but, he couldn't quite put his finger on what it was.

A rustling noise outside brought him out of the shelter to investigate. He pulled the knife out of its sheath on his belt with his free hand, pointing the camera into the woods with the other hand, revved up to confront the thief. The microphone picked up footsteps crunching on dead leaves.

"Hey bear," Floyd said in a deep, stern voice. His gung-ho desire for a confrontation suddenly disappeared.

The rustling stopped abruptly, but there was no sign of what caused it. Floyd backed away, switching out his knife for a canister of bear spray. He held it out in front of him, ready to strike anything that moved.

"Hey bear," he shouted, spooking the mystery animal. It stirred up and ran across the woods in front of him, hidden from sight by the thick brush and trees.

Floyd backed up, turning to follow the noise, trying to determine where the animal was going. At first, it sounded like it was running away from him, but then it turned around and got louder, coming right for him.

Before he could move out of the way, a galloping deer bounded out of the wall of green, almost knocking him over as it bounced through his camp and back into the woods on the other side. Floyd's heart jumped into his throat. He dodged the startled animal, diving out of the way. Rolling over onto his back, he laughed in relief for a moment. The laughter was short-lived as he realized he missed an opportunity to bag a deer.

"Damnit. I should have had my bow and arrow ready. I gotta stop being scared of every little noise out here and take advantage of all my opportunities. It's tough, though. If that had been a bear charging, head-on, a bow and arrow wouldn't have helped much. You gotta be ready for anything out here. You never know what's around the corner."

Floyd stood up and craned his neck, looking into the woods where the deer had fled, hoping for a second chance, but it was long gone. He had no choice but to let the matter go. It was too late in the day to go after it. He added some wood to the fire and resumed looking around camp, trying to figure out what else was missing.

"My clothes probably smelled like fish, so I can almost see how an animal might have dragged them away," he reasoned for the benefit of the camera. "But the axe? How could the axe be taken away by animals?"

He shook his head, perplexed. Dehydration, hunger, and sleep deprivation slowed his thought process, but through the haze he reminded himself of all three. He was slipping mentally. It was possible he had merely misplaced the missing items. The most reasonable explanation was probably the right one.

"I must have left the axe somewhere by mistake. Your mental faculties ain't quite...um...all together out here with little food and water. I ain't had water all day. I should have gone out to get some sooner. I was gathering wood earlier, too, over by the creek. I'll bet

I left the axe there," he deduced out loud. "It's the only thing that makes sense."

Floyd ducked into the shelter and rummaged around. He wasn't the neatest or most organized contestant. He always tried to keep everything in its place, but he often forgot and misplaced important items. After a little digging in the shelter, he found his headlamp and put it on. It wasn't dark yet, but it was getting there.

"I better go get the axe before it gets dark," he declared.

He swapped out cameras for one with night vision and brought it with him.

Chapter 8

Day 15

Feetprints

"How long before someone comes looking for us?" Hutch asked, leading the way through the forest.

Behind him, Sharon didn't seem to hear the question. Page continued trying to contact the Mothership, her pleas getting more desperate by the hour. Bringing up the rear, Doc seemed eager to hear the answer to Hutch's question.

Hutch stopped and turned to Sharon. "Well?"

"Well, what?" Sharon asked.

"How long before someone comes looking for us?" he repeated.

"How should I know?" Sharon challenged.

Hutch shook his head in disgust. Now that the going got rough, she was acting like she wasn't responsible for anything. "Well, how often do you check in?"

"Check in with who?" Sharon answered with a question again.

It was grating on Hutch's nerves. "The network, your family, anyone on dry land back home," he exploded, arms flailing. Getting answers from Sharon was like pulling teeth. She always acted like she didn't even understand why she was being questioned.

"I don't check in with the network and I don't have any family that I'd check in with," she snapped.

Hutch didn't have any family to check in with either. He had grown up in a children's home after his parents died in a plane crash when he was twelve—a difficult age to get adopted. A loner all his life moving forward, he learned to rely on only himself and live without any attachments. The few colleagues and friends he had wouldn't be alarmed by his disappearance. He was known to vanish for months at a time without warning and without letting anyone know where he was or what he was doing. He couldn't blame Sharon for not having any family or friends to check in with, but not checking in with the television network backing the show was a different story.

"How can you not be checking in with the network? You bring a boatload of people out to the middle of the Pacific Ocean like this with no backup, no communication with anyone?" Hutch reprimanded.

"I thought all we needed was you, Mr. Survivalist," Sharon spat, storming past him.

Doc interjected. "Don't worry, between all the crew members on the Mothership, the contestants, and their families back home waiting to hear from them, someone is bound to start asking questions if the network doesn't come looking for us first," he reassured.

"Yeah, but that could take weeks, months even. We're working on a show that could last a year," he reminded the doctor. "How long do you think it'll take before someone starts asking questions? And, then, how much longer will it take before those questions turn to action and someone actually comes looking for us?"

Dejected, Doc's shoulders slumped. "It might be a long time," he admitted.

Page didn't want to hear any of it. She was the only one, besides Sharon, who knew the state of the relationship between Sharon and the network. With her calls to the Mothership unanswered, Page grew impatient, on the verge of panic, the idea that it could take months before someone came to rescue them only making matters worse. The contestants came to Isolation Island to test their survival skills, but Page had no survival skills to test. She didn't want to be stranded in the wilderness.

"Come in, Mothership, dammit!" she shrieked, trying to resist the urge to smash the useless radio on the ground. "What the hell is going on? Why isn't anyone answering me?"

Doc grabbed her by the shoulders, trying to calm her down. "Everything's going to be all right. Give it some time. Try again later," he consoled.

Hutch was blunt, never willing to sugarcoat a situation. He had always believed the truth of the matter was essential to prepare everyone for the real challenges they were up against. "It's time to face facts. The Mothership is gone, Page. We're on our own."

Doc's bedside manner fought back. "No. We don't know that," he reassured Page. "The network will send someone eventually. They won't just forget about us."

Page broke down in tears, burying her head in Doc's chest, which was as high as her head could reach.

"Hey, hey, there," Doc consoled. "Don't worry. Someone will come. Until then, we'll be fine. This is a survival contest," he reminded her, putting on a happy face. "If the contestants can do it, we can do it, especially with a top-notch survivalist to help us. It'll be our own little adventure. Right, Hutch?"

Hutch patted Page on the back, getting her to lift her head up and stop sobbing for a moment. "He's right, Page. We're going to be fine. I'll make sure of that. But, make no mistake, the game is over. We need to round up the contestants one by one. We'll have a better chance sticking it out as a group."

Sharon shouted from up ahead. "Come on! We're almost to the river!"

*****

The river was easy to traverse. A downed tree provided a bridge the foursome shimmied across on their bellies. An hour later, they came to another river. It was also easy to cross because it was shallow, but it raised some disturbing questions.

"What the hell? This river isn't on the map," Hutch complained. The rudimentary map he had been relying on the whole time had been produced by his predecessor, Nelson Greely.

"Well, nothing's perfect," Sharon dismissed without a care.

"Nothing's perfect? This map is useless if it's not accurate. How can we trust it now?" Hutch asked.

"It's the best we've got. Deal with it," Sharon snapped.

There wasn't much else he could do. They were stuck on a remote island with shoddy communications equipment, an inaccurate map, and possibly a murderer on the loose, but they couldn't afford to come unglued. Hutch bit his tongue and led the way. They filled their canteens, crossed the river, and headed for the shore where they collected mussels and limpets for dinner as they made their way toward Floyd's territory.

"We've been walking all day," Sharon complained. "How much farther is it?"

"We need to find a place to make camp for the night," Hutch told her.

"What do you mean, make camp for the night?" Sharon asked, infuriating Hutch.

He ignored her rhetorical question, his eyes focused on something up ahead. Sharon hurried past him, stopping him for a confrontation.

"You said we'd make it to Floyd's camp by nightfall," she protested.

Hutch nudged her out of the way and continued walking, squinting at a disturbance in the sand forty yards away. "I said *if we were lucky*. We're not lucky. We need to find a spot to build a fire and a shelter for the night," he explained, speeding up.

Sharon rushed after him. "We've got to be close. Let's keep walking, at least until it gets dark." She looked back at Page and Doc, looking for support, but they were too far behind to hear her proposal.

Hutch ignored it all together, stopping at a line of footprints and drag marks stretching across the beach from the water to the tree line.

Sharon smiled for the first time since they landed on Isolation Island. "Footprints. See? I told you we were close," she gloated.

"I don't think these are Floyd's footprints," Hutch informed her, following the prints into the woods.

Sharon went after him, asking, "What do you mean, they're not Floyd's? Who else could they belong to?"

Hutch shook his head, finding it hard to believe Sharon was so unperceptive. "Why would you think they belong to Floyd? There's only one set of prints and they're coming *from* the ocean. You think he went for a swim? The water's freezing," he sneered, following a trail of flattened brush. It led to a round, orange, deflated life raft. He picked it up to make sure its passenger wasn't underneath.

"What is it?" Page asked, catching up with Hutch and Sharon.

Doc walked up behind her, answering her question. "It's a life raft, but did it come from the Mothership or our Medline?"

They all looked in different directions, hoping to find an

indication of which way the raft's passenger might have gone. Hutch kept on the same path and kept walking.

"Here I come Elizabeth," a raspy voice called out up ahead.

Hutch turned to shoot Sharon a perplexed look before rushing toward the voice. They made it to a clearing with tall grass and wet clothes strewn about. A man stripped down to his green boxer briefs paced back and forth in an agitated state, seemingly unaware he had company.

"Simon," Sharon exclaimed.

It didn't get the man's attention. He fidgeted with his fingers, muttering something incoherent to himself. His name was Simon Scoff, the Assistant Production Manager.

Normally, a small show like Isolation Island wouldn't have an Assistant Production Manager, but Sharon was being paid as the Production Manager—responsible for overseeing budget and personnel, among other things. She had hired Simon to do the Production Manager's work while she received the pay. She was claiming many titles to come away with as much money as possible while allocating the actual work to "assistants".

Simon was a short, fat, bald man who considered a delayed lunch a survival situation. He had no business on the island. Peeling off his last article of clothing, he complained, "Why is it so fucking hot?"

The girls watched Simon stomping around as Doc and Hutch both took off their coats and rushed over, trying to cover him up.

Simon pushed them away. "Leave me alone," he said, at first. Then, as if noticing there were other people around for the first time, he said, "Oh, hey. What are you guys doing here?"

Page asked, "What's wrong with him?" She took a few steps back.

Simon circled like a caged animal, licking his fingers and eyeing the women. It wasn't him. He was normally a shy, timid man.

"He's in the end stages of hypothermia," Doc explained.

Simon collapsed, falling flat on his back as if to illustrate Doc's assessment. Hutch pounced, using his coat to cover the stricken man. Doc laid his coat on the ground next to Simon and grabbed him under his arms, motioning to Hutch. "Lift him up."

Hutch took Simon's legs and they swung him onto Doc's coat.

"We need to make a fire," Hutch barked. "Give me your coats and get some firewood, quick!" he ordered the women.

Page complied without question, tossing her coat to Doc as Hutch cleared an area and collected some dry grass to get a fire started. Doc used Page's coat to cover Simon's legs and then held his hand out, expecting Sharon's coat next.

"Your coat," Doc blurted out. "Come on."

Sharon took a step back. "Are you crazy? We'll all freeze to death," she whined.

"No, we won't," Doc retorted. "Hutch is going to make a fire and the rest of us are going to get under the sleeping bag with Simon to warm him up."

Still reluctant, Sharon took off her coat and tossed it to Doc. He threw it over Simon's upper body. With his mouth propped open, taking shallow breaths, Simon stared at the sky with an unsettling look of amazement on his face.

"Go help Page get some firewood," Doc ordered.

As Sharon walked away, Doc turned to Hutch who was removing the sleeping bag from his backpack. "What the hell is wrong with that woman?" Doc asked, frustrated.

"She doesn't care about anyone but herself," Hutch asserted. He unrolled and unzipped the sleeping bag while Doc checked Simon's pulse.

"Is he going to be okay?" Hutch asked.

"His pulse is weak, but it's still there," Doc answered. Patting Simon's face, he asked, "Simon, can you hear me?"

Simon smiled, turning his head slowly, blank eyes staring at his caregiver. "You're the best. Did I ever tell you that?" he mumbled.

"That's good, Simon. Stay with me. You're going to be fine," Doc reassured.

Page and Sharon returned, each with their arms full of dead wood. Hutch wasted no time getting the fire started.

Sharon knelt next to Simon's motionless body, searching his eyes for signs of life. "Is he alive?" she asked.

Simon turned his head in response, lifting a hand to feel Sharon's face. "Sharon? Is that you?" he asked in a daze.

"Yes, Simon. It's me," she replied in a docile tone. It was the first time she had shown any sensitivity. Before she could offer any words of encouragement, Simon sprang up with a burst of energy, grabbing Sharon by the throat. "You fucking bitch," he growled. "This is all your fault."

Sharon struggled to pull away. Although Simon's grip was too weak to cut off her oxygen supply, she wasn't able to escape.

Doc had to pry Simon's fingers off her. "Simon, stop it. Relax. We're going to take care of you," he said, tucking the dying man's arms back under the sleeping bag.

"What the fuck?" Sharon complained, falling back to get away from the delirious man.

With the fire growing, Hutch got under the sleeping bag to help warm the freezing man. Doc crawled in as well, urging Page and Sharon to join them. Page did so without hesitation, Sharon ignored them.

She chose to warm herself by the fire. "I'm not getting near him," she insisted.

Doc assured her, "It's okay, He's just confused. It's normal with hypothermia." It fell on deaf ears.

Huddled under the sleeping bag, Doc monitored his patient. Simon's skin was cold and clammy, his fingers wrinkled like prunes from prolonged exposure to the frigid waters of the Pacific. The heat from the fire only made him more agitated. He squirmed in the arms of Doc and Hutch as they tried to keep him warm and stable.

Hutch grabbed Simon by the chin and turned his face. "Simon? Are you still in there?"

His eyes rolled back in his head for a moment, but he replied, "I'm over here."

"Listen to me Simon. What happened to the Mothership?" Hutch coaxed.

Simon attempted a smile and muttered, "Momma?"

Hutch rolled his eyes and tried again. "The ship, Simon. What happened to the ship we were on?"

Simon's mouth opened in slow motion, taking several runs at producing words. "It's…it's…it's…gone," he finally said.

"What happened?" Hutch asked.

Simon rocked his head side to side as if trying to shake the visions out of his head. "It blew up," he said, screwing up his face like he was about to cry.

Hutch and Doc shared a look. Page gasped and whimpered. Sharon didn't seem overly concerned or interested. She turned her head away.

"Did anyone else survive?" Hutch asked, but Simon was slipping away. His head fell to one side. "Simon," Hutch tried, lifting Simon's head again. "Did anyone else survive?"

Simon's face turned to complete anguish but, for the first time, his eyes gave an indication of awareness attached to intense fear. "It killed them all," he whimpered.

Page buried her face in her hands, bawling. Hutch and Doc remained stoic while Sharon seemed to ignore it all, holding her hands out to the fire, warming herself.

Simon's anguish melted off his face. Something in the sky had caught his attention. His glassy eyes widened and his jaw dropped open. "It's so fucking beautiful," he gasped before the last ounce of life drained from his body and he went limp.

EZRA GREER

Day 6

8:41am

Age: 51
Occupation: Truck Driver
Home: Alaska
Status: Widower, 3 children

"Everything happens in slow motion out here," Ezra Greer explained to the camera sitting on its tripod.

He was referring to the slow progress he was making on the boat he was building to cross the river to retrieve the treasure. The Alaskan truck driver had spent as much time as he could gathering materials and building on Day 5, but the never-ending list of essential daily activities left him little spare time. In the wilderness, even the smallest of tasks was time consuming and there were no guarantees of success.

The boat wasn't coming along as well as Ezra had hoped. He had lengths of wood cut to make a frame and he had spent hours after dark the night before whittling a paddle, but all he had was pieces of a boat.

On Day 6 he returned to the riverside early to put all the pieces together but, instead, he set up the camera and stood there staring at them.

"This is going to take all day," he moaned, scratching his head. "And, I still have to paddle across the river and dig. And then, I'm going to have to bring the treasure back. I'm probably better off just making a simple raft and cover it with the tarp. It'll be like a barge. Much quicker to make."

The camera captured his progress. While he worked, he told the camera about the worst period of time in his life. Some of the future audience was bound to recognize him from the old headlines and he wanted to take advantage of the opportunity to set the record straight. It was difficult to talk about, but it needed to be done and he just wanted to get it over with. He started at the beginning.

"My life took a turn for the worse on the third day of a week-long heat wave. It was July 21st and I was living in a small town outside Raleigh, North Carolina with my wife and three daughters. My wife and I were both pharmacists so, we were making good money and we had just moved into a very big house—5900 square feet. We had only been there a few weeks. Most of our stuff had been unpacked, but there were still boxes in the garage we hadn't gotten around to."

The mere mention of the boxes and the garage made him have to pause and collect himself.

"Our daughters had all gone to their friends' houses—friends with pools. They were trying to beat the heat. It was over one hundred degrees every day that week and humid as all hell. So, when my wife decided it was a good time to finish unpacking the boxes in the garage, I tried to talk her out of it. It was my day off and I had had big plans to take a nap in front of the fan in my den. The central AC in the house was broken. We knew it was broken when we bought the house. A repair man was supposed to come the following week. I begged her to let the boxes wait, but she was determined to get it done."

He laid the tarp flat on the ground and started lining up the skinny logs he had chopped down. Unsure of how many he'd need he decided to keep adding to it until it looked wide enough to carry him and whatever treasure he might find.

"I couldn't talk Penny into joining me on the couch for a lazy afternoon. She went to the garage and I stuck to my plan. We had bought a new couch for my den. They just delivered it three days prior and I hadn't had a chance to test it out, but I knew it was comfortable—that's why we had chosen it. I brought a glass of lemonade with me and retired to the den. I turned the ceiling fan on as well as a standing fan, both on HIGH. The standing fan oscillated, cooling me from head to toe. I was asleep within a matter of minutes."

"All the way on the other side of the house in the garage, Penny, had started unpacking the first box. I hadn't planned on sleeping for so long. I woke up about four hours later, chugged my lemonade and came downstairs to tell Penny how comfortable the couch was. She wasn't there. I checked the time on the microwave's clock in the kitchen. It was 6:19pm, exactly. I remember because I was surprised thinking she might still be working on the boxes. I had thought the heat would have discouraged her much sooner, but so much time had passed, she should have been finished."

Ezra paused in the middle of tying a couple logs together with cordage. He stared off into space as if his mind had traveled back in time to that fateful day.

"I filled a glass with lemonade to bring to her, thinking she'd be hot and thirsty after working that whole time. But, when I took it to the garage, she wasn't there. Only one box had been separated from the rest. It sat, half-empty, behind her car in the garage. I checked outside, called her name out repeatedly, but she wasn't there. I tried texting her, but there was no reply. I tried calling her cellphone but it went to voicemail. Frantic, I searched the entire house, room by room, under the beds, in the closets. She was gone. She just disappeared, from her own home, in broad daylight. And where was I? I was napping."

His eyes darted away, filling with tears. He turned his back to the camera. Although he had forgiven himself years ago, there was a reflexive feeling of guilt every time he thought about 'the nap'.

"I know it's ridiculous for blaming myself for taking a nap. I don't really blame myself, but I'll always regret it. I should have been there to protect my wife, but how was I to know? We were at home where we were supposed to be safe."

He pounded his fist on the raft, wiped his eyes and turned back toward the camera. Tying another knot as he sniffled, he continued the story.

"A guy and his son were fishing when they found her body dumped on the banks of the river about six miles away. She had been missing for sixteen of the longest days of my life."

He choked back another round of tears for a few minutes while the camera documented his grief. Deciding the best diversion was busy hands, he frantically tied knots while he continued the story.

"Of course, when a wife goes missing and turns up dead, the first person they look at is the husband. But, in a small town with a tiny police force with no experience investigating murder, the husband is automatically guilty. They searched my SUV, which had been parked in the driveway the day Penny went missing, and they found traces of her blood on the back seat. That was the end of the investigation. Guilty. They didn't look in any other direction, even after I explained Penny had cut herself while cleaning the backseat of the SUV days earlier."

His legs began to cramp from crouching so long. He stood up to stretch them, then knelt in the soft grass to continue securing the knots.

"As if losing the love of my life wasn't enough, I was charged with her murder and found guilty. I'll never forget the way those jurors looked at me, like I was the monster the prosecution made me out to be. I'm the only one who knows without a doubt it wasn't me. I'd never hurt Penny. She was my entire world. But, nobody else could know that with any certainty, especially not a bunch of strangers. They sentenced me to life in prison with no possibility of parole. I spent twelve years behind bars for a crime I didn't commit."

He had three logs tied to each other on one end—not nearly wide enough to cross the river unless he intended on dangling his legs in the water. Moving to the other end, he knelt down and looked right at the camera.

"The real murderer was finally caught after killing another woman. He confessed to killing my wife and seven other women in North Carolina, Virginia, and South Carolina. Norman Wayne Leddy was the piece of shit's name. He was sentenced to life in prison for murdering eight women, including my wife—the same sentence I got for supposedly murdering only my wife. They should have fried the motherfucker. Not a day goes by that I don't fantasize about torturing Norman Wayne Leddy to death."

The bitterness and anger showed on his face, producing wrinkles which told the tale of a long battle with the negative emotions of his past. He resumed tying the logs together with an intensity powered by raw hatred for the man who killed his wife, the police who arrested him, the lazy prosecutors who wanted a conviction at any cost, and the jury who believed it all.

"In the end, Leddy's confession was exactly what I had been saying all along. He had knocked Penny unconscious in the driveway, loaded her into my SUV, and drove away, using the keys he found on a hook in the kitchen, just inside the door from the garage. He sexually assaulted her, stabbed her in the heart and left her for dead by the riverside. Then he drove my SUV back to my house and parked it where he had found it and returned the keys as if nothing had happened.

"The cops who arrested me still insist I'm guilty. They fought against my release. They said Leddy's confession was fake. They said my theory of a stranger abducting my wife and returning the SUV was too much of a coincidence. They couldn't admit I had figured it out when they couldn't. Leddy must have been coerced into confessing because he had nothing more to lose, that's what they still think. They refuse to admit they were wrong. That just pisses me off to no end. There are thousands of people in prison who don't belong there, all because of stubborn and incompetent investigators. After I got out, I thought about joining groups to fight for reform, maybe even starting my own organization. But, I had had plenty of time to think about it while I was in prison and I came to the conclusion that reform is impossible. Everyone knows the justice system is broken, but they all act like there's nothing wrong. I even had some motherfuckers say to me that the system *does* in fact work because, in the end, I was found innocent and set free. Thanks a lot, after twelve years in prison. After more than a decade locked in a cage, surrounded by the scum of the Earth."

Ezra took a deep breath, checking his surroundings as if making sure he wasn't in a cage anymore. The lack of concrete and bars reenergized him. The telling of the story which had dominated his life had always gone through a wide range of emotions, but it always ended with renewed appreciation for freedom.

"I love it out here, away from all the bullshit," he said. "I might never go back."

10:45am

Ezra tested the durability of his raft. Each of the five-foot long logs were secured to each other with little play. Next, he wrapped it up like a present using the tarp. He had waders on, but he wanted to take as many precautions as possible to prevent getting wet. The tarp would also trap in some air, helping the raft stay afloat. The camera kept rolling as he worked.

"We all like to think that the justice system is like what we see on TV," he said, unable to put his ordeal to rest. He had never had the forum to strike back at all his accusers. This was as close as he'd ever get. "Someone dies and a crack team of expert detectives and CSIs come out and, even though it's really difficult, they figure out exactly what really happened using DNA and fingerprints and fibers and all kinds of lab tests. That's not reality. And that one detective that keeps the others from getting tunnel vision, from misinterpreting evidence and arresting the wrong person—he doesn't exist," Ezra explained.

"My own daughters didn't believe me. The cops and the media got to them and turned them against me. The media helped convict me as much as the police did. It was brutal and it's dangerous—the power of the media. They use it so irresponsibly. All they care about is ratings and being the first to break a story. They don't care if they've got all the facts wrong. They don't care who they hurt. The more sensational the lies they tell, the more attention they get and they're never held accountable when it turns out they were completely wrong. They ruin people's lives with false accusations and then shrug it off when it turns out they were wrong."

He started getting choked up again, the toll he had paid evident in his eyes. His entire body seemed suddenly drained of life.

"I'm hoping maybe my daughters will see this on TV and finally realize how much I loved their mother and know I had nothing to do with her death. I want my girls back," he pleaded, tears escaping his eyes no matter how hard he tried to hold them back.

On Day 6 of hard time in the wilderness, Ezra Greer broke down sobbing, releasing almost two decades of sorrow and pain. He sprawled out on the raft, letting it all out in one long uncontrollable outburst for the camera to witness. It ended as abruptly as it began, but it was therapeutic. He picked himself up and checked the raft to make sure everything was secure.

"I really needed that. I've had all this bottled up for so long. Isolation Island is exactly what I need right now and I'm going to make the most of it," he swore.

Tying the final knot to secure the tarp, Ezra flashed an endearing smile and a wink at the camera. "There. Now let's get some treasure," he said as if the future audience was coming along for the ride.

He dragged the raft over to the edge of the river. A simple task such as this was no simple task while filming a TV show. He had to make several trips back and forth, setting up the camera first to capture images of transporting the raft to the river and the rest of his equipment.

He had debated over what to take with him. The shovel was a definite necessity, but taking the tools he used to make the raft would mean risking losing it all if the raft sank or capsized. He loaded all the tools onto the raft, nonetheless.

"I know it's not the best idea to take all this stuff with me," he explained to the camera. "But, I don't want to come back. The plan is to paddle across the river, dig up the treasure, load it on the raft and float it down the river to get closer to camp. That's all going to depend on what the treasure is, but I'm trying to minimize the amount of times I have to cross the water."

With the raft loaded up and a camera strapped to his head, Ezra paddled across the river, the gentle current pulling him toward the fork. For all the work that went in to preparing for the trip, the actual trip took less than two minutes. He made landfall on the peninsula and dragged the raft ashore, tools and all.

A series of rocks formed an obvious, manmade X in the dirt, centered between the two forking branches of the river. On the other side of the fast, shallow fork Ezra spotted another manmade sight he hadn't expected. A ring of rocks framed in the charred ashes of an old fire. He zoomed in on it with a camera to examine it.

"That's odd. They told us we'd be separated, but that's definitely an old campfire. I wonder if we're competing for the treasure."

He shifted the camera's focus to the stone X. "This must be where the treasure is. The X looks undisturbed so, I'm pretty sure I've gotten here first."

Shifting back to the campfire, he searched for clues to indicate who had built it and how long ago.

"It's kind of overgrown," he told the camera. "See how there's grass and weeds hanging over the burnt spot? If there had been a fire there recently, it would have burned anything hanging over the top like that. Which begs the question, who made the fire? We've only been out here six days."

Ezra held his breath, looking and listening for any other signs of human activity. The forest was still and quiet. Only the trickling of water over rocks in the shallow river could be heard along with a pair of squabbling birds darting from tree to tree.

Focusing again on the fire, Ezra concluded, "Well, someone had to bury the treasure here. That someone must have built that fire. It's the only explanation."

Satisfied, for the time being, he set up the camera so that it could capture the triumphant digging up of the treasure. He plunged the shovel into the soft ground at the center of the X, marking the middle of his digging area before removing the stones and tossing them aside.

"I hope they didn't bury this very deep," he said, tossing the first shovelful aside.

ZOEY PRICE

Day 6

9:19am

Age: 24
Occupation: Dance Instructor
Home: Montana
Status: Single

Zoey Price had considered calling the cave home until someone came to rescue her, but alas the stars were telling her to keep moving. She woke up early on Day 6 and loaded up the rainwater she had collected in the plastic bottles.

"I'm actually lucky it rained. Otherwise I wouldn't have any water," she told the camera mounted on her hat. "Following the shore was a mistake. I should have followed the creek, instead, ensuring a steady water supply. I wouldn't be able to boil it, but I could at least filter it through moss to make it drinkable. Maybe I'm better off, though. If I had followed the creek, I wouldn't have found these bottles and I might have been stuck in the rain last night."

She wrapped the water bottles in her only tarp and put the makeshift knapsack on her back. Her hair got tangled up in the cordage and she struggled to release it.

"This cave looks like it gets flooded. In fact, it looks like flooding is what carved the cave in the first place. So, I'm going to keep moving. The only way is uphill. It's not going to be easy, especially with everything still wet, but it's the only way to go."

Zoey bid farewell to the cave, knowing she might have to return if she couldn't get past the obstacles she believed were dividing her from other contestants.

"I'm following the next stream or river I find," she promised as she began to climb the slippery hill through the woods.

4:24pm

Zoey had zigzagged uphill, over flatter land, and across dense patches of forest trying to find a way down or around the cliff blocking her way. A wide animal trail provided an easy route close to the edge. She turned on the camera mounted on her hat again.

"This trail is really wide. I hope that doesn't mean it belongs to a bear. Animals, like humans, take the path of least resistance. So, it might seem creepy to see a path like this, thinking it must be made by a human. But, it's perfectly natural for animals to use the same route over and over, making it easier for them to walk or run."

She stopped and turned her head, pointing an ear forward.

"Is that?" she whispered.

Her eyes widened as if she thought it would enhance her hearing. The camera captured the forest in jerky motions as she adjusted her head, trying to hear better. It took a moment for her to realize she needed to get closer to the source of the noise.

"I think I hear water," she said, moving in the direction she though the sound was coming from. As she got closer to the cliff, a steady Shhhhhhhh rushed somewhere through the trees. She hurried along the animal trail. If it was water she was hearing, the path should lead right to it. A short walk brought her to a clearing alongside a river rushing over the edge of the cliff.

"Great," she sighed, too fatigued and hungry to show any real enthusiasm for the beautiful sight. She dropped her tarp backpack on the ground and scurried to the edge to see how far down the water crashed.

"Under almost any other circumstances, I'd be thrilled to find a waterfall," she said, craning her head forward as her left foot ran out of ground.

"That's a long way down," she reported, tipping her head so the camera could see the dangerous drop.

"There's no way I'm getting down there."

The cliff was so steep, it disappeared halfway down to the plunge pool. Zoey scanned the area directly under her, searching for any sign of human activity. The broken tree that had fallen into the river near the plunge pool looked natural. She failed to notice the broken tree's stump alongside the river had been cut flat by human hands. She took a step back and searched the canopy below, but it was an endless sea of trees.

"Well, at least, I found water. But, I'm going to have to boil it," she said.

On the other side of the waterfall, the cliff went on as far as she could see. She shook her head and took one last look down before turning around.

"This is a dead end," she declared, disappointed. "But, I'm not turning back. I'm going stay close to the water's edge and follow it upriver."

She picked up her bag and let out a frustrated sigh. "This was a huge waste of time. I should have followed the river in the first place," she said, too disappointed to rest. Making the wrong move would eat at her if she didn't keep moving.

"Then again," she added, heading upriver. "If I had gone straight to the river from my burned-out camp, I probably would have followed it downriver, which would have just led me to this point anyway. That's how fate works. You think you could have made the opposite choice, but the results just turn out the same, no matter what you do. It's all up to the stars," she claimed.

Zoey Price left the waterfall at 4:34pm on Day 6.

STEPHANIE HAMILTON

Day 6

4:44pm

Age: 29
Occupation: Artist
Home: Colorado
Status: Single

Stephanie Hamilton arrived at the waterfall at 4:44pm on Day 6 with an axe in one hand and tripod in the other. She set up the camera and took a few shots of the waterfall from top to bottom before focusing on the task at hand—chopping into the severed tree stump.

She began by chopping at the seam between the tree's outer ring and bark, working her way around. Each chop split a chunk of wood and bark away. It was a tedious task, but once she made the correct chop, the nature of the stump revealed itself. A chunk of wood from the rings split away. When she removed it, she could tell the top two inches of wood acted like a lid. Underneath, the tip of the corner of the treasure chest peeked through.

"That's it," she said. "There's a box in there,"

She pried at the lid with the axe, trying to get underneath it, but it would take more than that. She kept chopping at the edge until it loosened enough to pull it up. Tossing the lid to the side like a heavy Frisbee, she rejoiced in her accomplishment. The Isolation Island logo, with its dark trees and green lettering stared up at her from atop the treasure chest.

"Yes," she yelped, fists pumping. "Woo hoo!" She took a tight victory lap, resting her arms with her hands on her hips. "Yeeeaaaahhhh," she bellowed to the woods; to the river; to the rest of the animals in the forest, but she couldn't be heard over the roar of the waterfall by anything except the camera.

She popped open the top of the chest, reveling in delight. The saw and the hammer and nails would speed up any construction project. The knives and fishing hooks would help with food gathering and processing. The extra cordage and fishing line meant new projects were in her future. But, the cans of food and bag of rice were the first items she hugged—new tastes and sweet carbs.

"Salt and pepper," Stephanie cheered, pulling the containers out to add to the pile outside the stump.

She swooned over the hammock, but she really lost it when she found the coffee and percolator. "Oh my god, oh my god," she exulted, galloping around, cradling the coffee like a football, waving the percolator around with her other hand. "I got coffee. I got coffee," she bragged and celebrated.

Returning to the treasure chest, she pulled out the last item, which she had already seen. She held up one of the rolls of toilet paper for the camera to see.

With a chuckle, she said, "I guess this is for the coffee."

She looked through her new stash again, imagining the advantages and new possibilities. After almost a week of solitude, the excitement was an exhausting overload.

Stephanie slumped on the ground and asked herself, aloud, "Now, how am I going to get all this stuff back to camp?"

WES WOOD

Day 6

5:11pm

Age: 57
Occupation: Farmer
Home: Mississippi
Status: Divorced, 8 children

Wes Wood pulled his boat out of the bay. It wasn't his usual docking site. He had chosen a new spot—closer to camp. Everything he had with him was in his backpack, except the axe. He threw the backpack over his shoulders, turned the boat over on land, and headed back to camp using a new route that would go undocumented. He hadn't brought any cameras with him.

The new route paid off. Hanging from a low-lying tree branch, Wes found the clues to a treasure in a glass bottle. He read the scroll to himself, taking his time, his lips moving, backtracking over the same words over and over. When he was done, he looked up all around him, examining the location and surroundings. There was nothing to be seen besides the same old forest landscape. He rolled up the scroll, stuffed it in his pocket, and resumed hiking back to camp, going over the clues in his mind.

6:25pm

Upon arriving at camp, Wes rushed to his shelter, pulling off his backpack, and bringing it inside. After fifteen minutes of rummaging around, he emerged from the shelter with a camera and set it up on a tripod.

The scroll was back in its glass bottle. He held it up for the camera and gave it a shake.

"I was out gettin' firewood," he lied, "and look-y what I done found."

He uncorked the bottle, let the scroll slide out, and unrolled it, performing for camera as if it was the first time. "Looks like clues to a treasure," he declared, holding the scroll up.

He read it out loud.

> A TREASURE SHARED BY TWO ISLANDS
> IS NOT FAR AWAY,
>
> IT'S ONLY ON *THIS* ISLAND
> A SHORT TIME EACH DAY,
>
> IF YOUR TIMING IS OFF,
> THE BRIDGE WON'T BE THERE,
>
> COME BACK TOMORROW,
> OR WHENEVER YOU DARE,
>
> FIND THE RIGHT SPOT,
> TRY NOT TO GET STRANDED,
>
> THE TREASURE APPEARS,
> JUST LIKE THE LAND DID

"Umm...this is...this ain't gonna be easy. A TREASURE SHARED BY TWO ISLANDS—I ain't got no idea what that means. Maybe they talkin' 'bout the barrier island."

He furrowed his brow and reread, "IT'S ONLY ON THIS ISLAND A SHORT TIME EACH DAY. That don't make no sense. What's it mean? The treasure is being moved every day?"

The simple Mississippi Farmer read the entire scroll two more times, his face animated with confusion and frustration.

"This ain't gonna be easy," he decided all over again.

Taking a minute to think about it, he froze, his eyes blank and unblinking. His lip curled up, exposing yellow teeth which were desperate need of brushing.

"I wonder if everyone got tough clues like this," he said, still in a trance while his brain struggled to compute.

Snapping out of his thoughts, his eyes came back to reality with a bit of a twinkle as a smile grew slowly.

"I wonder if everyone done found their clues," he said, trailing off into a scheme forming in his brain.

TUCKER JORDAN

Day 6

6:11pm

Age: 28
Occupation: Yoga Instructor
Home: Vermont
Status: Single

Tucker Jordan trudged through the forest, his face darkened with incoming facial hair, arms full of firewood. His expedition on Day 6 was mostly exploratory, but he never passed up a chance to bring back dry wood. The camera on his woolen hat was along for the ride. He enjoyed having something to talk to, if not someone.

"So…I didn't really find anything interesting on this trip, but that's to be expected," he said, looking around and changing direction.

He walked for a full minute before stopping again. The camera captured blurry images as it whipped back and forth.

"Uh oh," he croaked, his throat getting drier as anxiety set in. "I'm not sure if I know how to get back to camp."

He turned around and went back in the direction from which he came, but nothing looked familiar. Stopping again, he craned his neck, scanning the forest in every possible direction.

Trees to the left. Trees ahead. Trees behind. But, to his right, he spotted what looked like another animal trail. He forced his way through a series of bushes to get there.

"Great. Now, if I can figure out which way to follow this trail…" he muttered.

He decided to take his chances heading west. With the sun low in the sky, he followed it, squinting his way through the forest, keeping his head up to search for anything that looked familiar.

The camera was as blinded by the low sun as its carrier. The tripwire rigged across the trail ahead was virtually invisible.

Tucker's foot hooked the wire, stopping him in his tracks.

"What the…" he began, looking down. He knew it wasn't one of his own traps. Rattling branches overhead behind him made him turn around.

A log armed with thick wooden spikes swung down from the trees overhanging the trail. The spikes pierced through Tucker's neck and chest, out his back, picking him off his feet and continuing on. Blood spurted from multiple wounds from his chest and carotid artery as the morbid pendulum swung back and forth. By the time it came to rest, Tucker Jordan was dead, blood spattered in every direction below him.

With his head slumped forward, almost falling off, the camera kept filming the ground. It watched as scavengers came and went, taking advantage of the situation, tearing Tucker's clothes off to get to the flesh.

Black crows swooped in, pecking at the carcass between larger visitors. It seemed like every animal in the forest had taken a bite by nightfall. Wolves ultimately claimed the body, chewing through bone and muscle, tendons and ligaments. A younger one ate the neck meat away, right down to the vertebrae, until Tucker's head fell off. The camera smashed on impact with the ground, wrapping up the final morbid scene for one of the most cheerful and optimistic survivors in the game.

Chapter 9

Day 1 minus 12

Trouble Ahead, Trouble Behind

With twelve days left before Isolation Island was set to begin production, the contestants were ready to go, the location had been finalized, the treasures had been buried, and the clues were in place. Sharon Rose was surprised to be called in for a meeting with network executive Arthur Mallory.

Sharon got on a crowded elevator in the network's headquarters in Hollywood, wondering why Mallory had called her in. Each time the doors opened, she rehearsed a different scenario in her head, trying to be ready for anything Mallory might ask. There was a lot that could be questioned, but Sharon had managed to keep it all under the network's radar. She had her lies and explanations memorized, should questions arise and there was the blanket contingency plan to just play dumb if her creative accounting should be discovered.

I didn't think it would be a problem, she rehearsed in her head, over and over as the elevator emptied and the last few floors passed by on her way to the top.

I didn't think it would be a problem, she thought with a more innocent tone. She kept repeating the phrase in her head, searching for the most believable amount of ignorance to inject.

She straightened her skirt, dusted a few specks of lint from the lapels of her black business jacket, and took a deep breath, thrusting her chest out, looking for the right posture to have her body be a distraction. Arthur Mallory had shown some interest in her in the past. She was saving it for an emergency. If she could get him to make a move, she'd have something on him to be used as a GET OUT OF JAIL FREE card, should the time come.

Sharon was the last person left on the elevator by the time it reached the fiftieth floor. She stepped off, into the waiting room.

"Can I help you?" the receptionist greeted without looking up from her computer.

"I'm here to see Arthur Mallory," Sharon said.

The receptionist looked up and stopped clicking her keyboard. Looking over her glasses, she asked, "And you are?"

"Sharon Rose," she replied, annoyed the receptionist had to ask, but not surprised.

"Ah, yes. They're waiting for you. Go right in," the receptionist instructed as the phone started to ring.

"They?" Sharon asked, eyebrows raised. Arthur hadn't mentioned anyone else would be attending the meeting.

The receptionist just nodded her head, answering the phone and turning to her computer.

Sharon relaxed her face and took a deep breath, walking down the long, intimidating hallway leading to Arthur Mallory's office. The wood paneling on the walls was exquisite, but the real attraction was the hall of fame-like presentation of hit TV shows and movies the network was responsible for. *Jimmy Darwin*, led the pack. Although she wasn't a big fan of the movie, she appreciated its success and popularity. She scowled at the poster of *The Project*, a TV series she hated, jealous she had never achieved its level of success.

Her favorite current TV show had a slot at the end. *Being John Smith* was a thrilling science fiction mystery series in its third season, collecting awards along the way, including Best New Series. It was a show Sharon had tried to get in on at the ground level, but she had been turned down, repeatedly. Not only turned down—the network had let her go all together. She hoped Isolation Island would be her big comeback. Donning a fake smile, she entered Arthur Mallory's office ready for anything.

She hadn't imagined Nelson Greely would be there, but there he was—talking to Arthur Mallory. The two men were laughing about something, but Sharon's entrance put an abrupt end to it. Their faces turned serious in unison as if choreographed.

Nelson Greely was a tall, lanky man with an oddly-rectangular torso and graying hair. He stood alongside Arthur's desk, dressed in his usual attire, ready for an outdoor adventure at the drop of his safari hat. Clamming up when Sharon arrived, Nelson stood at ease with his hands behind his back.

Arthur Mallory remained seated at his Olympic-sized mahogany desk in his top floor office overlooking the smog settling over Los Angeles.

"Sharon," Arthur greeted cheerfully. "Come in," he waved her in and motioned for her to sit in the chair across the desk from him, making it clear he wasn't going to stand up or shake her hand.

Sharon looked to Nelson for a greeting, but received no reaction at all. He stood like a soldier—eyes forward, blank face, unengaging.

"What did you want to see me about?" Sharon asked, taking a seat.

Arthur leaned forward, hands folded. "I'll get right to the point, Sharon. We're pulling the plug on Isolation Island."

"What? Why?" she asked, her usual insincere, exaggerated tone coming through even though she was genuinely caught off guard. She had a way of sounding phony no matter what she said. Force of habit.

Mallory replied, business-like, "Our experts have informed us that the location you've chosen is too dangerous."

Sharon waited a moment for a longer explanation, but when it was apparent that was all she was going to get, she argued, "No, it's not. Don't tell me you've been listening to Nelson's ghost stories."

"You're in no position to decide what's safe and what's not. That's why we hire experts," Arthur reminded her.

"All right, then, lets pick another location," Sharon conceded.

Arthur sighed and sat back in his leather chair. "The location is not the only problem, Sharon. It's you."

Sharon's mind raced through the long list of things Arthur could have discovered or, perhaps, he discovered it all. She struggled to keep calm on the outside.

"It's me?" she asked, shooting Nelson a suspicious look he didn't engage with.

"Sharon, come on," Arthur said in a don't-embarrass-yourself tone.

"What did you tell him, Nelson?" Sharon barked, her panic manifesting as anger.

"Nothing that wasn't part of my job," Nelson answered.

Arthur held a hand up to stop the exchange. "Sharon, stop the act. You know this is not your forte. You know nothing about survival. If we sent a bunch of unsuspecting contestants out there with you, some of them would be coming back in body bags, guaranteed."

"That's why we hire experts," Sharon fired back.

"You're absolutely correct. That *is* why we hire experts to support you, but it does no good if you don't take their advice. We were willing to give you a chance on this. You blew it. It's over. We're not willing to risk the lives of innocent contestants," Arthur asserted.

Sharon opened her mouth to argue, but she was met by Arthur's hand. "I'm not finished. You know damn well where this is coming from," Arthur continued.

But, Sharon wasn't sure where it was coming from. It could have been a conversation about her creative accounting or cutting corners or just plain incompetence or it could have been something Nelson told Arthur.

"The network will not be held liable for your incompetence, Sharon. I'm giving you the benefit of the doubt by calling it incompetence. Perhaps you just don't realize how serious a show like this is. This is not the type of show to cut corners on when it comes to safety. The decisions you've made regarding equipment, personnel, and even some of the contestants—it's downright reckless. I mean, come on. Ezra Greer? The man was in prison for killing his wife."

"He was exonerated," Sharon defended, shrugging her shoulders. "It's a great story viewers will engage with."

"How about Wes Wood? A suspected serial killer? Are you serious?" Arthur questioned.

"He was only a person of interest. They never arrested him," Sharon rationalized.

"You don't send people like that into the woods on a deserted island to compete against each other for survival, Sharon," Arthur bottom-lined it.

Sharon tried to keep arguing, but Arthur had had enough. His voice drowned hers out with purpose.

"The discussion is over. I've made my decision. The show is dead," Arthur declared. "I suggest you stick to reality that takes place within civilization. Now, if you don't mind, there's the door."

Sharon stood and leaned on her arms over Arthur's desk, attempting to give him a view of her cleavage. "Can I talk to you alone?" she whispered.

"There's nothing to talk about. I have another appointment coming. Goodbye."

Dejected, Sharon straightened up, attempting to maintain a confident, professional demeanor. "Thank you for your time, gentlemen," she said, failing another attempt at sounding sincere and leaving without further argument. She wasn't the type of woman to take no for an answer. She stopped in front of the receptionist's desk without hesitation. "Mr. Mallory wants to meet with me again tomorrow," Sharon lied. "Perhaps you could find a slot to pencil me in."

"Sheila," Arthur's voice rang out of the intercom on the receptionist's phone.

She picked up the receiver. "Yes, Mr. Mallory."

Sharon couldn't hear Arthur's end of the conversation.

Sheila, the receptionist, repeated, "Yes, Mr. Mallory," several times. She hung up the phone and cleared her throat. "I'm sorry, Miss Ross," she said, getting Sharon's name wrong. "Mr. Mallory says he doesn't have time to meet with you again. You have a wonderful day." To make sure there was no further discussion, Sheila rushed to make a phone call.

Sharon took the hint and went to summon the elevator. As she waited, she counted her blessings. The meeting could have gone much worse, resulting in lawsuits and the end of her career. She had gotten off easy, but she was still in a pickle with Isolation Island canceled before it even began and less than twelve days to resurrect it.

The doors opened to an empty elevator. Sharon pressed the button for the ground floor, but before the doors could close, Nelson Greely rushed in, happy to have caught the elevator until he noticed he wasn't alone. The two passengers stood side by side in the elevator, looking up at the floor indicator.

"You're a coward, Nelson," Sharon said, devoid of emotion, unwilling to look at him.

Nelson took the same stance, calmly informing her, "I just

saved your life, you incompetent bitch, not to mention the lives of the contestants unfortunate enough to have applied for a contest run by someone who has no regard for human life. Do you need the money that badly or are you just a greedy bitch?"

"Fuck you, Nelson."

"Nice. Real professional," he smirked.

"Let me ask you one question, Mr. Survivalist," she said, finally turning to look at him. "Did you tell Arthur about your little trip to Isolation Island? Is that what this is all about? You're too scared to go back?"

The smirk faded from his face, his eyes still on the floor indicator as it counted down to 1, but it was obvious his mind had jumped somewhere else for a moment. "I haven't told anyone about that," he said.

The elevator doors opened. Without turning to look at him, Sharon got the last word as she left ahead of Nelson. "Good thinking. I wouldn't tell anyone, either, if I were you. You'd never be taken seriously again for the rest of your life."

EZRA GREER

Day 7

8:08am

Age: 51
Occupation: Truck Driver
Home: Alaska
Status: Widower, 3 children

"I'm bitter," Ezra Greer confessed to the camera inside his log cabin. "How can I not be? My life was torn apart, my wife was taken away from me by another human being, my freedom taken away."

Having successfully dug up the treasure, he had rafted it down the river, closer to his camp on Day 6, making several trips between the river and camp to get all the goodies home. As a result of his efforts, he was preparing to reward himself with a hot cup of coffee on the morning of Day 7. It had just begun to boil.

"And, for anyone who thinks everyone who is wrongfully imprisoned can sue the government and become a millionaire, you're sadly mistaken. People who haven't experienced it don't realize how expensive it is to defend yourself in this country. It took five different attorneys to try to defend me, file appeals, and, ultimately, get me out of prison. Then, another two lawyers to sue for wrongful imprisonment. In the end, almost every penny I was awarded, nearly six million dollars, went to the attorneys."

Ezra shook his head, poking the fire with a stick. "And they call that justice." He spat into the fire. It landed on a hot rock and sizzled for a moment.

"So, I'm bitter about the entire situation. The only people I can forgive are my daughters. I can't blame them for believing all the lies they were told by the prosecution. I wish they had known me better than to believe I was capable of killing their mother, but that's on me. I've always been a distant person; always assuming people know what type of person I am."

He grabbed a can of beans which he had opened for breakfast and "drank" whatever was left at the bottom.

"Maybe I just wasn't cut out for this society. It's hard to explain the way it feels when society turns against you on such a massive scale. We've all experienced betrayal by people close to us, but it's an entirely different story being betrayed by absolutely everyone—everyone you know and every stranger. When you boil it down, it was 'The People' versus Ezra Greer. *The People* and all the resources of their government. It wasn't *my* government anymore. It might as well have been The Whole World versus Ezra Greer."

Ezra poured a little bit of water from his canteen into the empty bean can and swished it around to clean it, but he didn't dump the water out. He drank it down. Apparently, he didn't mind water tasting like beans, but he didn't want his coffee to taste like beans. The treasure didn't include a coffee mug, so he planned to drink from the bean can.

"The whole system is fundamentally flawed," Ezra continued. "It's pathetic. I was supposed to have my fate in the hands of a jury of my *peers*. It wasn't in any way a jury of my peers. I'm an educated atheist. The jury was made up of Christians. More than half were women. How is that a jury of my peers? Worst of all, it was a jury of morons. You put twelve intelligent atheists on the jury and they would have reached the correct conclusion—not guilty."

He poured the coffee into the can. His gloves protected him from the heat, but he still had to put it down in a hurry and let it cool before drinking.

"Atheists are one of the most under-represented minorities in America," Ezra explained. "Only around four percent of Americans identify themselves as atheists. But, the real number is lower than four percent because, of the four percent who claim to be atheist, only eighty percent actually don't believe in *any* gods or a higher power. So, twenty percent of atheists aren't even atheists. They still believe in some kind of spiritual force or higher power."

The fire was dying down and he was letting it. With an excursion on his list of things to do today, he wanted to protect the embers but let the flames die down while he was away.

"Oh, and if you think atheists are bad people, consider this—they represent less than 0.1 percent of the prison population. That's *zero point one*—not even one percent—meaning 99.9% of the prison population believes in god. Make what you want out of that little nugget of information."

Ezra tested the coffee to see if it was cool enough. A tiny sip burned the roof of his mouth. He shook his head and put the can down.

Picking up where he left off, he explained, "The prosecutor and the media made sure everyone knew I was an atheist. I was shocked they were able to do that. The religiously devout automatically assumed I was guilty because I didn't believe in their gods. It tainted the jury. In some countries, atheists are still executed. Even in America, land of the free, atheists can't run for office in some states. It's a travesty."

Impatient, Ezra tried slurping the coffee a little at a time. The taste woke him up and the warmth soothed him from within.

He continued to complain, "They make you put your hand on a work of fiction and swear to tell the truth. But, it's so ridiculous because the lawyers don't have to swear to tell the truth. The prosecutors don't have to swear to tell the whole truth. The lawyers are free to lie the entire time."

Ezra stopped himself, taking a large gulp of coffee. "They could have put some sugar in the treasure chest," he criticized.

"I know how I'm coming across. I'm still angry. I don't know if it's something I can ever get over because it's still happening. Not to me, but there are plenty of other people going through what I went through and worse. I need to refocus this energy. It's such a waste getting worked up over the past and complaining. I need to let it go and move on. I just don't know how to do that. I guess that's why I'm here," he decided.

Ezra stood up and let the camera continue filming the spot he had been sitting in as he finished his coffee and prepared to leave the shelter.

"So, the plan for today is to hike back to the river, then follow it to the ocean. Just for the hell of it. It's always good to explore. I'll keep my eyes open for more bottles and maps. Maybe this isn't the only treasure they're going to make available. I'm hoping there will be more, eventually."

Leaving the shelter required a lot of prep work. He made sure the fire was at a safe level. He gathered camera equipment to take with him. The equipment he was leaving behind had to be plugged into solar chargers to replenish the batteries. Food had to be secured before leaving it unattended. When Ezra brought the treasure to camp, he had brought it all—even the treasure chest itself. He knew right away it would be perfect for storing food. It could be latched shut but, as an added deterrent, he had smoked the chest, giving it a scent unpleasant to animals. He also covered it with pine branches to further confuse the noses of scavengers.

The goal was to not only protect the chest and food, but to discourage animals from breaking into or damaging the cabin. He wedged the door in place and tied it shut with cordage, but a determined bear could walk right in if it smelled food.

Once everything was secured, Ezra Greer bundled up and set out to hunt and explore.

JILLIAN HILL

Day 7

11:10am

Age: 45
Occupation: Homemaker
Home: Kentucky
Status: Married, 6 children

Jillian Hill froze in place on an animal trail she had yet to explore. She suspected it wrapped around the lake and, while testing the theory, she heard a rustling in the woods behind her. She froze, scanning the forest, looking and listening for the faintest trace of movement. The forest was still, but she could hear a strange crunching, like slow footsteps through leaves. She searched for the source as it got louder, but it was buried behind a wall of greenery and it stopped just as abruptly as it had begun.

"Gosh dang it," she whispered to the camera filming from atop her head. "Somethin's followin' me. This ain't the first time I heard it, neither."

She inched away, backwards, eyes and camera aimed at where she thought the noise had come from.

"I done heard it creepin' around my camp. I heard it when I went to get water and now it's the same noise. Worse part is—it sounds like something walking on two feet—and that ain't right out here. There aught not be anything walkin' round here on two feet." Her voice was accompanied by an involuntary quiver, making her sound scared and frantically paranoid.

She didn't wait around to count the feet of her stalker. She hurried along the animal trail, checking over her shoulder, every few steps, one hand on the bear spray attached to her belt on her hip. Her heavy breathing came across as frightened gasps.

"What the heck is that?" she whimpered, fear overcoming her full throttle.

Up ahead, a straight stick, about four feet long, stuck out of the ground in the middle of the animal trail. As Jill crept nearer, the object impaled on top of the stick took shape and there was no mistaking it—a human skull. She approached with caution and vigilance almost paralyzed by disbelief.

"Dear lord, this better be part of the game," she hoped out loud.

She checked the skull for any indication of its origin, authenticity, or perhaps a message from the producers. Pulling it off the stick with trembling hands, she checked underneath the skull and weighed it in her hand.

"I ain't never seen a human skull in real life before," she explained with a sniffle. "I ain't sure if this one is real, but it feels pretty real. Like, it ain't plastic. But, I'm sure they got all kinds of Hollywood tricks to make things look real. This is gotta be part of the show, or somethin'." Her voice was getting more desperate with her desperate attempts to explain away what she had found.

She returned the skull to the stick and craned her neck, looking at the trail and forest beyond. There was nothing else out of the ordinary.

"Maybe this is the boundary. A head on a stick can only mean one thing—go no farther," Jill guessed, the deduction calming her down. "That's gotta be it. It's just a prop," she confirmed, trying to convince herself.

She screwed up her face, following her crinkled nose as she sniffed. "Dang, it smells somethin' awful, though." She took another few whiffs, hoping to identify the odor. "It's like, urine and a barn full of cows or somethin'. I can't rightly tell."

She checked behind her again. The forest was silent. Not a bird or insect made a peep, adding to the eeriness. The hair on the back of her neck itched as if standing on end. She scratched at the gnawing feeling, her wrinkled eyelids attempting to open wider as she looked around.

"I'm going back to camp," she whispered to the camera. "Somethin' ain't right here."

ZOEY PRICE

Day 7

2:47pm

Age: 24
Occupation: Dance Instructor
Home: Montana
Status: Single

Zoey Price dragged her feet through the leaf litter. She had been following the river all day, hoping it would lead to another contestant. She hadn't eaten more than the occasional handful of greens in the past few days. What little energy she derived from her vegetarian diet was gone and she slowed to a crawl—more like a drag. She didn't have the energy to turn off and deal with the camera, so it kept filming.

"I'm so tired. I can barely move my feet anymore," she told the camera, stopping on the animal trail she had been following. "I don't think I can go any farther today. I need food."

To add to her troubles, a rumble of thunder announced an approaching storm. Zoey looked up to assess the sky. Dark clouds were rolling in. The race was on.

"Oh, give me a break. I can't get caught out in the rain without fire or shelter," she explained, too tired to sound panicked.

Whatever was left in her reserve tank kicked in. She picked the nearest suitable spot to string up her tarp high enough to keep her dry but also shield a fire. Wasting no time, she rushed to gather firewood, piling it under the tarp but she wasn't fast enough.

The rain came pouring down all at once. There was no period of drizzle to take advantage of or warn her to get back to the shelter. It caught her out with an armful of firewood. She hurried back to the shelter but, in a matter of a few steps, the torrential downpour soaked her and rendered the wood she had gathered useless. Tossing the bundle aside, she lightened her load, using her last bit of energy to run back to the shelter. Unfortunately, she still needed to get a fire started. All her extra clothes had burned up, leaving her with only one outfit which was now soaking wet and sucking the warmth from her body.

She had her bow drill and enough firewood to make it through the night, but she'd have to dig deep to muster up the energy to get the fire started or else risk hypothermia. There was no time to think; no time to curse the rain or feel sorry for herself. She hurried through the steps of making a friction fire like clockwork and succeeded in record time. There was no celebration this time, but it was a potentially life-saving event.

KIMMIE ARDEN

Day 7

3:31pm

Age: 36
Occupation: Nurse
Home: New York
Status: Married, 2 children

"I like it here. It could be warmer, but it's nice and peaceful," Kimmie Arden admitted to the camera.

She had set up a nice shot of her shelter and fire and lounging area, where she sat back in the new chair she had built. The contest started off as a challenge, but Kimmie settled in and began to thrive. Food was plentiful and water wasn't far away. Her shelter was cozy and, so far, the animals had left her alone. It was all difficult. It was all a struggle, but she kept her eyes on the prize and did what she had to do without complaining.

"I really needed this time off. It may not seem like a vacation to most people, but it is to me," she said, keeping her hands busy, whittling a piece of wood.

With all the necessities taken care of, Kimmie was free to build things that would make her more comfortable. The chair was the first item, but she had plans to make a raised bed, a small table, and even toyed with an idea to make a musical instrument to entertain herself and help pass the time.

"Don't get me wrong, I love my children and my husband, but I needed this alone time," she explained to the camera. "And, I've come to a conclusion—I'm going to quit my job. Whether I win the million dollars or not. I'm done with doing things that stress me out. I want a peaceful life. A happy life. I'll bet the stress of my job has taken years off my life already. That has to end."

Her eyes never looked up as she fiddled with the piece of wood she was shaping into a spoon with a long, cylindrical handle.

"I'm going to buy a small resort in the Bahamas," she said and it sounded like a fact rather than a wish or a dream. "Just a place where my family can live, right on the beach, with some bungalows to rent and a pool and a bar. Nothing too complicated. For years, my husband and I have toyed with the idea of doing that. We talked about it before we even got married and had kids. It turned into something we only dream about because we're always worried about the impact it would have on the kids."

She flipped the spoon and worked on making the bowl deeper.

"Being out here, even though it's only been a week, it brings a certain type of clarity. It's like," she said taking a deep breath, looking for the right words. "You really get your priorities in order. Maybe it's because that's what survival is all about—getting your priorities in order—fire, shelter, water, food, etcetera. But, the longer I'm out here, the longer the list goes. You have your life back home and you think about it and the people you miss and you realize what's truly important."

She chased away an annoying fly with her hand, swatting it away from her face. It returned as soon as her hand went back to whittling.

"I don't want to live a life of stress. I don't want my children to see me stressed all the time. We're always worried about the impact of uprooting our kids and moving to a tropical island, a foreign country, but what impact is having on them, seeing Mommy crying again after another stressful 14-hour day at work? What impact is it having on them to not see their mother for five days straight at times because Mommy's working the nightshift this week?"

She held the spoon out at arm's length to examine it for a moment, continuing her soliloquy.

"I want to set a good example for my children. Otherwise, they'll grow up making the same mistakes I've made, thinking things like hating your job and dealing with stress is all part of a normal life. I want to teach them that change is good; that you can turn your life around if things aren't going as well as you'd like; that dreams are not just something to fantasize about, but goals to strive for and accomplish."

A chilling breeze swept in, steady and strong. It didn't faze her. She checked the sky for the weather forecast. It looked like rain.

"When I was a little girl, my parents took us to Disney World. We drove all the way down, got to see most of the states on the east coast. My father was driving and, when we got to Orlando, he announced that we were almost there. My brother and I were bouncing off the walls in the backseat. I pressed my face up to the window so I could see and remember the arrival to the hotel, but we still had a little way to go. I watched as we passed a long, brick building adjoining a baseball field and football field."

She looked up at the camera and animated her words with a free hand. "My eight-year old brain couldn't figure out what it was. What kind of building could it be, in a place where people come for vacation? I asked my father what it was as our car passed by. 'It's a school,' he answered matter-of-factly and I was absolutely shocked. 'A school?' I asked. 'Why would a school be here, where people go on vacation?' Both my parents laughed. My mother explained that people live here, right next to Disney World."

The sky turned dark and gray, distant thunder sounding out a definitive warning.

Kimmie looked up and went right along with her story. "I'll never forget that moment. My brain went into overdrive. The information did not compute. *If people can live here, why don't we live here all year round instead of just one week out of the year for vacation?* And, I thought about all the vacations we had taken to beaches in Florida. *People live there, too,* it dawned on me. *How is that possible? Why would anyone live anywhere else?* I had to reevaluate everything I thought I had known about living life. Of course, I was only eight, so I didn't really know anything yet."

She laughed at her own lost innocence.

"When you're growing up, your parents are often your only example. My parents went to work every day, worked hard all year to have enough money to take the family to these beautiful places on vacation. We lived outside Albany, New York, which is a fine place, but it's far from a tropical paradise. I always equated beaches and warm weather with paradise. So, I developed a better idea right then and there. I thought about it the whole vacation. Why not live in my favorite place instead of just visiting once a year? That's where my dreams for my future began and, now, almost thirty years later, I still think it's a great idea. Somewhere along the line, I had grown up and lost sight of it, like we all tend to do. But, it's time to do it. No more excuses. It's long overdue."

The rain was overdue, as well. Kimmie could hear it start pounding the forest from afar and she knew it was coming fast. She gathered the camera equipment, tools, and chair and hurried into the shelter to wait it out. The rain came crashing down in buckets a minute later.

DERRICK BOND

Day 7

5:16pm

Age: 29
Occupation: ex-Marine
Home: Texas
Status: Single

"Son of a bitch," Derrick growled, throwing his 'digging axe' to the ground inside his latest attempt at finding the treasure. Hole number three didn't unearth anything but rocks and more rocks. The curious spot he had been working on turned out to be a tangle of roots from the tree he was no longer calling the treasure tree.

He plopped down on the cold soil at the bottom of the hole, leaned back against the side, and unrolled the treasure map.

"What am I missing? Is this even the right tree?" he asked in frustration, the map not revealing anything new. "This is insane. I don't know if this is the right spot. I don't know what the treasure is. I don't even know how big it is. It could end up being a cigarette lighter for all I know."

The frustrated ex-Marine crumpled the scroll into a ball and threw it hard across the new ditch, which wasn't far. His energy was running dangerously low. He had only dug around three feet down, which wasn't deep in his estimation. He had no way of knowing other contestants had found their treasure relatively close to the surface.

"Aaarrrrrrhhhhhh," he howled in frustration. The camera watched from atop the tripod, only catching Derrick's head and shoulders in view.

With his head in his hands, he broke down in tears, trying to hide it from the camera. "This is not how I wanted this to go. I was supposed to dominate this competition," he said, editing what he had told his friends and family before leaving for Isolation

Island—"I'm gonna make Isolation Island my bitch."

Derrick had tried to give up on digging to focus on acquiring food, but the allure of the treasure kept calling him back for another try. The nagging idea that he was 'so close' kept eating at him. The strategy, if it could be called that, wasn't paying off. He had wasted half the week digging and now he was close to starving.

"I don't know why I can't give up on this treasure bullshit," he confessed, not caring about his choice of words which would need to be bleeped out. "I know I should give up on it. I've tried to give up on it, but I've spent so much time and energy on it already…I don't know what to do."

Another round of weeping ensued. Cold, tired, and hungry, he was slipping into a difficult state to recover from.

"Maybe it's time for me to tap out," he considered out loud. "I've never been a quitter, but it's game over for me. I took a gamble, choosing to go for the treasure and I got burned. Maybe there is no treasure. Maybe I was supposed to remain disciplined and stick to survival. I can't believe how everything has fallen apart so quickly. I thought I'd be out here for months and look at me. I've only been here seven days and I'm already wasting away to nothing."

He wasn't exactly wasting away to nothing—his chest and biceps were still ripped, but all those muscles needed a lot of fuel to continue functioning. Derrick had only had two small fish during his first seven days on Isolation Island and he was just beginning to lose muscle mass. His cognitive function, however, was deteriorating rapidly. The mood swings he had been experiencing were leveling out to pure depression. His thoughts were slow and hindered by the fog clouding his mind.

"I don't think I can turn this around. I don't think things couldn't get much worse," he told the camera.

As if provoked by Derrick's statement, dark clouds rushed in out of nowhere and began dumping rain on the frustrated contestant. He shielded his head with his hands, hunkered down in his bunker, and shouted at the top of his lungs, "Fuuuuuck!"

Chapter 10

Day 16

Floyd's Camp

Hutch and Doc woke up at the same time, as if their circadian rhythms had synced. They both immediately noticed Page was missing. Sharon still slept stretched out into Page's spot.

Doc shimmied his way out of the shelter. Hutch followed, bumping Sharon on purpose with his knees as he crawled over her. She woke with a groggy groan, but everyone else was gone.

Hutch and Doc found Page tending the fire right outside the shelter.

"Good mor…" she began, forgetfully cheerful. There was nothing good about the morning after another crew member had died. "Well, morning, anyway," she corrected herself. Her demeanor turned appropriately somber. "I got the fire going."

Hutch gave her a halfhearted, "Good job."

Knowing they were going to pack up and keep moving, Doc didn't wander far to relieve himself on a tree.

"I also checked in with the contestants," Page added. "No one reported anything unusual. Still no answer from Floyd Benson or any of the missing contestants."

"Great," Hutch uttered. He seemed lost in thought, scanning their surroundings.

"What are we going to do?" Page finally asked.

Hutch replied with questionable confidence. "That's what I was thinking about all night. Our best bet is to round up all the contestants and pick a spot to build a camp together. We'll be safer all together."

"Unless one of the contestants murdered Derrick Bond," Doc added, returning to the conversation with his fly half open.

"I've thought about that. If someone murdered Derrick it must have been to increase the odds of winning the competition. With the competition cancelled, they'd have no reason to kill anyone else," Hutch deduced, but he sounded like he was trying to convince himself as well as the others.

Page pointed discretely at Doc's zipper.

"Or, they'll murder us all to cover up Derrick's murder," Doc suggested, struggling to unstick his zipper. The teeth were caught on fabric, but he managed to free it and run it up to the top.

"We won't let that happen. We know there might be a murderer among the contestants. We just have to stay vigilant," Hutch countered.

Page flinched and both men noticed. They shot each other a look.

"What was that?" Hutch asked, both men looking at Page, expecting an answer.

Page kept her eyes on the fire as she poked it with a stick, trying to look busy. She didn't answer.

Hutch tried again. "Page, what was that for?"

"What was what for?" she dodged.

"That flinch. You flinched," Hutch kept on her.

Page sighed and groaned, hesitant.

Hutch didn't relent. "This is not the time or place to withhold information, Page."

She tilted her head back and forth as if weighing the best choice of words in her mind. "Derrick might not have been murdered because he was competition," she spilled carefully. "We do background checks on all the contestants. One of them was a suspect in a serial killer investigation."

Hutch and Doc shared another quick look.

"Who?" they demanded in unison.

Page answered, "Wes Wood."

"Why the hell was he accepted into the competition?" Hutch asked, irate.

"There were no charges against him. He had never been convicted of anything. We couldn't discriminate based on suspicion and rumor," Page defended.

"Great. Wonderful. That's really smart," Hutch complained throwing his hands up, letting them slap down on the sides of his thighs. "At least, we know who to keep an eye on, I guess."

"We should probably keep an eye on Ezra Greer, as well," Page suggested, cringing a bit.

"Ezra Greer? What did *he* do?" Hutch demanded.

Page answered with her teeth clenched in a worried grimace, "He was convicted of murdering his wife…"

Hutch threw his hands up again in frustration and dismissal letting them slap down purposely louder.

"But, the conviction was overturned. Someone else confessed to the murder. Ezra was exonerated," Page hurried to explain.

"Oh, that's better," Doc grumbled.

Sharon emerged from the shelter with an angry look on her face, freezing all conversation. She fixed a cold stare on Page, walking slowly and deliberately toward her.

"Are we giving away confidential information, Miss Hawkins?" the groggy producer asked.

Hutch stepped between them. "Don't you take that tone with her," he growled.

"They needed to know," Page defended from behind Hutch.

"This isn't a game anymore, Sharon," Hutch insisted. "We've got three dead bodies on our hands, a boatload of missing crew members, and four missing contestants. Lives are on the line here, including our own. This is no time for your confidentiality bullshit. I need to know about any contestants who might pose a threat."

"Wes Wood is harmless," Sharon claimed. "He's no serial killer."

"Why take a chance having someone like that in the competition?" Doc asked.

"We're making a TV show, Ben—entertainment. What's more entertaining than being alone on an island with a potential serial killer and a man once convicted of murdering his wife?" Sharon explained, folding her arms.

"The only entertainment that might come out of this is the string of lawsuits you're going to have to endure if we make it out of here alive," Hutch spat. "Now's your chance to come clean. Is there anything else I need to know?"

Sharon answered without hesitation. "No."

Hutch kept staring at her darting eyes, but they made no contact with his. She turned away, muttering something about the need to get going.

"Do you believe her?" Doc asked.

"Not at all," Hutch admitted.

"Me either," Doc confirmed.

Hutch turned to Page who was still hiding behind him. "Check in with the contestants again. Tell them we have an emergency situation that calls for a halt to the competition and to stay put. Let them know they'll have to survive for possibly a few weeks before we can get to them on foot and if they see a passing ship, do whatever they can to flag it down. Tell them to build signal fires and use their flares if they have to."

"What should I tell them if they want to know why?" Page asked.

Sharon stood with her arms folded, listening and staring from afar, but she didn't object.

Hutch stared her down with eyes that said he didn't want to hear a word out of her. "Tell them we've lost contact with the Mothership and we're working on the problem. Make sure they all know about the buried treasure. We're going to need every resource possible."

"Are we going to get moving, or what?" Sharon huffed.

"Yeah. What are you waiting for?" Hutch asked her. "Start packing up. Start breaking down the shelter. Don't just stand there making demands. This is going to take a team effort. I'm not letting you stand around barking orders anymore. You got that?"

Sharon rolled her eyes. "Whatever," she said, ducking into the shelter to gather her things.

Hutch and Doc left the women to break down the shelter while they tended to the unpleasant task of dealing with the newly-acquired corpse.

The previous night, they had wrapped Simon's body in a tarp, carried it away from their shelter, and covered it in pine branches to disguise the scent from scavengers. Hutch didn't like the idea of sacrificing a tarp for a decomposing body, but he was counting on making it to Floyd Benson's camp where, even if Floyd was dead, there would be another stash of supplies, tarps included.

The plan was to make a stretcher to carry Simon's body to Floyd Benson's camp. It would slow them down significantly, but they didn't want to lose another body to the animals.

They found the point was moot when they returned to the area they had left Simon's body. It was gone. Only the pine branches and mangled tarp were left behind. Neither Hutch nor Doc said a word but they were probably both thinking they were better off without having to carry a dead body around. They returned to the shelter to help pack up and explain Simon's body was gone. Nobody seemed surprised or particularly heartbroken. They were on their way to the beach within a half hour.

The foursome rejoined the beach, making slow progress along the rocky coast toward the area they believed Floyd Benson's camp to be. The progress was slow because they took the opportunity to collect limpets, mussels, and useful debris along the way. They snagged a few plastic bottles, a useable section of fishing net, and various cans.

Hutch grabbed a piece of bull kelp—a long, thick, dark-green tube of ocean vegetation that resembled a tail—but, upon inspection, decided it was way beyond its expiration date for eating.

They marched up the coast all day, a chilling breeze pushing them along. With the sun lowering over the ocean, it was looking like they'd have to set up camp for another night but, out of nowhere, Hutch recognized a tangled mass of dead trees sprawled out on the edge of the water.

"We're close," he said, pointing out the landmark. "This is Floyd's insertion point."

Hutch would know. He had been along for the insertion of each contestant. From there, he could find each contestant's camp with the details they reported on Day 2, or so he hoped.

"Do you think you can find his camp?" Sharon asked.

"I think so," Hutch answered. He couldn't resist reminding her why it's an uncertainty. "It would have been a lot easier if we had proper tracking equipment."

There had been many arguments between Sharon and Hutch about the lack of proper tracking equipment, but it was too late to change it on Day 16.

"You're a professional survival expert, Mr. Adalwolf. Don't tell me you can't track someone without fancy electronic equipment," Sharon gibed.

Hutch ignored her, searching the edge of the forest. "It looks like he cut a path right here," he said, pointing to a semi-worn path. "This will probably lead us right to his camp."

Sharon went first, taking another verbal jab at Hutch as she passed him. "See? That wasn't so hard."

The path did, indeed, lead right to Floyd Benson's camp, but the camp was empty. Floyd was nowhere to be found. They called out for him, repeatedly, as they examined the state of the camp.

The fire pit showed no signs of recent activity. Floyd's clothes were gone. So was his sleeping bag and most of his tools. The camp looked like it had been vacant for some time.

Sharon sat down on Floyd's 'sitting log' while everyone else called out for him. "Enough," she shouted, frustrated. "He's obviously moved to a new camp."

"Really?" Hutch challenged.

"Really. All his clothes are gone. The tools are gone," Sharon argued.

Hutch pulled a first aid kit out of the shelter. "You think he'd leave this behind?" he asked. "Or how about this," he continued, pulling out the canister of bear spray. The flare gun was next. He shook it in Sharon's face.

"Okay, I get it," she said, batting his hand away. "So, where is he?"

Hutch pulled the case of camera equipment out of the shelter. "Maybe this will give us a clue," he hoped, but without an exact location and fading daylight, there wasn't much they could do to locate the missing contestant until morning.

Hutch started a fire while everyone else gathered firewood and they prepared to spend the night at Floyd's camp without Floyd.

ZOEY PRICE

Day 8

4:29pm

Age: 24
Occupation: Dance Instructor
Home: Montana
Status: Single

The pounding rain which began on Day 7 had let up, but a lighter, steady rain persisted. The wind had died down, making the situation a little more manageable but still unpleasant, to say the least.

Zoey Price sat in her makeshift shelter, huddled next to the small fire she had been nursing to keep warm. Her clothes reeked of smoke after drying them over the fire the night before. She turned on the camera, from time to time, to have 'someone' to talk to and keep up her morale. It didn't help much, but she grasped at any little shred of motivation to keep her going.

"I am so done with this shit," she told the camera. "I just want to get the fuck out of here. It's been raining all day. I've got no rain gear. I barely made it through the night even with a fire and I'm running out of wood. I went out to gather some, but I had to go naked so my clothes wouldn't get wet again and the wood is soaked. I'm hoping the fire will help dry it out enough to burn tonight. I don't know what else to do."

Tears began streaking down her cheeks, but her face remained stoic. She didn't have the energy for a full-blown weep.

"If I had a choice, I would have tapped out by now. I'm stuck in this pathetic shelter. I'm freezing. I'm exhausted. I didn't get any sleep last night. I'm starving. I don't know how much more of this I can take," she vented.

Wiping the tears from her eyes, she donned a fake smile.

"But, I'm still here. I guess that's a plus. I just hope this rain lets up soon."

The shivering blonde sat in silence, too tired to continue talking, her mind too clouded from lack of food to think of anything more to say. There was nothing more to say that didn't involve repeated the same complaints over and over. Rather than waste the camera's batteries, she switched it off and tried to take a nap.

7:11pm

"I should have gone in the other direction to begin with," Zoey told the camera, switching it on to check in with the revelation she had decided was the lesson she was meant to learn. "I should have stayed in the cave. I should have been more careful with my fire. Talk about a rookie mistake. Survival is all about decisions and I've made all the wrong decisions so far. So much for using the stars as guidance."

She pulled another stick off the pile of drying wood and set it in the fire, her hands trembling from a combination of cold and low blood glucose.

"I've never been in a situation like this," she sniffled. "This isn't a game anymore. I can't just press a button and have someone come rescue me. This is life and death and I feel like I'm leaning more toward death than life, right now."

She curled back up into a ball, hugging her knees in a sitting position at the edge of the fire. The 'nest' of leaves that served as her bed did little to prevent the ground from sucking the heat from her body.

"Now, I find myself second guessing every decision I've ever made in life. I'm second guessing everything I believed in. Look at where it's gotten me. I came out here all bright-eyed and bushy-tailed, thinking I was going to prove to the world how tough and capable I am. This was supposed to be my big break, my life-altering adventure. I could do it. I could do anything I put my mind to. I had an ace up my sleeve, too. The stars would guide me and give me an advantage over everyone else. I was naïve, really."

She shook her head, stuck between tears and anger. Had she

had more energy she would have used it to throw a violent, cleansing tantrum.

"Not naïve. Naïve is too gentle a word. I was stupid," she lashed out at herself. "I'm not sugarcoating anything anymore. I was plain stupid. Really, really stupid. I wanted an adventure like I saw other people having on reality shows. I applied for Survivor four times, but they didn't take me. I had so much to prove. I wanted to come to Isolation Island and show everybody that a petite, blonde, vegetarian girl could be just as tough as the bearded survivalist hunter man. But, all I've proven is that I'm stupid and I make poor decisions. I don't know what to do with that information, but identifying the problem is half the battle, right?"

The sound of the rain pelting her tarp intensified, intruding on her ears anew, reminding her that nature was in charge and there was nothing she could do about it.

She grabbed the sides of her hat and pulled it down tight, trying to block out the sound. "Argh! I wish it would stop raining," she yelled. Lifting her head to the camera she added, "On the bright side, at least I've got plenty of drinking water," she jested.

After flashing a fake smile at her only companion, she turned off the camera and let the mood swings continue undocumented.

11:51pm

Zoey curled up in a ball in her pathetic shelter with her eyes wide open. The cold and the rain kept her from sleeping. She turned on the camera again. "I don't want to be one with nature anymore," she confessed. "Mother Nature is a mean bitch. She doesn't care. People say nature always provides but that's baloney. Nature has no obligation. Nature makes no promises. Nature is brutal and violent."

With another sleepless night ahead of her, she was delving into deeper thoughts, to her life before Isolation Island, to the universe and the grand scheme.

"I've always considered myself spiritual and enlightened, in touch with nature, guided by the stars—whatever you want to call it. But, that's all garbage. The stars don't mean anything. They're just…stars, billions of lightyears away. Our planet and our sun is also shining in *someone's* sky at night. Maybe not advanced aliens, but stupid, egotistical animals like us that *think* they're intelligent. Us—just another species of animal trying to survive on a little blue dot revolving around a star. Maybe there's an alien looking up at us, thinking somehow our tiny little light billions of light years away is affecting their lives. But they're wrong, just like I was. It's meaningless and now that I really think about it, it's stupid to think otherwise. The stars we see in the sky might not even exist anymore. They could have burned out long before we came along. I can't believe I was so self-centered that I thought this vast, infinite universe existed solely to influence and guide this tiny, little creature called Zoey on this insignificant little planet called Earth."

Her voice grew weary and fainter, unable to sustain the outburst. Deep in despair, she turned off the camera and tried to rest her eyes, if not fall asleep.

SEATON ROGERS

Day 9

4:20am

Age: 33
Occupation: Screenwriter
Home: Utah
Status: Single

"I've never been a good sleeper," Seaton Rogers admitted for the camera. He had been hunkered down in his shelter since the rain began a few days ago and he was running out of things to talk about. "Waiting out a rainstorm is worse than waiting for the sun to come up—it could take days or weeks for the rain to stop. There's no way to know. There's no weather app to tell you the forecast out here."

With nothing else to keep him occupied through the sleepless nights, Seaton often turned to his camera like a therapist.

"Back home, if I sleep seven nights in a week, it's a miracle. Feels like I average five nights at best. That really accumulates over a lifetime. I'm only thirty-three and I'm exhausted every day from the moment I get up in the morning. I can't imagine how tired I'll be when I'm fifty."

Unwilling to get out of his sleeping bag, Seaton swung his feet over the side of his raised bed and sat up like an inchworm in mid stride. He had to take an arm out to operate the camera which had been lying near his head for a too-close close-up. He set the camera on his lap, pointing up at his face. The night vision picking up his eyes and nose, the only part of his face not covered. His hat was pulled down over his eyebrows and a scarf covered his chin and mouth.

"I wonder if my sleeping problems have anything to do with being an introvert. Insomnia is a lonely condition. It feels the same no matter where you are. Even out here, it's the same as at home—

the rest of the world, around you, is asleep and quiet. It's peaceful and nerve-racking at the same time. It feels like you're missing out on something. As I've gotten older, I enjoy the nighttime more and more. It's like being out here. There's no threat of a phone call coming in unexpectedly. No threat of the doorbell ringing. I'm not expected to do anything at night, except sleep."

The rain pattered on his tarp roof as it had for several hours, seeming to be in the process of tapering off, but it never quite stopped. In fact, it was beginning to pick up again, the drops getting heavier and louder.

"When you have something that reoccurs through your entire life, especially if it started when you were a kid, you just assume it's normal," Seaton continued his therapy session. "Ever since I was a kid, it took me hours to fall asleep. Two to six hours to fall asleep was normal for me. I remember one day, my pediatrician asked me how long it takes for me to fall asleep. He was shocked by my answer. He told me ten to twenty minutes was normal and that shocked *me*. It didn't seem possible. What a luxury it would be to be able to fall asleep in twenty minutes. That would be something. Actually feeling awake and reenergized after a night's sleep would be even better."

He reached off-camera to grab another log to add to the fire, growing the flames bright enough to disable the camera's night vision feature. All the camera captured for a moment was Seaton zoned out and frozen in place. If not for the sound of the fire crackling, a viewer might think it was on pause.

He suddenly snapped out of his temporary, open-eyed coma. "What the fuck is charisma?" he asked, shifting subjects like he was apt to do in the wee hours of a sleepless night. "Like, I know what it means in a…a…" He twisted a clawed hand held up under the side of his face, "…a vague sense." He paused, looking for a thought. "But I don't *really* know what it is. Anytime someone says, 'That guy's got charisma,' they're usually talking about a complete douchebag who's full of shit. So, to me, if you have charisma, you're pretty much just full of shit. That's part of *my* definition of charisma. I don't know what else it means. I know when other people use the word they mean it as some kind of compliment. They say it with admiration, as if it's a virtue to have a vague, undefinable quality that people are inexplicably drawn to.

"I think it comes down to people not listening to what the charismatic person says. Or maybe just believing the charismatic person's bullshit. They always talk about cult leaders being very charismatic and that's where I think the word really exposes an error in thinking. Cult leaders aren't charismatic. Any person with half a brain would know cult leaders are full of shit. Getting idiots to believe your bullshit should not be the definition of charisma."

Switching to a nasally voice he used for comedic impersonations, he said, "He's very charismatic."

A second made-up voice answered. "No, he only seems that way to stupid people."

Seaton yawned, nearly inhaling his scarf, knocking him off balance. The camera almost tumbled to the ground, but he caught just in time.

"I don't know. I'm going to try to sleep again," he told the camera with it focused on one eye. "Goodnight."

He turned off the camera and set it on the ground next to the bed, hoping to drift off and sleep through the upcoming rainy day.

STEPHANIE HAMILTON

Day 10

4:19pm

Age: 29
Occupation: Artist
Home: Colorado
Status: Single

The rain continued into Day 10, varying in intensity, but never ceasing. Stephanie Hamilton had ventured out in her raingear to check the gill net she had strewn across the river. She brought two fish back to her shelter—enough to last her through a few more days of rain, if need be.

Stephanie's shelter had gotten a bit cramped with all the equipment inside hiding from the rain, including the treasure items she had spent a full day lugging back to camp. She passed the time by carving utensils, little wooden animals to keep her company, and a set of five small dice to play games with. All of it would be sacrificed to the fire if she ran out of firewood.

The pile of firewood she had been saving for a rainy day was almost depleted, but she had new, wet wood drying over the fireplace. Keeping the shelter warm was a never-ending chore, but the real challenge was the isolation and confinement. Like most contestants, Stephanie dealt with it by talking to the camera.

"I don't mind rainy days, normally. At home, a rainy day is a good excuse to relax and curl up with a good book and a hot cup of tea. But, there are no books here. Not much to do. I still don't mind a rainy day, even here but three days in a row? That's too much."

She stopped a moment to think, checking on the fish stew she had cooking in a pot. "I think it's been three days. I'm losing track. Maybe it's been four days. Either way, it's too much. I can't go out hunting because the other animals don't want to come out in this weather either. Taking a walk in the rain and mud is no picnic.

Plus, I have to get all bundled up with rain gear. It's best just to stay in my little shanty and wait it out. I've got food and there's no end to the water supply as long as it's raining. Going to the bathroom is a pain in the behind, getting all dressed in rain gear and then still getting wet, anyway. There's not a whole lot to do. I play games in my head. Like, I'll try to name all fifty states or recite the alphabet backwards. Anything to pass the time and keep my mind off of how much it sucks to be stuck in the rain on a remote island with no electricity or entertainment of any kind."

She lifted the cover off the pot and stuck her nose close for a whiff of the enticing aroma. She let out a satisfying *ahhh* which seemed to soothe and cleanse her.

"You know how food tastes better when you eat outside?" she asked the camera. "It's the same with the *smell* of food. My shelter smells like fish stew and I love it. My stomach is growling waiting for it, but I kind of enjoy the waiting part. Anticipation is an underrated feeling. Some people prefer surprises, but it robs you of that period of anticipation when you can revel in what's about to happen. Looking forward to good things is almost as much fun as experiencing it. Sometimes it's better because you find the real thing doesn't measure up to your expectations—your anticipation. I book my vacations way in advance so I can daydream about how awesome it's going to be. I looked forward to coming to Isolation Island for months. And, now, when the going is getting tougher and frustrating, I can remember the anticipation and excitement. It reminds me to stop and smell the roses. It reminds me to enjoy this experience as much as possible because one day it will all be in the past."

She taste-tested a wooden spoonful of the saltwater/fish broth with a loud, satisfying slurp. "Oh, that's good. I love soup. If I can catch a bird in my bird trap, I'll make chicken soup...er...or bird soup, I suppose."

Returning the cover to the pot, she licked the spoon clean.

"When you're out here in the wilderness and everything is a hazard, surviving from day to day is difficult. It always makes me think about how much human life expectancy has increased and why. Out here, a small cut could get infected and kill you. A tree branch or the entire tree could fall on you and crush you. An animal could attack you. You could get sick from drinking contaminated water and die. You could die of exposure, hypothermia. There are so many things that could kill you, just waking up to face another day is a triumph and you feel it. You *should* feel it. It's good for morale. When you're in a survival situation, you can choose to let it bring you down. Heck, it can creep up on you and bring you down even if you don't want it to. But, it's better to embrace the challenge and enjoy overcoming it. I choose to embrace it, but I sure wish it would stop raining. I'd embrace some sunny days right about now."

She paused to listen to the rain hitting her roof, trying to determine if her request was being answered with an end to the rain. It wasn't.

Stephanie sighed an exaggerated sigh for the camera. "Maybe tomorrow."

WES WOOD

Day 11

5:05pm

Age: 57
Occupation: Farmer
Home: Mississippi
Status: Divorced, 8 children

The rain didn't stop Wes Wood. Every morning, he dressed up in his forest camo raingear and headed out on his DIY boat without any cameras, returning well before nightfall with no record of his activity.

At 5:05pm on Day 11, Wes pulled his boat ashore and emptied the water which had accumulated inside. He left the boat upside-down, grabbed the axe and shovel and hiked back toward camp. Arrows rattled in the quiver tube slung over his shoulder. Anytime was a good time for hunting in his mind. No opportunity should be wasted, especially when food supplies were so low. He had been living off of fish, unable to catch anything in the traps on land. His arch nemesis, the fox, continued to help itself to the scraps of food left in the traps as bait.

On the way back to camp, Wes checked his traps, as usual. The first trap along the way was empty. No kill. No bait. Mr. Fox had struck again. "Dash nab-it!" he spat with only the trees to hear him. He looked around as if he expected to see the fox watching and reveling in victory. The hapless hunter began to wonder if the traps were worth the effort. All he was doing was keeping the fox fed and wasting his own time and energy in the process.

The rest of the traps looked the same as the first. The fox knew where they were and made his rounds every night, collecting free meals. Wes kicked the last one, a wooden bird trap, to pieces, venting his frustration. He collected the wood and brought it back to camp for fuel. A drying rack he had built over the fire was almost full. He stripped out of his wet raingear, and redressed in dry clothes. Grabbing a camera, he climbed into bed, lying on his side as if he had been there all day, and pointed the camera at his face.

"Welp, it's Day 11 here and the dang rain ain't lettin' up. I ain't left the cabin in four days and I ain't aimin' to," he lied. His pride wouldn't let him mention the fox which was outsmarting him and he preferred to keep his daily excursions a secret.

"There ain't nothin' to do but wait when the weather's like this. I got me enough food and firewood fer a couple or three more days. If it don't let up by then, I guess I'm gonna have to go out."

Wes used the camera to report in every day in this manner to make it seem like he was hunkered down in his shelter the entire time. The message was the same each time—nothing to see here, just sitting around doing nothing while it rains. Boring and uneventful.

DERRICK BOND

Day 12

2:40am

Age: 29
Occupation: ex-Marine
Home: Texas
Status: Single

Derrick Bond was still awake at almost three o'clock in the morning. The rain pounding on his tarp had become deafening after countless hours without letting up. He tossed and turned, confined to his tiny lean-to shelter. He turned on the camera for companionship.

"If it ever stops raining, I'm going to build a bigger shelter. Being cooped up in here for…a million hours, I have no idea long it's been. It feels like forever. I'm going to lose it any minute. I just keep reminding myself this is for the money, one million dollars. It's the only thing keeping me from tapping out. I didn't sign up for this shit, being locked in a tiny shelter while it rains for the rest of my life."

He sneezed and scratched his nose. Closing his eyes tight, he tried to block out all the negativity, but it was impossible. He was surrounded by it with nothing to think about but his failures and misery.

"If it doesn't stop raining soon, I swear I'm going to hang myself," Derrick threatened. "I've had to take a leak for the past three hours, but I don't want to go out in the rain again. This fucking rain won't fucking STOP!" he growled, starting soft and weak but ending with a howling scream. He wanted the relentless clouds to hear him. He wanted the bears and wolves to hear him and fear him. He had had enough.

A drop of water landed right in his eye. His roof was leaking. He knew it upon impact and he lost his mind. The video camera captured the tantrum after being kicked to the corner.

"Mmmother!..fucker! God damn bullshit, fucking, fucking, bull-fucking-shit," Derrick began his verbal rage. He went on cursing every bad word he could think of, tacking on fuck or fucking to each. If the video ever aired, it would be one long bleep. He pounded his fists on the ground and threw his equipment around the confined space. Luckily, his back was to the camera when he stuck his crotch out the front door and peed on his own doorstep.

The curses continued long into the night. Anger turned to sobbing, then to laughing at his self-inflicted predicament and back to anger again. The cycle repeated several times.

Derrick Bond finally cried himself to sleep at 4:09am on Day 12. The rain stopped a few hours later.

Chapter 11

Day 17

This is Getting Serious

Hutch woke up on Day 17 with Sharon curled up next to him and Doc on the other side of her. They had had a hard time fitting into Floyd Benson's tiny shelter for the night, but they endured. On the plus side, packing themselves in like sardines helped keep them warm.

Page was already awake outside, making her rounds on the radio, getting a head count, hoping to make contact with the missing contestants or at least break even without any more coming up missing in action. As she tried making contact with Floyd Benson, she listened all around her for sounds coming from his radio in case he was injured or dead nearby.

There was an eerie quiet to the morning. The location seemed haunted by Floyd's disappearance. What happened to him? Where was he? It was possible he was the victim of an accident or foul play but another possibility had to be considered. Perhaps Floyd Benson was gone because he was wreaking havoc on the other contestants.

Hutch emerged from the shelter hoping to find Floyd chatting away with Page, joking about how he had dropped his radio off a cliff by accident and the minor hardships that caused him to relocate his camp. Instead, Hutch was greeted by Page's somber expression and the reality that Floyd was still missing.

"Did you get a hold of anyone?" Hutch asked, wondering about the other missing contestants.

"No," Page answered, short and sour. Her face was filled with worry, threatening to overflow with tears, not only for the missing contestants but the predicament she was also mired in.

Hutch knew he should put his arm around her and comfort her, tell her everything was going to be okay, but he couldn't bring himself to do it. He was too honest and he was a realist, incapable of being stupidly optimistic in such a serious situation—both were side effects of being a survivalist. The words would come out empty and hollow if he tried. He knew they were stranded and in serious trouble. Telling her everything was going to be fine while dead bodies were accumulating all around them just seemed wrong to him.

Dr. Rodney crawled out of the shelter just in time to deal with Page's breakdown. He comforted her like only a doctor with a good bedside manner could while Hutch built up the fire.

Hutch had to bite his tongue, hearing things like, "Don't worry" and "We're going to be all right," and other lies about how everything will magically work itself out. The longer it went on, the more he wanted to get out of there before he said something honest and damaging to morale.

"I'm going down to the shore to see if I can scare up some food," he announced gently. "We'll all feel better once we get some food in our stomachs."

Page lifted her head off Dr. Rodney's shoulder and said with a sniffle, "We should look for Floyd's treasure chest. Maybe he didn't find it before he…" She didn't have the strength to speculate, as if saying Floyd met his ultimate demise would somehow make it true.

"That's a good idea," Hutch agreed. "Doc," he said, looking for confirmation and acceptance of the assignment. If nothing else, it would keep Page busy and focused on something other than how screwed they were. He spared them the lecture about how, in a survival situation, there was no time to dwell in sorrow or worry. They needed food and water. They needed fire. They needed shelter. They needed to make contact with the outside world or signal for a rescue somehow. There was an endless list of things that needed to be done. In addition, they still had nine contestants to locate, which meant they'd have to do it all while on the move, complicating matters even more.

The treasure would make it all a little easier, if Floyd hadn't found it and used it up already. At least, they could forego the time-consuming hunt. They didn't need clues or a sketchy map. Page had found her notes with the location of every treasure chest, along with where shovels could be found. She hadn't left them on the Medline after all.

Hutch wasn't giving up on finding Floyd Benson. While Doc kept Page busy searching for treasure, Hutch was in full tracking mode. He searched for signs of recent activity on his way to the nearest shore, but found none. It was as if Floyd Benson had turned into a ghost and vanished, leaving no trace except for the camp.

There were no clues to Floyd's whereabouts at the shore either, but Hutch managed to find some limpets and mussels. Their hard shells plunked in the pot as he collected them, walking the shore northward until it turned to the east. The shore changed from mostly rocks to hard, packed gray sand, a welcomed change as the rocks were slippery and difficult to navigate. Washed upon the shore, he found a tangled ball of fishing line. It broke when he tugged on it—too old and weak to be any use. He also found an old, thin tin that looked to have contained some kind of mints or candy at some point in its lifetime. The lid was faded, except for a logo written in Korean. The writing didn't matter. He pocketed the tin with a use in mind.

After decades of experience, Hutch's survival instincts were reflexive, which was a good thing considering his mind was occupied with so many questions.

Where was Floyd Benson?

If Floyd was hurt, why didn't he use the radio to call for help?

If Floyd was dead, what happened to all his supplies?

Could Floyd be responsible for Derrick's death and/or hanging?

Perhaps Floyd or one of the other contestants had gone on a killing spree and then, stole the Medline and destroyed the Mothership to cover their tracks.

The lack of evidence supporting any theory made the thoughts and possibilities get wilder and wilder the more he grasped at straws to explain what was happening.

Hutch continued to search the shore for food and clues when a faint flash of light hit his eye. It seemed to have come from the forest. He froze in place, searching the tree line, but saw nothing. Taking a step back, he lined up with the reflection again. This time, it wasn't as bright, but he pinpointed the source at the edge of the forest and hurried over to find it came from the lens of an abandoned video camera. The camera was turned on its side, pointing at the ocean.

Hutch flipped the viewing screen out and tried to turn it on, but the battery was dead. Hoping it would contain clues to Floyd's whereabouts, he brought it back to camp without delay. The camp was empty once again.

Hutch radioed to Page to check up on them.

"How's the treasure hunt going?" he asked, doing his best to convey a lighthearted tone.

Page answered. "We've found the spot. Dr. Rodney is digging. How are things on your end?"

"I found a video camera on the ground near the shore, but the battery is dead. Over," Hutch replied.

"I've got some extra batteries in my backpack. It's in the shelter. Help yourself," Page responded.

"Will do. Over and out," Hutch ended abruptly. He was anxious to see what the camera had captured.

The batteries were right where Page said they would be. Finding them made him wonder, not for the first time, how someone as professional and organized as Page ended up working for someone as incompetent as Sharon. He came to the same conclusion he had come to before—she must be well-compensated.

He changed out the batteries on the camera and pressed the playback button, but the screen just flashed a sideways shot of the empty beach in night vision mode and shut down. The memory card was full. There was no telling how long the camera had been abandoned. It could have been recording up until the battery went dead or the memory filled up, which would have meant it was dropped on its side while recording.

Hutch rewound one minute and pressed play again. The same sideways shot of the beach filled the screen. He turned the camera so that he could examine the footage right-side-up. There was nothing but empty beach, tinted green by the night vision, with greenish waves turning over and crashing on their way to shore. No new information. He rewound the video a minute at a time, finding nothing new after several attempts.

Realizing it was going to take a while, Hutch sat on Floyd's 'sitting log' and settled in, rewinding the video five to ten minutes at a time until he saw something change.

After rewinding through over four hours of the same footage, the only change was the lighting. Night vision gave way to the normal grayish gloom of Isolation Island's western shore. The only activity was from two birds fighting over some scrap of food before one prevailed and flew away, chased by its opponent.

Hutch rewound another hour, pressed play, and finally found a new scene—Floyd walking through the forest. He was in the middle of a sentence.

"...is such a waste of time and energy," Floyd said. "I've got to be more careful with my tools, but it's not easy. The thing that can't be captured on video properly is the toll this contest takes on your mental state. Lack of food, lack of restful sleep, it all messes with your head. You just become absent-minded. Your thoughts get cloudy. It's the perfect recipe for making stupid mistakes, like leaving one of your most important tools in the woods. At least, I *hope* I left it in the woods. If I didn't...well, that's a whole other problem. No point in getting ahead of myself. I'll worry about that if the time comes."

Hutch had to take it on faith that the person speaking was really Floyd Benson. He had no reason to think otherwise, but the cameraman never showed his face. The camera captured a bouncy picture of the trail ahead until Floyd stopped to rest.

"Even with my strategy of conserving energy, I'm still exhausted," he said through labored breaths. "I'll rest tomorrow. I don't like doing too much in one day and today, I did more than I had planned to."

Floyd started walking again, but the microphone picked up more than his footsteps. Hutch turned up the volume, trying to discern what the extra noise was. Floyd seemed indifferent, apparently not noticing the sound. Something was scurrying through the brush, but on video it was impossible to determine which direction it was coming from. Hutch dismissed it as a squirrel or a larger animal rustling dead leaves nearby. The sound dissipated as Floyd kept walking along the animal trail, picking up his pace for the first time. The camera waved up and down with the same shot of passing greenery. It could have been filmed almost anywhere on the island.

"I hope it doesn't start rain...," Floyd said.

His sentence was cut short with a hard thump. The screen blurred with rapid motion. Either Floyd had fallen to the ground or he had dropped the camera. All Hutch could see on the screen was a close-up of the leaves of a fern living on the edge of the trail.

Floyd provided no explanation. In a heartbeat, the camera was on the move again, waving around, providing only a blur of green and flashes of Floyd's lower body. Hutch paused the video to scrutinize the shot. It appeared as though Floyd was lying on the ground, the toes of his boot pointing up among the scrambled frame. Hutch pressed play again.

The video continued with blurry flashes. There was a guttural groan, almost a growl, followed by a horrifying scream. The camera lifted off the ground and began swinging back and forth, faster and faster, in sync with the sound of boots hitting the ground. The side of Floyd's leg flashed by over and over as he sprinted through the forest. Hutch could hear something heavy chasing him.

The camera lifted and turned for a quick shot behind him. Hutch paused and examined the frame, but there was nothing but empty forest behind the fleeing man. Floyd let out a blood-curdling scream as if he had just woken from a nightmare. The camera turned back and dropped to his side again, swinging as he kept running. His panicked screams were drowned out by branches whipping by.

The motion of the camera suggested Floyd had it strapped to his hand as he ran. The screaming gave way to a controlled whimpering, coupled with heavy breathing. Hutch hit pause on the backswing, trying to get a look behind Floyd to see what he was running away from, but the video was too blurry to make out anything.

Floyd continued to sprint through the forest, presumably using every ounce of energy he had in him. He screamed out again. This time it was a hair-raising, "No!" repeating as he slowed down.

Suddenly, the camera was no longer swinging. It stopped with a thump, coming to rest turned on its side in the spot Hutch had found it. With a clear view of the shore, it captured Floyd running away without it. He turned for a split second to look behind him.

Hutch paused the video to get a look at the fleeing man's face. There was a look of horror and surprise but also confusion. The video resumed with a sideways shot of Floyd rushing into the cold ocean, breaking into a swim while the sound of running feet came to a slow halt off camera.

Hutch watched and rooted for Floyd, but he knew the frigid water would kill him if his pursuer didn't get to him first. Floyd kept swimming, disappearing behind waves and reappearing after they crashed and eased their way to shore.

Floyd had made it out past the breaking waves, slowing to a halt, nothing but a head sticking out of the ocean. Hutch expected the cold would get to him or his muscles would seize up and he'd drown. Instead, Floyd turned around, checking to see if he was clear of his pursuer. His head bobbed just above the surface, panicked hands flailing to tread water before he disappeared—yanked under by the owner of a pointed fin that poked out of the water for a brief moment. The size of the fin suggested it was a rather enormous shark.

Floyd surfaced again, arms reaching to the air looking for something to grasp to get him out of the water, screaming in pain. Then, he vanished into the dark water, pulled back under. This time, for good.

Hutch's stomach sank watching helplessly, hoping the poor man would somehow, miraculously fight off the shark and make it back to shore safely without freezing to death. The survivalist in Hutch knew it was impossible. The tinge of crimson washing up on shore with the waves, Floyd's diluted blood, confirmed there were no miracles on Isolation Island that day. The red faded quickly as if to illustrate its insignificance.

The crunching of a few slow footsteps passed the camera, leaving only the sound of calm ocean waves lapping the shore, indifferent to the violent death which had just occurred.

Hutch watched dutifully as the sun set on the horizon and the camera automatically switched to night vision. His eyes widened, lifting his head from the camera, tilting an ear to the wind. The faint, familiar sound of footsteps crunching through leaves made him spring up and spin around. His hand instinctively reached for the knife he wore on his belt, but it was only Page and Dr. Rodney returning from the treasure hunt, their arms full of useful items.

Page's satisfied smile ran away as soon as she got a look at Hutch's bewildered face. "Oh my god. What happened?" she asked, clutching the blanket and toilet paper she had retrieved from the treasure chest.

"You'd better sit down," Hutch instructed with a sigh. He

didn't want her to see what happened to Floyd, but there was no point in hiding it. They needed to see it for themselves. They deserved to see it for themselves.

They piled the treasure supplies into the shelter and sat on Floyd's 'sitting log' to watch from the time Floyd got knocked over to when he rushed into the ocean and disappeared.

Doc commented about the risk of hypothermia before Floyd's ultimate fate unfolded. Page covered her gasping mouth with one hand and her stomach with the other, on the verge of vomiting when Floyd got pulled under for the last time.

As the three of them sat huddled around the camera while the sun set on the screen, Doc lifted his head and looked around camp. After a second lap, it caught Hutch's attention and he shot the doctor a quizzical look.

Doc returned the same look and asked, "Where's Sharon?"

Hutch looked around to see for himself. "I don't know. I thought she was with you."

ZOEY PRICE

Day 12

9:15am

Age: 24
Occupation: Dance Instructor
Home: Montana
Status: Single

Zoey Price opened her eyes, early in the morning. The sound of rain pounding the tarp was replaced with sparse drips rolling off the tree leaves which hung over the thin, droopy dwelling she called her prison over the past few days. Five days of rain had finally come to an end overnight, while she slept. She crawled out of her tarp shelter, squinting and shielding her eyes from the bright light in the sky shining down on her for the first time in days. Her hair was frazzled and matted down. She hadn't moved much during the last two days. The prospect of a day without rain drew her out like an oasis in the desert.

When she saw the clear blue sky, she clasped her hands together, bowing to the sun as she knelt, thanking whatever force placed it there. She wasn't sure of anything anymore, but she knew sunshine was better than rain. Her cold, pruney fingers would have a chance to dry.

Zoey hadn't had much to eat other than the wet greens she had picked days earlier. She had used the rainy days to build a bird trap and a fish trap. Still struggling with the idea of betraying her vegetarian lifestyle, the very real possibility of starving to death outweighed any lingering moral objection she could come up with.

The ground was still wet, but it didn't seem to register in her head. She remained kneeling with her eyes closed, basking in the first warmth she had felt since her fire went out early yesterday morning. She began a hysterical laugh which quickly progressed to crying and back to laughter, alternating in waves of conflicting emotions.

"It stopped raining," she finally said, as if a camera was recording. "I can't believe it."

Her last battery had lost its final bar of energy yesterday, but she continued to talk to the camera—her last remaining connection to the real world. She held it in her hand, pointing it at herself when she talked or at whatever she was talking about. She turned it straight up to the sky to document the momentous occasion.

The clear sky meant she had a chance. She could pull herself out of the misery of the past week and possibly survive long enough to find rescue. But, first, she needed food.

Without a fire to cook over, she was limited to foraging for greens. She took her time combing the unexplored areas she hadn't hit during the rain storm. Needing more than just food for herself, she hoped to find something to use as bait in the traps she had made.

"So, here's the plan," she told the dead camera as she foraged. "If I can find something to eat, I'll see if it gives me the strength to pack up and keep moving. I've got to keep moving, but I'm just so drained from lack of food and shivering all night, I don't know if I'm up to it."

After a short period of exploration, Zoey was already winded and had to take a break. She leaned up against a tree and sunk down to the ground. It was there she found a rare treasure—an orange cluster of mushrooms growing like wavy shelves with yellow edges. Her eyes lit up. She pointed the camera at the mushroom, taking care to get a 'good shot' of the detail.

"Oh my god," she exclaimed. "I don't know what the technical name of this is, but the common name is *chicken of the woods*. It's a mushroom and it's edible," she said, her voice quivering with a combination of joy and relief. "I can't believe it. I thought chicken of the woods only grew in North America. Supposedly, it actually tastes like chicken when cooked. Unfortunately, you're not supposed to eat it raw. It could be harmful. But, if I can get a fire started, this could save me from starvation."

Tears streamed down her face. Realizing it, she turned her head away and wiped them with her sleeve. Another round of tears began when she looked at the clump of chicken of the woods again. It wasn't the most appetizing thing to look at, but it could be life-saving, and Zoey knew it. Before harvesting the mushroom, she let the emotions consume her and run their course, crying for as long as necessary before it passed.

With her pockets full of chicken of the woods, she smiled at the camera with a left-over sniffle of despair. "Now, I need to build a fire, but everything is still too wet. Maybe I can find something else to eat that doesn't require cooking."

Zoey found little more than the same greens she had been eating all along, but it was better than nothing and she found an added bonus. A large greenish-brown grasshopper jumped across her field of vision and she pounced on it like a cat on a mouse. She held it up for her friend, the camera, to see, its legs wiggling in hopes of escaping.

"Look at that," she said, smiling with a newfound burst of optimism. "A grasshopper. It's enormous."

It wasn't enormous for a grasshopper, but to Zoey's eyes it was a giant, the biggest grasshopper that had ever hopped the world. But, it was more than that. It was, technically, her first ever successful hunt. Even if it was only an insect, she had never killed an animal large than a spider in her adult life.

"I can't eat this, either," she said with a sigh, no sign of vegetarian's remorse in her voice. "Raw grasshoppers could have harmful parasites. But, I can use it as bait."

She stuffed it in her pocket and zipped it shut.

The smile ran away from her face for moment. The little voice within her that told her killing and eating animals was wrong was only a whisper now, but she could hear it and feel it. She shook it off, rationalizing what she was planning to do.

"The thought of killing this grasshopper to catch a bigger animal to kill and eat makes me feel bad, but I'll die out here if I don't eat. I won't have the energy to get out of here if I don't eat. I'm finally realizing being a vegetarian is a luxury. I don't have a choice anymore."

She patted the pocket she had put the grasshopper in, her thoughts more concerned with the grasshopper getting away than any guilt associated with killing it or offering it as bait.

"This is an emergency. You have to do what you have to do in a survival situation. I have to eat whatever is available, whatever will help me survive. I'm as hungry as a hippo. I swear, I'd eat a handful of white marbles at this point just to have something in my stomach."

3:05pm

"I'm checking my fish trap to see if I caught anything," Zoey explained to the dead camera. She stopped pretending to hit the record button and now spoke to the camera whenever she felt like it, as if the camera was voice-activated.

"I'm also curious why the water sounds so much louder. Maybe it's just my imagination," she wondered dragging her tired legs along.

"I've decided to stay put for one more day. Actually, I didn't really decide. I *tried* to decide for so long that it's too late to start walking now. Indecision could kill me out here, but I think my indecision just shows that I'm too tired to be hiking today. I should be fine here for another night or two. I managed to get a fire started using some of the dry wood I had left over in the shelter. It wasn't easy, but it's done."

She didn't explain why she thought the non-functioning camera missed filming such events. Her camp wasn't far from the river, but she moved at a sloth's pace, her head woozy and exhausted. The world seemed to be coming at her in slow motion and she was focused on matching its speed.

"If there's no fish in the trap, I'll eat the chicken of the woods and check the fish trap again tomorrow," she said. Even her words sounded tired with long, random pauses. She froze for a moment, looking for a word. "I'd hate to spend another night here, but I'm too weak to move on just yet. I have to get moving again soon, though. I need to find help somehow."

She repeated the mantra as if she needed to remind herself what she was doing out there, in the middle of nowhere.

"Oh, no. No, no, please no. Oh my god," Zoey stuttered, rushing to the river upon first sight. Four days of rain had been filtering its way through the island, causing the rivers to rise. The water flowed deep and fast, threatening to spill over the outer banks.

"It was fine a few hours ago," Zoey lamented. "I can't believe how much the water has risen and sped up."

She had placed the fish trap in a shallow corner where the water had been still, but the entire area was flooded and indistinguishable. She looked up and down the river, hoping to spot her fish trap snagged on a branch close to land, but it was gone and so was the grasshopper she used as bait.

"The fish trap I worked so hard on is gone," Zoey said, monotone and emotionless. "Shit, and now I'm gonna have to move my shelter and find some higher ground. The last thing I need is to get swept away by a flash flood in the middle of the night."

She looked up river again, reconsidering.

"Well, maybe not a flash flood, but it might as well be in the middle of the pitch-black night while I'm sleeping," she droned on.

She didn't have the strength or time to break down crying. She sucked it up and got to work.

KIMMIE ARDEN

Day 12

9:45am

Age: 36
Occupation: Nurse
Home: New York
Status: Married, 2 children

Kimmie Arden woke later than usual on Day 12, a habit she had picked up from sleeping late every day during the four days of rain. A clear blue sky was a welcomed sight when she climbed out of her shelter, camera first.

She immediately scanned the camp's perimeter and found another treat in store. Two deer heads popped up from grazing in the tall grass just outside what she considered to be her property. Their mouths chewed on autopilot, ears at attention as they examined Kimmie's motionless figure.

"Oh my god," Kimmie whispered to the camera, mouth barely moving. "Look at that."

She remained frozen in place with the camera on the deer. When the deer dipped their heads to search for more chewing material, Kimmie took a slow, careful step back towards the entrance to the shelter.

"I don't want to spook them," she said softly, but it was enough to get one deer's head to pop back up.

Kimmie froze again, staring back at the doe. It kept chewing and dipped its head again.

Kimmie whispered, "In this situation, you don't necessarily have to get into the mind of the deer if you can get into the eyes of the deer. That is, if you understand what a deer's vision is like. It's fuzzy, blurry, and kind of pixilated. Or so the experts say. I saw a rendered video of what it's like to see like a deer and it basically looked like snow on a TV screen, that white noise interference, and objects just had an outline around them. So, it's like seeing a bunch of shapes with no discerning characteristics. I look like everything else does, to the deer, because I'm not moving. If I stay still, the deer won't even know I'm here," she explained at great length, taking a step back whenever the deer weren't looking.

They played a game of Red Light, Green Light until Kimmie was deep enough inside the shelter to disappear into the shadow. She set the camera on the ground and scrambled to get her bow and arrow ready, taking care not to make too much noise.

"They probably can't see me in here," she continued whispering.

The camera had a hard time seeing her, as well. It was trying to adjust to the lighting contrast caused by the sunlight coming in through the door and the cold shadow within the shelter. Kimmie left it on the ground, more focused on capturing some protein than worrying about capturing the moment on video.

"What a treat this would be after four days of rain and smoked fish?"

She went down to one knee, took a deep, stabilizing breath, and drew an arrow back.

"I'm quite proficient with a bow, normally," she whispered, "but, I'm not exactly operating at one hundred percent here. I could miss this shot. Wouldn't that be embarrassing on national TV?" She was assuming the show would air and be a big hit.

She waited until the smaller of the two deer lifted its head again. Then, she let the arrow fly. A direct hit to the neck took the deer down, sending the other running for its life.

"Got him," Kimmie confirmed for the camera, even though she knew the deer was a doe.

She picked up the camera and hurried over to get a shot of her kill and finish the job if need be. The deer was still by the time Kimmie got to it. A quick, clean kill. She knelt down, laying a hand on the animal, bowing in respect.

"Thank you for your life and sustaining me," she said to the dead deer. "Now, I have to skin it, cut it into manageable pieces and..." she went on, pausing while the ramifications of dealing with so much meat hit her all at once. "When you're hunting for food and your survival depends on success, you get so focused that you forget about the practicality of having this much meat around without a refrigerator. This little guy will probably yield around fifty pounds of meat or so. I'll need to preserve as much as I can, but the biggest challenge is keeping it out of the mouths of the rest of the wild animals out here. Scavengers would love to come across a nicely butchered deer like this while I'm asleep. Protecting the meat won't be easy, but if I can do it, I just extended my stay here by a lot."

Kimmie raised a fist in victory, her own words sinking in.

"This could be a million-dollar deer," she smiled. "This is good."

JILLIAN HILL

Day 12

10:54am

Age: 45
Occupation: Homemaker
Home: Kentucky
Status: Married, 6 children

"This is bad," Jill Hill complained. "The wood's soaked right through." She lifted a broken branch she had found in the forest while looking for firewood. It crumbled in her hand, the wet chunks breaking apart further upon impact with the ground. She wiped her hand on her coat and moved on.

Several yards away, she stopped again. "*That's* what I been looking fer," she said, grinning a satisfied grin.

She filmed her find—a branch that had broken in the stress of the storm, but got caught up in the other branches on its way down. It hung low enough to reach.

"Look what the good lord done brung me. He hung it here to dry for me," Jill claimed. "This is better than any wood I could find on the ground."

She yanked the end of the branch and the whole thing came crashing down, almost landing on her head.

"Shoot. That was close. I guess that's why they call 'em Widowmakers. Gotta be careful."

Jill knelt down, holding the branch still with one hand as she wielded her axe with the other, ignoring her own advice. She chopped down on her hand between the thumb and forefinger. Blood gushed out, obscuring the size of the gash. She sprung up, dropping the axe on her foot, holding her injured hand.

"Dang it. Oh, gosh dang it. No, no," she gasped, turning indecisively in every direction as if looking for help.

Putting pressure on the wound, she winced and left everything behind on her way back to camp to tend to the cut with the first aid kit. The camera mounted on her hat followed along as she staggered through the damp forest. Blood streamed down her forearm, dripping off her elbow. She lifted her hand to uncover the wound. Wiping away the steady blood flow, she caught a glimpse of white that make her heart sink. She had hacked right down to the bone.

By the time she got back to camp, she was in tears, praying to god out loud. Using a bandana, she tied a tourniquet around the afflicted arm and applied pressure with gauze to stop the bleeding.

"I'm finished. I done chopped deep down to the bone. I need stitches. A cut like this will get infected out here, fer sure," she said with a sigh.

She was beginning to calm down, but the calm brought with it the reality of tapping out, which brought another wave of tears. Game over. No million dollars.

"I don't wanna leave like this. All I prayed for was to not have to leave 'cause of an injury," she lied. She had prayed to win the million dollars, repeatedly, thinking she would get her way if she asked nicely.

Worried the bleeding wouldn't stop, Jill Hill pulled the radio out of her pocket to tap out on Day 12. "Is anyone there? Hello? I need help," Jill spoke into the radio at regular intervals with no reply. Her voice got louder and more desperate with each attempt.

Had her radio worked, she would have been the first contestant to officially tap out. The radio turned on, but she was unable to contact anyone. The fall into the water and/or impact almost two weeks ago had rendered the radio useless. She was on her own and bleeding profusely.

12:22pm

The injured Jill Hill hiked in search of higher ground, hoping it would help her radio's transmission and reception. The only hill she had seen was in a direction she seldom traveled. Traversing new territory while her hand throbbed was the last thing she wanted to do, but it was the only hope she had left of contacting the Mothership with the radio. At least, she had managed to stop the bleeding.

The hill got steeper and steeper, but she managed to pull herself up with her good hand. Over the top hump, she breathed a sigh of relief over how short the climb had turned out to be. A wide, grassy plateau greeted her. The camera mounted on her head captured one of the highest points on Isolation Island. It was like being on top of the world, no trees obstructing the view of the sky and no higher ground visible anywhere.

"If'n the radio don't work here, it ain't workin' nowhere," she said through winded breaths to the camera. "Here goes nothin'."

She held the radio up, spinning around, trying different spots on the plateau, walking around the tall grass, but her attempts to contact the Mothership, or anyone, failed. With her eyes on the radio lifted in the air, she almost backed right into a ditch. She caught herself on the edge, stopping at the last possible moment.

"What the heck is this?" she asked, capturing the hole on camera.

It was about three feet deep and squared off, obviously not a natural feature. On the other side, she spotted a piece of weathered parchment and scooped it up. It was a treasure map meant for her, but someone had beaten her to it. She stood at the edge wondering if the treasure depicted on the map was a first-come-first-served reward that other contestants could cash in on even though it was in her territory.

Her next thought came after a thump in her chest had knocked the wind out of her. She looked down and wondered why there was an arrow sticking out of her chest, bloody point first. She would never know who shot it, only that it came from behind.

At 12:57pm on Day 12, Jill Hill dropped to her knees and flopped forward, tumbling into the ditch that would serve as her grave if someone would be considerate enough to throw some dirt on her dead body. The camera died next, eventually, as its battery drained while it captured nothing but darkness, lens-down in the dirt.

WES WOOD

Day 12

6:06pm

Age: 57
Occupation: Farmer
Home: Mississippi
Status: Divorced, 8 children

Wes Wood returned from another private excursion and pulled his boat ashore. The producers of the show had encouraged all the contestants to take their cameras everywhere they went and film everything they do, but Wes found it to be an unnecessary nuisance and too time consuming to bother with. He also didn't want anyone to see what he was doing during his daily excursions.

At the end of the day on Day 12, he returned to camp with two dead fish. A watermelon-sized patch of blood covered the forest camouflage pattern on the bib of his overalls. He zipped up his coat before he checked in on camera.

"Finally stopped rainin' so I been tryin' to find dry firewood all day," he said, sitting outside his shelter in a close-up hand-held shot. "There ain't nothin' interestin' about it. There ain't nothin' interestin' much about survival in the woods. The days is borin' when you're stuck in the shelter cuz it's rainin' and it's borin' when it stops rainin' and ya gotta go walkin' around all day findin' firewood."

He scratched his face and spat on the ground, the tail end of the spit sticking to the facial hair on his chin.

"If it don't start rainin' again, tomorrow, I aim to start lookin' fer the treasure. I ain't got around to doing that yet," he told the camera.

He held up one of the dead fish for the camera to see.

"I caught me two fish today, too, down by the water," he explained, as if future viewers might mistakenly think he found the fish in a tree.

"Gotta cut 'em and gut 'em," he sang, emphasizing his rhyming ability. "Gotta git the fire goin' and cook 'em up," he added, getting to his feet.

The camera fell from his hand, a dizzy spell almost knocking him over. He leaned a hand against the shelter, catching his balance, the camera pointing up at him from the ground. He sunk back down to a sitting position, a borderline unconscious look in his eyes.

Breathing heavy, he said in a labored voice, "But, first, I'm gonna set here fer a spell and rest."

Chapter 12

Day 1 minus 10

Rumors and Assignments

"Calm down. We go ahead as planned. We just need to make a few minor adjustments," Sharon Rose explained to Simon Scoff via cellphone. She had to compete with the street noise in a busy section of Los Angeles, on her way to meet with Dean Bates, Executive Producer of Isolation Island. He was the man providing the capital to film the show.

"We'll need to purchase our own equipment," Sharon dictated. "Keep it as cheap as you can. Some crew members will have to be replaced. We need a new survival expert since Greely threw us under the bus." The list of orders went on and on.

She listened to Simon's complaints and objections, but brushed them all off. She was determined to milk the project for as much money as she could.

"I know you have reservations. Just do what I tell you. We're in too deep to back out now. Get the equipment. Get the crew ready and keep your mouth shut," Sharon barked and ended the call without warning.

*****

Dean Bates was a man of questionable integrity, but he was a rich man in a city where money could buy anything he desired. He was the kind of eccentric millionaire you'd suspect of having a private island somewhere on the planet where he brought people against their will so he could hunt them for sport. The forty-nine year old enjoyed projecting such a creepy aura. He thought it made him mysterious.

When Sharon arrived at Dean's office, he was wrapping up a phone call. She pretended she wasn't listening as she sat in a small, rickety chair on the other side of Dean's enormous antique desk.

"We wouldn't use real guns. We could shoot them with paintball guns, but I don't see the harm in having them think it's a real gun. How else could we make the fear look authentic," Dean said to whoever was on the other end of the line. He held a finger in the air, acknowledging Sharon's wait time. "Well, give it some thought and get back to me. It'll be the edgiest show on TV, guaranteed."

The devious smile on his face faded quickly. It was obvious he didn't like what he was hearing. His tone changed to match his face. "Well, if you're too much of a pussy to pull it off, I'll just have to find someone else and you can go fuck yourself," he said and slammed the phone down.

He stood up and approached Sharon with a new smile and open arms. "Well, hello there, Sharon. Aren't you looking especially lovely today," he said, slithering over to her.

Sharon obliged him with a phony Hollywood hug which Dean held for an inappropriately long time. It wasn't the first sign of his physical interest in her, but Sharon was willing to put up with it for the money he was putting up to finance Isolation Island. She couldn't withhold a cringe as the hug seemed more like a grope from the creepy millionaire.

"Sit, sit," he said, as if commanding a dog. "I hope you're here to tell me the rumors aren't true."

"What rumors?" Sharon asked, playing dumb. She knew full well what rumors he was talking about.

"People are telling me the network is pulling the plug on Isolation Island."

"Oh, that was just a misunderstanding. Seems Nelson Greely, the so-called survival expert chickened out because he thought it was too dangerous. Not to worry, though. He's easily replaced. I met with Arthur Mallory and we still have the green light. We're still on schedule."

"The survival expert chickened out?" Nelson asked, improvising a new idea. "Hey, we could use that when we advertise the show. I can see it now—a survival contest so rugged, so dangerous that even self-proclaimed survival expert Nelson Greely didn't have the balls to undertake."

"That's certainly one way to go," Sharon said in true yes-man fashion. She had been playing Dean Bates all along, knowing he knew nothing about the entertainment industry. Dean was a patsy with pockets full of cash and Sharon was desperate enough to pick those pockets. She had a list full of excuses ready for when he inevitably finds out the network really did pull out of Isolation Island. Knowing Dean's penchant for putting people in extreme conditions like plastic game pieces, she actually considered telling him the network pulled the plug just to see if he would finance the endeavor just to watch people struggle and compete for his own amusement.

"I can't wait to see the finished product," Dean gushed with a sick excitement. "And, I've got some interesting ideas for Season Two. What if we purchased some lions and let them loose on the island?" he suggested like a mischievous child out of control.

Sharon did her best to keep her eyes from bugging out of her head. "Let's see how Season One goes first. There'll be plenty of time to discuss the future of the show later."

With his bubble burst, Dean folded his hands on the desk in front of him and took a professional tone. "So, if everything is a go, why did you insist on seeing me today?" he asked.

"I just wanted to reassure you that everything was going smoothly. There's just one wrinkle I wanted to run by you."

"What's that?"

"The contestant you hand-selected, Wes Wood. It turns out he was a suspect in a series of murders in Mississippi. Did you know that?" Sharon asked.

"I know," Dean said, the sinister grin returning to his face. "Won't that be an interesting twist?" he added, rubbing his hands together, reveling in the idea.

Sharon masked her revulsion for Dean and his psychotic ideas once again and left in a hurry, pretending to be late for another appointment. She always made a point of not staying long enough for him to start making passes at her. She was in and out in less than the ten minutes she had allotted.

*****

Sharon hurried back to her car which she had parked a few blocks away so that no one from Bates's office would see it. She often rented a Mercedes to bring to business meetings to create the illusion of success, but her actual car was an old, broken-down Toyota Camry. She gave a vigilant look in each direction before getting in, her phone ringing as the door creaked open.

"Now what?" she answered, knowing it was Simon again according to her Caller ID.

"Hutchinson What-a-wolf?" she asked, seemingly annoyed at the number of syllables in Hutch's name. "Oh, wait, I think I've heard of him. Can't you find anyone cheaper?"

Sharon paused for a lengthy explanation she seemed too impatient to let continue.

"I don't care how much experience they have," she interjected.

Another short pause came as Simon continued to voice his concerns.

"Listen, keep looking and put this Hutchington guy on the back burner as a last resort," Sharon said before hanging up without saying goodbye.

EZRA GREER

Day 13

9:59am

Age: 51
Occupation: Truck Driver
Home: Alaska
Status: Widower, 3 children

"There's something about eating meat off a bone. It provides some kind of primitive satisfaction," Ezra Greer explained to the filming camera. He was chewing the meat off the leg of a grouse he had shot with an arrow. Even the tiniest shred of meat was picked clean by the hungry survivalist.

Ezra had been doing well hunting, fishing, and trapping enough food to continue hunting, fishing, and trapping. The irony of thriving was that it burned a lot of energy, but Ezra knew how to get the most out of his harvest.

Holding up the bare bone for the camera to see, he said, "I'm not done with this bone yet. I'll take all the bones from this bird and boil them to make a delicious broth."

He snapped the leg bone with his hands before tossing them into the cooking pot. "It's easier to get the benefits of the marrow if you break the bones open."

He sat back and started on another leg, talking to the camera like a friend. "This competition is more than a contest for a million dollars. Although I'd really love to win the money, I don't want it to be easy. I'd hate for everyone else to tap out quickly. I want to really test myself and see how long I can do this for. Could I live like this forever? I think so, if I absolutely had to. But, do I *want* to live like this forever? That's an entirely different question I hope to find an answer to."

2:32pm

Ezra Greer turned on the camera mounted to his chest. With controlled breaths, he whispered, "Look at the size of that bear."

Fifty yards away, on the other side of a stream, a full-grown black bear sniffed around, turning over rocks and vacuuming up the worms and insects hiding beneath.

Ezra remained in a crouching position, bow and arrow in hand, but this wasn't the animal he had hoped to hunt.

"I'm almost tempted to take a shot, but it's too risky. I doubt I could take down a three hundred pound bear with an arrow from this distance. At most, I'd hit him and he'd run away and I'd lose my arrow. Then again, he could get pissed off and come after me. Either way, it doesn't spell dinner for me, so, I'm just going to leave him alone, find another place to hunt."

3:20pm

"There are still animals among us humans," Ezra told the camera from a rocky shore where he had been gathering mussels and limpets in his pot of seawater. They were meant to be added to the grouse broth for dinner. He had set up a camera on the tripod to capture the 'action'.

He sat on a boulder watching the waves crash, striking up a conversation with future viewers. "When I was in prison, I'd see these guys all the time. They can't control themselves. They act on impulses like animals do. You hear these guys talk about how they were just walking down the street one day, saw a woman, and decided to rape and kill her. And I'm like—how can a human not have something within them that says, 'No. Don't do that.' Do these people really lack something to stop them from committing heinous acts of violence? Why do they act like they have to obey the voices in their head? It's not all that complicated to choose not to rape someone. But, there's more to it than that. Raping and murdering isn't easy. A lot of effort is involved. These people have to really enjoy it. I think they're full of crap when they act like they don't know why they did it."

Ezra paused, contemplating his own line of thought. He had lived side by side with the type of people he was talking about. For over a decade he had analyzed them, formed hypotheses, and reconsidered those hypotheses. The memories continued to haunt him. The only way he could deal with it was to keep thinking until he had some answers that made sense to him.

"They're animals. If there's nothing within you that can stop you from raping and/or killing someone, you are an animal, plain and simple. That's why we have to keep these guys in cages. And they still don't get it. If you find yourself locked in a cage at any point in your life, you have to take a good hard look at yourself. These animals in prison don't do that. They get more violent, lash out, rape each other, beat each other up, kill each other—they get *more* animalistic."

He shook his head, trying to dodge a barrage of haunting memories from his time in prison. The attacks on him. The years he spent in solitary confinement voluntarily to avoid the other inmates.

"I understand the whole thing about how locking people in cages could be the cause, but not everyone who gets locked in a cage turns into an animal. I was in solitary for most of my time and I didn't turn into an animal."

Ezra smiled and gave the camera a strange look.

"Although, if you're watching me now, in this contest, you might actually make the argument that I *have* turned into an animal—living in the woods, killing to survive."

His face turned serious again, flooded with deep thought and self-evaluation. He twiddled a handful of small rocks therapeutically.

"But, one of the things that separates us from 'animals' is that animals have no remorse for killing. But, *I* do. I feel bad every time I kill something to eat."

He chucked one of the flat rocks, skipping it across the water until it got eaten by a wave.

"And," he added, "I still have a short list of animals I wouldn't eat because I like them too much. Dogs, cats, turtles, penguins...well, that's about it. I'd eat anything else I could think of right about now. Well, maybe not a koala bear or a sloth, either, but there's none of those on Isolation Island. I think that counts for something, though. The ability to make friends with animals of another species has to be some sort of positive evolutionary advancement."

He waited for another calm interval between waves to skip another rock. It hopped across the surface seven times—a new personal record. Filling time by the ocean with only his mind, a few rocks and a camera seemed calming but his brain was in overdrive. After years in solitary, he had learned to entertain himself by jumping from one deep thought to another, but there was always the risk of ending up in dark corners. Other times, he just bounced from topic to topic as the sparks went off in his head.

"I once had a religious person ask me, since I don't believe in god, what's stopping me from raping and killing people all I want. This was before I ended up in prison. That was disturbing because, to ask a question like that, I had to think that guy must walk around all day with the overwhelming urge to rape and murder people and the only thing stopping him is the threat of god's punishment, or judgement, or whatever. I have to wonder if that's normal for religious people and I'm the odd one for not having such thoughts. It's scary. Human society scares me more than anything. I'd rather be out here with the wild, four-legged animals."

His head dropped to his hands, mentally exhausted. His voice cracked and whined amid tears. "I don't want to go back to civilization. There's nothing that appeals to me back there anymore. I don't like anything about it anymore. So, yes, maybe I can stay out here forever and maybe I *want* to stay out here forever."

He lifted his head and wiped away a sniffle, recomposing himself. "Well, not necessarily here, but out in the wilderness somewhere. Preferably somewhere warmer."

STEPHANIE HAMILTON

Day 13

11:30am

Age: 29
Occupation: Artist
Home: Colorado
Status: Single

"It's Day 13 and I'm still alive," Stephanie Hamilton reported to the camera in her high-pitched but pleasantly soothing voice which seemed to be in tune with the background noises of nature. Her attempt to sound dire and distressed failed, betrayed by a smile she couldn't quite hold back.

"I slept late this morning because, well, I felt like it. Plus, there's nothing I have to do today. I'll check my traps for food, but I've got fish and meat smoking in my handy, dandy smokehouse," she explained.

Stephanie had converted her temporary shelter into a smokehouse to preserve fish and meat while discouraging scavengers. She turned the camera for a shot of it. Smoke seeped out through the intentional cracks in the roof.

"I'm thinking of building a little sauna or a sweat lodge. It's been getting colder every day since that long rain storm."

Turning the camera back on her, she sat back, relaxing in her wooden chair, enjoying a second steaming cup of coffee. She only allowed herself one cup per day to ration it, but she decided today would be a day of leisure—a day to relax, reflect, and enjoy. One extra cup of coffee wouldn't break the bank. It was made from reused coffee grounds anyway. It was weak, but relaxing and sipping it slowly on a lazy day gave her time to stop and smell the roses.

"I'm not doing any work today. I've been keeping myself busy with projects and food gathering all day, every day and I'm set up pretty well now, barring any unforeseen circumstances."

She paused to blow on her coffee, holding the cup with both hands, the steam rising to warm her cold nose.

"I don't want this experience to go by without stopping to really appreciate it. I may never have a chance to do anything like this again. Being out here, surrounded by nature, it's so calming. This is the part of the contest I'm really going to enjoy. I can tone down my work load and focus on what I love about being here. I think that's the key to winning this contest. I'm not going to think about the things I miss or anything I don't like about being out here."

In Stephanie's corner of the island, there wasn't much to hate. The contestants had been assigned their insertion points at random, but some spots were better than others. Stephanie was lucky enough to land on prime real estate—her own, private peninsula 'fenced off' by the cliffs and waterfalls behind her camp.

"I'm more of a realist than an optimist. I have a positive mental attitude," she said, using two fingers on one hand to put *positive mental attitude* in air quotes. "But, I don't use it to delude myself. I'm not going to pretend there aren't animals out here that would like to eat me. I know it's dangerous out here. To me a positive attitude just means focusing on the good things, rather than dwelling on the negative things. You can't be in denial, pretending everything is peaches and cream. You have to focus on the positives and let go of the negatives. Stressing and worrying doesn't do any good. Beating yourself up over past mistakes is useless and self-defeating. I prefer to roll around in the flower petals of positivity than waste one breath fanning the flames of pessimism. It's the same attitude I've always had back home. It's always worked for me. So, there's no reason to change for this environment. The more I can make this like home, the longer I'll want to stay."

She raised a finger to emphasize her point. "That's an important part of my strategy. I didn't come here to see how long I can suffer. I came to see how long I can enjoy the ride."

The bubbly survivor finished her last sip of coffee, closing her eyes to savor it all the more. A decompressing sigh followed, the perfect soundtrack for a lazy day.

"I know what I'm going to do today," she said, a tinge of

excitement in her voice. "I'm going to make a ukulele. I can carve out a piece of wood and use fishing line for the strings. I've never tried it before, but I think it'll be fun. It'll give me something to do that's not on a deadline or imperative for my survival."

Stephanie cleaned up, shut off the camera and walked off into the forest to find a suitable piece of wood to make an instrument.

DERRICK BOND

Day 13

11:58am

Age: 29
Occupation: ex-Marine
Home: Texas
Status: Single

Derrick Bond sat motionless beside the fire pit in front of the camera.

"This is always a difficult day for me. I knew it would be especially difficult coming into this competition," he droned, devoid of emotion.

A tear escaped his eye. He wiped it away, obscuring his face, trying to hide it from the camera. A deep breath, meant to cleanse and reset himself, quivered instead, threatening his balancing act on the edge of a breakdown. He looked away from the camera all together.

"Today is the...anniversary...I hate using that word when I talk about today. My mother murdered my father on this day, eighteen years ago," he edited.

The statement hung in the air as Derrick wiped more tears from his eyes. Each breath produced a sniffle. "I can't remember the last time I said that out loud. It's not something you want to share with anyone. I'm always afraid people will see me differently if they know. It's...I don't think *embarrassing* is the right word for it. Maybe *shame* is a more accurate word. Which is messed up because I didn't do anything wrong. Still, I usually opt to tell people my parents are both dead rather than admit my mother is in jail serving a life sentence for murdering my father."

Derrick steeled himself and looked straight at the camera for a moment, but he couldn't hold it. Looking away, he scratched his chin, the heavy stubble audible after almost two weeks of not shaving.

"People see these types of stories all the time, but they never seem to think about the ruined lives left behind. What happens to the children of parents who kill each other?"

His legs turned antsy, his discomfort with talking about it building, but it was a part of him that would be there forever. The camera was becoming an intimate companion after almost two weeks and he felt the need to open up. He was more than a faceless soldier. There was an injured child and lonely heart under all the weapons and camouflage.

"I'll tell you what happens to the children. They grow up to be like me, fucked up in the head, depressed, full of guilt and shame. Your mother is supposed to love you and protect you, not murder your father. How can someone do that to their own kids? How does a mother murder the father of her own child? I was only eleven at the time, but I knew there was no good reason—if there's such a thing as a *good* reason. My father was a saint. My dad was my hero. He was a Marine. He never raised a hand to me or my mother. All he did was love us and take care of us, but that wasn't enough for my mother. She killed him for the insurance money, planning to use it to run away with some guy she was cheating on my dad with. Two hundred thousand dollars. It's not even that much money, but it was more than my father's life was worth to mom. It was all *my* life was worth to her. I visited her in prison, once, on my eighteenth birthday. I don't even know why I went there. I was planning on joining the Marines, following in my father's footsteps, and because I was only eleven when it all happened, I never had the opportunity to confront her. I had been offered the opportunity as I got older, but I never wanted to speak to her again. I wanted to pretend I never had a mother."

Derrick bowed his head, pulling his wool hat down over his eyes, trying to hide, his body language becoming more animated, putting his agitation on display.

"She had the nerve to tell me she did it for me. She wanted to use the insurance money to give *me* a better life. What a fucking bitch. Who does that? I told her to go to hell. I told her she'd never see me or hear from me again. And here I am, on the anniversary of my father's murder, hiding in the forest on a remote island. Hiding from my fucked up life, trying to find a way to move on.

This game is not the reset button I was looking for. It's harder than I could have ever imagined. I've been to war, but war keeps your mind occupied. All you're thinking about is the enemy and keeping your friends alive. Out here, you're stuck with your own mind and all your past troubles bubble up over and over. There's nothing to do but dwell on it."

Derrick went silent for a full minute, his eyes indicating he was somewhere in his own head, in a memory or a dream.

"I can't change what happened, but sometimes…" he said, pausing because he was too choked up. His second attempt was less emotional. "Sometimes I wish she had killed him *before* I was born. How am I supposed to go on? How am I supposed to have a normal relationship with anyone?"

His eyes teared up all over again.

Looking right into the camera, he asked, "How can you ever trust anyone in your life ever again, when your own mother killed your father?"

1:23pm

Derrick Bond froze in place in the middle of the forest on his way back from gathering firewood, startled by a noise behind him. The camera on his hat scanned the woods along with his own eyes.

"Hey, bear," he said in a deep, confident voice, but he was anything but confident.

"I swear I feel like I'm being followed all day or watched," he whispered to the camera. "Maybe I'm being stalked by a hungry bear. It's really giving me the creeps. Every time I hear something, I turn to look and there's nothing there. Maybe this place is haunted or something."

He gave a last look behind him, all around, and moved on, sneaking through the forest as quietly as possible. His ears were on alert for unwanted sounds.

"I'm not tapping out. I am *not* tapping out," Derrick whispered, repeating his mantra for encouragement. It didn't stop the constant tic in his face acquired in the meltdown after the rainstorm.

"I'm losing it. I'm fucking losing it," he said, more to himself than to the camera.

A head rush almost knocked him over. He dropped his bundle of wood on his own feet but no pain seemed to register. Hugging the nearest tree, he checked behind him as he rested and regained his bearings.

"Hey," he hollered to the woods behind him and held his breath, expecting an answer.

"Something's following me," he claimed again.

A loud rustling coming towards him made his heart jump, but it was only two squirrels chasing each other through the leaf litter. They took the chase up a pine tree and disappeared.

"Maybe I'm just losing my mind. Isn't paranoia one of the signs that you're losing your mind? Maybe I'm just hungry. I need to get some protein in me," he guessed and reasoned.

His cloudy head wasn't cooperating. Derrick hadn't eaten in days. What little surplus food he had was gone before the rain stopped and he had no luck hunting or fishing after the rain stopped.

He made a mental note of his location, planning to return with a trap to capture the squirrels, but the round trip would require a lot of energy. Energy he didn't have.

He picked up half the firewood he had dropped and shuffled back to camp, but there was one more pit stop he had to make.

"I got one more trap to check along this trail," he explained to the camera between labored breaths. "I hope to god there's something in it. I don't care if it's a rat. I'll eat anything at this point."

He almost smiled, seeing the trap from afar. "Hey, look at that." It was simple snare trap and it looked like something had was caught in it.

"Oh, no. What the hell, man?" Derrick moaned, approaching the trap. He looked down and all around in every direction.

A squirrel's head was still caught by the neck in the trap, but the body was gone. Blood stained the ground around the severed head.

"This is bullshit. Look at that," he complained, pointing the camera to document the theft. "I trapped a squirrel, but I got robbed," he summarized.

Upon closer inspection, he paused for a moment. It didn't make sense to his slowed mind. He sprung up, head darting in every direction.

"This doesn't look like the work of animals. This squirrel's head looks like it was cut off with a knife and...I know I didn't do it."

He knelt down for another look. Holding the squirrel's head in one hand, he poked around the neck, lifting the fur. Even the camera could see it was a clean cut.

Dropping the severed head, Derrick threw his hands up, saying, "Okay, that is messed up. Nobody told me there'd be other people here stealing my food."

He scratched his head through his hat, causing the camera to wiggle.

"It can't be. The whole point of Isolation Island is to be isolated. It looks like this squirrel's head was cut off by a knife, but to be honest, I don't know what I'd expect it to look like if it got chewed off by an animal. Still, though, you'd think the animal would have eaten the head, too."

Derrick gave the area another onceover to appease his paranoid mind and scurried off with his firewood.

11:58pm

"I been trying to fill my stomach up with water to ease the hunger pains," Derrick explained to the handheld camera. It lit the way for him through the darkness. "I don't know if it really helps any, but it makes me have to pee every few hours."

He was only a few feet away from the edge of his camp at his designated "Peeing Tree" when he saw it way in the distance.

"What the heck?" he asked, unable to stop the flow of urine.

He squinted a better look and decided, "Either I've totally lost it or there's a flashlight shining out there."

He turned off the camera's light to better catch the faint beam lighting up the fine evening mist. A tiny, glowing ball waved around, disappearing and reappearing from behind bushes and trees as it 'walked' through the forest toward Derrick and his camp.

"Heeeyyy!" he shouted, instinctively, happy to see signs of human life.

The glowing ball steadied and turned to shine in his direction. He couldn't see anything beyond the light, but he had no reason to be alarmed.

"It must be the producers," Derrick told the camera. "I wonder what they want. Hey, maybe I won. Maybe it's over."

He shook off, zipped up, and started creeping cautiously toward the light. After a few steps, it disappeared and the forest went dark, the narrow crescent of moon barely creating a dim shade.

Derrick furrowed his brow and turned on his camera's light again, but the beam didn't penetrate far enough to see more than six feet in front of him.

"Hey," he tried hollering again. "Over here."

Crunching his way back to the beaten trail he knew was there, he kept his light shining on the spot he last saw the glow of the flashlight. He tried switching to night vision but the camera's screen only displayed a hazy, dark green blur beyond ten feet.

He continued to call out, following the trail, hoping to meet up with whoever the flashlight belonged to.

"I wonder if it's another contestant by any chance," he said in a hushed tone to the camera. "We're not supposed to have contact with each other, but maybe the edge of our territory is overlapping. That would explain my stolen squirrel, but in my mind, raiding someone else's trap is cheating, even worse than making contact with another person. That's probably why they're not responding."

Derrick proceeded to march over to the son of a bitch who stole his squirrel, now more focused on confronting him and getting him disqualified. If it turned out to be the producers of the show coming to talk to him, he was prepared to make a formal complaint about other contestants encroaching on his territory and stealing his food.

When he got to the spot he estimated the flashlight beam came from, there was no one there and no indication anyone had been there. Derrick looked up and down the trail. He directed his light into the woods doing two laps in a circle.

Nothing.

"What the heck?" he complained to the camera. "The light was definitely coming from somewhere around here."

He pointed the camera up the trail, trying night vision again. Nothing.

His ears perked up. Holding his breath, he turned his head catching a sound coming from behind him. Footsteps were coming his way. He whipped around, pointing the camera in the direction of the noise, but he was blinded by a flashlight that suddenly pierced through the darkness.

"Holy shit, you scared the hell out of me," Derrick gasped, holding a hand up to shield his eyes from the intrusive brightness.

Flicking his camera's light back on, he tried to get a look at who was holding the flashlight and how many of them were there, but the camera smashed in his hand. Stricken by a large stone, the light and lens broke, almost knocking the camera out of his hand.

"What the fuck?" he barked, the flashlight coming to a stop several feet away.

The hooded figure behind the light didn't reply. Derrick squinted, his pupils not responding to the brightness fast enough to make out much, but he did see the head of an axe rear up over the figure's hood.

It all seemed to happen in slow motion. Derrick's eyes bugged out of his skull. In a split-second his fight or flight reflex took over. He turned around and ran as the axe came down, just nicking the back of his bulky parka. He didn't even take the time to scream. He sprinted away, trying to navigate through the dark forest, the useless camera still in his hand. His instinct whispered a plan to use it as a throwing weapon of last resort.

The figure with the flashlight seemed to bounce through the woods, falling behind because of Derrick's head start.

Derrick hurled through the forest, tripping on a log while running at full speed. He tumbled to the ground, bowling over and springing back to his feet almost as if the stunt had been choreographed. He lost the camera in the process, but it didn't slow him down much. He continued to sprint until he couldn't sprint anymore.

Checking his six, he slowed to a jog. The light was still hot on his tail, the carrier invisible in the darkness.

A plan formed in the ex-Marine's head as he slowed. What

little energy he had in reserve was tapped out, but if he could make it to the Treasure Tree, perhaps he could guide his pursuer to fall into one of the deep holes he had dug.

It wasn't the best plan, but it was something. It gave him a decisive direction to go. It might have even worked had he not began to stall as he got there. His will was strong, but his body gave out after thirteen days of meager rations.

The light caught up to him in the clearing where the Treasure Tree grew. The blunt end of an axe smashed the back of his head, sending him to the ground.

It didn't knock him out, but his head spun as he flipped over and looked up at his assailant. The darkness under the hood revealed nothing. There was no face—just a black ski mask—but there was a scream. More like a bloodcurdling shriek harmonizing with a deep roar. It formed no words. It didn't respond to any of Derrick's pleas and questions.

"Stop. Why are you doing this?" Derrick cried out, unable to register what was happening. "Don't," he groaned, his own voice sounding like a slur in his injured mind. He didn't have the strength to fight back. His head was too woozy to move at all.

Out of the corner of his eye, a pant leg flashed by. The forest camouflage pattern oddly soothed him before his eyes closed for the last time.

He felt the cordage being wrapped around his neck. Not an ounce of strength was left in his body to resist being dragged and hoisted up.

Derrick's mind began a death protocol the whole world is familiar with. His life flashed before his eyes but not the bad things. He didn't recall anything about the wars, death, or destruction he had seen and been a part of. There was only peace as the body's natural, calming neurotransmitters worked their magic. It showed him the bright light and made him feel like he was leaving his body. He didn't look back as he floated off into the warm calm of death, his carcass left behind, dangling near the empty hole the treasure had been buried in.

Chapter 13

Day 17

Watch Your Head

"How could she disappear in broad daylight?" Page asked as if they were back home in public on a busy street when Sharon disappeared.

"Don't panic. She's probably just going to the bathroom," Doc guessed, trying to remain optimistic.

"She better hurry up," Hutch grumbled. "We need to get moving. We've got to round up all the contestants. Page, get on the radio. Contact each contestant and tell them what's been going on. Full disclosure." He pounced on the opportunity to give the order while Sharon wasn't around to object. "Tell them to be on the lookout for any unannounced humans or predators. They should carry their radio and a weapon with them at all times…"

Page pulled out her radio before Hutch finished barking orders but not to follow his instructions. "Sharon? Where are you?" she asked on the channel designated for the crew. They waited, but there was no reply. She threw an annoyed look in Hutch's direction. "Why isn't she answering her radio?" she asked before making a second attempt.

No one had a good answer. Doc picked a direction at random and began calling out for Sharon while Hutch searched Floyd's camp for new clues—drag marks, a piece of torn clothing, blood, anything to indicate Sharon had been taken against her will or harmed. He found nothing.

Fixed on the small pile of treasure items, Hutch asked, "Is that all the treasure?"

Page replied, "There's more, but we couldn't carry it all."

Hutch walked off into the forest without another word leaving Page and Doc to share a look of concern. They resumed calling out for Sharon.

Hutch returned a minute later with a long, straight stick. He sat next to the fire and worked on sharpening the tip to make a spear, good for keeping predators at a distance or for use as a throwing weapon.

Page watched him, lips pursed in a display of disgust. "You can't be serious. You plan on protecting us with a pointy stick?" she asked sarcastically.

"You have a better idea? Something or someone is lurking in the forest, killing contestants and now Sharon is gone. We're not going out looking for her unarmed. A long, pointy stick is better than nothing," he explained.

They weren't exactly unarmed. They had a knife, a hatchet, bear spray, a bow and arrows, among other potential weapons, but there was no harm in adding a spear to the mix. It was also the quickest weapon to make. Hutch was done in a few minutes.

"Let's go," he said, marching past Page.

"Go where?" she asked.

Hutch stopped and huffed. He wasn't a fan of stupid questions. "To look for Sharon," he said, nearly biting her head off.

"Where?" she demanded. Apparently, she knew they were going to look for Sharon. "How do you know where to start looking," she clarified.

"I don't," Hutch said, walking toward the animal trail which led to the treasure. "But, we've got to start somewhere and we've got to get the rest of the supplies from the treasure so, we might as well start there." He handed the spear to Doc. "You know what to do with this, right? If something's coming at us, you just keep it at a distance and I'll do the rest."

"We just came from the treasure," Page protested. "We would have noticed her."

"Not if whoever took her was trying to avoid you," Hutch explained. "Doc, you go first. You know the way. Page, you stay in the middle and I'll watch our backs."

Doc was smart enough to let Hutch run the show just as he'd expect Hutch to step aside in a medical emergency and let the expert take the lead.

The search for Sharon along the path to the treasure turned up nothing. They weren't just looking for Sharon. They were looking for any sign of her. The only indication of activity came when they reached the open treasure chest and discovered the remaining items had disappeared.

"What the hell?" Page complained. "They took our stuff, too?"

Hutch scanned the woods hoping for a trail to follow. Something wasn't right and it was gnawing at him. "How well do you know Sharon," he asked Page.

"Well enough, but she doesn't tell me everything."

"Doc?" Hutch redirected the same question.

"I was hired at the last minute, like you," Doc answered.

"Do you think Sharon would be stupid enough to go off on her own?" Hutch asked.

Doc shrugged his shoulders but Page answered, "No way. She wouldn't be that stupid. I know she can be…difficult. She doesn't always make the best decisions, but she's as scared as I am. I can tell. She just didn't want to show it. She might have returned to camp by now. I should have stayed behind to wait for her."

"No. From now on, no splitting up. We stay together, no matter what. If you have to pee, we'll guard you," Hutch dictated.

"Terrific," Page grumbled.

"What items were left behind?" Hutch asked.

Doc was quick to answer. "We took all the food, blankets and toilet paper. That leaves the hammock, building materials and…" He was crestfallen at the thought of the last item.

"And?" Hutch urged him on.

"There was a set of knives, too."

"A set of knives?" Hutch asked in disbelief. "You left behind a set of knives?"

"I thought you and I would come back for it and take the whole chest to camp. We could use it for firewood if nothing else," Doc explained, not defending his actions but laying out his reasoning.

"Great," Hutch sighed. "There's a killer on the loose and he has a brand-new set of knives." He took a last look around, but there was no indication of which way the thief had gone. "Well, this was a wasted trip. Let's take a different route back. Keep your eyes peeled."

"Shouldn't we take the chest?" Doc asked.

Hutch replied, "There's no point. We're not staying at Floyd's camp very long."

Doc and Page shared a look. "Why not?" they asked in unison.

"Our number one priority is gathering the contestants together. We can't leave them on their own for the killer to pick them off one by one," Hutch explained. "Our chances of survival are much higher if we all work together."

Hutch turned to Page who was inching her way around, looking into the woods. "Remember what I told you to do, Page? You need to start alerting the contestants now."

"Do you really think that's the best idea? We don't want them to panic," Page resisted.

"No. Do *not* suggest that garbage to me. Absolutely not. We're not doing that 'let's not worry the others' bullshit. You don't lie to people to protect them from a threat," Hutch roared. "You warn them of the threat. You prepare them for the threat," Hutch rattled off like it was part of some survivalist code of conduct.

"You're right, but we don't know what the threat is, exactly," Doc chimed in.

"We know someone stole our boat. We know someone is on the loose, murdering contestants and stealing things. Is that not enough information?" Hutch argued.

"What would we tell everyone?" Page asked. "We don't know what to tell them to look out for."

"We tell them not to trust anyone aboard the Medline, for starters. Then we take the time to tell them everything we know," Hutch answered without hesitation.

"Sharon wouldn't want that," Page argued. "She would want the contest to go on at all costs."

"Sharon's not here anymore, is she?" Hutch snapped. "Even if she was, I don't give a rat's ass what she wants anymore."

"Just because Sharon's gone, doesn't mean you're automatically in charge," Page protested.

"You're right. Even if she was here, I'd *still* be in charge," Hutch barked. He turned to Doc who was doing his best not to interfere. "Is that alright with you, Doc?" It was a genuine question, rather than a threat or bullying technique. Hutch and Doc had a mutual, professional respect for each other.

"That's fine by me," Doc said, nodding his approval eagerly.

"There. It's unanimous," Hutch said. "Are you going to

contact the contestants or do I have to do it myself?" he asked Page.

"What if one of them is the killer?" Page continued to argue. "We don't want them to know we're onto them."

"Who cares? Until we know who or what is responsible for the deaths, we have to treat each contestant as a target, not a suspect," Hutch countered and turned to Doc for support. "How would you like to be out here, thinking you're alone, but there's a killer lurking in the woods that no one bothered to tell you about?"

Doc couldn't argue with that logic. Perspective flips easily when you're in someone else's shoes. "You're right. I'd rather know about it," he conceded.

Hutch led the way this time, Doc bringing up the rear in his place. It wasn't the first time they were reduced to wandering the forest, yelling out a missing person's name, but there was a lot less confidence this time.

Page began the task of warning each of the contestants of the added danger and the apparent murders, leaving out specific details. As Hutch instructed, she ordered everyone to stay put, carry a weapon at all times and keep their radios with them at all times. She also reported Sharon's disappearance, telling everyone—if they see Sharon with someone, don't trust that person.

"This is stupid," Page complained to Hutch after she was done fielding questions from the first contestant, Stephanie Hamilton. "If someone took Sharon, they have her radio, too. So, they can hear everything I'm saying."

"If the killer is one of the contestants, he's had a radio all along," Hutch countered. "Make sure you report to the missing contestants' radios, as well. They might not be able to answer us but maybe they can hear us."

Page obviously didn't like the idea, but she did as she was told, starting with the female contestants and stalling as much as possible. Next up was Zoey Price, whose radio had perished in a fire. Unknown to Page, the warning couldn't be heard.

Not far from Floyd's camp, Hutch spotted something in the distance and stopped. "Try calling Sharon again," he ordered, holding up a hand to stop and silence his crew.

Page followed his orders, her voice echoing from up ahead as she spoke into the radio. There was no sign of Sharon except for a curious swatch of pink which was what had caught Hutch's eye from afar.

They approached with caution, led by Hutch while he watched out for indications that it could be a trap. Nearing the pink which stood out in the brownish leaf litter, they discovered an unsettling scene.

It was Sharon's pink panties on the ground, left behind, along with her shoes, pants, and radio. Upon closer inspection, Hutch found signs of a struggle—broken off bits of Sharon's fake painted nails peppered a bloody area a few feet away.

Page hid her face in Dr. Rodney's chest. Peeking at the evidence with one eye, she said, "Well, this narrows down our search for the murderer. It's obviously a man, if there was any doubt."

"What makes you say that?" Hutch asked.

"Her pants and panties were torn off. She was probably raped," Page speculated.

"Not necessarily. Maybe, she pulled her pants down to squat and pee when she was attacked. She might not even be dead," Hutch countered. "Look, she put up a fight." He pointed to the broken nails and drag marks. "Whatever it was, it dragged her off in that direction," he added, pointing deeper into the forest, away from Floyd's camp.

They followed the trail of broken branches and drag marks until they disappeared, a disturbing puddle of blood in their place. It was too much blood to imagine someone could have lost it and survived, but it provided a new trail to follow. The blood trail led them further away from camp and then dried up. They kept searching but they couldn't find any more traces.

"That's it," Hutch said. "The trail's gone."

"That can't be it," Page argued. "Let's keep going."

"No. We should head back to camp," Hutch said.

"Head back to camp? We can't just leave her here," Page protested.

"We can't waste any more time or energy. With the amount of blood we found..." he trailed off, hesitating to announce the obvious. "We need to get out of here. Keep alerting the contestants. Tucker Jordan's territory is closest. We need to check on him next."

Before they could act, their radios came to life. It was Kimmie Arden and she sounded stressed out.

"Hello. This is Kimmie Arden. I'm tapping out. Come get me immediately," she insisted. "Can anybody hear me? Please hurry. Over."

"I hear you, Kimmie. What's wrong?" Page asked, detecting fear in her voice—not what was expected from someone making a calm, rational decision to leave the game.

"Please, get me out of here as soon as possible," Kimmie repeated with a desperate whine. "I...I found something."

# ZOEY PRICE

Day 15

7:25am

Age: 24
Occupation: Dance Instructor
Home: Montana
Status: Single

Zoey Price trudged through the heavy morning fog. Setting out early, she was eager to cover a lot of ground, hoping to make up for wasted time. Unfortunately, the thick, low-lying fog was slowing her down.

"This is thick as pea soup," she complained to the imaginary camera, her stomach rumbling at the mere mention of food. Each heavy breath seemed to add to the fog. It was difficult to distinguish the river from the trail. She decided to veer away from the river in hopes of increased visibility, but she tripped and fell, knocking over a pile of rocks.

Her kneecap knocked against the stones, giving her a jolt of pain. She flipped over and propped herself up on her arms, eyes bulging when she saw what she had tripped over. Only one tower remained from the Triplets rock sculpture she had made the first week on Isolation Island. The others were toppled over, but she recognized them right away.

Her frustration rang out through the fog. "Aaaaahhhhhhh!" Realizing she had walked in a big circle, she bellowed her frustration over and over, pounding the ground with her fists like a two year-old throwing a tantrum. But, what else could she have expected to happen given the route she had chosen?

"Dammit. I can't believe this. I'm so stupid," she scolded, pounding the sides of her head in panic and frustration.

It took a while to calm down, the wet ground urging her to get up. She brushed the debris off her butt, explaining to the nonexistent camera, "I should have realized the river I was following was the same river near my camp. I should have, at least, crossed to the other side, but it looked pretty treacherous over there."

She shook her head, rubbing her eyes with the palms of her gloved hands.

"I can't believe this. I just wasted…I don't know how many days…walking in a stupid circle," she said with a sniffle.

Her instinct was to breakdown and cry in a pitiful display so future viewers would know the pain and frustration she was feeling. That would never happen since she didn't have a real camera. Instead, she sucked it up and composed herself, a new, fierce look in her eyes.

"Okay…okay. I'm okay. I'm still alive. I can't let this stop me. So, I walked in a giant circle. So what? Now I know which direction to go," the renewed Zoey said, forcing herself to be positive.

She laughed at a new realization "So much for letting the stupid stars guide me. I've been out here, what? Two weeks? It didn't take long out in the wild to find out everything I was raised to believe is a stupid load of horseshit. It's my mother's fault. She was really into astrology. She's the one that taught me about it. When my father up and left us, she said it was all in the stars, as if these little balls of light billions of light years away somehow controlled the fate of everything on Earth. Everything that ever happened to me, she blamed it on the stars. I was looking for real answers. Instead, she taught me to dismiss everything as fate."

She continued as she walked toward her original camp, looking up at an imaginary camera periodically as she explained, "Going through all this, all the hardships, all the highs and lows, I'm realizing something else. I may have made some poor choices. I walked in a big circle, but I'm surviving out here *by myself*. Any way you slice it, I've survived on Isolation Island for over two weeks with minimal equipment. This was all me. The stars have nothing to do with it. There aren't any magic powers in the universe controlling what happens to one pathetic little creature on one pathetic little planet in the corner of the universe. The magic is within us. It's within me. And it's not magic. It's simply a condition we call life. The will to survive. I *will* survive. I can make it another two weeks if I have to."

7:48am

Zoey checked in on her old camp, hoping to find something useful she may have left behind or, better yet—signs the producers were looking for her. The camp looked just as she had left it, with the exception of having been rained on for days. There was nothing left to salvage.

"I can't believe the producers haven't noticed I'm missing and come looking for me," she expressed to the imaginary camera, but by Day 15 the crew already had problems of their own she could never have imagined.

"Well," she wrapped up, hands on her hips. "At this point, I might as well keep following the river, but I'm crossing to the other side as soon as possible."

SEATON ROGERS

Day 16

11:31am

Age: 33
Occupation: Screenwriter
Home: Utah
Status: Single

Seaton Rogers shuffled out of his shelter, scratching his stomach with one hand, the other raised in a fist for a stretch while he yawned. The groggy-eyed survivalist proceeded to build up the fire so he could make coffee—waking up seemed to take priority on the morning of Day 16.

Once the coffee was on, Seaton sat down and did what he should have done as soon as he exited his shelter—he scanned the woods around camp for signs of predators and potential prey. Luckily for him, the forest was quiet and empty.

"I don't wake up well," he said out loud.

Looking around, he realized he hadn't set up a camera yet and took to the task. He positioned it to get a shot of himself sitting by the fire.

"I don't wake up well," he repeated. "I'm not a morning person, to say the least." His drooping eyelids confirmed the claim.

"To make things worse, someone from the production crew called to check up on me early in the morning and woke me up. I wish they wouldn't do that. Like, why do they have to call so early? That's the second day in a row they did that. I wonder if something is wrong. If it happens again, I'm going to tell them not to call me until after 12pm," he promised, drawing an imaginary line with his hand. "That's standing orders for everyone I know back home—don't call before 12pm."

Home. The word conjured up so many feelings. Warmth, security, food. So basic, but when those things are gone they are missed dearly.

"However," he added with a mischievous smile, "I prefer no one call me at all, ever. I hate the phone. I hate talking on the phone. I hate having to make phone calls. I hate the fact that the phone could ring at any moment and I always hate it when it does ring. I actually changed my ring tone to a recording of me yelling, 'Noooo!' because that's my usual reaction when someone is calling me. I'm more of a texting kind of guy. But, don't expect me to answer your text until I'm good and ready."

The inside joke made him laugh and wonder if the other contestants were explaining their odd quirks on camera for the whole world to eventually see.

"Sometimes…correction—*most* of the time…it's just nice to be alone and think in the peace and quiet of solitude. That's something that's not very popular anymore, or maybe it was never popular. My parents used to worry about me because I didn't flock to other kids and make friends. I always enjoyed playing by myself. It's funny because anyone who knew me when I was a kid and they were an adult, they always say the same thing—"You were so quiet when you were a kid, always playing by yourself."

He glanced up at the camera with a shy, almost embarrassed look as if he were undressing in front of strangers.

"Like, so what? People act like anyone who enjoys time by themselves is some kind of weirdo or…I don't know what—a serial killer or something. I'd really like the world to know and understand—there's nothing wrong with being an introvert. I grew up thinking something was wrong with me because everyone insisted being alone was the most horrible thing in the world. People still think that."

He wiggled his fingers, using a mock-scary voice. "Isolation leads to depression, madness, suicidal tendencies, and all that bullshit." Back to his normal, unamused voice, he continued, "No, it doesn't. Maybe it does that to extroverts. Maybe it could do that to *most* people, but it doesn't apply to everyone. And, always remember, the threshold for *most* is only 51%."

Seaton's face became visibly annoyed and animated, distaste with the subject evident. Or, perhaps, the "people" he was thinking about. To him, "people" were often the source of all the world's problems.

"I see people in introvert groups online all the time, asking how they can overcome their natural tendencies and be more like others expect them to be. I know the feeling. The whole world wants you to be like them. I'm not one to dish out advice, but since I have a captive audience here, this is for all the introverts out there."

He straightened his posture, positioning himself in an attempt to create a professional mystique, using a clear, stern tone which was intended to sound like a public service announcement.

"Embrace your introverted-ness—your inner introvert. There's nothing wrong with you. It's perfectly okay to be alone. It's okay to celebrate being alone. Brag about how great it is to be alone when people criticize you for it. Maybe if introverts seemed happier about being alone, everyone else would just leave us alone and let us be happy instead of scolding us for being alone and not leaving the house."

Seaton's eyes darted, an awkward grin on his face. Feeling exposed and vulnerable, he was suddenly self-conscious again.

"Okay, so I'm gonna be alone now, bye," he signed off and shut down the camera, abruptly.

4:04pm

Seaton Rogers cast a line into the river with his makeshift fishing pole, wondering if the risen river and faster current had swept all the fish away. He stood within the camera's view in a Captain Morgan stance on two boulders large enough to still be above water.

"I must say, I didn't think I'd like the video portion of this competition, but I'm enjoying the captive audience—the power of yielding the camera and letting my thoughts spill out without anyone interrupting me or arguing with me. Contrary to what you might think of me by now. After what?" He pretended to look at an imaginary watch on his wrist. "Sixteen days? You might think I don't like to talk but that's not really true. I do like to talk but not useless, polite chit-chat just for the sake of talking. I've got no use for that. I like deep discussions about interesting things in life. I want to talk about the cosmos and evolution. I want to talk about philosophy and what the future might look like. I'm kind of tired of the way the world is. I'm more interested in where it's going to lead and how it's going to change. I like to think about 'what if's' like—What if Earth develops a giant storm like Jupiter's red spot and it just sits on Florida all the way through the Gulf of Mexico to Texas? Imagine a never ending hurricane sitting in one spot over land. How would we deal with it? I like that sort of mental exercise. I guess that's why I became a writer."

He pulled in his empty line, rebaited it with a crushed grasshopper and cast it out again without complaining the original bait had been stolen.

He looked back at the camera and said, "So, since I've got you here, let's explore some of the things that have been stuck in my brain. I really want to make the most of this experience. I didn't come out here just for the money. This is an adventure and a growing experience. It's therapeutic. So, what's going on in my brain? You may be wondering. So, here it goes. I've always wished something interesting would happen. I don't mean here during the contest. I mean in general. I'd love to see a discovery that is so earth-shattering it changes everything we thought we knew about the universe. Like, how about some aliens or proof of life outside Earth? How about some UFOs that we can confirm are really real. Let them land on the White House lawn or take over the broadcast of every TV station at the same time to convey their message. Give me *something*. Wouldn't it be incredible if we picked up a transmission from outer space and, at least, were able to *communicate* with life outside our solar system? I wonder about all the logistics that would go into it. How could we prove it wasn't a hoax? How would we be able to learn the aliens' language? I love questions like these."

He shook his head slowly, a glimmer of yearning in his eyes, like a child hoping against all logic that Santa Claus was real and on his way with a bag full of presents. His excitement for the subject and the lack of evidence left him deflated. His shoulders slumped.

"Nothing interesting ever happens, but even if it did, they wouldn't tell us about it anyway. Everyone is too afraid that people would panic if they got any new information. It's ridiculous. From what I've gathered in my thirty-some-odd years on this planet, humans are a stubborn species. We don't like change and it's to the point that people kill to keep things from changing. We've had almost endless wars trying to change things, which means we've also had endless wars trying to stop things from changing. I always wonder what a sudden, drastic change would look like. Preferably a change for the better. Unfortunately, I can't recall the last time things changed for the better, globally-speaking. Maybe the life of a species is similar to a single life—aging and dying as it gets older. Maybe death is the only way for change to take place."

Seaton pulled his line in to find he had only succeeded in feeding the fish in the river. He gave the camera a disappointed look and laughed it off.

"I imagine this entire segment is going to end up on the cutting room floor." He turned off the camera and headed out.

KIMMIE ARDEN

Day 17

9:12am

Age: 36
Occupation: Nurse
Home: New York
Status: Married, 2 children

Kimmie Arden spent the morning searching for mussels and limpets on a stretch of shore she hadn't visited before. A bodycam was along for the ride, shooting from her chest.

"It's a good thing I don't really need food right now because it's slim pickins here, on this beach," she complained, hopping from rock to rock.

"I was hoping to supplement my diet a little. That's something you have to be conscious of. It's easy to get complacent when you make a big kill. The deer meat will meet my protein needs for quite a while, but there's more to long term survival than merely protein. Variety is as important as ever. I'll keep collecting edible greens, fishing, whatever I can do to keep some variety in my diet."

She squatted to pry a limpet from its hiding place between two rocks. It was only the third one she'd found. Upon standing, she pulled her hat back, off her forehead, trying to decide if her eyes were deceiving her.

"Oh my god. Is that…a coconut," she exclaimed, pointing to the brown hairy ball floating in the ocean. She grabbed a stick and hurried over to fish it out. "How could a coconut make it this far north?" she wondered aloud. "I mean, I know they're long distance travelers but this seems a bit extreme."

Bending down, stick extended, she guided the find closer to shore, the lapping waves keeping most of it hidden under water. A quick poke and a pull brought the object in. Kimmie lifted it out of the water by the brown hairs and let out a shriek. A bloated, eyeless face stared back at her. She flung the severed head on shore, the disturbing clunk of cranium hitting stone made her shutter and convulse in a jittery dance.

"Oh my god. That can't be real," she wished looking back at the ocean for the rest of the body. "That's got to be some kind of Halloween decoration or something. The ocean is full of floating garbage."

With no body in sight, Kimmie inched closer to confront the object again. It was considerate enough to have landed facing away from her. She turned it over with her boot, covering her mouth, muffling another scream. The putrid smell of wet, rotting flesh almost knocked her over.

She turned around and paced away repeating, "Omygod, omygod," over and over. Pulling her radio out of her pocket, she turned back toward the head, pressing the call button without hesitation.

"If this is a joke, some part of the show they didn't tell us about, it's not funny at all," she informed the camera.

"Hello. This is Kimmie Arden," she said into the radio.

Chapter 14

Day 17

Heads Up

"Hello. This is Kimmie Arden. I'm tapping out. Come get me immediately," she insisted. "Can anybody hear me? Please hurry. Over."

"I hear you, Kimmie. What's wrong?" Page asked, detecting fear in her voice—not what was expected from someone making a calm, rational decision to leave the game.

"Please, get me out of here as soon as possible," Kimmie repeated with a desperate whine. "I...I found something."

"What did you find?" Page asked.

Kimmie replied in a panic. "Just come and get me. I'm done. Get me out of here," she shouted.

"Calm down. Tell me what you found," Page tried again.

Hutch pushed Page's hand down and took over the conversation on his own radio. "Kim, this is Hutch Adalwolf. I need you to relax. Take a deep breath and tell us what's wrong. We can come get you but it's going to take a while. What did you find?"

"It's...a head. I saw it floating in the ocean and I thought it was a coconut, but it's a severed head. It looks like it's been floating around for...," Kimmie reported almost breathless before shifting to relief. "Oh, thank god you're here. I see your boat coming now. Can you see me?"

"Kimmie, don't attract attention to yourself," Hutch blurted. "That's not us. I repeat. That is *not* us. You need to get out of there. Do you understand? Over."

"Then, who is it?" Kimmie asked.

"I don't know, but one of our producers is missing and multiple contestants have been murdered. You have to run. How far away are they?"

"Oh my god. They're not far," Kimmie reported. "Did you say

contestants have been murdered?"

"Listen to me, Kim. Run back to your shelter and grab whatever you can to make it through the night. Do you have a weapon on you?" Hutch asked.

"I don't know. I...I have a knife on me and bear spray. My bow is back at camp," she whimpered, the pulse in her voice suggesting she was on the move. "Over."

"Get whatever you can to defend yourself, take some food if you have any, but travel as light as you can. Get to the river and follow it upstream. If you find a safe place to cross, do it and, keep in contact with us. We're leaving now to meet up with you," Hutch instructed. "Over."

"Does this person know where my camp is? Are they going to follow me?" Kimmie asked.

"Hopefully not, if you get a head start. If you're lucky he hasn't seen you," Hutch said. "Over."

"Oh, no. I waved to him thinking it was someone coming to extract me," Kimmie reported. "They might have seen me. Over."

"Okay, there's nothing you can do about that now. Just go, hurry. Put some quick distance between you, but then, pace yourself. You could be walking all night, into tomorrow. Did you get a look at the person?"

Breathing heavily, Kimmie explained, "No, the boat was cutting across the water too far away to make out anyone onboard." The sound of leaves and cracking twigs stopped. "Maybe I should go back and check it out? Maybe it's not what you think. Over."

"No, Kimmie," Hutch replied, giving it no thought. "Don't go back. You need to keep out of sight. Over."

There was no reply.

Page laid a hand on Hutch's shoulder, her brain working on something her face was trying to express. "Maybe you should let her check it out. What if it's Sharon?"

"What?" Hutch asked narrowing his eyes.

"What if Sharon found the boat...and..." Page started to explain, petering out when she realized the idea made no sense.

"You think Sharon found the boat and left us here so she could go cruising around the island by herself?" Hutch asked, trying not to sound sarcastic but it was impossible.

"Maybe the killer still has Sharon. Have you considered that?" Page persisted.

Doc intervened, "Maybe the boat will just keep going. Either way, we need to keep tabs on it if at all possible."

Hutch pursed his lips, unsure how to proceed. This was a new situation for him. He'd never been in the military; never been hunted by humans, but Doc's suggestion made sense. Risking Kimmie's life was a different matter. Hutch struggled with the idea, but given Kimmie's silence, she was taking matters into her own hands regardless.

"Kimmie," he whispered into the radio. "Keep yourself hidden. If you see the boat coming toward shore, get out of there. Do you read? Over."

"Okay," came the reply.

Doc and Page froze, waiting for the next transmission. Hutch wasn't waiting. He turned back toward Floyd Benson's camp.

"Hey," he shouted back, realizing they weren't following him. "Let's go. We gotta move. There's no time to waste."

Kimmie's whispering voice crackled over the radio, "It's coming this way."

"Get out of there, Kimmie," Hutch urged.

Page interjected with her own radio. "Can you get a look at his face?"

Hutch rushed back and snatched the radio from Page's hand. "What the hell do you think you're doing?"

"We need to know who it is," she defended.

"You're not risking someone else's life to find out," Hutch growled.

"He's huge," Kimmie whispered. "I couldn't get a look at his face. He's wearing a hood and a knit ski mask and I don't know what else. Over."

"That's good enough," Hutch said, a sense of urgency in his voice. "Get out of there. You're losing your head start. Over."

"I'm going," Kimmie reassured him. "I tried to get a close up with a camera. I…I don't know what to make of it. It looks like he's wearing another mask under the ski mask. Very strange. I got it on video. Over."

"You're a brave woman," Hutch told her. "Just don't get yourself killed. Over."

"Roger that. I think I'm far away enough and I've got a clear trail. I'm gonna make a run for it. I'll check back in after I leave my camp. Over and out," Kimmie signed off.

"Copy that. Good luck. Over and out," Hutch replied. He shared a concerned look with his crew. "We've got to get to her before the killer does." He pulled out the map to plan as they hurried back to camp.

"Who do you think it is?" Page asked, struggling to keep up with Hutch's long strides. They were all running on fumes but there was no time to stop and rest or eat.

"It doesn't really matter right now," Hutch dismissed.

She turned to Doc, slowing down to get alongside him. "What's your guess, Doc?" she asked.

"Kimmie said he was huge so, it has to be a man. That narrows it down to Ezra Greer, Wes Wood, or maybe Tucker...what's his name," Doc deduced. "The only other man left is Seaton Rogers, but I can't imagine anyone calling him huge. It must have been someone threatening enough to force Floyd Benson into the freezing ocean."

"What if it's not one of the contestants?" Page asked.

"You think a crew member snuck away to wreak havoc on the contestants? I suppose that's another possibility," Doc conceded. "I'm wondering whose head Kimmie found floating."

Hutch interrupted, "You two can play the guessing game later. We need to warn the rest of the contestants. Doc, you call Seaton Rogers and Stephanie Hamilton. Page, you call out to Tucker Jordan, Zoey Price, and Jill Hill. If any of them reply, hand the radio to me," Hutch instructed, leaving the suspicious Ezra Greer and Wes Wood for himself to contact and feel out.

KIMMIE ARDEN

Day 17

9:47am

Age: 36
Occupation: Nurse
Home: New York
Status: Married, 2 children

Kimmie Arden rushed back to her camp, shocked by the sequence of events—first, she found a severed head, then she found out the person who might be responsible for its removal was on a boat headed for her nearest shoreline. By the time she got to camp, it was finally sinking in.

The first thing she went for was the bow and arrows. There were three arrows left—one had been lost when it narrowly missed a bird perched in a tree days before. Kimmie's hands trembled as she emptied the cooking pot, dousing the fire with unprocessed water. It wasn't enough to put the small fire out. The loud sizzling made her cringe. She kicked dirt and old ashes onto the fire pit, smothering it as best she could, but smoke still rose thick enough to give away her location.

She shoved the pot and cover into her backpack, frantically looking around her shelter, trying to decide what else to take. There wasn't much to consider. She grabbed a hunk of smoked meat she thought would fit in the pot. It took some effort, but she managed to force it in. Pulling her sleeping bag off her raised bed, she laid it on the ground outside to roll it up.

Every little common forest sound made her head dart. Two squirrels chasing each other in the leaf litter nearly gave her a heart attack. She hurried the packing process, attaching the rolled up sleeping bag to her backpack. Anything that could be used as a weapon was coming along with her.

She zipped up the backpack and grabbed the long, wooden axe

handle to make her escape, but detecting a noise behind her, she froze.

Holding her breath, she turned her head, unwilling to move any other body part or make a sound. The noise got louder and became unmistakable. Something with two legs was walking through the forest not far away. Kimmie stifled a whimper. The killer was closing in.

Best case scenario—the killer would pass her by far enough away without seeing her, but with smoke still rising from the fire, it was more likely she'd be found if the killer was indeed looking for her. She didn't stick around to find out.

With a strong pull, she extracted the axe from the log it was impaled in and ran in the direction of the river. It only took a few strides before she decided against running. The equipment in her backpack made too much noise rattling around. She switched to a power walk, taking care not to jostle her belongings, choosing the path she hoped to be the quietest—a path she had been using all along to get to her water supply, the river.

Fear moved her forward, but curiosity tugged from behind. She kept checking over her shoulder until her camp area was almost out of sight, but curiosity got the better of her. She hid behind a layer of bushes, crouching out of sight, and pulled out the one camera she had brought with her. Zooming in on her camp, she focused on the only area that wasn't obscured by the forest.

She watched the camera screen and listened for any movement around her. She could see the entrance to her shelter and smoke from the dying fire. A hooded head and shoulders walked into view, barely visible in forest camouflage if not for the movement. It came in and out of view as it searched the camp.

With her heart pounding in her chest a thought crossed her mind—what if this is all a hoax, just part of the TV show to spice things up? What a cruel joke that would be. She pushed the notion out of her head. She needed to treat the situation seriously. If it turned out to be a trick, so be it.

Kimmie could see the tarp coming off her shelter, pulled out of view. Her heart sunk. There was no denying the culprit meant her harm—stealing equipment she depended on for survival. She wanted to march down there and confront him, but the thought of her kids growing up without a mother stopped her. A plan to lay in wait and ambush the killer was unacceptable for the same reason. A survivalist like Kimmie had only one viable option and that was to flee as quietly as possible, leaving as little a trail as possible.

Unfortunately, the rest of the animals in the forest promised no cooperation. Two squirrels—perhaps the same two squirrels as before—scurried through the dead leaves a few yards away, causing a ruckus. Kimmie held her breath and froze, watching the camera screen.

The hooded head in frame spun around. Squinting black eyes that seemed to know exactly where she was, landed in her direction. The squirrels took the chase up a nearby tree, but the eyes of the killer ignored them, Kimmie's bright blue parka not helping to conceal her. The masked face shot forward, out of view, reappearing in flashes through the forest.

Kimmie turned and ran, the heavy axe weighing her down. She flung it into the woods, off the trail with a mighty heave that lunged her forward, almost knocking her off balance. Peering over her shoulder, the killer was out of view. She sped up, trying to put more distance between her and her pursuer, but she knew she wouldn't make it far on little sleep and her deep woods diet.

There was no place to hide. Her legs were already begging her to stop. With little choice, she slowed. The well-worn animal trail would lead the killer right to her, but veering off the trail would be dangerous and slow her down even more. She knew, if she was going to survive, she was going to have to fight.

Tired and winded, Kimmie pulled her backpack off along with the bow and what was now only one remaining arrow. Two arrows had been lost in her hasty escape. She scoped out a spot to take cover behind a tree with a clear, direct look down the trail. She pulled back an arrow, taking aim where she expected the killer to appear and waited.

Within seconds, the tall shadowy figure lurched into sight and froze, black eyes staring directly at Kimmie. She let the arrow fly without hesitation. The figure's hand flashed in reflex, catching the arrow in midair. Kimmie gasped, stricken with fear. The killer flipped the arrow in his hand, stalking up the trail.

Kimmie dropped the useless bow, stepping out from behind the tree while pulling the skinny bottle of bear spray from its holster. She removed the plastic safety and took aim, startled by her first close-up view of the alleged killer.

The oversized black eyes behind the mask were framed in by a sliver of white on each side and scaly, green lids which looked painted on. The only other feature she could see was the lipless mouth which matched the eyelids—thick scaly and dark green. If the creature approaching her was human, it had to be covered in some kind of protective armor.

Kimmie had no time to dwell on the stalker's appearance. She aimed and fired a blast of bear spray right into the vacant, shark-like eyes. The stinging chemicals brought the attacker down to one knee, at first, and then the other, letting out a growling shriek that sounded half man and half velociraptor. Kimmie gave it another zap with the spray and closed in to finish the job with her hunting knife.

The stricken creature clawed at its eyes with gloved hands, flailing around on the ground like a panicked fish. Kimmie approached, one hand armed with the knife, the other reached out to pull the mask off the assailant to determine who or what it was exactly.

The creature grabbed her arm as she neared, pulling it in closer to its mouth and bit down. Snake-like fangs pierced her skin like two hypodermic needles followed by the pressure of blunt molars holding her arm, in place. The pain was immediate and intense, radiating up her arm and hitting her chest. She staggered away holding the stricken arm, her mind trying to process what had just happened. In a desperate attempt, she pulled the radio out and called for help, her words slurred as her perception slowed to a crawl.

"Help," she moaned, dropping to the cold ground, her legs giving out like they had been switched off. The world went out of focus as she tried to warn the others, "It got me."

ZOEY PRICE

Day 17

12:25pm

Age: 24
Occupation: Dance Instructor
Home: Montana
Status: Single

Zoey Price dragged her feet through the woods alongside the river, her once white boots scuffed and soiled from the trek. They matched the rest of her outfit. Her light pink snow suit looked like it had been dragged through mud ten years ago. The "nose" had fallen off the face of her bunny hat. The long tassels which had once dangled from the hat were gone—cut off a few days ago because they kept snagging on branches.

Zoey's face and hair weren't in better shape. Dirt had accumulated in the fine lines of her face. Her shiny, blonde hair had turned greasy and grimy and started falling out in disturbing clumps. She barely had the energy to move on, but she was still alive and as determined as ever to find help. She spoke to her imaginary camera from time to time about her struggle on Isolation Island and life in general, shedding the old views of the world she had been taught to believe her entire life, trading them for what she was learning on her own in the harsh wilderness.

Zoey hadn't had a decent meal in days, surviving only on the small batch of mushrooms she had found after abandoning her camp, which amounted to one small snack per day. Surviving on the move was much more difficult than it had been at camp with equipment. A temporary shelter had to be erected every night and taken down every morning. A new fire had to be started every night and extinguished before moving on the next day. Worst of all, the constant hiking through rough terrain was exhausting. She had to stop to rest every twenty minutes and the lack of food was slowing her down to a crawl.

"I'm so hungry, I'd eat a rat at this point," she said, pretending a camera was on her as she shuffled along. "And, that's really saying a lot considering I haven't eaten any kind of meat since I was eight years-old."

Reconsidering her wish, she amended it. "On second thought, maybe rat meat isn't the best place for a vegetarian to start being a carnivore."

The river grew louder but narrower, turning to whitewater trickling over large boulders and smaller stones. She kept it in view through the woods as she had done for days hoping to find something or someone to help her. It led her to the only lake on Isolation Island. It was a welcomed sight after days of the same monotonous scenery over and over.

"Oh my god," she exclaimed. "Do you see that?" she asked the imaginary camera, expecting the imaginary cameraman to get a shot of the lake.

The lake was still, the noonday sun reflecting off the dark water like a mirror. There were no signs of other contestants, but Zoey was confident the lake wouldn't have gone unused by at least one of the other nine survivalists.

She found an animal trail hugging the shoreline and followed it until she came across one of Jillian Hill's snare traps. The remnants of an eviscerated squirrel covered with flies emitting a foul odor. Zoey held a gloved hand to her nose.

"Yuck, that is nasty," the vegetarian said, examining the carcass to determine how old it was. There was nothing to be salvaged other than blackened bones and clumps of matted fur. "Poor guy. Looks like he's been here for days. As morbid as it sounds, this is a good sign. I must be near someone's camp." She smiled at the prospect. With tears threatening to fill her eyes, she looked around for other signs of human activity. She could be near the end of her harrowing journey. Finding nothing encouraging, it suddenly dawned on her. "Maybe it's *not* a good sign. Why didn't anyone come to check the trap?"

A few minutes up the trail she began to see skinny stumps—the remnants of young trees cut down by Jill's axe. Any footprints had been washed away by the storm, but there was no mistaking the matted vegetation and chop marks left behind, even if they weren't fresh.

"I don't know what to think," Zoey said, moving slowly along the trail. "Someone was definitely here, but they could have tapped out."

The lake overflowed into a wide, shallow creek, directing Zoey toward the bay presenting a new opportunity. The clear, rocky creek was home to crayfish—easy to catch, easy to cook, and safe to eat. Zoey pulled one from the creek and held it up for the fake camera to see, the creature's claws open and outstretched in defense.

"I haven't eaten meat since I was eight years-old, but I have to have food and this might be the least painful place to start. Sorry little guy," she said and continued looking for more along the way, stuffing them into her pockets.

Soon, her pockets were full and the hunt for firewood and a spot to make camp began.

1:42pm

Zoey Price fell to her knees, gripping a bundle of firewood, the sight ahead of her like an oasis in the desert. Jill Hill's shelter still stood sturdy and, compared to Zoey's tattered tarp, looked like a five-star resort. The exhausted traveler picked herself up and approached with her tired arms stretched out for a hug.

"Hello?" she attempted, her voice cracking with emotion. A lump in her throat held her back but she tried again. "Hello? Is anyone here?" There was, of course, no reply. Jill Hill's lifeless body was in a ditch at the top of the hill.

"I need help," Zoey kept trying. After a few attempts, she resorted to hollering into the wilderness around the camp, her weakened voice not carrying far.

Taking a closer look at the camp, it became apparent no one had been there in a while. The pains of another failure stabbing her heart, she checked inside the shelter to confirm nobody was home. There were a few supplies left behind, lifting her spirits back up for a moment until she saw the cases of camera equipment identical to the ones she was familiar with.

"This is not a good sign," she said, opening the cases to discover most of the equipment was still there. "If this was someone's camp and they tapped out, why is this still here?"

Zoey ignored the sinking feeling in her stomach in exchange for dealing with the rumbling hunger pains. She rummaged around hoping to uncover any useful items, laying it all out on the ground in order of importance. There was a ferrorod, two crusty fishing hooks, the tarp roof and cordage holding it in place, and a head lamp. She clicked on the head lamp to make sure it worked, stuck it in an inside pocket and zipped it up. But, there was one item that almost brought tears to her eyes—a cooking pot. She grabbed it and emptied the passengers from her pockets, receiving several pinches in the process. The crayfish clamored over each other, trying to climb up the tall walls of the pot, clinking their shells against the bottom each time they failed.

It only took one bottle of unprocessed creek water to submerse her meal, ensuring they wouldn't die before she could get a fire started. The ferrorod and dry wood from inside Jill's shelter made starting a fire seem easy after having to make friction fires with damp wood night after night.

Zoey took a last look at the crayfish in the pot, legs and claws wriggling everywhere. She thought about the remorse she might feel, staring at the lives she was about to take. She was starving, but it was still a big deal. A tinge of guilt welled up from her gut, threatening to make her chicken out. A long, grinding growl from her stomach stifled the guilt and triggered her mouth to water.

"Sorry guys," she apologized before setting the pot on a rock among the flames of the growing fire. She didn't have the heart to watch them cook. Instead, she opened the camera equipment and watched Jill's footage, hoping to find out what had happened to her opponent. The camera with the crucial footage was still with Jill's remains, but the sight of another human was uplifting. Zoey watched with hope building up.

She let the camera play back Jill's experience while preparing her meal. It was a useful distraction. Breaking the tails off the cooked crayfish had less of an impact on her, but when it came to eating the flesh inside, she hesitated. Looking at the reddish-white piece of meat the words *life or death* echoed in her head, but the decision to move forward came through logic. She had already killed the animal. Backing out of eating it now would be the worst thing she could do.

She slipped the little piece of meat into her mouth and chewed slowly with her eyes closed. Unable to hold back an ecstatic moan, she had to admit out loud, "I've never tasted anything so amazing. It's not the crayfish. This is the taste of life."

The rest of the crayfish went down without an ounce of guilt.

WES WOOD

Day 17

1:45pm

Age: 57
Occupation: Farmer
Home: Mississippi
Status: Divorced, 8 children

"So, here's the new situation," Wes Wood informed the camera, mispronouncing the word *situation* as sichee-ay-shin. He was filming while getting into his boat. The bodycam on his chest caught a glimpse of the weapons on display on the bottom of the blue, tarp covered boat. "We's got ourself a killer on the loose," he said with an exaggerated southern twang as if announcing *a good old fashioned 'coon hunt*.

He shoved off and paddled toward the mouth of the bay, armed with every weapon available to him. The bow and arrow was his weapon of choice, but he was prepared for anything.

"Somebody's been killing the other contestants and, I tell you right now, it ain't me. I ain't had nothing to do with it. I been through this before. Dead bodies coming up everywhere, a killer on the loose. I ain't gonna set here an' wait to be accused. This camera's gonna be my witness, my alibi (pronounced a-lee-bye)." He didn't delve any deeper into the previous accusations against him.

"The producers called me to tell me about this killer on the other side of the island. So, this is me on my side of the island. Fer the record, it's around two or three o'clock PM, I reckon, on Day 17. They sayin' the Isolation Island game is over, but they gonna pay me fer this one way or a other. Since I had 'em on the radio, I axed 'em where this dang treasure is at and they told me."

The camera shot wasn't much of an alibi. His arms obscured the view and shook the camera as he paddled.

"Now, I didn't want to admit it before, but I been lookin' fer this dang treasure for days and I can't find it nowheres. I ain't been filmin' much on account of I wanted it to look like I done found it on the first try," Wes confessed. "But, it's time to come clean. I ain't had no luck at finding the treasure and I been wasted all my time lookin' fer it."

The elusive second island described in the clues to the treasure appeared in the distance, right where he was told it would be, about fifty yards away from the main island. It was tiny, home to a lone sickly gray tree and a patch of moss and grass. The tiny island was protected from the waves by a narrow peninsula jutting out into the mouth of the bay like a single, long sabretooth made of stone.

Wes stopped paddling long enough to complain about how difficult the clues were and read from the scroll out loud to the camera to prove it.

> A TREASURE SHARED BY TWO ISLANDS
> IS NOT FAR AWAY,
>
> IT'S ONLY ON *THIS* ISLAND
> A SHORT TIME EACH DAY,
>
> IF YOUR TIMING IS OFF,
> THE BRIDGE WON'T BE THERE,
>
> COME BACK TOMORROW,
> OR WHENEVER YOU DARE,
>
> FIND THE RIGHT SPOT,
> TRY NOT TO GET STRANDED,
>
> THE TREASURE APPEARS,
> JUST LIKE THE LAND DID

"I still don't know what the hell this is talkin' 'bout. They said it's on that little island over yonder," Wes said, pointing out the gray tree's miniscule piece of real estate. He set the scroll down and paddled hard.

Pulling up next to the piece of rock and dirt protruding from the salt water, he used a chop of the axe into the dirt to anchor himself and pull the boat closer. A length of cordage tied to the axe kept the boat from floating away as he searched for the treasure. A wide ditch in the center of the island was filled with water, making the island look like a donut. Wes stuck a booted foot into the hole, hitting the top of the treasure chest with a thump. He stomped down on it several times in celebration.

"There it is. Whoo hoo," he howled, ecstatic.

Laying down on the ground next to the hole, he plunged an arm into the cold water, feeling around for a handle or something to grab onto, but he couldn't find anything. Trying to grip a corner of the chest didn't give him enough leverage to lift it out. He sat back on his knees, frustrated.

"They said the water will drain out at low tide. I was hopin' I could pull it out before then, but it ain't budgin'. Gonna have to wait. At low tide, all the water is supposed to drain from here and I can walk back and forth to shore. I reckon there ain't nothin' else to do but wait."

Chapter 15

Day 17

Five Contestants Remain

Kimmie Arden's weak raspy voice crackled over the radio, "It got me."

Hutch almost fumbled the radio, pulling it off his beltline to reply. "Kimmie, this is Hutch. Where are you?"

"I can't feel my legs," Kimmie slurred.

"Hang in there Kimmie. We're coming for you. Just tell us where you are," Hutch reassured.

"No. Don't come," Kimmie answered, keeping the talk button depressed so Hutch couldn't argue. "I'll be dead long before you can get here. I tried…Nooo!!!"

Kimmie's scream was accompanied by an unearthly shriek. Then, the transmission cut off.

Hutch shouted her name into the radio over and over, but there was no reply. They waited and listened for more, but the radio remained silent. Doc tried making contact using his radio, but received no reply either.

Kimmie Arden was presumed dead and Hutch was stuck in the middle of the woods with his bewildered crew, wondering what to do next. Page's legs turned to noodles. She crouched down into a ball, hugging her knees, crying over the loss of another contestant.

Doc squatted next to her with his arm around her in consolation, looking up at Hutch. "Now what?"

There were five contestants left alive—Ezra Greer, Wes Wood, Seaton Rogers, and Stephanie Hamilton—all on the other side of the island. Then there was the wandering Zoey Price at the deceased Jill Hill's camp. The closest camp to Hutch and his crew was Tucker Jordan's. Since he hadn't responded to repeated attempts to contact him, they knew their chances of finding him alive were slim. Given Kimmie Arden's discovery of a brown-haired severed head, the chances of finding him with his head attached were even slimmer but they were duty-bond to try.

Hutch led the way and his weary crew followed him through the forest in the silence of disbelief. There was definitely a killer out there attacking the contestants and the crew could be next.

"I know who the killer is," Page muttered, breaking the silence as they marched. "Maybe not. I don't know. It *might* be him. You definitely can't count him out."

"Who?" Doc asked.

"Dean Bates. One of the executive producers. He's a really weird rich guy. I only met him once, but Sharon told me stories about this guy. He's one of those rich bastards that enjoys treating people like puppets and pawns in games for his own amusement. He probably set this whole thing up so he can get a group of people he could hunt on a remote island," Page accused based on hearsay and rumors.

"That's a stretch," Hutch contended. "Did you hear that shriek when Kimmie screamed and the radio went dead?"

"Yes, don't remind me. What about it?" Page inquired.

"Kimmie said, *It* got me," Hutch pointed out, pondering at the same time.

"So, what?" Page asked. "Are you saying the killer isn't human?"

"I don't know. Why did she say *it*?" Hutch demanded.

"So, it's an animal that can kill people, hang people, and drive a boat. Yeah, that sounds much more likely than my rich freak theory," Page said, sarcastically.

"I don't know. Maybe it's a human in disguise. I'm just saying, there could be more to this than a contestant or crew member murdering people. What if it's neither? What if it's someone that was here *before* we got here, before the contestants? What if this wasn't a deserted island in the first place?" Hutch suggested.

The idea alone was frightening. They marched through the forest in silence, afraid to keep guessing, afraid to let their imaginations go wild. They needed food and water. They needed shelter and a fire. They needed to get to Tucker Jordan's camp unscathed and decide what to do next.

ZOEY PRICE

Day 17

5:47pm

Age: 24
Occupation: Dance Instructor
Home: Montana
Status: Single

While the other contestants were learning about the technical difficulties and murders taking place on Isolation Island, Zoey Price searched the forest around Jillian Hill's camp, hoping to find a contestant returning from a hunt with food. Thinking the owner of the camp may have moved to higher ground, Zoey hiked uphill. A gust of wind met her when she pulled herself over the top of the hill, the innocent-looking grassy plateau laid out before her.

Approaching the ditch where Jillian Hill had died, the edges revealed the scene one step at a time. A shredded, bloody, bright-orange coat marked the spot, announcing the story wasn't going to be pretty, stopping Zoey in her tracks.

"Oh my god," she whispered to the real camera she had brought along strapped to her hat.

It captured everything her eyes could see as she inched closer—a video camera with straps indicating it had once been mounted to the cranium of a contestant—not a good sign.

A step further revealed a half-eaten, decaying torso with a bloody arrow still sticking out between collapsed ribs. Zoey gasped and stifled a scream.

More shredded clothes, torn apart and bloody, she was afraid to take the next step. Her legs went numb, threatening to collapse underneath her. She had to turn away.

With her hand over her mouth and nose, she braved forward, the worst of the scene already discovered. Last, but not least, a florescent yellow boost of hope with a short, black antenna peeked out from under a torn piece of clothing drawing her near with widened eyes. The stench and the mere thought of dead human flesh was overpowering. She doubled over, holding her stomach.

"Oh my god. A radio," Zoey managed between dry heaves. She had to look away and find a breath of fresh air to stabilize herself, swallowing incessantly as her mouth watered, preparing to lose the first meal she'd had in days.

She refused to give it up, normalizing her breathing to a slow, steady rhythm. "I'm fine. I'm okay," she reassured the camera with her eyes closed, a tear streaming down one cheek. "A radio," she said, again, the word itself evoking emotion. "All I have to do is get that radio and I'm saved."

She did her best to not make a big production out of the retrieval, but the decaying human flesh and discarded bones made it difficult. Slow movements were important, like a thief trying to rob a sleeping victim. Staying low to the ground, Zoey reached in and snatched the radio away, retreating with it to the corner.

"Oh my god, I'm saved. I'm saved," she wept, hugging the radio. She clicked it off and on, a red light indicating there was still power, but the cracked screen flickered in and out with a low power warning in the upper right corner. Cranking up the volume, she cried out for help.

"Hello? Is anyone there? This is Zoey Price. I need help."

She let go of the talk button and waited, praying for a reply. The lack of any noise or even any difference when the talk button was activated was cause for concern.

She closed her eyes and muttered, "Come on, come on," but she couldn't will an answer.

The cracked screen displayed *no reception*. Holding the radio up at arm's length and waving it around didn't help, but she tried, lacking any better option.

"I need to get out of this hole," she said, squinting at the radio held to the sky. She tried flicking through different channels, repeating her calls for help and waiting for a reply. The speaker didn't make a sound all the while.

She had one more item to retrieve while she was down there. With another unnecessarily stealthy approach, she reached over the carcass of her former competitor and gently plucked the camera from its resting place. She took a moment to document the scene with the camera on her head.

"This is a real mess, but it looks like whoever this was, they were shot with an arrow," Zoey explained to the camera, eyebrows knitted in confusion. "I don't know how that's possible. Did two contestants have a dispute over territory or supplies or what?"

She looked up and around the perimeter of the hole then, back at the remains. "It's not safe to stay here," she whispered.

She didn't just mean down in the hole. If the owner of the camp was murdered, the camp wasn't safe; the entire area wasn't safe. After hoping to find another human for so long, now, she had to wonder what kind of human she might run into. The thought of throwing her arms around the first person she found and crying in triumph disintegrated.

6:47pm

Back at camp, Zoey Price rewound Jill's final video through several hours of darkness—the bottom of the pit which would serve as the dismembered survivalist's final resting place.

Stop. Rewind. Play. Stop. Rewind. Play.

Eventually, she found the part where Jill had cut her hand. Watching the last moments of Jill's life sent shivers down Zoey's spine. She touched the screen for the illusion of contact and watched, cringing when the axe came down on Jill's hand.

Zoey had been trying the radio every few minutes after finding fresh batteries for it in the camera equipment case, but seeing Jill struggle with it on video wasn't exactly encouraging. When the arrow came piercing through Jill's chest, the thump was audible. The camera on Jill's head tilted down. Zoey could see the bloody arrow and watched Jill go crashing down into the ditch before the screen went black.

"I can't stay here," Zoey said, looking up to see how low the sun was. She didn't have much daylight left, but she had Jill's headlamp.

The decision was difficult. Spending the night at Jill's camp would be most comfortable, physically, and warm, much warmer than Zoey's weathered tarp. But, would she get any sleep, wondering if a murderer was lurking in the dark woods all night? It might already be stalking her. Option two was to find a spot to pitch her tarp. She could camouflage it and stay hidden until morning, but it still involved trying to sleep through the night wondering if a killer was near.

The only option Zoey could get behind was the third option—pack up and keep walking.

But which way?

Unwilling to change her initial direction, she chose to go around the north end of the lake. She took everything she could carry, including an ember from the fire before putting it out. There was too much camera equipment to drag along so, she took a few cameras, the solar battery charger, and Jill's footage.

STEPHANIE HAMILTON

Day 17

7:47pm

Age: 29
Occupation: Artist
Home: Colorado
Status: Single

Stephanie Hamilton sat, bundled up, by the fire outside her shelter. It was getting dark for the first time since she found out a killer was on the loose. The fact that the killer was last seen on the other side of the island was little consolation.

After she finished checking in with Hutch and his crew, she did her best to stay calm, but she could feel her heart pounding in her chest. Seven people had already died. *At least* seven that they knew of. And no one knew how many more had died on the Mothership.

The news was unreal. It hit Stephanie particularly hard. This contest was supposed to be her escape from reality—a much needed break from society.

She explained the new situation to the camera in a droning, monotone voice she hadn't used since her last bout of depression when she was a teenager. "The best thing about being out here was—at least, one of the best things about being out here—was being away from the toxic culture that's been developing for so long back in the real world. Seems like the whole world is offended these days, bickering back and forth over every single issue, inventing new issues to be divided over."

Staring into the fire, her eyes stopped seeing, receding into her mind. Although she had seemed happy, positive and cheerful since Day 1, she was fragile, like a balloon full of joy—easily burst by a needle.

"Fighting. There's so much fighting. Over everything. It's

tiring. I have no desire to go back to the, quote-unquote, 'real world' with all the drama and violence."

She wrapped her arms around herself, hugging tight.

"I thought I could, *at least*, escape the violence, even for a little while. I guess I did, *for a little while*. I spent around two weeks, waking up each day without any news about who killed who or how many people were raped and murdered yesterday. That was great, but I should have known I couldn't escape it for long. Today's news, even here on Isolation Island, is disturbing and terrifying."

The fire crackled, shooting an ember right at her face. She didn't flinch. The ember fell short and arched to the ground near her feet.

"Wherever there are humans, there's violence. We are the most dangerous animal on the planet, by far. Most people think mosquitos are the deadliest animal in the world to humans, because of their ability to transmit diseases like malaria. But, if disease transmission counts, then you have to count deaths due to diseases transmitted from human to human—HIV, tuberculosis, the flu, COVID-19, all of it. Add all those deaths to the murders and suicides. And, while you're at it, throw in accidental deaths like car accidents, plane crashes, whatever. That's still humans killing humans no matter how you slice it. Heck, you could even count deaths from tobacco, drug overdoses, and pollution. Add it all up and I'm sure it blows away the harm any other animal could possibly do to us."

She snapped out of her trance for a moment, blinking away the dryness in her eyes caused by the smoke from the fire. Taking a deep breath, she scratched her nose and went right back into the trance.

"Even here, on Isolation Island, I'm still not safe from humans," she continued, her upper lip curled up in disgust. "I hate that. I never would have thought that I'd have to worry about contact with other humans during this contest. That was supposed to be the fun part."

She shook her head, her own words sinking back into her mind. "It really pisses me off. I know other contests probably struggle with not having contact with people, but I counted that as one of my biggest strengths. I'm much happier without people around. Not because I'm afraid of people. I just prefer to be alone. Being alone is so underrated. I often wonder how people function without alone time. I need it. I crave it. From time to time, it becomes absolutely essential to the point I consider getting away from people an emergency."

Her head fell to her hands without warning. She covered her eyes, letting out a long sigh of relief as she rubbed them. It was her reset button—a way to collect herself and refocus.

"Or, maybe I *am* afraid of people. I don't know. But, I can tell you this—I won't hesitate to kill anyone who comes near, intending me harm." A bit of fire flickered in her eyes. She was sensitive but by no means weak.

She looked up, right into the camera with a warning. "If you try to hurt me, I will claw your eyes out." She laughed at the words coming out of her own mouth. She had never threatened anyone in her entire life, but she had never needed to. Murder wasn't the only crime taking place on the island. There was also robbery. Stephanie and all the contestants were being robbed of the experience of a lifetime.

Extending her arm to make sure the bow and arrow on the ground next to her chair were still within quick reach, she rephrased her will to survive. "Seriously, if that killer comes around here, I will fuck him up."

11:22pm

Stephanie Hamilton reached around for a weapon by the light of the fire inside her shelter. Something had jolted her awake after a long, miserable time trying to fall asleep with visions of murderers dancing in her head. She opted to have the bear spray be her go-to weapon at night. It could stop whatever came at her with minimal effort. If anything stuck its head through the front door, she was ready to spray it in the eyes, stopping it long enough to assess the situation and strike with deadly force if needed.

Mounted to the wall next to her bed, the knife would come out next. She planned to spend a few hours on knife-throwing practice the following morning, should she survive the night. She took both the spray and the knife and got up.

A metallic clank rang out, making Stephanie's heart jump. Something was outside and he, she, or it must have knocked over the cooking pot. A deep exhale like a frustrated mule came next. Stephanie peered out the small peephole she had created in her front door for just such an occasion. It was a cloudy night so, what she saw was what she had expected—darkness. But the darkness moved. She had been looking a moose right in the snoot, the majestic beast sniffing around her door.

Stephanie almost fell back, jolted by the close proximity. Backing away, she clutched the bear spray with both hands, aiming it at the door. If the moose got spooked it could trample its way into the shelter. She wasn't confident the bear spray would stop it, but she had little choice.

The good news—it was *only* a moose. She almost laughed out loud at the irony. Yesterday, she would have been petrified by a moose so close to her shelter, but today, it was preferable to a human poking around.

The moose had no desire to enter the shelter. It would have been a tight fit for the towering male, its antlers wider than the front door. It sniffed around the camp for a few minutes and moved on, but it was enough to prevent Stephanie from falling asleep again. She spent the night guarding her shelter, tending to the fire, and singing songs in her head to stay calm.

SEATON ROGERS

Day 17

9:10pm

Age: 33
Occupation: Screenwriter
Home: Utah
Status: Single

Isolation Island, the game, was over, but the fight for survival was on like never before. After longing for human contact for over two weeks, the challenge looked totally different. The strategy had changed for the remaining survivalists. They were now at war with an unknown enemy and everyone was a suspect. Some dealt with it better than others and they all dealt with it in different ways.

The first night after finding out about dead and missing contestants was especially rough, but Seaton Rogers had progressed along the list of emotions quickly to a sobering place. He knew he was the farthest away from where the killer was last reported. For him, Day 17 was not about being hunted, but about *preparing* to be hunted. He spent most of Day 17 gathering information and arming himself. The bow and arrows, knife, axe, bear spray, and a spear he had made were at his disposal and multiple weapons were always within reach.

He had set up long tripwires circling his camp using fishing line. They were tied to the handles of the pot and lid hanging from a tree. If anything touched the wire, the metal clanging would alert him.

By bedtime, he focused on one last method of preparation—resigning himself to the reality of the situation. This wasn't a nightmare. It wasn't a game anymore. It wasn't a TV show. He might have to kill another human being. He might die himself.

The thought compelled him to take to the camera in the hopes that, if he died, someone might find it—a last testament on video.

"I am *not* dying out here. I have the best chance of surviving. I'm currently farther away from the last murder than anyone else. I've got the most time to prepare. That includes eating. I can't fight for my life on an empty stomach. There's a distinct possibility it might come to that—not just surviving but *fighting* for my life," Seaton began, holding a camera in the air over his face, laying on his elevated bed covered with a sleeping bag.

He went silent for a moment, looking off to the side. There were so many things he wanted to say, but all the thoughts were cluttering his mind. Pulling the camera in a bit closer for a more personal shot, he only had the top half of his face in frame.

"Just in case I die out here," he continued with a quiver. He swallowed away the lump in his throat. "I wanted to share with whoever finds this footage, if anyone finds this footage, I wanted to share with the world my favorite moment since I've been on this planet. A few years ago, I was in a band. I played bass and did some of the lead and backup vocals. The guys in the band, we all loved the TV show *Breaking Bad*. So, we put a set list together of all the songs in the entire series—"Baby Blue", "Boots of Chinese Plastic", "Major Tom", etcetera—and we played it at a show on Halloween. We were all dressed like characters. I was Badger. The people in the audience were dressed like characters, too. There were a few hundred people there and dozens of Walter Whites and Jessie Pinkmans. It wasn't Carnegie Hall, but for me, it was the greatest stage on Earth at that moment in time."

His face turned to absolute delight, freezing with his mouth dropped open, time traveling to his memory. The camera shifted to capture the whole thing as if someone had hit pause.

Blinked his way back to reality, he continued. "It was so awesome. The crowd was loving it. The guys in the band were all in the zone. I remember thinking at the time that I'd remember this moment for the rest of my life. That's when you know something is special. Sometimes you don't realize it until after the moment has passed, but I knew it at the time and it made me enjoy it all the more. It was a magical night. I need pleasant memories like that. My mind is haunted by bad memories. Maybe that's overstating it, but my mind remembers every stupid little thing I've ever done in my life. It keeps me up at night. I wish I could just erase all the unwanted memories. I've learned what I needed to from those situations and now I want to just remember the rules I learned and forget the actual events and how they transpired and how stupid I was."

The indoor fire dimmed, the large flames lighting the room flickering low now. The camera automatically switched to night vision mode.

"I've been learning to deal with those unwanted memories. Alcohol helps, but it's not the healthiest solution. Now, when I remember some stupid thing I did fifteen years ago, I just remind myself of that Breaking Bad concert and I feel a little better."

He hung in the memory a moment longer and then snapped himself back to the present.

"Don't worry, this is not a confession. I don't care to review all my mistakes. Nor would I want the world to know about them. I just want to remember my favorite thing ever and tell all you good people—should anyone ever find this."

It was unlike Seaton to open up to anyone. The feeling made him clam up just as quickly as his shell had shown signs of cracking. He shifted gears to reciting lyrics to songs from his favorite unknown bands. It came off as a bit bizarre, but in Seaton's mind, the video he was recording would be famous if anyone found it and he wanted to take care of his fellow musicians by mentioning their work.

Chapter 16

Day 18

Divided Sky

Hutch led his dwindling crew northeast, toward the last known location of Tucker Jordan's camp. They weren't expecting to find him alive. The description of the severed head Kimmie had found and its proximity to Tucker's camp, coupled with the fact they couldn't contact him, all pointed to one outcome. They were on a salvage mission more than a search and rescue mission. There was little reason to believe they'd find any useful equipment left behind if Tucker had been murdered, but they had to be sure.

They approached Tucker's camp with caution, treating it like a crime scene.

"I'm going to circle around for a closer look," Hutch whispered to Doc and Page, hiding in the bushes within a stone's throw from the back of Tucker's shelter. "You two stay back. Get in position for a good view and cover me."

He handed the bow and arrows to Doc and pointed out a good vantage point. Circling around the camp, Hutch took an inventory of everything he could see. The fire pit looked like it hadn't been used in some time. No signs of current or recent activity anywhere, but there were supplies in plain view.

He moved in for a closer look. "Hello? Tucker? Is anyone there?" There was no reply. He glanced in Doc's direction, nodding his head toward the shelter. Creeping closer, he announced himself again, this time stating his name. With no reply, he checked inside the shelter. Tucker Jordan's supplies remained just as he had left them with no indication of what had happened to their owner.

Hutch waved Doc and Page over.

"Is anyone here?" Doc asked, hitching a thumb at the shelter.

"Nobody," Hutch replied, deflated. "There's video to look through, some supplies."

Page suggested, "Maybe he's just...out. You know? Fishing, hunting, collecting firewood. He might come back."

"It doesn't look like anyone has been here in a while," Hutch explained, pointing to the flattened ashes in the fire pit. The rain had matted them down days ago.

Doc emerged from searching the shelter. "I don't see his radio anywhere."

Hutch surmised, "He probably had it on him when he..."

He didn't want to say the words *died or dead.* The words were too final. He avoided them until he had definitive proof in front of him. They were too tired to deal with another death, having walked through the night to put distance between themselves and the killer. They were still reeling from losing Kimmie Arden. Their repeated failed attempts to contact her again on the radio confirmed she was one of those words they didn't want to say out loud.

"What if he's not dead? What if Tucker is the killer?" Page proposed.

"Mr. Yoga?" Hutch mocked. "I doubt it." Hutch had seen Tucker on the Mothership, doing yoga all day, every day on their journey to Isolation Island.

They didn't discuss it any further. What little energy they had left was better spent on maintenance. They settled in—as much as anyone could settle into a dead man's camp. They needed fire, food, and drinkable water. All the while, they had to stay on guard from both animal and human predators while keeping the remaining contestants up to date. It was a lot to deal with on little to no sleep.

"So, what's the plan?" Doc asked.

Hutch responded as if it were all part of survival protocol. "We spend the night here, wait to see if Tucker returns, search the area, sift through his video footage for clues. We should take turns catching up on sleep. We'll need to take turns standing guard overnight, as well. The next closest contestant is Jill Hill, about a day's hike from here. If Tucker doesn't turn up, even if he does, we move on at daybreak tomorrow. It's too risky to stay in one place for too long. Once we've got everyone together and numbers on our side, we set up a line of defense and then hunt this killer down." Looking up at the sky, he added, "I just hope it doesn't rain."

The wind was picking up and the temperature was dropping noticeably. The sky was still clear, but they knew that could change at any moment and they had to be prepared. Rummaging through Tucker Jordan's equipment, they took an inventory, delighted to find his raingear.

Page tried it on over her clothes. She nearly disappeared in a sea of bright yellow. The raincoat alone, covered most of her body, coming down to her knees. The pants were falling off her, but she used a cordage belt to tie them on and chopped the legs to a manageable length. The pieces she cut off were perfect for Hutch and Doc to use as head coverings. For the rest of their bodies, Hutch cut up a tarp to make ponchos.

The problem with their raingear was the color. They were decked out in bright blue and yellow.

"Good luck hiding from the killer," Page commented, modeling her tailored rain suit. "I look like I was dipped in highlighter ink."

"The killer won't come out in the rain," Doc speculated. "If we're lucky, that is."

"If we're *lucky*, the killer won't find us," Page argued.

"If we're *lucky*, the killer won't come after us at all," Hutch edited.

"How does the killer know where each contestant's camp is?" Page asked, tilting her head as if it had just dawned on her.

"That's a great question," said Doc. "The killer has to be a crewmember. None of the contestants could have located everyone else's camp within 14 days."

"Who says the killer knows the location of every camp?" Hutch responded. "Either way, it could still be someone who was on the island before any of us. We need to put together a timeline of who was killed and when. But, it looks like the killer hasn't been to the other side of the island, yet."

He pulled out the map and they gathered round as he explained and pointed out, "This lake is almost exactly the middle point of the island. Everyone west of the lake is dead. Zoey Price is unaccounted for. Hers is the only camp north of the lake. Directly to the east is Jill's camp, also missing. The next closest contestant is Stephanie Hamilton, all the way in the northeast corner. She's alive and well."

He tapped the X marking Stephanie's camp. It was tucked away on its own peninsula and protected by a sprawling cliff by land.

"And, we're here," he continued, pointing to Tucker's camp close to the lake's western-most shore. "It seems the killer hasn't made it past the cliff. So, if he started from Jill, he went: Jill, Zoey, Tucker, Floyd, and then Derrick, which is where he ran into us and took our boat." He traced the area with his finger, connecting the dots from Jill's camp to Zoey, who was actually alive and currently, at Jill's camp. Zoey's camp and Tucker's camp were separated by ocean, a thin peninsula and another stretch of ocean, making the trek by land twice as far.

"Floyd's last video footage was from Day 5," Doc interjected. "Could the killer have located four camps on foot in five days? Never mind the time it takes to stalk and kill four people."

"Right," Hutch agreed, holding a finger up for control of the conversation. "And he couldn't have started with Derrick. His body wasn't hanging there for nine days by the time we found it, no way. So, that would put Floyd and Derrick's deaths far enough apart for the killer to have started with Floyd, proceeded to Tucker, Zoey, and Jill and then circled back to Derrick. Also, you have to wonder why Kimmie Arden was bypassed, initially."

"Then again, Zoey and Jill might not even be dead," Page reminded them.

"True," Hutch concurred. "But, either way, the timeline is strange. I don't think the killer knew where to find any of them. It's too disorganized."

"Oh my god. Maybe it's Nelson Greely," Page blurted out, as if it hadn't even crossed the filter in her mind yet.

"What?" Hutch asked, dubious.

She thought it through out loud. "What if Nelson Greely came here with the advanced crew to bury the treasure chests, but he found something valuable, something he wanted to keep to himself? He goes back to LA and tries to get the network to pull the plug on the show, arguing the island is unsafe. Then, he comes back to the island hoping to cash in, but he finds we're filming anyway. He starts killing the contestants, steals our boat, and sinks the Mothership before anyone can find out what he's trying to hide here. He would know, at least roughly, where each camp was located based on where he buried the treasure chests."

"Interesting theory," Doc agreed, reprocessing it again.

Hutch was less convinced. "I don't know. It sounds a little too Scooby Doo-ish. Are we going to pull off the killer's mask when we catch him and find out it was some greedy old white guy the whole time?"

"Well, you said it could be someone that was here before us. Nelson Greely was here before us," Page reasoned.

"Someone could have been here before Nelson Greely," Hutch argued.

"Like, who?"

"Anyone in the world. We're not on another planet here. This is prime real estate for someone who wants to live off the grid. An escaped fugitive, Russian pirates, refugees, castaways, Malaysia Airlines Flight 370, *anything* is possible. One thing's for sure, sitting on our asses talking about it isn't going to help. We need to get back to work. Food, water, fire, sleep. Let's get to it before it rains."

*****

With food, water, and fire taken care of, the crew searched the surrounding forest together. No one was allowed to go walking off alone, not even to relieve themselves. They were armed and hypervigilant, following an animal trail which brought them to a cliff overlooking the ocean.

Down below, their Medline rocked back and forth over choppy waves, anchored and unoccupied. No sign of the killer. No one said a word. They scanned every inch of the panoramic view.

Black clouds formed a straight line across the sky, like a blanket easing in from the east, but Hutch and his crew were still dry under clear sky. A deep rolling rumble of thunder churned out a warning. Dusk would be coming early and it might be a cold, wet evening.

"Let's make a run for it," Page suggested. "Just run to the boat and go. We can pick up the other contestants and get out of here."

"Are you crazy?" Doc asked. "How far do you think we'll get in that little boat on the open ocean?"

"We won't even make it to the boat if the killer is watching," Hutch interjected. "We don't even know how to get down there. We can't climb down this cliff. It's too dangerous. We have to scope out the area first. If we can find the killer before the killer finds us, we'll have the advantage."

Page turned around, looking back into the darkening woods. "What if the killer has already found us? He could be following us. Waiting for us to get into a vulnerable spot, like this one. We're practically cornered here."

"You're right," Hutch agreed. "And, we're out in the open. But, the first place the killer will look is at Tucker's camp if he's been there before. The bastard probably knew we'd end up coming here next."

"He's probably listening to us on one of the missing radios," Doc surmised, the darkness around his eyes crying out from lack of sleep worse than his days as an ER doctor.

"Follow me," Hutch whispered. "We take it slow. No talking. Try to be as quiet as possible. Eyes open. If you see me hold a closed fist in the air, it means get down and keep your mouth shut, immediately.

They crept through the tall yellowing grass, back to the trail they had followed to get there. Hutch froze, freezing Page behind him and Doc behind her. A scrape against dry leaves almost made them jump had it not sounded so far away. It was distinct enough to make Hutch throw a fist up and drop to one knee.

Another dry crinkling of leaves came from the same direction, like someone raking in the forest. After a few strokes, it stopped. Hutch's eyes widened in search, scrutinizing every bush and every tree. Was there someone hiding there?

Another sound announced two legs walking through the leaf litter, swishing as feet dragged along. Hutch waved his crew over, leading them to take cover. He could see movement far away through cracks in the bushes and trees.

He bobbed his head around, trying to get a better view as the sound grew. Not taking any chances, he drew an arrow back in his bow, ready to shoot anything that came near them.

Through the woods, a hooded figure appeared, pushing an obstructing branch out of the way, lumbering forward, covered in a brown tarp poncho, looking down, face hidden from view.

Hutch whispered over his shoulder, "If things go bad, I'll keep him occupied. You two make a run for it."

Before anyone could object or ask questions, Hutch jumped from cover, onto the trail, confronting the stalker with an arrow aimed at the chest.

"Stop right there," Hutch shouted. "Take another step and you're dead."

EZRA GREER

Day 18

5:05pm

Age: 51
Occupation: Truck Driver
Home: Alaska
Status: Widower, 3 children

"I'm not going to stand around here, waiting to be killed," Ezra Greer affirmed. He had returned to camp with a batch of gutted fish caught in the river with the gill net. This single survival item had been bringing in a steady supply of protein now that he had it set up in the perfect spot.

The camera continued to roll while he prepared to cook. Ezra had no interest in filming for the TV show anymore. The camera was now a tool. He set it up to monitor his camp for unwanted visitors while he was away. He was away a lot, hunting and securing his territory with traps for both animal and human predators.

"I know I'm a suspect. I can tell by the way they're talking to me on the radio. The producers know about my past. If people are really turning up dead, they probably think I had something to do with it. I'm in a no-win situation here. If the crew comes for me, they'll treat me like a criminal. If the killer gets to me first, I'll have to defend myself, probably kill him and then try to prove I'm not the original killer. Either way, I'm screwed. This is not what I signed up for."

He ducked into his shelter to retrieve the salt and pepper while two fish fillets sizzled in the pan over the fire.

"I'm completely on my own now," he said, returning to the chair next to the fire.

He had built a "jungle dining room set"—a small table and one chair—so he could enjoy his meals al fresco. A lot of work had gone into his camp and he had settled into an effective rhythm, not only surviving but thriving. With the contest cancelled and a killer on the prowl, all that was about to change.

"Completely on my own," he said, again. "Why does this keep happening to me? When I was released from prison, it was a dark, somber day. I was happy to be getting out of jail, happy to be exonerated. It sounds like a story with a happy ending—freedom, justice, but it was far from happy. It was far from acceptable. Everything I worked for my entire life had been taken away from me before being imprisoned. I was coming out with nothing. My home was gone. The lawyers took every cent I ever earned. The prison just spit me out on the street with nowhere to go."

He scratched at the graying beard which was getting thicker and grayer day by day. Leaving his chair for a moment, he pushed the fish fillets around the pan to keep them from sticking.

"So, there I was, finally being released, completely on my own. Outside the prison, a group of reporters were waiting like vultures. One of them asked me why I didn't look happier. After all, I was a free man. 'The nightmare is over,' she said with a fake smile on her stupid face. I looked at her and said, 'my wife is still dead. My relationship with my children is irreparable. I've lost absolutely everything I ever cared about and I have nowhere to go.' That little soundbite never made the news. I guess they were expecting a happy, triumphant story where they could tell everyone at the end to never give up and keep fighting. But, no one really cares. My life is just a story to temporarily entertain people, maybe outrage a few of them until they move on to the next news story, all along forgetting the characters in these stories are real people who have to continue living somehow."

Ezra slid one of his hand-carved, wooden spatulas under the fish fillets and flipped them over one by one. They each received a dash of salt and pepper.

"The way I see it, my options are the same as they were when I got out of prison—lay down and die or keep surviving. I'm going to keep surviving. I refuse to surrender this territory. It might not look like much, but I worked hard for this. I'm not finished living my life. It's time for a little offense. I won't be sharing that with anyone. I'm done with this stupid game and these stupid cameras. So, for all the reasons you've seen documented on these videos, this will be my last communication of any kind. It's every man for himself now. I can't trust anybody on this island. I don't know anybody on this island. Everyone is a potential enemy. Goodbye and good riddance."

And, with that bitter farewell, Ezra shut down the camera.

ZOEY PRICE

Day 18

6:30pm

Age: 24
Occupation: Dance Instructor
Home: Montana
Status: Single

Zoey Price had chosen to hug the shoreline of the lake until she got a view of how close the ocean was. She didn't want to end up walking in a circle again. Her overnight hike continued into Day 18. Fueled by another feast of crayfish and greens she had harvested along the way, she had covered a lot of ground.

"I'm not stopping until I find another live human being on this god-forsaken island," she promised the camera, dragging her weary feet along. Finding help wasn't her only motivation. She was racing against a blackened sky which threatened to drop buckets of rain any minute. The only pit stop she had made was to turn the extra tarp she got from Jillian Hill's camp into a rain poncho.

Her pink snow suit had turned a mangy brown. Dirty wisps of insulation squeezed out like cotton candy through tears in the legs.

"I'm not stopping," she repeated again, urging her own body to keep moving. "I just have to keep putting one foot in front of the other. There has to be someone out here with a functioning radio."

The trail she had been following took her to the west over hilly terrain. Another steep incline appeared before her, slowing her down, but she kept moving at a snail's pace to get to the top.

"There better be something good at the top of this hill," she said, winded. "Someone's camp, maybe a nice Starbucks and a supermarket," she joked. "I feel like I've been walking forever."

What she found at the top was a downhill trail sloping gradually to a hideous mess.

"What the hell is that?" she asked the camera, squinting. "I swear, I'm so tired my eyes won't even focus."

Using the camera's screen, she zoomed in on the object. There were blackened wooden spikes intermingled with bones, rotting flesh, and torn clothes. "Damn. It looks like a giant wooden porcupine landed on someone," Zoey described, her face more concerned than her words. Scanning the site, she noticed the severed neck and lack of head. Her heart nearly jumped out her throat. She squatted on her feet, hugging her knees and rocked back and forth, trying to keep it together. "Not another dead body. I can't deal with another dead body. What the hell is going on here?"

She buried her head in her knees, pulling the tarp hood over it like a turtle hiding from a predator. The camera only picked up muffled whimpers and desperate whining. She picked up her head again, tears in her eyes. "What the hell kind of TV show is this? Where is everyone?" she cried, anger building beneath the tears.

She sprang to her feet, looking for something to hit or break. "They just dump you on this stupid fucking island and forget about you? They just leave you here to die? Why isn't anyone looking for me?"

The tantrum was short lived, resulting in smashing a large, fallen branch against the trunk of a tree. It was like pulling someone's arm off and beating them with it, but it vented some frustration. Cooler thoughts prevailed in the end. She knew she didn't have the energy to spend.

Braving on, she steeled herself, willing her feet to bring her closer with the hope that the dead body had a functioning radio. The closer she got, the more apparent it became there'd be nothing useful left intact. There were yellow shards of plastic all over the ground on the other side of the log. One of the spikes had pierced right through the radio, leaving it impaled next to a piece of cloth hardened with dry blood.

"Poor guy. Or girl. Can't really tell which," Zoey said, examining the mess.

A few feet away, a pair of boots stood upright as if their owner had been knocked right out of his shoes. She checked to make sure they didn't contain a pair of feet before comparing them to her own shoe size. Too big.

"Damn it. But, I'm sure I can find a use for these," she claimed and wrapped them up in her makeshift tarp backpack. It was almost filled to capacity and getting heavier. If she found anything else, she'd have to jettison something.

She rooted through the torn clothes, searching for pockets. There was a ferrorod in one and a headlamp in another.

"Interesting," she commented. "A headlamp, but no head. No camera. I wonder if this was one of the crew members."

The only thing left to salvage was a canister of bear spray. She had one holstered on each hip now under her new poncho.

The excursion took long enough to allow the blanket of dark clouds to catch up to her, spurting a light drizzle upon arrival. Zoey pulled the hood over her head, the raindrops pelting the stiff tarp material.

"Just what I needed," the weary survivor sighed.

Thunder rumbled across the sky, mimicked by a churning in her stomach. A sharp pain in her abdomen doubled her over. Staggering into the woods in pain, trying to get away from the nauseating sight of Tucker's remains, she looked for a spot to unload the suddenly urgent delivery, unsure which end it wanted to come out. Her mouth watered, preparing for the upheaval. She bent over and let it erupt, spilling in a pathetic little pile blackened by bile. There wasn't much left in her stomach to reject.

Upon straightening, she caught a glimpse of another trail through the thick brush. Bobbing her head around, she couldn't get a good view, torn between curiosity and another possible emission. She took a swig of treated water from a plastic bottle and swallowed hard, willing her stomach to settle down. Focused regulating her breathing, she evened out and kicked some leaves to cover her vomit.

"I don't know why I'm covering it," she mumbled, feeling the need to explain to the camera.

She didn't want to end up like the dead body in the 'wooden porcupine' trap. With her head down, she kept watch for tripwires and booby traps as she made her way to the new trail, hoping it would lead to salvation. A man jumped out onto the trail before she got there, aiming an arrow at her.

"Stop right there," he shouted. "Take another step and you're dead."

Chapter 17

Day 18

Crossroads

"Don't shoot. It's me, Zoey, Zoey Price," the girl under the tarp hood shouted, tilting her head back to see, hands in the air.

Doc and Page emerged from the woods. Page recognized Zoey right away and lunged forward to block Hutch's shot. Doc tried to hold her back from interfering, grabbing her by the shoulders.

She let him hold her back, but shouted. "That's Zoey Price. Put the bow down, Hutch."

"In a minute," Hutch replied, cool and calm. "Pull your hood off, Zoey. I want to see your face."

Zoey kept her hands up, using one to pull back the hood. The new, weathered lines on her face were highlighted by dirt, her lips dry and chapped. Her eyes were half-closed and sleepy, drooping even in surprise. She didn't respond, following his orders.

"We've been trying to reach you on the radio. Why haven't you answered?" Hutch asked.

"I don't have a working radio," Zoey explained, keeping it simple. Full explanations were lengthy and best saved for a time when weapons were not being pointed.

"What happened to the one we gave you?" Hutch continued to interrogate.

"It melted when my shelter burned down," she explained, on the verge of tearing up.

"What are you doing wandering the woods around Tucker Jordan's camp?" Hutch asked, lowering his weapon.

"I've been on the move since my camp burned down. I lost all my supplies." Her voice was fading into exhaustion. "I can't hold my arms up anymore. I'm going to put them down," the weary traveler said, lowering her arms. "There's a camp near here?"

Hutch turned to Page, asking, "How did you recognize her so quickly?"

"Her nose. She's got that cute little knobby nose. I'd recognize it anywhere," Page explained, taking a step away from Doc's loosened grip.

Doc threw a single wave to Zoey accompanied by a nod, but before he could speak, he dropped to his knees, a bewildered look on his face. He fell forward like an old tree coming down, an arrow sticking out of the back of his head.

Page shrieked in horror.

Hutch yelled, "Run!" taking cover behind a tree. He looked back at Doc, just a few feet away, face down on the trail. The good doctor's body convulsed on the ground, his arms flat at his sides, flopping around like a harpooned fish.

Zoey turned and ran back the way she had come. Page followed her as fast as her legs would take her. They zigzagged through the forest, making themselves difficult, moving targets.

Hutch squatted behind the tree, taking a deep breath. He peeked out, trying to get a fix on the killer's position. It was like trying to locate the Viet Cong in the Vietnam War. The arrow had come from nowhere, perhaps shot by one of the bushes or trees. There was nothing else in sight. He ran across the arrow's path to another tree, taking cover again and readying his bow and arrow.

"You fucking coward," he screamed, hoping to coax the killer from his hiding place. "Ambushing people like a fucking animal." Poking his nose out into the open, he held his breath, wide-eyed, listening for the killer's movements. He was met with silence and a blank, green canvas, not a creature stirring. Even the birds were quiet.

The sudden tranquility was eerie. Doc's body had stopped convulsing. But, not far away, Page and Zoey were running for their lives.

Hutch wanted to go after the killer, hunt him down and kill him, but which way to go? Trace the arrow back to where it came from and hope to take the killer by surprise somehow?

Impossible.

The women were getting farther away and the killer could have taken off after them. That left Hutch with only one option—catch up with Page and Zoey. He broke out in a sprint, half-expecting to catch an arrow in the back as soon as he broke cover.

Fumbling with the radio as he ran, Hutch called out, "Page,

where are you? Over."

An answer didn't come quickly. If the girls were hiding, they may have even turned their radios off if they were in close proximity to the killer. Hutch didn't risk trying again. Zoey's deteriorated physical appearance told him they couldn't have run for long. Hiding could be their only option.

A confirmation came over the radio in a whisper. "We're hiding."

It sounded like Page's voice. He slowed to walk, trying to catch his breath. There wasn't much left in his tank either after four grueling days on the move. It was a rare taste of nature most humans are lucky enough to never experience—the decision between fight and flight when you don't have the physical strength to do either, but your life is still on the line, no matter what you do. There is little security in nature. Even less when you're being stalked by another human—the most formidable predator in the world.

It was new ground for Hutch. He was a survivalist, not a soldier, in what was turning into a war against an enemy he had yet to see. If he had been alone, he surely would have taken a different approach, but with everyone else scattered around the island, there was little choice but to survive long enough to unite and make a stand. If they had to worry about the basics—food, water, shelter—on top of security, they'd all be as good as dead.

Hutch walked through the forest, with all this in mind, trying to decide what to do next. When he came across an animal trail, he followed it without giving it much thought.

Page's whisper came across the radio. "Where are you, Hutch? Over."

Over. She had determined it safe to answer, Hutch had to assume.

"I couldn't get eyes on him. I ran in the same direction as you. I just came out on a trail," he explained in a precautionary whisper. "Is Zoey with you? Where are you? Over."

No answer. He checked behind him, his flanks, scanning the woods for signs of Page and Zoey as well as the killer. Following the trail around a bend, he came upon Tucker Jordan's remains strewn around the trap that had killed him.

He pressed the talk button on the radio and said, "I think I found Tucker Jordan."

After a short delay, an answer followed. "Keep going."

Hutch perked up, a vigilant eye scrutinizing every bulge and crevice as he walked, anywhere two petite women could be hiding. He understood their hesitation to divulge their location over the radio. The killer could be listening. The killer could be watching, following Hutch for the perfect opportunity to take them all out at the same time. Their only saving grace was the dwindling daylight and reduced visibility.

Off in the distance, Hutch noticed a good hiding spot—a cluster of large boulders protruding from the ground. An old downed tree added a second wall to the natural shelter, its leftover stump indicating it had been growing atop one of the boulders at some point in its lifetime.

If Page and Zoey weren't hiding there already, they would be soon, once Hutch found them. He gave another look around for stalkers and then left the trail, traversing the dense vegetation. His leaf-crunching footsteps were difficult to minimize, but another sound whistled through the woods. A hollow, timid sound like that of a dove.

Hutch recognized the sound. Someone was using their hands to create a type of whistle. With hands cupped together and thumbs positioned just right, it creates a crude wind instrument which can be manipulated by the wave of one hand, similar to a conch shell. He knew it well since his childhood when a Cub Scout leader had taught him how to do it.

The hollow whistle sounded again. Hutch kept his eyes on the downed tree. The top of Page's head popped up as Zoey sounded off again. He gave a single nod of confirmation and scanned the area again before hopping over the log. Page and Zoey sat up, Zoey's legs covered with leaves. They had been trying to camouflage themselves as they waited for Hutch to find them.

"Are you okay?" he asked them.

"We're fine," Page answered.

"Fine? We're not fine," Zoey growled. "Page says half the contestants are dead and we're next. I've come across two dead bodies in the last few days and now the doctor gets killed right in front of me. I'm far from *fine*." Her outburst died as quickly as it had erupted, her last shreds of energy expended.

"Do you think he followed you?" Page asked.

"I can't be sure," Hutch answered. "We have to assume he's following us until we can confirm."

"If he's following us, we're screwed," Zoey grumbled. She pulled out a plastic bottle with water, took a swig and passed it to Page.

"Not necessarily. We can turn the tables on him, lead him into a trap," Hutch explained.

"How do we do that?" Page asked, passing the water bottle to Hutch.

"We radio ahead to the remaining contestants, have them set up an ambush."

"What if the killer is listening to our radio chatter?" Page asked.

"That's a good question," he answered before turning to Zoey. "How did your camp burn down?"

"My own carelessness," she said, keeping her answer short.

"You certainly don't look like the Zoey we dropped off on Day 1," Hutch commented.

"That Zoey was a little girl. People grow up fast when they have to survive on their own."

"You said you came across *two* dead bodies?" he inquired.

"The body in the trap on the trail you just came from was one. The other was a woman in an open ditch. An older woman. It looked like she had been shot with an arrow through the chest. I'm lucky I didn't run into the killer myself. Who is he?"

"Did the body have a head?" Hutch asked.

"Which? The woman? Yes."

"Where did you find her?"

"There's a lake not far from here. She's on the other side up a hill on a plateau in a ditch. I'll tell you right now, I'm not going back there. I've been wandering around, walking in circles for too long."

"There's no need to go back," Hutch assured her.

Page interjected, "The only contestant left that fits that description is Jillian Hill. That's roughly where her camp would have been, around the bay and the lake."

Hutch pulled the map from his pocket, nodding in agreement. "Okay. So, we know which direction to go. There's no reason to go into the northeastern part of the island," he said pointing to a portion of the island sectioned off by two bays. Thee bay—the long, narrow bay separated Stephanie Hamilton and Wes Wood. Then there was the smaller, short bay where they had seen the Medline before Doc got sniped. "We have to head toward the remaining survivors."

There was no time to mourn the loss of the fallen. There was no talk of going back to bury Doc. No one had the energy to grieve and follow rituals, even if they had known the dead better. They were down to the few supplies they carried. Zoey had more than Hutch and Page put together now.

The temperature was dropping, but there would be no fire tonight. It was too risky. The best they could hope for was no rain. In their weakened state, all they could do was rest and keep an eye out for predators—both animal and human.

They sat huddled together while Zoey whispered her harrowing disaster story—the ups and downs of surviving on her own with almost no supplies. Page brought her up to date on the crew's tale from the moment they had made landfall.

In the last moments of dusk, a howl carried through the forest, not like the whine of a wolf which they were used to. It almost seemed to be mocking as it swelled and repeated, "Yooooooooo!" A cackling laugh followed, remaining stationary and distant, repeating and alternating with the unsettling howl. It echoed all around them, bouncing off the trees, moving past them, making them feel surrounded.

"That's him, isn't it?" Zoey whispered, watching Hutch's shadowy face for a reaction to the noise.

"It doesn't sound like any animal I've ever heard," Hutch confirmed.

"Maybe we should track him down," Page suggested. "It should be easy if he keeps howling. It'll be harder for him to see us in the dark. We could sneak up on him. This is our chance."

"No. That's what he wants. He's toying with us. Taunting us. Trying to draw us out. He doesn't know where we are. That means we're relatively safe for the night. At least, I hope. We're going to have to sleep right here. I'll bury the two of you in leaves and drape the tarp over top. That'll provide sufficient warmth to prevent hypothermia and keep you dry, but it's not going to be comfortable."

"And where will you be?" Zoey asked.

"I'll be on guard duty."

SEATON ROGERS

Day 19

3:04am

Age: 33
Occupation: Screenwriter
Home: Utah
Status: Single

Seaton Rogers was jolted awake by the metallic clanking of his "Early Warning System". Using fishing line, he had rigged up trip wires across the trail that led to his camp. Inside his shelter, the alarm was nothing more than a carved stick with small rocks balanced upon its length. If the fishing line is disturbed, so too is the stick it's tied to, causing the rocks to fall off and into the metal cooking pot. The system only covered the "Georgia Border" of Seaton's tiny Florida-shaped peninsula which is only useful if an intruder comes by land.

He hadn't decided what to do about the three shores the killer could land on. If Seaton's peninsula was Florida, he was living in Orlando with a thirty-minute walk to either Daytona Beach or Tampa. The system which surrounded his camp was still in place and would have to suffice until he came up with a better idea.

When the Early Warning System sounded, Seaton sprang up, clutching a knife. He had fallen asleep with the knife in his hand less than an hour ago. The warm glow from the fire lit up the room. Except for the warning system, nothing was disturbed. He got out of bed and grabbed the bow, dressed head to toe as usual.

Seaton's backpack had turned into a bugout bag, hidden in the forest near some dense bushes. He called the area "the security booth" because it provided him a narrow spot to hide with an excellent view of his campsite. If an intruder showed up Seaton would have the advantage of surprise as well as the option to flee. Until then, he had a vantage point and a few lonely crickets keeping him company.

"The toughest thing," Seaton would later tell the camera, "is making the decision. Stay and fight? Should I run for my life and leave behind everything I worked so hard for? I've thought about it. You *have* to think about it ahead of time. There might not be any time for hesitation. It's not easy to decide to abandon everything. Maybe it's easier when your life is on the line one hundred percent, without a doubt. But, if I think I stand a chance fighting, I'm fighting. Surviving in the jungle while on the run is perhaps just as dangerous."

He sat on a stool made from narrow logs, a feature he had installed in the "security booth" after contemplating how long he'd have to wait to be sufficiently satisfied it was a false alarm. He wouldn't feel safe until daylight.

And so, the virtual standoff began. He wouldn't sleep a wink, wondering if someone was there. A never-ending blanket of clouds kept the forest black as a void, leaving him to wonder if there was anything there at all. Every little noise rattled him. He'd hear something moving, then it would go silent, but Seaton repeated the noise in his head, replaying it over and over, scrutinizing every aspect to conjure up an explanation for it.

It was just a deer walking by.
It was two chipmunks fighting.
It was a bird landing and then taking off again.

When all else seemed impossible, to calm himself, he would default to blaming the inexplicable noises on squirrels.

It was a long, nerve-racking wait for dawn. His sleep deprived imagination ran wild and deep into corners of his mind he didn't care to explore. Would it be better to die, quick and clean? Dying slowly from a serious injury would buy him extra time for someone to come along and help, but it could be agonizing and there was no guarantee anyone would come. He tried to push the endless possibilities out of his head and focus on the sights and sounds of what he called *the jungle*.

9:29am

Although it had been getting progressively colder day by day, Day 19 saw a jump in temperature into the mid-sixties. The leaf bed on the forest floor was dry and crisp. Seaton Rogers had worn a path circling his camp. He called it the Patrol Path.

"I wonder if I've ever spoken to a murderer," he contemplated, the camera his only witness as he patrolled, bow and arrow ready for action. "I'm often curious about the things that cross our paths which we're unaware of."

Hutch's voice squawked over the radio. "Where are you Zoey? Over."

Seaton turned the volume down. He had been monitoring the crew's chatter all morning. They seemed to have lost each other. First, Hutch and Page went back and forth, explaining Page's location. Now that they found each other, Hutch and Zoey began a conversation. Seaton stayed out of it all together.

"I'm by the lake," Zoey answered, half-buried in static. "Where the big river flows out." She continued to describe the area in great detail.

Seaton turned the volume down some more and let his mind wander out loud. "What are the odds of me crossing paths with a killer in the forest while filming a TV show? Some people would say the odds were one hundred percent. Some people think everything happens for a reason. And it's true, technically, but they have it backwards. Everything happens for a reason and the reasons are the events leading up to what happens, not the events that happen after. A window breaks because it was hit with a rock, not because there's some magic plan being played out that you'll reap the rewards from sometime in the future. People always assume that fate has something wonderful or special in store for them. In reality, we all have the same fate—death. If you really believe everything happens for a reason and the reason is something in your future, then everything happens for your ultimate fate—the end of your future—and that's death. I don't believe in that. I don't believe in fate."

Seaton perked up a bit, seeing one of his deadfall traps had been triggered up ahead. His food supply had remained steady, but every little bit was a welcomed victory.

"I believe we control our own destiny," he went on. "I almost didn't come to Isolation Island. I was having second thoughts, doubting my own ability to survive. In the end, I decided it would be worth it just to get away from people for a while and to test my abilities. That's the reason I'm here. I wasn't destined to come here. I made the decision."

He approached the deadfall trap with caution. Paranoia whispered in his ear, waring him the killer could have triggered the trap to serve as a distraction. A scan of the woods only revealed no one was visible among the dense vegetation.

"Some people believe I didn't have a choice. No matter what happened, I would have decided to come here. Well, then, why bother thinking about anything if our choices are predetermined? People believe in a lot of things that don't make sense if you think about it, even briefly. People ask me what I believe in and they get all bent out of shape when I tell them I don't believe in anything. I'm still thinking about everything. I enjoy the mystery of life. I don't think anyone has figured it out yet. If anything, I believe in facts, but facts are facts whether you believe them or not. There are things I'd *like* to believe. I'd like to believe aliens are among us or watching and waiting for the right time to help humankind. I'd like to believe that we live on in some way, shape or form after we die. But, I don't believe any of these things because there's no proof. That's a great tragedy I see affecting the entire planet and population—people are killing each other because of things they simply believe with no proof whatsoever. It's sad and it's scary."

"I'll wait right here for you," Zoey said over the radio. "How long do you think it'll take you to get here? Over."

"At least four hours. Maybe longer," Hutch replied. "Hang tight until we get there. Over and out."

Seaton was delighted by the little tail he found sticking out from under his deadfall trap. He lifted the heavy stone revealing a dead, flattened mouse underneath.

"Was it fate that led this mouse to my deadfall trap? Hey there, Mickey," he joked, turning the flattened mouse over. "Or is it Minnie? Was it fate that led you to my deadfall trap?"

He switched to a high-pitched squeaky mouse voice to answer. "No. It was the bait. I love fish guts."

"And there you have it folks," Seaton concluded in a serious news anchor voice.

STEPHANIE HAMILTON

Day 19

1:15pm

Age: 29
Occupation: Artist
Home: Colorado
Status: Single

Stephanie Hamilton made contact with the crew and broadcasted her message over the radio while she stood in front of a filming camera on a tripod. Her shelter was the backdrop for her final video diary entry.

"My name is Stephanie Hamilton," she said, steady and monotone—a combination forged by fatigue. "I'm from Silverton, Colorado in the United States of America. I came here chasing a dream that involved a future, but now I see there is no future. I've always been happy in the present, but that was assuming there was a future. The only possible future I see now is being stranded on this island for the rest of my life and even that wouldn't be so bad if it wasn't for the possibility that I'll be hunted down and die a painful death any day soon."

She spoke in a strange state of calm, her words floating and wandering like telling a fairytale, but fluctuating between depression and indifference.

"I lived on this planet in peace, as much as I could. I'd like to die a peaceful death, as well. I'd rather die on my own terms than let some psycho killer decide when my time is up. Life is a game of survival and sometimes, you have to know when to tap out. I've had a good run. I only wish it had lasted longer."

Even the camera could tell she was tired and a bit loopy—not the best mental state for making life and death decisions, but that's how survival goes.

"Goodbye world. And, good luck." She signed off the radio.

Not wanting to hear the pleas of Hutch and his crew begging her not to go through with it, she switched the radio off altogether.

To the camera, she had a few more things to say. "I'm going to throw myself in the frigid, unforgiving Pacific Ocean. If anyone finds this, let my family know I loved them and that I lived the way I wanted to and I died the way I wanted to."

Her voice fell away and faded out like a sudden case of strep throat had struck her. She was only able to produce one teardrop which didn't even make it down the dry, cracked skin of her left cheek.

"Oh, and, if the killer finds this—who the fuck are you to end someone else's life? Next time you have the urge to kill, do the world a favor and kill *yourself*."

She turned off the camera and picked up her backpack, its weight almost causing her to topple. If she jumped into the ocean with it on, she'd sink like a stone. She took one last look around camp, taking her time. At 1:33pm on Day 19, Stephanie Hamilton abandoned her camp and disappeared into the woods on a path to the nearest shore.

Chapter 18

Day 19

1:55pm

"Stephanie, please, if you won't answer me, at least, take some more time to think about it. Over," Hutch finished his plea after almost half an hour of begging Stephanie Hamilton to not kill herself. With no reply from her, he didn't have anything left to say. Part of him respected the decision. Stephanie had a good point. Who wouldn't rather die by their own hand than be murdered? If he talked her out of it and she died a painful death, it would be his fault, he decided. Still, he was surprised that a survivalist would choose to not survive.

Page and Zoey stared at him while they waited, again, for a reply. Hutch kept his eyes moving. The task at hand prior to Stephanie's speech was more important than ever. They had spent the entire morning testing the theory that the killer is monitoring their radio communications. They pretended to be separated and gave away their exact, fictitious locations while watching those locations to see if the killer would show up.

After the first attempt failed to coax the killer out, they tried the location they currently had under surveillance—a conspicuous corner where the lake emptied into a wide river which flowed west, past Tucker Jordan's camp and emptying into the ocean near Kimmie Arden's camp. There's no way the killer could miss it the way it was described over the radio. Zoey had pretended to be the one waiting in this location, guiding Hutch and Page to her and, thus, the killer. They had been waiting for hours, but the killer didn't bite.

Now, it appeared they had lost another contestant. Only four remained and Hutch wondered if he could stay alive long enough to save a single one. Sleep deprivation and malnutrition couldn't be willed away no matter how determined he was. They only built up and took their toll.

"She's bluffing," Zoey suggested.

"Bluffing?" Page asked, trying to provoke elaboration.

"She wants the killer to think she's dead. No need to go after her," Zoey explained. She looked to Hutch for a reaction.

He remained stoic, staring straight ahead, deep in thought. "We need to get the boat back," he decided.

"You said it was too risky," Page reminded him.

"We're going to have to take a risk if we're going to save the others," Hutch explained.

"The others are fine. They're all far away from here. We're the ones in danger right now," Page argued.

"That's why we need to get the boat back. If we don't get out of here, *we* will be in constant danger. All of us," Hutch spelled out.

Without another word, he saddled up his backpack and led the way. He still wasn't one hundred percent sure the killer wasn't watching them and listening over the radio, but they had lost almost a full day testing the theory. Hutch cursed himself for what he determined had been wasted time. They hadn't learned anything. The killer might as well have been invisible.

"Hey," Zoey said, something dawning on her. "Can't we use the boat's radio to call for help?"

"We can try, but it's only got a range of about thirty miles or so," Hutch explained.

"But, can't we drive out a few miles and try it?" Zoey asked.

"This was a deserted island for a reason. It's remote. Ships don't just pass by. There's no reason to get anywhere near this damn island. The chances of a ship passing by are slim," he replied.

"But, you said we could try," Page pointed out.

"Yes, we *will* try," Hutch promised.

3:03pm

Step one in getting the Medline back was scoping out the area. Hutch had decided the best vantage point would be the spot they last saw it from—the tall cliff.

"What if it's not there anymore?" Zoey asked as they approached the clearing atop the cliff. No one wanted to ask the question out loud, but Zoey didn't believe in jinxes anymore.

"Then we go to Plan B," Hutch answered.

"What's Plan B?" Page asked, stopping ahead of Zoey and Hutch. She was already looking down on the empty "Tucker Bay" as they had named it. The other, larger bay, they had dubbed Jillian Bay to tell them apart. The lake and some treacherous terrain were between the two, according to the map which had been proven to not be 100% accurate. They'd have to take their chances trusting it and take the long way around the lake to get to the last corner of the island where the remaining three contestants were still alive.

Hutch had to see the empty bay for himself. There it was—Tucker Bay and no boat. Time for Plan B. "Come on," he said, turning around, offering no reaction to the missing boat.

"What are we going to do?" Page asked.

"If the killer is going in that direction with the boat, we'll go in this direction on foot." He ended pointing to the forest where he hoped they'd be able to get around the lake and the heart of the island.

"Why don't we go back to Tucker's camp and get our equipment?" Page challenged.

"For two reasons. One—the killer could be waiting there to ambush us. Two—the killer probably took everything we left behind. We have to keep moving forward."

WES WOOD

Day 19

3:06pm

Age: 57
Occupation: Farmer
Home: Mississippi
Status: Divorced, 8 children

"The killer is back on the Medline, the boat you should all remember from Insertion Day," Hutch's dire voice came through the radio. "That means, he's on the move along the north to northwest coast if he's coming toward you. I want every remaining contestant to band together to make a united attack."

Wes Wood listened with a questionable grin on his face. "We's gonna fight back, Yeehaw Motherfucker," he twanged with his thickest country accent for the camera filming from his left side as he sat slapping his knee for emphasis.

"Seaton, follow your nearest river north. Wes, you follow your nearest river south. Find a spot near the river where you can build a fort. Stock it with food and water. We're going to be on the move without food for a long time. Do you copy, Seaton, over?"

"Copy. Will do. Over." Wes assumed it was Seaton.

"Good. Do you copy, Wes?"

Wes answered, "Copy that. We's gonna rip this guy a new asshole. Over."

Hutch continued the roll call. "Ezra, if you're listening, follow your nearest river north. We'll meet you at the fork near the lake. Bring food. Do you copy?"

A long pause followed. Hutch tried a few more times with the same result—silence. He also tried to get a response from the MIA Stephanie Hamilton. More silence. He signed off by telling Seaton and Wes to start moving first thing in the morning. The rendezvous point was a twisted part of the river where it made a U-turn forming a bulge.

"This here's gonna get intristin' I tell you what," Wes told the camera. "The contest is over, but sure as shoot, the show's still on. Gonna get it all on camera and make my million dollars one way er another."

Giddy as a child on their first trip to Disney World, Wes Wood wasted no time getting down to the business of preparing for the trek to the rendezvous point to prepare for battle. The idea of building a fort in the woods gave him a much needed jolt of energy.

EZRA GREER

Day 19

3:06pm

Age: 51
Occupation: Truck Driver
Home: Alaska
Status: Widower, 3 children

Ezra Greer sat on a chair at his camp, sharpening the point of a stick as he listened to the instructions over the radio. There was a small pile of sharpened sticks next to him. He didn't reply when Hutch singled him out. He didn't spring into action. He didn't even flinch. He just listened and took note.

Ezra had an every-man-for-himself philosophy ever since his wife had been abducted and murdered and everyone abandoned him, assuming he was guilty. The attitude was only strengthened by his time in prison. Helping the others, banding together in a united front against the killer would go against everything his best judgement was telling him. Part of him was expecting to be accused of being the killer and joining up with the crew could only increase the likelihood.

He moved forward with his own survival, looking out for number one while continuing to contemplate his options.

Chapter 19

Day 19

4:45pm

Hutch led the way down a worn path which had been getting wider and more prominent. He kept a vigilant eye out for traps and tripwires as Zoey brought up the rear, making sure no one was following them. Ahead of them, up a slight hill, an obstacle appeared, protruding from the trail. Even from afar, Hutch could tell what it was. He stopped abruptly, eyes darting in every direction rather than scrutinizing the head on a stick in their path.

Behind him, Page gasped and ran toward the impaled head, disregarding Hutch's pleas to stop. Focused on the grizzly sight, she didn't appear to hear him or simply chose to ignore him. She stopped two feet away, frozen in place with her hand over her mouth. Although the face looked like animals had been nibbling on it, Page recognized Sharon's long, jet black hair framing in a ghastly mid-scream expression, jaw propped open.

Hutch pulled Page back, her legs not budging until forced to move. "Don't stand there," he whispered slow but stern.

"Wha…" Page began.

Hutch cut her off. "Whoever put that there did it for a reason. Not just to scare people away but to stop you in your tracks, probably within good view. It's a diversion tactic. While you're standing there like an idiot, staring at it, he's watching or on his way to kill you. We're probably close to where he lives."

Page broke Hutch's grip and marched right past the stick, her chin jutting out—the kind of look that's often followed by rolling up sleeves.

"What are you doing?" Hutch demanded, chasing after her.

"He's on the boat, which means, he's not home. If this is where he lives, I'm going to check it out," she insisted.

"And what if he's not alone?" Hutch posed. "The killer could have an accomplice; a whole family or tribe or who knows what.

I'm not walking into another ambush."

"Then what the hell are we going to do?" Page asked, whipping back around in frustration.

"First, we're going to get out of here, out of sight. Let's go," he ordered, pulling her away again.

Zoey had been hanging back, absorbed in watching and listening for any sign of movement. An eerie tranquility bathed in silence. A breeze rattled a symphony of leaves. Zoey didn't seem to notice the commotion Hutch was dealing with. He called her over, snapping her out of the trance cast by the location. He led the women into the woods for cover and the reconnaissance mission was on. They kept the path within sight, following it around the western-most point of the lake.

Cradled in a corner, overlooking the lake, the brick façade of an old, broken-down building peeked through vines and ivy overgrowth atop a slight hill. Hutch counted at least three floors if there wasn't a basement level. A wide, stone staircase led to the double doors in the center of the building on the second floor. A burnt out fire pit at the bottom of the staircase suggested nobody was home.

Hutch stopped his crew and they huddled in the bushes examining the building. The panes of glass in the double doors were gone, as well as most of the windows. Part of the moss-covered roof and top floor had been caved in by a giant fallen oak tree—an old injury judging by the looks of the rotting wood. The exposed interior walls had long since decayed. It was a wonder the entire west end of the building hadn't collapsed yet. Above the doorway, a disturbing set of lettering was etched into a concrete slab.

"Oh my god," Zoey whispered in awe. "Aliens."

Hutch's face displayed an instant "have you lost your mind" look. "What?"

"Look at the writing above the front doors," Zoey instructed, pointing a finger which poked through a hole in her glove at the tip. "It looks like some kind of alien language."

"I'm pretty sure that's Korean," Hutch said.

Zoey's eyebrows raised to full mast. "How do you know it's Korean? Not Chinese or Japanese?"

"Korean looks more like mathematical equations than Chinese

or Japanese writing. I've spent extensive time in all three countries. It's just a semi-educated guess. Chinese is more decorative looking. Japanese…" He shook his head searching for an adequate description, but the words were out of reach in his sleep deprived brain. "Japanese looks like Japanese," he finally settled. "The writing above the door looks Korean. I think we can rule out aliens for now."

"Damn. That would have been cool," Zoey said.

Page looked at Zoey and rolled her eyes.

"What?" Zoey asked, annoyed by the look. "Wouldn't you rather die knowing aliens exist?"

"I'd rather not die at all," Page snapped.

"Watch the windows," Hutch interrupted. He picked up a hefty rock and hurled it onto the front steps. It fractured upon impact, sending shards in multiple directions.

Three sets of eyes watched the windows for movement.

Nothing. If there was anyone inside the building, they weren't startled by the noise.

"Okay, let's go," Zoey said, starting forward.

Hutch grabbed her arm and pulled her back. "No. You two wait here. Be still and quiet. Watch for any movement in there. I'm going to circle around and check out the other side."

Page protested, "There's no one in there. That rock smashing on the front steps would've brought someone out to investigate, for sure."

"Just wait here and let me check out the other side. There's no reason to go in there in the first place," Hutch grumbled, trying to keep his voice lower than his frustration level. No reason other than curiosity.

"No reason?" Zoey interjected. "Maybe there's a radio or a phone or some way to send out an S.O.S."

"Or food. I'm starving," Page mumbled.

"We're not rushing into a mysterious building on an island that's supposed to be uninhabited," Hutch insisted. "Wait here," he commanded. "And stay down."

He climbed through the thick brush, hiding behind a wall of green as he made his way toward the center of the building, trying to get a peek in through the windowless doors. Anything could be inside, hidden by the shadows. Still, Hutch was determined to make his rounds and exhaust every angle before entering the building as if it was standard procedure.

Page and Zoey had other plans. They had circled around to the west end and were creeping up against the outer wall toward the front doors.

Hutch stifled a few four-letter words when he spotted them. They weren't exactly stealthy. He rushed back to his previous position—lined up with the staircase—readying an arrow. It was too late to stop them. All he could do was cover them and hope nothing popped out and killed them.

They opened one of the doors, a rusty creak announcing their arrival to the entire forest. Hutch cringed in anticipation of a trap going off but it never came. Zoey was the first one to enter, disappearing into the shadowy belly of the building. Hutch watched the windows for movement. So far, so good.

Zoey reappeared waving Hutch in. He, in turn, waved her to come back, mouthing, "Get out of there."

Zoey replied with more gestures encouraging him to join the exploration. Against his better judgement, he took a deep breath and broke cover, wondering if he'd be shot with an arrow as soon as he was out in the open. The dead quiet wasn't exactly encouraging, but at least, he could detect any nearby movement. Zoey and Page waited for him to climb the stairs.

"Well, I guess the front doors aren't booby trapped. Good job," he said, sarcastically out of frustration. "He must not be concerned with us finding his home," he added, assuming the killer lived in the building.

They walked into the cramped lobby, puke green tiles crumbling off the walls. There was no front desk or check-in area. Anyone who had arrived there in the building's heyday must have known where they were and why. But, what was this place? An apartment building? The world's smallest military base? The lobby held no clues.

"Follow me. Watch your step and do NOT wander off on your own," Hutch instructed.

They had entered from the north entrance. Stairs were straight ahead. The last hours of daylight filtered in through a cracked, dirty window, shedding light on the steps leading downstairs. With lots of options, Hutch chose to check out the west wing first. A short hallway led to an open doorway. A single, cavernous room stretched to the end of the building. Long counters and stools filled part of the room, broken glass sprinkled like confetti everywhere. Whatever had been there, not much was left behind, certainly nothing useable. The ventilation hoods lined up against the far wall suggested the room had been some type of lab. The ceiling bowed and sagged, threating to cave in at any moment. The only written clue as to the nature of the building was not in English. Small plaques on the walls labeling the different areas were engraved— Russian on top and Korean underneath.

They spread out and searched through drawers, finding most of them empty. Some had broken test tubes and bedding which looked to be laid down by mice.

"What is this place?" Zoey asked, completing a lap around the room.

"It must have been a lab of some sort," Hutch guessed. "Maybe some kind of school."

"What would anyone be studying here, on a deserted island?" Page asked.

"Probably something they didn't want the rest of the world to know about," Hutch answered. "Let's check out the rest of the building."

They crept back through the hallway to the east side of the building, dirt, broken glass and chips of tile crunching under their shoes. The musty air had already seeped into their clothes. The scent of stale urine wafted by.

Hutch opened the door to the first room off the eastern hallway. Except for an old desk and rickety chair, it was empty. The next room was significantly larger, filled with giant computer columns and control panels reminiscent of the technological dinosaurs of the 1950s, all labeled in Russian.

"Where did they get the electricity to power this stuff?" Page wondered out loud. She flicked a few switches as if expecting the machines to come to life.

The large room at the end of the hall once served as a cafeteria. The kitchen equipment was falling apart. Long tables with benches lined the walls in an odd configuration. Hutch rushed over to a table laden with treasure.

"This is our stuff," he said examining the equipment.

There were cans of food from the hidden treasures, axes, knives, pots and pans, gill nets, fishing equipment, hammocks, saws, an axe, and other tools. Zoey opened her backpack and reclaimed anything she thought would be useful.

"What are you doing?" Page asked. "He's gonna know we've been here."

Hutch joined Zoey, filling his backpack as well, leaving the axe for last. "Who cares?" he said. "Let's take as much as we can carry. And, don't leave behind anything the killer can use as a weapon."

Page located the can opener and went straight for the food. She opened a can of beans and they gathered around scooping out handfuls with their dirty fingers, gobbling up every drop.

Next, they checked upstairs, a gruesome story unfolding. The west wing was off limits, the sky exposed through the collapsed roof. Crumbling walls housed beds with thin mattresses and straps set on frames with wheels. A few IV hanger poles were left behind.

"It looks like an old military hospital," Zoey suggested.

"Maybe left over from WWII," Page added.

Hutch reserved judgment, looking past the ruins to the lake outside, keeping an eye out for the killer. It would have been a beautiful view if they weren't in mortal danger.

The entire east wing of the second floor was a corridor lined with small cells, each with an iron door you'd expect to see in the solitary confinement wing of a supermax prison.

Hutch tried the first door, but it was locked. A peek through the tiny, dirty window revealed a seven by seven cell with only a toilet and a pile of human bones.

Two doors down, Page gasped. A set of large bones accompanied by two childlike skeletons were strewn about, the walls and floor stained and caked with dirt.

Zoey found a similar scene in a room across the hall. "Good grief, kids? What the hell were they doing here?" she mumbled as if repeating the inquiry would summon a realization.

One cell stood out above the others. Not only because the door had been removed, but inside there was a bed made from multiple, decomposing mattresses and articles of stolen clothing. Little carved wooden figures of wolves and bears sat like an audience in the corner. There was a fresh pile of bones, possibly from a rabbit, in a pile on the floor near the "bed" like the remnants of a midnight snack. Someone had been there recently. Someone who, apparently, didn't mind the smell or the filthy scraps of foam mattresses. Hutch snatched up a knife from the floor. Judging by its age, it belonged to one of the contestants.

"This must be where he sleeps," Zoey said of the killer.

"Looks like it," Page muttered in response.

Hutch moved on to the room at the end of the hall and stopped short a few steps in. Rusty, four by four cages stretched to the ceiling with no space between them, like kennels, several with human skeletons locked inside.

Page crept up behind him, taking in the scene. "Why'd they leave so many people behind…in cages no less?" she asked.

Hutch didn't have an answer. None of it made much sense or looked like anything he'd ever seen before.

"We got some supplies and food. There's nothing else for us here. Let's go before he comes back," Hutch said and started back down the hall toward the stairs.

"Wait," Zoey urged. "He's bound to come back here. Why don't we wait and ambush him?"

Hutch shook his head. "Ambush him? We don't even know who or what we're dealing with. You think you're ready to fight to the death after a few handfuls of beans? Look at you. You can barely lift your legs to walk."

Zoey deflated and fell into line, following Hutch and Page. He had a point. They were all too weak to overpower the killer, especially on the killer's turf.

"What about a trap? We could set a trap to get him when he comes back," Page suggested.

Hutch stopped halfway down the stairs as if he couldn't walk and think at the same time. "That's not a bad idea. We could…Shit! He's coming."

Through the windows above the double doors to outside, Hutch spotted the killer following one of the worn paths to the front steps, accompanied by two wolves. They followed like loyal pets behind the forest camo-clad figure.

"Dammit. One of us should have stood guard," Hutch muttered, cursing his own mental fuzziness, hurrying down the stairs.

It was too late to go out the front door, but it was the only exit they had seen in the entire building. Jumping out a window at that height was risky. It was an option of last resort. Instead, Hutch led the women down another flight to the bottom floor. They could crawl out a window from there.

Part of the bottom floor was underground but the top half had the windows they had spotted from outside. It was dark and dingy and when the odor hit them, it was obvious where the previous urine smell had come from. They had found the wolves' den—a series of caged rooms along the south wall of the building. The rooms along the north wall were empty, but the killer was approaching from that direction. Hutch chose the closest caged room, the rusty door propped open. A square of light on the ground indicated there was a window, but the striped shadow within could only mean one thing—the windows on that side of the building were barred. They went in anyway.

Page stifled a scream, covering her mouth with her hand. Pieces of a half-eaten human body were on the floor, torn bits of clothing strewn about. She recognized them as Sharon's.

Hutch turned to Page and raised his index finger to his mouth to shush her. Then the heavy footsteps landed on the floor above them, clunking their way around the lobby. If they proceeded toward the cafeteria the alarm would be sounded when the killer realized his stolen tools had been raided. They had to get out now, but the room they were in had only a barred window.

Page's eyes widened, petrified, looking past Hutch. A deep, menacing growl came from behind him and he knew what to expect when he turned around. One of the wolves had circled around to the south side of the building and was now staring Hutch in the face through the barred window halfway up the wall. It showed its teeth, large fangs dripping with saliva.

Hutch knew better than to look the animal in the eyes, but he couldn't help recognizing the mismatched irises—one brown, the other a bright, empty gray. He eased down slowly, picked up a section of Sharon's arm—hand to elbow—and offered it to the wolf through the bars. It latched on without hesitation, yanking the meat away and trotting off to enjoy the meal alone. Everyone let out a quiet sigh of relief at the same time.

Above them, the footsteps stomped down the hallway toward

the cafeteria and faded.

"We gotta get out of here," Hutch whispered.

Upstairs, the killer scurried about in a panic, a guttural growl making it obvious he was angry.

Hutch pointed out the door. "Go. Across the hall. I saw regular windows on that side. We can get out before he figures out we were here."

Page rushed out the door, crossing the hall. A blur of angry wolf zipped by in a flash, tackling and attacking in a fury, barking and growling, knocking her sideways a few feet onto her back. She raised crossed arms in defense, but the wolf took it as an offering to sink its teeth into, taking bite after bite as it lunged and weaved.

Hutch pounced into the hallway behind them and wielded the axe, slashing it down on the back of the wolf's neck. It chopped in through flesh and bone to a halt, blood spurting like a hose with a thumb partially blocking it. The wolf let out a piercing yipe, letting Page out of its grip.

Hutch tried to pull the axe out, lifting the dead animal off her before the weapon popped out. The blood continued to spray, but it wasn't coming from the wolf. Page held a lacerated hand to the side of her neck trying to stem the bleeding, a bewildered look on her face. Hutch knelt and tried to help stop the bleeding but the amount of pressure needed would have strangled her. She gurgled a raspy plea for help, blood oozing out of her mouth.

"Hutch!" Zoey screamed, heavy feet thumping quickly on the stairs down the hall.

Hutch whipped around picking up the axe again. "Try to stop the bleeding," he shouted to Zoey.

The killer appeared in the middle of the hallway, axe in hand, mask and hood off, exposing the dark, scaly armor covering its face and head. He, or it, bared its teeth with a growling hiss. White fangs flashed through the dark.

"Stay back," Hutch warned with feigned confidence, glancing to his right through an empty room. A windowless frame provided an escape route, but could they get out in time? Escaping would mean leaving Page for dead.

Zoey cried out, "There's too much blood. I can't stop it."

Page's labored breaths slowed, growing fainter.

The killer took a slow step forward, toying with them or

perhaps sizing them up. It lifted the axe in one hand, leaning it over its shoulder.

"Just leave us alone," Hutch bargained.

Page's whimpers ended with a final rattle, lightening the load should they attempt an escape. Zoey abandoned her efforts and shifted her focus to defense, slowly pulling a canister of bear spray from a hip holster.

The killer rumbled a low guttural growl like an agitated crocodile, advancing slowly.

Hutch whispered to Zoey, "When I say so, zap him with the bear spray. Aim for the eyes. Then, make a run for it. Out the window on your right, around the lake. Don't stop until you come to a river or stream."

"What are you going to do?" she asked.

"If I can't kill him, I'll meet you there. Ready?"

"Okay."

Hutch waited until the killer was within range and gave the signal. "Now!"

Zoey shot a stream at the killer's eyes but it wasn't the first time killer had encountered such an attack. It shielded its eyes and turned away, the spray wasted on clothing.

Hutch charged forward, wielding the axe, screaming for Zoey to run as he blitzed. She darted into the empty room as he swung down with all his might, but the killer caught the axe's handle with one hand, short of contact, and delivered a kick to the stomach, sending Hutch flying back several feet without his weapon. He landed arched over his backpack, dislodging the bow and snapping arrows in half upon impact.

With an axe in each hand, the killer advanced. Hutch pulled out a hunting knife and hurled it, end over end, striking the killer in the shoulder. It only managed to penetrate a few inches. The killer swung an axe, chopping down. Hutch rolled out of the way, grabbing a broken arrow as the axe came crashing down on the ground beside him. He stuck the arrow into the killer's foot and rolled again as the other axe came down.

The killer let out an ear-piercing, inhuman shriek. It pulled the arrow out of its foot and the knife out of its shoulder, dropping the axes in the process. Hutch scurried to his feet.

Zoey screamed from outside the window, reaching a hand out.

"Come on. Hurry," she urged him out as the killer regathered its weapons.

Hutch grabbed her hand and heaved himself out the window. The killer followed, but halfway out the window Zoey gave it a shot of bear spray right in the eyes sending it falling back into the building. Another shriek echoed out of the building, into the forest.

Zoey helped Hutch to his feet and they took off running toward the tree line. The other wolf gave chase, summoned by the killer's screams. They ran through the forest, around the lake into territory they weren't familiar with. Hutch led them toward the river that would link up with the remaining contestants, hoping the map wouldn't let them down. He pulled his backpack off as he ran, letting Zoey get ahead of him as the wolf gained on them. He knew they'd never outrun a wolf, even on their best day.

With the wolf on his heels, Hutch scrambled to find and unravel a gill net and threw it over the pouncing wolf, tripping the predator up. Its front legs collapsed, sending the animal into a roll, tangling up in the net until it was rendered helpless.

They kept running, afraid the killer would pursue them. Just as Hutch was catching up to Zoey, she stopped short and let out a startled groan. She had almost fallen into a pit. When Hutch got alongside her, he realized it was more than a pit—it was an open, mass grave. Bleached bones peeked out of weathered clothing—faded green uniforms which looked to be some branch of military. A snake slithered around among the bones, disappearing into the depth. There was no telling how many bodies had been dumped there and there was no time to count.

"What the heck is this?" Zoey asked.

"It doesn't matter. We have to keep running," Hutch answered and urged her away by the arm.

She unglued her eyes from the death pit and they resumed running for their lives through the forest.

SEATON ROGERS

Day 19

10:10pm

Age: 33
Occupation: Screenwriter
Home: Utah
Status: Single

"Seaton? Wes? Ezra? Is anybody listening? Over," the voice came over the radio. It was Hutch.

Seaton Rogers had been waiting for an update since before the sunset. With his camp packed up and ready to go, he bedded down for the night, wide awake but warm and cozy in his sleeping bag inside his shelter. The comforting glow of the fire flickered off the walls with mellow, crackling ambiance. It was the closest to safe as he had felt all day.

"I'm here. It's Seaton Rogers. What's the scoop? Over," he replied, chipper as he was hoping for good news—something along the lines of the killer is dead and a cruise ship is coming to pick everyone up.

"We had another run-in with the killer. We found where he lives. He's...*it's* not exactly human. I don't know what it is, but we managed to injure it. Unfortunately, we're down to just me and Zoey..."

Seaton cringed. Another loss.

"The plan remains the same. We're hiding out for the night. Tomorrow we're going to work on building a raft to bring us downriver to you, but it might take a couple days. You need to be ready to strike. We're going to try to get the killer to follow us. Will you be ready to move out tomorrow? Over."

Seaton hesitated. Yes, he was ready to move out, but he wasn't ready for a fight with the unknown creature that had been killing everyone in sight. "It's not exactly human?" he asked.

"What do you mean by that? Over."

"I don't know what this thing is," Hutch admitted. "It looks like some kind of human, lizard hybrid or something. It lives in a strange abandoned building. An old lab or a hospital with cages. We really don't know what to make of it. We can try to figure out what it is after we kill it or else it's going to kill us. That's all that's important for the time being. Over."

"And how are we supposed to kill this mystery creature? Over." Suddenly, the thought of a normal human murderer on the loose didn't sound so bad to Seaton.

"We're going to have to take it by surprise and outnumber it. Our best bet is to try to trap it first. The good news is, it doesn't appear to understand our language. So, at least, it's safe to communicate via radio. I'll let you know when and where to expect us. Over."

"Last time I heard from you, you said the killer was back on the boat. If it's not human, how does it know how to operate a boat?" Seaton asked. He was having a hard time swallowing the whole story. It could all be part of some twisted plot to film people in a horror movie situation. After all, they were all there to make a TV show in the first place. He thought he may have caught a hole in their ruse.

"I wish I had an answer for you, Seaton. This thing has been able to build sophisticated traps, operate the boat, destroy the Mothership and keep wolves as pets. There's no telling what else it's capable of. Over."

"Wolves as pets? Are you saying we should expect a hybrid human-like creature along with a pack of wolves? Over," Seaton asked, unable to believe the words which were coming out of his own mouth.

"I'll keep you updated on that aspect. We saw the killer with two wolves. We killed one. We'll try to take out the other one before we bring him to you, but for now you can expect the worst. Will you be ready?"

Seaton sighed. It wasn't too late to opt out and disappear into the forest. He felt like he'd stand a better chance of survival trying to swim the Pacific Ocean to Hawaii. With no good options available, he answered, "I'll be ready to move out first thing in the morning. Keep us updated as much as possible. Over."

"Listen Seaton, you and Wes are our only hope. Ezra has gone silent. Stephanie is…gone. If we can't make this work somehow, we're all done for. You relay this information to Wes tomorrow morning and get ready. We're counting on you. Over."

"Don't you worry," another voice interrupted. Judging by the southern accent, it was Wes Wood. "I heard everything y'all was talkin' 'bout. We'll be ready fer that sumbitch. Y'all just be careful gittin' here. And I suggest we all get us some sleep. We ain't gonna do nobody no good if we ain't rested. Over 'n out y'all."

Seaton let that be the last word and tried to take the advice, but as usual, sleep would be hard to come by that night.

Chapter 20

Day 20

6:46am

The sun came up on Day 20 but it refused to make an appearance. Cold gray clouds loomed over the island and sat like a stubborn old man, unmoving, as if the wind currents decided to take the day off. The sun was somewhere on the other side of the clouds, providing little light but even less warmth.

Zoey and Hutch woke in the same embrace they had fallen asleep in—wrapped in tarps and clothes and covered in leaves to stay warm enough to avoid hypothermia. Sometime during the night, the trembling from fear and adrenaline had turned into shivering from the cold, but they made it through somehow. They had that little bit extra needed to survive—the intangible quality called luck. But, luck can run out and Hutch knew it. Zoey didn't believe in luck anymore. The truth, however, was in the fine print. The rule of threes—three minutes without air, three days without water, and three weeks without food—only defines averages. In reality, everyone is different and while one person perishes, others can beat the odds and survive in the exact same conditions.

"Jesus," Zoey mumbled, still half-asleep. "You really reek." She cracked her eyelids open and took a deliberate whiff to analyze. It kicked her in the face like a bucket of smelling salts. "Wait, or is that me?" she asked, lifting her arm slightly. The cold air whooshed right in through the crack she made. She tightened her grip on Hutch.

"It's both of us," Hutch croaked, a puff of vapor floating away from his mouth, confirming it was as cold as it felt. "We gotta get moving."

"No!" she cried, refusing to let go of him. "Not yet. It's too cold." It was more than the cold she feared. They were hidden and as secure as they could possibly be under the circumstances. It may have only been the illusion of security, but it was something and more than she had experienced in the first nineteen days of her harrowing adventure. Once they broke cover, the pause button on the world would be undone and reality would grab them by the throats again.

Hutch was antsy. There were so many things to do and timing was important, but he understood Zoey's need for a few more minutes of peace and the comforting warmth of another body. "We're going to be okay," he reassured her, but he wasn't as confident as he sounded. Too many people had died on his watch. He didn't want to think about it. He was supposed to be an expert survivalist, ready for anything. At one point, he had worried about how his reputation would suffer. No other reality survival show had ever lost a contestant, let alone several contestants and the entire crew. His reputation didn't matter anymore. People's lives were more important. All he worried about was protecting the remaining contestants, even if he had to sacrifice his own life.

"We're going to need to split up today," he told Zoey.

"Split up? Are you crazy?" It wasn't what she was expecting. After spending so much time surviving alone, she wasn't ready to separate.

"We finally know what we're up against," Hutch explained.

Zoey cut him off before he could go any further. "No we don't. We have no idea what that...*thing* is."

"We know more than ever. We know it doesn't understand us. We can communicate from afar with the radios without worrying about it hearing us. Most importantly, we know where it lives. We have to go back..."

Again, Zoey interrupted with an objection. "Go back?" she exclaimed.

Hutch talked right over her. "Listen. We need to go back and watch from the other side of the lake. If we've got eyes on him, he can't take us by surprise. While you're watching him, I'm going to build a raft. We'll follow the river as far as we can. It'll get us closer to Seaton and Wes."

"How long will it take to make a raft?" Zoey asked, uncomfortable with the idea of being left alone, uncomfortable with the idea of being on the water, and absolutely petrified of the implication of having to spend another night so close to the killer.

"It could take all day, but I'm not starting until we have some kind of shelter built for tonight," Hutch replied.

"I don't like it."

"What part?"

"I don't like any of it. I don't want to spend another night here. I don't want to take a chance going out on the water—on a moving river no less. There are rapids and waterfalls out there. We don't know how rough the water will be. We don't know how deep it is or if it's even passable. What if you spend all day making a raft and it only takes us a quarter mile before we hit a waterfall or a wall of boulders we can't get by. I've been around this island. There's a million obstacles."

"If we run into an obstacle, we pull the raft out and carry it to the next safe spot," Hutch explained.

Zoey pushed him away and climbed out of their leaf cocoon, regretting it right away when the cold air hit her.

Released from the embrace, Hutch wasted no time collecting the supplies they had buried under a giant pile of leaves a few feet away from their bed. "If you've got a better idea, I'm open to suggestions," he conceded.

"We know where this thing lives now. What if we stay here and keep an eye on it like you said and have Wes and Seaton come to us. Then we attack."

"They'll wear themselves out getting here and then what? You know firsthand what it's like trying to survive while on the move in a place like this. They'll be zapped of any energy. It'll take away any chance of an advantage over this…monster," Hutch reasoned. "You and I can travel more easily with the flow of the river. The longer we stay here, the greater the risk of another attack. We can watch this thing, but if it comes after us, we're too weak to defend ourselves. We're lucky we made it out alive yesterday, but we lost…"

Hutch wasn't the type of man to cry, but tears filled his eyes as his voice faded, cut off by the lump in his throat. He couldn't say the words, couldn't say her name. He never had the chance to get to know Page well, but he knew she was a good person and didn't deserve to be mutilated by a wolf and some freak human-hybrid killing machine. He didn't dare let the thought of what happened to her body after they escaped enter his mind. The loss of Dr. Rodney also weighed heavy on his heart and mind.

"It's not your fault. At least you managed to injure it," Zoey offered, wrapping her arms around him again. She was so much shorter than him that her nose ended up right near his armpit. A cloud of ripened man-sweat kicked her in the face again, but she didn't smell any better after twenty days without a shower. Somehow, her own odor didn't bother her as much. She had to let him go and search for a breath of fresh air.

Hutch gathered the rest of the supplies. "That's another reason we need to go back—to see how injured it is," he said, pulling his overfilled backpack over his shoulders. "Are you with me?"

Zoey put her makeshift tarp backpack on with a groan. "I'm with you. Let's go."

The trip back wasn't long. They had only managed to get about an hour away before settling down for the night and they only needed to walk back to the lake. They shared a can of tuna along the way and checked in with the remaining survivors.

Ezra and Stephanie were still MIA. Wes and Seaton were both on the move. Hutch went over the plan with everyone who was listening and signed off, keeping the radio transmissions short and to the point to save the batteries. Sheer determination kept them putting one foot in front of the other, making progress back toward the lake.

Hutch studied the map again, wondering how many more mistakes there were. They still hadn't reached the river they were counting on to take them to Seaton and Wes. "There's no indication of the building on this map," he complained, flicking the withering paper with his fingers.

"Maybe nobody found it. They wouldn't have sent us here if they knew about it," Zoey reasoned. "Right?"

"It's not *just* that. The lake is nothing more than a generic oval. Obviously, it wasn't explored. There are rivers missing, blank terrain. That Nelson Greely is a clown. He should have mapped out the entire island thoroughly. This is all just guesswork—another cut corner."

"Who's Nelson Greely, again?"

"My predecessor. He's supposed to be a survival expert, but no true expert would run such a shoddy operation. He should have scouted the location better."

"Oh, I remember meeting that guy. Why are you here instead

of him?"

"They told me he quit for personal reasons."

"Personal reasons? Talk about vague," Zoey said, ducking under a low-hanging branch. "Maybe he *did* find the building and backed out."

"Anything's possible. I never should have trusted Sharon. This is what I get for assuming people are doing their jobs properly," Hutch lamented. "If there's one lesson I've had to learn over and over in my life, it's that you can't count on anyone else to do things the right way."

"If you want something done right, you have to do it yourself."

"Exactly. But at the same time, in this business, you *can't* do everything yourself."

Just as he was losing all faith in the map, he heard the inviting sound of trickling water. The river they were looking for did exist, although not where the map indicated. Nonetheless, they found a spot to cross and followed it upstream until they came to the lake. Across a thinner part of the lake, they found the killer's building again. Had they not been looking for it, they might not have found it. Overgrown and tucked between the tall trees, it was barely visible from their vantage point. A burning fire outside helped mark the spot.

Hutch and Zoey crouched, taking cover behind bushes, away from the exposed shoreline. The killer soon made an appearance, limping over to add wood to the fire. His pet wolf padded behind him, sniffing the ground, circling the fire. It didn't look like it had been injured after getting tangled up in the net.

"Watch him," Hutch whispered. "I'm going downriver to find a spot to set up camp for tonight and launch the raft. If anything happens, if he leaves headed in our direction, let me know immediately with the radio and get out of here. Follow the river until you find me. Got it?"

"Got it," Zoey nodded, keeping her eyes on the killer, trying to squint more details into focus. The monster looked small from across the lake and moved slowly, like a person with sore muscles after the first workout in years. It favored the injured shoulder, pausing to lift and stretch its left arm gingerly. It was hurting, but not immobilized.

Plopping her butt down on a nearby rock, Zoey settled in for what she hoped would be a long day of surveillance. The reprieve was much needed, her feet thanking her but throbbing through cold numbness. As long as the killer was in sight, her mind was at ease. The killer sat on the front steps, the wolf prancing around like an excited overgrown puppy.

Zoey used the reprieve to remove her boots. A waft of foot odor floated up instantly, hitting her in the nose. She had to pull her head back. Turning to take a breath of clean air, she reached down again to peel off her damp, dirty socks. The pale white feet staring up at her with wrinkled toes looked like they belonged to a rotting corpse. Underneath each foot she found broken blisters with thick, calloused skin peeling off. The backs of her heels were red and irritated. She rolled up the cuffs of her pants to let the clammy mess breathe, cursing herself for not tending to it days ago.

She kept one eye on the killer, noting the wolf had calmed down, laying down at its master's feet like a loyal companion. The surreal sight of the monster petting the hundred-pound dog did not compute. She couldn't believe any of it was real. It had to be a nightmare or a hallucination—perhaps she had never left her camp and was still lying there, half-dead, waiting for the last shreds of life to escape her body while she hallucinated.

With time to think, a common saying intruded and echoed in her head—*be careful what you wish for*. For almost a year during the selection process for Isolation Island, she had wished and prayed and consulted the stars, hoping for what she thought would be the chance of a lifetime to come her way. It was certainly touted as such by the producer. She had begged to be a part of it. Uprooting her life for an indefinite amount of time was never an issue. She needed and craved a life-altering experience to guide her to the next chapter in her life, but she had no premonitions it would turn out like this.

Her mind zoned out, wandering into what ifs and whys, in the end concluding life was all random. There is no fate awaiting her, no grand plan. She was in control of her own destiny for the rest of her life.

A cracking twig snapped her out of the trance. Looking up, horror struck her heart when she realized the killer was gone from the front steps and something was rustling leaves behind her. How long had she zoned out for? Could the killer detect her and locate her so quickly?

Crunching leaves and rattling bushes brought her to her bare feet, looking for an escape route, readying the last bottle of bear spray. The water would be cold, but the lake provided a last resort should she get cornered.

"Hutch?" she whispered with a quiver.

The sound didn't stop. She knew she wouldn't get far running through the forest with bare, injured feet. Bracing herself, she aimed the bear spray at where she thought the sound was coming from.

The matted fur of a fat, stocky black bear flashed by the dense brush to her left. The four hundred-pound beast spotted her and stopped in the clearing she and Hutch had used to get there.

Zoey froze, arms outstretched, ready to use the spray should the intruder come any closer. The bear lifted its snoot, nodding its head as it sniffed the air, assessing the threat. Zoey's heart rate jumped but she showed no outward sign of fear, reminding herself not to make eye contact. Bowing her head, she kept a peripheral view of the animal.

The stalemate seemed to last forever. The bear lifted its front legs off the ground, rocking back and forth before settling down. The innocent face didn't fool Zoey. Another step forward would earn it a shot in the eyes.

"Go away," she said, stern and confident, but not too loud.

The bear backed away and returned to the path it had been on before noticing her. The furry, waddling rump eased slowly away until the forest swallow it up. Zoey exhaled a long sigh of relief. Another disaster averted, but she didn't feel safe until she had eyes on the killer again.

Across the lake, the wolf was peeing on a tree at the corner of the building. The killer was bobbing in and out of view at the top of the stairs, absorbed in a task she couldn't make out from so far away.

"Hutch?" Zoey whispered into the radio.

He responded right away. "Go ahead. Over."

"A bear just went by. It's headed toward the river. Over."

"What's the killer up to?" he asked.

"I can't tell but I can see him. Wait..." she paused,

scrutinizing the killer's movements. "I think he might be setting up a trap around his front door. He seems to be using paracord or tying something. It's hard to tell. Over."

There was a long pause before Hutch replied. "Okay. Keep up the good work."

12:47pm

Hutch was nearly tapped out of energy, but he persevered, setting up camp and cutting down young trees to build a raft. He had found an excellent spot about an hour away from Zoey. Their camp was set up on the other side of the river where a fork presumably sends a secondary river toward Ezra Greer's last known location. If the killer wanted to get to them it would require crossing a waterway. It was as safe as possible.

Hutch had three lengths of wood chopped to size and lashed together using cordage to form a narrow raft. At least two more logs were needed. He found a young pine tree with a straight, narrow trunk which would be perfect. It was tall, but cut in pieces, he was sure he'd have more than enough without having to cut down additional trees.

Having lost the axe, he was reduced to using a hatchet he had reclaimed from the killer's home. He already had blisters from days of chopping and working. Each chop at the pine tree reverberated through his damaged hands, threatening to make his blisters pop and the skin slough off, but he kept at it.

"Hutch. Are you there?" Zoey's voice crackled through the radio, breathy like whisper.

He stopped chopping and pulled the radio off his belt. "I'm here. Over," he said, winded by constant effort.

"I thought you'd be back by now. Over."

Hutch wiped the sweat from his brow, wincing from exhaustion. "I'm doing the best I can. I got our camp set up. We should be able to get some sleep tonight. What's the killer up to?"

"He's been limping around, fortifying his shelter. There's traps at the front door and possibly on the other side of the building. I couldn't see what he's been doing on the other side. The wolf follows him around like a puppy dog," Zoey reported.

"Good. Let him set up the traps, as long as he stays put. Over."

"He looks like he's hurting pretty badly. I think we bought ourselves some time. Maybe we should go on the offensive—attack him tonight while he sleeps. Over."

Hutch was too fatigued to entertain such a notion. "It's too dangerous. He's setting up traps and we're both in poor condition. Over."

"When will you come get me?"

"In a couple hours. I have to down this tree and prep it to add to the raft. Over."

"You're already working on the raft?"

"Yeah, but don't expect much along the way of shelter. Over."

"As long as it's warm and keeps the rain off of us, I'll be fine. Over."

"We need to save the batteries in these radios," he reminded her and signed off, urging her not to use the radio again unless it was an emergency. The radio showed two out of five bars of battery life left, but there was no telling how much they'd need it and the solar charger Zoey had nabbed from Jill Hill's camp hadn't been working well under constant cloudy skies. He clipped the radio back on his belt and resumed chopping away at the pine tree.

The bottom third of the tree and right side was almost bare, with only thin, dead branches and no needles, making it easier to prepare for the raft. Hutch chipped away at the trunk about three feet from the ground, notching out the side he wanted the tree to drop in. Satisfied, he backed up and began hacking away at the other side to weaken the trunk. It took many more whacks than he had anticipated.

"You gotta be kidding me," he mumbled to himself, exasperated. He straighten from his chopping stance, hyperextending his back and twisting to stretch his stressed muscles. Pushing the tree to topple it didn't help. He stifled the desire to shout in frustration, instead, turning the frustration into a burst of energy. With wider swings he hacked at the tree six more times before he was spent. A slow cracking sound indicated it was enough. The pine tree leaned away from him in slow motion, easing its way down until its healthy upper branches got caught up on its neighbor—a big old oak tree.

As if someone hit a fast-forward button, the pine tree separated from its stump, changed direction and came crashing down on him along with a long, dead branch from the oak tree. Hutch tried to throw himself backward, ending up on the ground, out of the way of the pine tree, but the jagged end of the oak tree's broken branch slammed down on his lower leg. The disturbing crack of breaking bones was louder than the thump of the pine tree hitting the ground.

Hutch let out a scream through clenched teeth. The branch pinned down his left leg below the knee. The other end of the branch was stuck under the pine tree. He tried to pull himself out, but the pain was excruciating and he feared tearing his leg apart. Lying flat on his back, he tried to regulate his breathing as dizziness threatened a blackout.

A single thought repeated in his mind—*it's not that bad, it's not that bad.* It calmed him enough to stay conscious. Staring up at the gray sky a moment of delirium brought him a sense of peace and tranquility. The silence of the forest, only intruded upon by the faint sound of the nearby river, was like a security blanket draped over him, oddly serene and inviting. It only lasted a moment before the pain forced its way in again, throbbing and stabbing.

He needed a plan, something to focus his mind on. Step one—call for help. His hand felt around his beltline but the radio was gone. His heart sank. Whipping his head back and forth, he located the fluorescent yellow beacon of hope under the thin branches of the pine tree a few feet away. He reached out with his left hand, falling just a few inches short. Another try yielded similar results. He had to wiggle his way closer on his back. Each jostle produced a shot of painful protest from his injured leg but he only needed a few inches. Reaching out again, he laid two fingers on the radio, pulling it along the dirt until he could wrap his hand around it. His brain noted everything was going to be more difficult now that he was injured, but somehow he believed he'd be all right.

"Zoey, I need help," he moaned and let go of the talk button.

"What's wrong?" Zoey returned, obvious concern in her voice.

"I think I broke my leg. Over," he said, amazed at the effort involved.

"Oh, no. Where are you? I'll be there as soon as possible. Over."

"Follow the river. Just past the fork, you'll find a downed tree you can use to cross over. I'm about ten minutes east of camp pinned by a tree. Over."

"Okay. Hang tough. I'll be there in no time," Zoey reassured him.

2:23pm

Hutch stared up at the sky, the forest canopy reaching out to the void where the pine tree he had cut down used to live like thin, dark fingers searching for light. The ground was cool and comforting, like the earth was cradling him, consoling him in a prolonged moment of distress. This was the best he'd come to having a time-out to rest.

He did another quick checkup. He could move all his limbs, even wiggle his toes on the injured foot. Diagnosis—one broken tibia. He minimalized it as much as possible in his mind and kept a positive though—*the body has an almost miraculous ability to heal*. It was true, but in the wild every injury was potentially life threatening and he knew that, as well.

It seemed like hours since he had called Zoey for help, possibly days. Maybe she forgot about him or couldn't find him or was injured on her way. Worst of all, maybe the killer had gotten to her, sucked the life out of her and fed her to the wolves. She was a good person. She didn't deserve that.

Hutch's eyes narrowed, his body numb and still. What a planet he lived on, his mind wandered with wonder. It felt as though the earth could just swallow him up and return him to harmony with the forces of nature. He wanted to just fall asleep and rest. Drowsiness lulled him to surrender—just let it happen.

"Huuuutch!" a voice rang out through the wilderness. It sounded like he was hearing it from underwater.

He recognized it as his name but he gave no reply. Floating on a trippy cloud, he wondered why the woods would howl his name. What more did the wilderness want from him. He had given it his all, tried to live a natural life but what an unnatural position to end up in. Some extraordinary creature, possibly created in a lab, had attacked him and the people in his charge. It seemed so unfair that something outside of nature, something artificial would threaten his existence—he who had given his all to be a part of the natural order of things.

"Hutch?" the voice came again, this time closer, but still outside of reality somehow.

He tried to focus; to remind himself he was still part of this Earth. His head was too heavy to lift. A deep state of relaxation was the only thing stifling the pain.

"Oh my god. Hutch. Are you okay?" the voice ranted, accompanied by a heavenly touch of his face and head. There was nothing like it—a caress from the stars, the universe.

His eyes came back to focus, awoken by the smell of the unwashed young woman, a sobering reminder. "Zoey?" he asked as if wondering how she had made her way to the same afterlife he was experiencing.

"I'm here, Hutch. Don't worry. You're going to be okay. It's not that bad," she rattled off, reassuring him without much basis.

"Water." It was the only thought left in his head.

Zoey unscrewed the cap from one of the water bottles she had found and poured the contents slowly into his open mouth. He swallowed as if it was a chore, but he wanted more.

She gave him dose after dose until his wits began to return. The injury was difficult to assess, as it was covered by his pants and the end of the broken branch. Feeling around, it seemed the bone wasn't protruding. She straddled the branch and tried to lift it but it wouldn't budge.

"You need to get the pine tree off it," Hutch instructed.

Zoey took her backpack off and positioned herself at the top end of the pine tree, preparing to heave it off the broken branch. She pulled and pulled making slow progress while Hutch grunted and groaned with each jostle. Only managing to lift the trunk a few inches, it slipped from her hands and came crashing back down on the branch, crushing his shin again. He let out a gasp instead of a scream, as if the wind had been knocked out of him and then it was lights out.

"Sorry. Sorry," Zoey repeated, frantic, but there was no reply.

She rushed over to him, hovering over his face. "Hutch?"

WES WOOD

Day 20

2:30pm

Age: 57
Occupation: Farmer
Home: Mississippi
Status: Divorced, 8 children

Wes Wood trudged through the forest, lugging with him every item he could carry. He let the head-mounted camera roll, documenting his slowing progress. After an early, fast-paced start, the old farmer had tired himself out.

"I got half a mind to turn around and go back. I got me a good shelter, a boat, and lotsa food. Them city slicker Hollywood bigshots done screwed up, bringing us to this crazy island with some kinda monster critter, lord knows what. I ain't got no obligation to help 'em," he ranted, trying to convince himself to bailout.

"On the other hand, if'n I can bag this crazy critter and bring 'em home, I'll be rich. I reckon there's lotsa scientists what would pay millions to get a look at this thing, even if it's dead. Course, getting' off the island ain't gonna be no picnic, but when there's a will there's a way."

He stopped to catch his breath and make sure the river was still within earshot. His age was starting to show, his gray hair seeming grayer as it got longer and more straggly. The dark lines on his face began to show twenty days of weight loss and dirt build up.

"That thing would be even more valuable alive," he reconsidered. "I don't care what it is—a freak of nature, a generically ingineered bigfoot warrior or somethin'. Don't matter. It all adds up to one thing. Money. I reckon with a little help, we can build us a cage and trap that motherfucker. That'd be one helluva payday, I tell you what. I'd be famous, too. Maybe even write a book about it. They'd make it into a movie. I kin see it now, the part of Wes Wood played by Clint Eastwood. Boy howdy. That'd be the shit." Apparently, he wasn't aware of the drastic age difference between his go-to idol and himself.

He took a swig of water from his canteen and continued on, boring the camera with repeated fantastic fantasies of fame and fortune in between radio conferences with Seaton Rogers. They planned to coordinate a rendezvous the next day.

Chapter 21
Day 20
4:28pm

"…on, Hutch. Don't die on me now," the words increased in volume, echoing through the darkness. He recognized it as female but wondered who it was and who she was talking to.

And why was it so dark?

The voice rambled on for a while and then stopped. After some time, he finally thought to open his eyes. Not too fast. A small crack let some light in, reminding him there was a world out there, but he couldn't remember where he was or why his bed was so firm. He lifted his head, causing a chain reaction of pain and soreness shooting up from his leg. Now he remembered. His leg was broken, but it felt strange, out of his control.

Zoey had split a thin log in half, using each half to sandwich his leg in a splint tied and secured with cordage to immobilize it. The branch that broke his leg was already chopped up for firewood.

Hutch was laying on Zoey's coat, covered with a tarp in an attempt to keep him warm. She had her back to him, working on making a crutch, testing the Y at one end for comfort under her arm.

"Rise and shine," she said, noticing he had awoken when she turned around. Trying out the crutch, she hopped around, putting all her weight on it. It was too long, but she planned to customize it for her patient as soon as she could get him on his feet. "How are you feeling?"

Hutch grunted a confirmation of consciousness. "Thirsty," he mumbled in a gravelly voice.

Zoey was prepared with the last of the treated water. She handed him the bottle and he helped himself. "What do you think?" she said, modelling the crutch under her arm.

He swallowed a gulp of water and cleared his throat. It was all coming back to him. Isolation Island. The killer. The tree landing on his leg. "You're going to have to leave me behind."

Zoey laughed at the notion. "Yeah, I'm not leaving you behind. That's not negotiable. Let's get you on your feet and test this thing out."

Hutch didn't protest. He wanted to see how bad the injury was and how much his mobility would be hindered. Zoey needed to see for herself if he was going to convince her to leave him behind.

She helped him up and they found the crutch to be about six inches too long. A little chopping rectified the situation and he was hobbling around in no time, but he couldn't ignore the pain. Wincing with every step, he tried to "walk it off", an absurd notion, but there wasn't much more he could do.

"You have to promise me, if we get into trouble, you run. Don't wait for me," Hutch negotiated.

A weak nod from Zoey wasn't enough. He grabbed her by the arm and spun her around emphasizing the seriousness of the situation with bold eyes. "Promise," he insisted, needing to hear the words.

She looked him right in the eyes. "I promise. But, we're going to be fine. You should soak your swollen leg in the cold river. I'll finish the raft and we can be on the water first thing in the morning."

"We're not ready to leave. We need to give Wes and Seaton time to prepare. Tomorrow, you need to go back and keep an eye on the killer. I'll finish the raft."

"How are you going to do that?" Zoey asked, her voice jumping an octave higher.

"Just help me get these last two pieces back to camp and I'll manage."

"What two pieces?"

"You need to chop two lengths off the pine tree and drag them to camp," he explained, marking the spots where he wanted her to cut with a wave of his hand.

"Yes, sir," she replied with a mocking salute. "Right after I make you a second crutch."

"Good idea. Thank you, Zoey."

7:09pm

Hutch settled down next to the fire to dry and warm the injured leg he had soaked in the river. Even while tending to his injury, he wasn't totally useless. Using some fishing line and one of the hooks he had swiped from the killer, he managed to pull a decent-size fish from the river for dinner. Zoey cooked it in the pan while water for drinking boiled in the pot. Although still short on supplies, it was more than she had had while trekking through the forest alone so, she was content and her face showed it, a fearless grin flickering by the light of the fire as daylight ran out.

"You're a remarkable woman," Hutch said, suddenly struck by her resilience. She seemed to be holding up better than he was, although, she wasn't the one with the broken leg.

"Not really. I'm just doing what I have to do. Surviving," she claimed, adding a can of beans to the pan. "Look at that. It's practically a full meal. Too bad it's dark already, I could have wrangled us up a salad, too. But…" she teased, ducking into the lean-to shelter Hutch had set up before his injury.

She came back out hiding something behind her back. "We may not have a three course meal, but we've got something even better." She revealed the treasure—a tall, dark green bottle of wine reclaimed from the killer's home. "It's the closest thing to a painkiller as I could find," she said, handing him the bottle.

"Oh, that's…" He shook his head, not sure what to say. Getting drunk wasn't a good idea, but he didn't want to burst her bubble and a few sips of wine couldn't hurt. He faked a smile and finished his sentence. "Great." Pulling a Swiss Army knife from his pocket, he used the corkscrew to pop the cork out. His head swam from a mere whiff of the rich burgundy bouquet. He passed the open bottle to Zoey. "After you," he insisted.

She waved the open bottle under her nose, her eyes rolling back in her head as she departed to some happy place she didn't feel the need to reveal. "Wow, this is going to be good. I could just sit here smelling it all day." Raising the bottle by the neck for a one-sided toast, she proclaimed, "To survival," nodding decisively. "Nova Scotia." She turned the bottle upside down in an exaggerated motion, taking a good, healthy gulp. A satisfied, close to orgasmic moan followed.

Hutch had to laugh. Accepting the bottle back, he asked, "Nova Scotia? What's that about?"

Wiping an escaped rivulet of red from the corner of her mouth she giggled. "It's supposed to be *na zdorowie*," she explained. "It's Polish. It means *to health*. It's like saying *cheers*. I had a Polish friend in college. She was the one who introduced me to my boyfriend. We were playing a drinking game that night. It was a really simple game but it was so much fun. You take a deck of cards and one person flips the cards over one at a time. Every time a Jack comes out everyone has to slap the table. Last person to slap the table has to drink. Every time a 9 comes out, everyone has to shout, *Nine!* Again, the last one has to drink. You go through the whole deck that way and it's easy at first, but for the next round the deck gets passed to the next person and they have to pick another card and name an action that must be performed when that card comes up. So, each round there's more things to remember and you're getting drunker and drunker which makes it even harder. The next thing you know, you're drunk off your ass, slapping the table, shouting and pulling your ear or touching the tip of your nose, not sure what to do. I'd never played the game before. Neither had my boyfriend. We had so much fun that night."

She trailed off, drifting to another place, the smile on her face fading and returning with a quiver. Snapping out of it, she continued, "Anyway, my friend taught us the Polish way of saying *Cheers*. But, my boyfriend was really getting lit," she laughed, "and he couldn't pronounce na zdorowie. He kept screwing it up. Naddersofa, nadravosya. Eventually, it morphed into him just lifting his glass and shouting *Nova Scotia!*"

She acted it out, raising an imaginary glass her hand was cupped around. "Nova Scotia! Nova Scotia!" She took an imaginary sip each time.

Hutch could tell she was flickering in and out of the past. A tear escaped her eye, but it was impossible to tell if it was due to happiness, nostalgia, or sadness. Perhaps it was a little bit of each.

She let the tear streak without acknowledging it. "When it was his turn to pick a card and an action, he chose the queen, he said because he was sitting across from a beautiful queen—me. And the action was to shout *Nova Scotia!*" The hurried, eager story slowed suddenly, her next words more solemn. "I'll never forget that night. After everyone else left, he and I sobered up and we ended up talking all night long until the sun came up. He always called me the Queen of Nova Scotia forever after."

"Well then, to the queen," Hutch jested, raising the bottle. "Nova Scotia." He took a sip and passed it back to her. "What's your boyfriend's name?"

She stared into the fire, taking a swig. "His name was Cal, short for Calvin. Calvin Morris."

Although his mind was hazy, Zoey's choice of words didn't get by him. "Was?"

"Was. He died in a motorcycle accident last year," Zoey elaborated, tearless and devoid of emotion as if she couldn't let it take over out there in the wilderness when she was expected to be strong—when she *needed* to be strong.

"I'm so sorry. That must have been hard for you," Hutch offered. He had never really had anyone die in his life. He had never really let anyone in. A lone survivalist, it always seemed easier than having other people to worry about. Hearing stories about loved ones dying tragically made him not in the least bit regretful.

"It was. It is. I don't know. Death is just part of life. Our days are numbered, even if we weren't on this lousy island. I wonder if anyone will notice we're gone." When offered the bottle again, he waved it off so, she took another large gulp and then turned to ladylike sips.

"I'm sure people will notice. I'd be surprised if anyone will notice *I'm* missing," he said with a nervous laugh. "But they'll notice other people missing. They'll come looking, eventually."

"And what will we tell them? A monster killed the crew and half the contestants?"

"I don't know. I haven't thought that far ahead. It's best to focus on what's right in front of us. Take it one step at a time," he explained.

Zoey nodded absently. "I'll drink to that," she said, raising the bottle.

The night grew darker and the wine drained inch by inch until words began to slur and topics changed midsentence. Zoey was the only one feeling it as Hutch had chosen to be the sober one.

Zoey sat by the fire, propping her head up with one hand, the almost empty bottle in the other. She was stumbling over words and concepts. "I wanna...I wannawa...I just wanna to do something...uh...somefing...like, somefing different with my life," she struggled to spit out. Being a dance inshtructor just seems like...um...I don't know. I wanna do somefing more impor-int, Somefing more specialer. Ya know?"

Hutch pried the wine from her hand. "You've had more than enough tonight Zoey. Maybe it's time to get some sleep," he suggested.

"I misth my mom," she cried suddenly, shifting gears.

Under normal circumstances, Hutch would have scooped her up, carried her to the tent, and tucked her in for the night, but there was no chance of that happening with his broken leg. He had underestimated how drunk she'd get, but she needed the break from reality. If they could make it through the night without an attack from the monster or wolves or bears or hypothermia, she'd be fine. She fell asleep on Hutch's shoulder near the fire, where he was stuck for a few hours not wanting to disturb her peaceful unconsciousness.

SEATON ROGERS

Day 20

5:33pm

Age: 33
Occupation: Screenwriter
Home: Utah
Status: Single

"I've been trying to communicate with this guy, Wes Wood," Seaton Rogers explained to the camera as he hiked. "And, let me tell you, it's not easy. I can barely understand what he's saying. He sounds like he's got a mouthful of marbles. It doesn't exactly fill me with confidence. I mean, *we're* supposed to be the last line of defense? Seriously? A hundred fifty pound bean pole and an old redneck farmer? I'd stand a better chance turning around and disappearing in the jungle."

He arrived at a good spot to rest and eat and set up camp for the night. It was close to the river in a clear area he wouldn't have to hack down make habitable.

The shelter was nothing more than a tarp hung in an A like a tent, using cordage tied to trees. On one side, the opening was blocked by a live tree. The other side would remain open to the fire he was working on. His bedding and weapons were laid out in an orderly fashion, ready to defend.

A pot of rice had finished soaking up the salty water, providing the warm, inviting aroma of a hot meal to which he added a can of beans. It was more than he planned to eat in one sitting. The leftovers would be tomorrow's breakfast so that he wouldn't have to waste time cooking again. He ate the mixture with a wooden spoon he had carved in the first few days of the competition. It made him a bit nostalgic.

"I miss the good old days," he said to the camera he had set up, slightly askew on a rock on the other side of the fire. The tripod was back at his original camp—useless weight. "Remember the good old days? Back when all I had to worry about was starving to death or freezing to death or being attacked by bears or wolves. I was afraid I'd run into a moose back then. Big deal. It wouldn't bother me now. It wouldn't seem like a danger compared to the description of this half-human monster killer thing."

He licked the back of the spoon and looked directly into the camera as if looking into the eyes of the people who had given it to him. "If this turns out to be a hoax, just a part of the TV show meant to throw contestants for a loop, I swear I will sue the shit out everyone involved," Seaton promised with inflated chest. "If it's not part of the show," he shifted gears, slumping his shoulders. "Well, maybe I can turn it into a screenplay if I survive. Provided I can get back to civilization." His voice quivered a bit as it tapered off.

Deep down, he was proud of how he was holding up. The full reality of the situation hadn't hit home yet. Safe and sound in his own corner of the island, he hadn't even seen a dead body yet. Now that he was purposely moving closer to the killer, he was starting to doubt the decision. First and foremost because it wasn't his decision. He was following Hutch's orders.

One thing he knew for sure—the camera gave him an artificial strength. While filming, he maintained a strong façade, a quiet courage, or so he thought. It also provided a distraction. He could talk about anything he wanted and from time to time, he wandered into old memories and stories from his youth, growing up as an introvert. These began to take shape in a special segment he called his *Daily Reality Check*. He tried to keep the topics positive or use them as a reminder of how things could be worse.

He launched into one of these while he took his time eating dinner. The slower he ate, the more satisfying the meal, in his mind. With a distant gaze, the hopelessness of the situation crept in, threatening to bring down his spirits.

"I think it's time for my Daily Reality Check," he introduced, his blank face saying he had gone back in time. "I may be out here in this desolate location. I might be stuck here forever, but there's only one real problem and that's the killer. Remove the killer, eliminate him, and I'm left in a peaceful place with very few people, if any of them survive. I can tolerate a small amount of people. I may be an introvert, but that doesn't mean I never want to see another person again. I just prefer to keep the list of people I maintain contact with to a minimum."

He scooped another spoonful of rice and beans into his mouth like a robot, unblinking, and chewed slowly, unafraid to talk with his mouth half full.

"Sometimes I look back and wonder if the things that happened to me shaped who I am or if who I am makes me remember certain things as more important. In my freshman year of high school, my social studies teacher asked a question of the whole class. I can't even remember what led up to it, but I'll never forget the response. The teacher posed a scenario—there's a little old lady walking down the street with a thousand dollars in her purse. There's no one else around. If you're absolutely guaranteed to get away with it, would you rob her? He asked for a show of hands. Who would rob this poor little old lady if they knew they could get away with it?"

The bulge of food in his cheek switched sides as he spoke and chewed. His face came back to life, animating disgust and confusion.

"Now, this was one of the few classes I had that wasn't an honors class so, it was a mixture of kids, but I still couldn't believe the response. When the teacher asked the question, I kind of laughed it off. Like, who would rob a little old lady? But the show of hands appalled me. Out of about thirty students, me and four or five others *didn't* raise our hands. I couldn't believe it. The majority of the class held their hands up proudly. Several students even got quite worked up over the notion of getting away with such a crime. One kid was bouncing on his knees in his chair, whipping himself up into a frenzy, describing how he'd hit her upside the head, too. There was chatter all around the class about how much fun it would be."

Seaton shook his head, as if he was embarrassed for the whole human race. His eyes glassed over while his heart broke all over again.

"The few of us who didn't raise our hands looked at each other in astonishment. Some of us sank in our chairs, but I was too shocked to do anything except look at the teacher. My expression must have said it all. He shot me this look. It was so telling. It said he knew exactly how the question would go over. It said the whole thing was a lesson for the few decent people who didn't raise their hands. It was something our young minds needed to know. The world is full of malicious people and opportunistic predators that would take anything they wanted, harm anyone they felt like if they could get away with it. And then there were people like me—the minority. People who *don't* go around robbing old ladies, not because of fear of punishment but simply because it's not a nice thing to do. I regret that the teacher didn't dig deeper or maybe he had in the past with unsatisfactory results. He should have asked how they'd feel if it was their own grandmother or mother getting robbed. He should have asked what the fuck was wrong with them. He should have made note of each person who raised their hand and suggest psychiatric counseling. The fact that he didn't was very telling, as well. He was telling us, the good people, that there's nothing we could do about the bad people. Maybe it wasn't the most politically correct lesson for a teacher, but it was realistic. In fact, it was quite the wakeup call. I never looked at people the same again."

He finally snapped back to the present time, shoveling another spoonful of rice and beans into his mouth.

"So, the question I'm left with now—almost twenty years later—did that make me afraid of people? Did that turn me into an introvert? I often wonder about it, but I usually end up with the same answer. I was like this *before* that experience. And, for the record, I'm not *afraid* of people. I just don't like many of them. So now, after twenty days on my own, I'm filled with anxiety because I have to meet a stranger in the wilderness tomorrow and try to work with him. I have to try not to hate him and, odds are, he'd rob an old lady if he could get away with it."

Chapter 22

Day 21

1:10pm

    Zoey Price watched from her hiding spot across the lake from the strange building the killer used as a home base. The wolf was sprawled out on the front lawn, basking in the limited sunlight on a frigid morning. The temperature had dropped significantly overnight. Zoey and Hutch had woken to frost on the ground before splitting up. Zoey was charged with monitoring the killer's activities while Hutch made good on his promise to finish the raft back at camp. It was a slow day on both ends.

    The killer stayed close to home and was still limping on the injured foot. He spent the morning cooking over the fire and rigging up some kind of trap or alert system in the woods surrounding the building. It was difficult to tell exactly what it was from across the lake two hundred yards away, but the killer worked on it steadily, digging holes and sharpening sticks intended to do damage.

    With the killer busy, Zoey decided to take a bathroom break. She crept away from her hiding spot quietly and answered nature's call deeper in the woods. Two deer watched from afar. Zoey knew it was an opportunity to acquire some protein. Creepy, crawly crayfish weren't difficult to harvest and eat, but she hadn't graduated to killing big, furry mammals yet. She let the deer prance away and made a mental note to not mention it to Hutch, but the encounter reminded her stomach of food. It growled in protest of her decision to let the deer escape. She opened a can of tuna and ate it on the way back.

    As she eased back into her hiding spot, she ran her finger around the bottom of the can, trying to get every last scrap of tuna. On the second attempt, the can slipped out of her hand, tumbling down to the rock she was going to sit on. Swatting at it, she only managed to get a piece of it, increasing the force with which the tin can hit the rock. The metallic plink rang out like an alarm bell. The can bounced and rattled off adjacent rocks, causing even more noise. Zoey crouched behind a bush and froze, eyes wide and fixed on the killer.

The wolf jumped to attention as soon as the can hit. It sprang to its feet and zeroed in on the direction the noise came from, barking, bobbing, and stamping its feet in a frenzy.

The killer whipped his head around, seeming to stare right at Zoey despite her attempt to hide. The wolf refused to let the sound go. The staring contest continued. The killer kept his eyes on her hiding spot as he dropped the shovel he was using and grabbed a bow.

Zoey flinched, but she knew an arrow couldn't reach her at that distance. She wasn't even sure she'd been spotted. Her pink outfit wasn't helping, but it was so dirty after twenty days in the wild it was almost camouflage. Her brain dished out orders.

Stay calm.
Stay still.
Don't panic.
Get ready to run.

The killer prowled closer to the edge of the lake, his limp almost non-existent suddenly. The wolf darted back and forth like a dog behind a fence and Zoey was the mailman on the other side.

She calculated her options. Perhaps running was the wrong move. That *thing* is injured. It could be the right time to strike. She could lure him out easily—just stand up. Find a new hiding spot and ambush him from behind. Zoey had gained confidence but she wasn't delusional. The idea was too risky.

And, what about the damn wolf? She wasn't sure she could handle the injured killer, let alone a healthy wolf. The animal also removed the option to hide in a new spot. The wolf's nose would find her. Even a human nose could find her with one stuffed nostril given how much she reeked after twenty days without a shower.

The sizable head start she had left her with only one logical option—run. But, where to? The quickest route would be the trail she had blazed over the last couple days.

She knew the standoff wouldn't last forever. The creature would come to investigate such an unnatural noise. Who would make the first move?

Unwilling to give up her hiding spot, she remained still, but the killer was pacing like the wolf now, looking from different angles. Without warning, the killer broke into a sprint along the edge of the water. The injury only seemed to slow him down to the speed of a normal, uninjured human. The creature disappeared into the woods. In the direction it was headed, it'd have to round the short end of the lake. The wolf followed at wolf speed.

Zoey took off, her makeshift backpack rattling around, threatening to come undone, but she couldn't slow down even if it meant losing her supplies.

She clutched the radio and shouted to Hutch, "I've been spotted. It's after me." She let the distress in her voice convey the fact that she was running for her life.

There was no reply.

"Hutch!" she shouted. "What should I do?"

"Come back to camp," Hutch responded. "I'll have the raft in the water ready to go. Keep me updated on your progress."

"The wolf is coming, too," she warned, already zapped of energy. Slowing, she looked over her shoulder, expecting to see the wolf on her tail already.

A small can of tuna and some breakfast beans doesn't get a person very far. Zoey slowed to catch her breath, her legs threatening to stop moving all together. With her hands on her hips she keeled over, coming to a halt as her tiny lunch threatened to escape its acidic prison.

The forest was alive with movement as if Zoey's running had startled every creature within a quarter mile radius. Her salivary glands were working overtime, lubing up from an expulsion. She swallowed hard, willing her stomach to calm down, and kept moving. Her eyes darted with every sound. Small creatures rustled leaves on the ground as well as in the trees above.

The wolf and killer would catch up to her if she couldn't move faster. She dragged her feet into a jog, running on a dwindling amount of adrenaline.

Keep moving.

Keep moving.

SEATON ROGERS

Day 21

1:30pm

Age: 33
Occupation: Screenwriter
Home: Utah
Status: Single

"There he is," Seaton Rogers announced to the camera. He had stopped along the riverbank when he spotted a man fishing up ahead.

Two hours ago, Wes Wood had reported in via radio on their shared channel saying he'd be fishing in the river while he waited for Seaton to show up. Making his way west, Seaton followed the river, in no particular hurry while Wes stayed put.

"Last chance to back out," he confessed his true desire.

He could turn around now, disappear into the woods and not be a part of the danger which was fast approaching, but along with the danger, there was a feeling of adventure which called out to him. What an epic story it would be if they managed to come out of this alive. He had to be a part of it.

More than that, Seaton felt a sense of duty. It was every person's moral obligation to help their fellow humans. It was something Seaton had always listed as an essential component of a successful society and this was his chance to put his money where his mouth was, even though they weren't exactly within the confines of society.

There was also a strong curiosity within him. A perpetual yearning for a new discovery, something different and exciting had always eaten away at his heart. This was something different. This was something exciting and it called his name, like the sense to explore calls a child into the unknown, the unexperienced. How many people could say they not only encountered an unknown humanlike creature, but they fought for their life against it and won?

The intrigue and promise of adventure pushed him forward. He raised the radio to his mouth and whispered playfully, "look behind you."

Wes Wood turned around, makeshift fishing pole in hand. Seaton waved to him with a gloved hand. Wes howled in celebration, whipping himself into a frenzy all by himself, pumping a fist in the air. "There you is. Git yo ass over here, boy," he shouted.

Seaton dropped his hand and moved forward, looking for a spot to cross. He shot the camera a look of disapproval, reluctance, and regret all at once.

Wes was never one to make a good first impression. He went full loudmouth, unable to contain his excitement over making contact with another human being. His howling made Seaton cringe. What a great way to draw attention.

"Here's goes nothing," Seaton said, shaking his head. Then he corrected himself, mumbling, "Here goes *everything*."

"I seen a place to cross over yonder," Wes shouted, pointing upriver. He pulled in his fishing line and set the pole on the ground to help guide Seaton across the river. The varying depths provided good fishing spots and shallow areas to cross.

Seaton had been hiking in his waders and regretting it up until then. They gave him poor traction and were uncomfortable, not designed for long treks. The only plus side was the ability to stay dry. It seemed every bush and branch in the forest was wet and brushing through played a number on absorbent clothing.

The cold, rushing water surrounded him as he plunged almost waist-deep, holding his equipment over his head. Wes hopped from rock to rock to meet him part of the way and relieve him of the heavy equipment. The water got shallower closer to shore, only ankle-deep.

Safely on the other side, Wes greeted Seaton with an overly-firm handshake. "How y'all doin'? Y'all have a rough time gittin' here?"

They had been in contact every step of the way. Seaton wasn't sure why Wes was asking such a redundant question. "Um...you know the story. I'm here," Seaton shrugged.

Wes lifted a large rock. The tail that had been sticking out from underneath it belonged to a fish the farmer had caught. He picked it up by the gills and showed off the prize. "Lookie here. We's eatin' good tonight, my friend," he exclaimed, slapping Seaton on the shoulder, almost knocking the poor guy over.

"Have you heard the latest?" Seaton asked.

"I ain't heard nothin' lately," Wes replied, spitting on the ground for no apparent reason.

"The killer is after Zoey." He had heard the commotion on the radio. "They had split up for some reason. She's trying to get back to Hutch and they're getting on a raft to come downriver. We need to be ready."

"How much time you reckon we got?" Wes asked.

"No idea, but it's safe to assume we don't have any time to waste."

"Well shit then. We better git gone."

Chapter 23

Day 21

1:58pm

Zoey hurried along the path next to the river, propelled by only the sheer will to live. On the other side of the river, the wolf emerged from the brush, barking and running up and down the bank. The deep rushing water kept the animal at bay.

Zoey picked up the pace with a whimper. Looking over her shoulder, she saw the killer join the wolf. He quickened his pace trying to catch up with her and readied an arrow for launch.

She turned into the woods obstructing his shot and cried into the radio, "He's right across the river from me."

Hutch replied, "Run Zoey. Don't stop. You can do it."

"I can't," she complained. "I can barely lift my legs."

"Yes you can, Zoey. Don't give up," Hutch encouraged.

She dug deep, but all she could muster was a light jog. It was better than nothing. An arrow zipped by her face, impaling itself in a tree she was passing.

"Dammit! Leave me alone," she shouted, injecting a short burst of speed into her legs she couldn't maintain. Off the beaten path, rocks, bushes and trees created an obstacle course, slowing her down. She hopped over a downed tree and almost fell flat on her face. With her heart pounding in her chest, her legs turned to wet noodles, begging to surrender.

The killer and his wolf slowed, passing her on the other side of the river as they searched for a spot to cross.

Up ahead of Zoey, a cleared path snaked in from the river's edge. She dropped her backpack. There wasn't much left anyway. Steeling herself for one last sprint, possibly the last of her life, she pulled the survival knife from its sheath and clutched it in her hand, resolving to put up a fight. She took a few deep breaths and ran for her life.

2:11pm

Hutch was covered in dirt from head to toe from squirming around on the ground all day trying to get the raft finished. It was a long, tedious process, but the raft was wrapped in a tarp and ready to launch in the river.

The tips of one of his crutches had been modified. He sharpened it to a point to use as a weapon, then hardened it in the fire to give it more stabbing strength. There was no time to build a trap and he was in no condition to set up an effective ambush. All he could do was wait. He rechecked the knot in the cordage tied around a boulder which kept the raft from floating away. The shelter was already dismantled. The equipment was loaded. All that was missing was Zoey.

He depressed the talk button on the radio, wanting to ask her where she was, but instinct stopped him. What if she was hiding, trying to be quiet? He let go of the button, cursing the situation.

It would have been nice to test the buoyancy of the raft with both himself and Zoey, but he was confident it could handle the load. There was only enough time to carve one paddle and it wasn't quite finished. The other navigating tool was nothing more than a long stick he planned to use to push along the bottom and brace against rocks to avoid smashing into them. He checked it all over again. Was there anything he was forgetting? There wasn't time to do anything else.

Zoey's voice came screeching through the radio's speaker. "I'm almost there. They're right behind me."

Hutch waited a moment for more information. Nothing. He replied, "Keep running Zoey. Get right on the raft when you get here. Don't stop for anything." He craned his neck, looking in the direction he was expecting the chase to come from.

Zoey appeared first, flashing between the trees and brush on the other side of the river. One thing she had going for her was her size. She was petite, down to under ninety pounds.

The wolf was next, padding along the river's edge in the distance. It looked like it didn't know where Zoey was exactly. The killer was even farther behind, jogging like a marathon runner.

Zoey broke from the tree line. The wolf tore right after her.

The killer sprinted trying to catch up. It was an all-out race to the fallen tree bridge. Hutch positioned himself on the receiving end. The wolf was gaining on her.

Zoey did an impressive balancing act with her arms stretched out to both sides as she hurried across the bridge. The wolf hesitated to follow her. It pounced around the other end of the tree until it built up the confidence to attempt a crossing.

"Go! Get on the raft," Hutch shouted, urging her on.

The wolf ran across with much less hesitation, nipping at her heels as she jumped off the tree onto solid ground. Hutch lifted his sharpened crutch and rammed it in the wolf's open, panting mouth before it was within reach of an attack. With an extra shove, he forced the sharp end down the animal's throat to inflict maximum damage and pushed it over into the river, bloodying the water in a short-lived streak.

On the other side, the killer came running up to the bridge, readying an arrow. It stopped near the downed tree and launched the arrow. Hutch dove out of its way, hitting the ground with a thud and a groan. He squirmed to get vertical again and used his remaining crutch to hop as fast as he could to the raft. Zoey had collapsed at the front with the last of their equipment, breathing heavy.

"Hurry," she gasped when she turned around to see the killer crossing the bridge. It scurried across using its arms and legs like a lizard on hot sand.

Hutch swung his injured leg onto the raft first, pushing off land with his good leg. The killer got across the bridge, drew back an arrow and launched it into Hutch's back. Zoey screamed in terror, the arrow piercing out of his chest. Falling to his one good knee, Hutch pulled his knife from its sheath and hacked at the cordage tethering them to land.

The killer moved a few steps closer, tilting its head to one side, black, vacant eyes making contact with Zoey's as she screamed. It pulled out another arrow as Hutch's bloody hand slipped on the knife. The killer took aim.

One last hack and the raft was finally cut loose. With all his might, Hutch sat up waving his arms around, trying to make himself as big and obstructive as possible. "Get behind me," he tried to shout, but his lungs couldn't carry the message.

The killer let the arrow fly. It glanced off the side of Hutch's head, deflecting it away from Zoey but taking a huge chunk of flesh and part of his ear with it.

The killer readied its last arrow, but it was too late. The river swept the raft into fast water, pulling them out of range. Hutch collapsed on his back pushing the arrow out his chest, blood oozing down the shaft.

Zoey rushed to his side, thrown back and forth as the raft jostled from the shifting weight. "Hutch! Hutch! Talk to me, Hutch." Her shouts turned to whimpers. Lacking a medical background all she could think to do was apply pressure to the wound to stop the bleeding. But, what about the arrow? "Hutch, tell me what to do."

The injured man raised a bloody hand toward her. "Just…" he tried with a wet, gravelly gurgle. "Just hold my hand."

Zoey obliged, petting his head with her other hand. The flesh from his scalp wound flopped on her lap. The warm, greasy blood squirting on her was almost comforting in the cold afternoon.

"Stay with me, Hutch," she begged over and over until his hand went limp and lifeless. His eyes shut gently like he was dosing off for a nap.

Hutchinson Adalwolf was dead and Zoey Price was, once again, on her own—on her own and hurling down the river out of control. The raft had spun around, white water splashing over the edges.

There was no time to grieve. Zoey let the tears fall, but they didn't register. She crawled to the middle of the raft and grabbed the paddle. They were going backwards, but it didn't matter. She stuck the paddle flat in the water, trying to slow down and keep from turning sideways. Something thumped against the new front with a small splash. Hutch's crutch pointed straight up out of the water, then spun around, the dead wolf bobbing with it. Zoey whacked at the crutch, pushing it to the side. She caught a glimpse of the dead animal's face as she drifted past—mouth open, bloodstained fangs protruding from wet, matted fur. She'd have no problem butchering it and eating it for dinner, but there was no time for that.

She drifted down the river. After forty-five minutes, the water calmed and widened, surrounded on both sides by endless trees and wilderness. If not for the dead body onboard, it would have made a nice photograph for a postcard.

Zoey kept the raft under control around the bends twisting through the forest, snaking back and forth. This wasn't on the map, but it was calm and manageable—up until the raft ran aground.

The river had been getting shallower as it got wider. Zoey almost toppled over when she ran out of depth to keep afloat. There was nothing more than shallow water and white caps cresting protruding rocks ahead as far as she could see.

She released the tension from her shoulders, letting out a cleansing sigh.

WES WOOD

Day 21

4:33pm

Age: 57
Occupation: Farmer
Home: Mississippi
Status: Divorced, 8 children

Wes Wood and Seaton Rogers made their way west, following the winding river. Wes led the way and filled the air with chatter about himself, his family, and his farm. Seaton let him talk, but offered little along the lines of conversation in return. Wes filmed most of it while Seaton put his cameras to rest.

"What time you reckon it is?" Wes asked.

"4:20," Seaton replied with a grin, the first words he had spoken in almost an hour.

"Really?" Wes looked at the sky, trying to figure out where the sun was behind the cloud cover.

"It's always 4:20 somewhere," Seaton reassured him, sounding like he wanted an escape from Wes and his constant chatter.

"I reckon yall's right 'bout that," Wes quipped, not quite getting the joke. He came across as overly friendly and overly chipper given the situation, as if the threat of the upcoming conflict had been exciting him in some perverted way. "So, what's the story with y'all?" he asked flat out. "Y'all not a big talker."

"I think we should be talking about…" Seaton tried, quiet and subdued, his usual tone among strangers.

Wes talked right over him, despite his invitation to contribute to the conversation. "Where y'all from anyways?"

Seaton seared an annoyed look into the back of his unwanted companion's head. "Utah," he answered, short enough to not be interrupted.

"Oh, Utah. Y'all Mormon then," Wes returned, as if geography and religion were the same thing.

"No. I'm not Mormon," Seaton replied with an aggravated sigh. It wasn't the first time he'd had someone assume he was a Mormon, or even the hundredth time.

Wes stopped at a dead end where clear ground disappeared in a wall of greenery. "So, y'all Christian then?"

Seaton turned into the forest away from the river. "What's the difference? We should be talking about how we're going to fight this creature."

Wes followed, laughing out loud for show. "Don't worry 'bout that. We'll whoop its ass. Don't matter what it is." From behind, he couldn't see Seaton rolling his eyes.

Seaton hacked through a stretch of bushes and weeds until he came out in a field of tall, yellowing grass. They were surrounded by the river on three sides. He stopped and looked at Wes.

"Hold up now," the old farmer ordered and hurried ahead to survey the land.

The river wound around a bend past them on one side and made its way back, blocking their forward path leaving them in a peninsula of sorts.

Wes returned, shouting, "I reckon this is it."

They weren't sure it was the exact spot Hutch had been talking about, but it was good enough to set up a line of defense and they were running out of time to prepare, not to mention daylight. They needed to get to work. Step One—set up camp.

Zoey's trembling voice crackled over the radio. "Seaton, Wes? Is anybody listening?"

"This here's Wes Wood. How y'all doin' out there? Over."

"Not good," Zoey replied. "Hutch is..." she began, fading into a sob. Then, she forced the words out. "Hutch is dead."

For the first time, Wes's face turned to concern. He didn't know what to say. He shared the look with his partner.

"Hutch is dead," she repeated. "Do you hear me? Over."

"Are you hurt?" Seaton asked.

"I'm okay. I floated down the river for a while, but I got stuck. The water's too shallow. I pulled the raft onto land, but I don't know what to do now." There was a long pause before she remembered to say, "Over."

"Where's the killer? Does it know where you are?" Seaton asked.

"I don't know. Hutch managed to kill the other wolf. The killer is a good distance away, unless he followed me. I...I have no idea. Over."

"Don't panic," Seaton said, calmly. "We've found a spot to set up camp. We're going to surround it with traps. You just need to get here. Do you think you can do that? Over."

"Not today. I'm too exhausted. I can barely move. I made a fire and strung up a shelter for the night, but I'm about to collapse. Over."

"Do you have food and water?"

"A little."

Seaton turned to Wes. "Maybe we should try to find her."

"When? Tonight? 'Less she's only a couple hours away, we ain't gonna make it before dark," Wes pointed out.

"I'll go," Seaton volunteered. "You stay here and set up camp. I'll walk through the night if I have to." He relayed the information to Zoey.

"No. I'll be fine. It's only one night. I'll try to get back on the water first thing tomorrow mor..." she said, stopping abruptly mid-sentence. "Shit. Someone's coming," she whispered.

Chapter 24
Day 21
4:58pm

Something was stirring in the forest near Zoey Price. It was on two feet and clothed, moving slowly behind bushes and trees. She stood up, her legs protesting, a hatchet in one hand and the radio in the other. With the talk button depressed so Seaton and Wes could hear what was happening, she looked for the best escape route, but she knew she couldn't get far before she collapsed again. Hiding behind a tree, she watched and waited to attack.

"Zoey?" a voice called out.

She didn't recognize it, but whoever it was, they knew her name. Flattening herself against the tree trunk, she braced for a battle.

"Zoey?" the male voice repeated, louder and unthreatening. "Don't be afraid."

Fear struck her heart, not because of the man approaching but because of the realization she might be hallucinating.

"It's Ezra Greer, Zoey. Are you there?" the voice tried again.

Zoey peeked her head out from behind the tree.

Ezra appeared in the clearing next to her gear. He was dressed in forest camouflage, much like the killer, but the killer didn't have a gray beard like Ezra. "It's okay. I'm here to help," he reassured her.

"Where the hell have you been?" Zoey asked, breaking cover. She took a step forward. Her foot landed on a rock, turning her ankle and sending her down to one knee. "Dammit."

Ezra hurried over to help her. "Easy now." He threw her arm around his shoulder and walked her to a soft spot to sit down. "Settle down. You need to rest." Pulling his backpack off, he sat in front of her and let loose his sleeping bag to cover her up. Bundled up, she clutched the sleeping bag like a life preserver while he removed her shoe and sock to check the foot she had twisted.

Her feet had dried since dipping into the river, but they felt like they had just come out of a refrigerator. Ezra watched for a reaction as he manipulated her foot. She seemed to have full range of motion without any pain—a good sign. He ran through the procedure again to be sure. "That doesn't hurt?" he asked for verbal confirmation.

"No, but my feet are pretty numb from the cold."

He took off the other shoe and sock, massaging some life into both feet. She purred like a kitten from the relief it provided, thanking him repeatedly. When he was done, he gave her a pair of his own dry socks. They had been worn before but he had cleaned them in the river—as close to clean as it could get on Isolation Island.

He helped her to her feet and she tested out the twisted ankle. "How does that feel?" he asked.

"It feels totally fine," she replied, surprised she was able to put full weight on it without a problem.

The radio which she had left on the ground crackled. "Zoey, are you okay?" It was Seaton.

"I'm all right," she reported. "Ezra is here." She held the radio up toward his mouth.

"Everything's okay. I'll take it from here, boys," Ezra said, directed toward the radio. "Over."

"Good," Seaton replied. "We need to set ourselves up here, too. We'll check in with you a little later to go over the plan. Over."

"Thank you," Zoey said into the radio. "Over and out."

She sat down again, keeping the radio in her hand resting on her chest. "So, where the hell have you been? Why didn't you keep in touch on the radio, at least?"

"I didn't want the killer to know where I was," Ezra claimed, rummaging through his backpack. He pulled out two cans of food and opened one.

"So you just show up unannounced?" Zoey asked, confused and annoyed even though she knew she should be grateful she wasn't alone.

"Look, if you don't want my help, I'll go back to my camp," Ezra snapped, unwilling to explain his actions.

"Sorry. Of course I want your help. Thank you for coming."

"I heard you on the radio, running from the killer. Hutch told you to get on a raft. I put two and two together, followed the river. I figured you didn't get past the shallow part and then I heard you talking to Seaton and Wes. I couldn't let you stay out here by yourself."

"The killer is not human. It doesn't understand what we're saying on the radio," Zoey explained, accepting a can of corn beef hash and devouring it.

"Maybe not, but it sounds intelligent enough to keep count of how many different voices are coming out of the radio," Ezra countered.

"Hmm. I hadn't thought of that," she replied, trying not to let food fall out of her full mouth.

"Yeah, well, at first I was going to just stay away, save myself. But, after seeing how many people he's killed, I thought if he was after you, I could get behind him and take him by surprise. I wasn't fast enough," he explained. "These old bones don't move as quick as they used to. The rough terrain didn't help either."

"I don't think that thing is going to stop until we're all dead. We have to kill it." Her eyes filled with a residual fear remembering the encounter in the abandoned lab. Then there was the chase through the forest and Hutch dying in her arms. He had sacrificed himself to save her and it didn't go unnoticed. A tinge of guilt mixed with the fear and showed in a peculiar expression.

Ezra didn't fan the flames. It was obvious she had been through a living nightmare, but the story could wait. He didn't need to make her relive it at that particular moment. "I know. I'll do everything I can to help," he reassured her. "Hutch was right, the best move we have right now is to get farther away, buy us some time to regain our strength and set up a line of defense with Seaton and Wes."

"I'll be good as new after a good night's sleep," Zoey promised bravely.

"I'm sure you will. You go ahead and get some rest. I'll get us set up for the night."

9:11pm

Zoey was jolted awake from a sleeping nightmare into the waking one. A flickering light highlighted a naked human foot sticking out of the fire. The leg it was attached to was engulfed in flames. A scream stuck in her throat like she was being strangled. A dark figure hovered about, back turned to her on the other side of the fire. She wiggled out from under the sleeping bag draped over her, tripping as soon as she got to her feet.

The dark figure turned around. It was only Ezra, the shadows cast on his face dancing around like a demented clown on fire with a crooked smile. "Oh, hey," he said like it was a pleasant surprise to see her awake.

"What are you doing?" she shouted, backing away.

He followed her glances alternating between him, an escape route, and the foot sticking out of the fire. Raising his open palms he replied, "I'm sorry, Zoey. This is the only way."

"Who is that? Who did you kill?" she demanded.

"I didn't kill anyone. It's Hutch," he explained. "I'm sorry, but it had to be done. What else could we do with the body?"

She didn't answer, staring at Hutch's foot in the fire. He deserved better, but maybe he preferred being surrendered to a fire in the wild.

"What would Hutch tell us to do with the body?" Ezra tried again. "We don't have the time or energy to dig a grave. I'm sorry, but cremation is the only option."

Zoey didn't protest his decision. Instead, she broke down crying. Ezra approached with caution and put his arms around her for a warm embrace. She buried her face in his chest and let it all out. The tears weren't only for Hutch. They were for the most difficult twenty-one days of her life. It took a good ten minutes to dry up.

"We're going to be okay," Ezra reassured her.

She rubbed her red, irritated eyes. "How long was I asleep for?"

"About three or four hours," he informed her, pushing Hutch's foot deeper into the fire with a stick where it disappeared into the glowing orange. He motioned for her to sit on the log on the other side of the fire.

She cringed with disapproval. "Did you have to burn him in the fire we're using to cook and boil water?"

"Sorry, but fuel is fuel. Try not to think about it," he said, handing her a half-empty can of green beans. "Or, if you prefer, think of it as one last way he's taking care of us, keeping us warm."

She stared at the can of beans for a moment and then looked up at him.

"Don't worry. They're cold," he reassured her. "Come on. You need to build up your strength."

Her hunger outweighed her reluctance and she accepted, eating slower than her last meal. She pulled out one green bean at a time with her dirty fingers, biting each one in half to make it last longer. Ezra sat down next to her, holding his hands open to the fire to warm them up.

"So, how'd a young woman like yourself get into the art of survival?" he asked, trying to distract her with a change of subject.

"My dad," she replied, her eyes transfixed on the fire. "He was really into nature. He used to take me camping all the time, taught me everything about building shelters and making fire. But, when we got to the hunting part of the curriculum…it just wasn't for me. I love animals and I hate the idea of taking a life, any life. I couldn't do it. He's been disappointed in me ever since. I came out here to show him I could survive without hunting or eating meat. I figured I could impress him, even if I didn't win the million dollars. I just wanted him to be proud of me like he was when we used to go camping together."

"You made it this far. I think you qualify for badass status already. Don't live your life seeking the approval of others, not even your own father. It's impossible to meet other people's expectations. Believe it now, otherwise you'll inevitably realize it one day when you're older and it'll be too late to get back all the wasted time and energy," Ezra lectured her as if *he* was her father.

She nodded, but it was difficult to tell if the words were sinking in. "What about you? How'd you end up on this godforsaken island?" she asked as she finished the green beans.

He sighed, took a swig from his canteen and passed it to her before answering. "A long series of unfortunate events. Nothing worth talking about."

"Are you sure? Talking about it might make you feel better," she suggested. Any distraction from their current predicament was welcomed.

"I'd feel better *not* talking about it," he politely declined.

"Sorry," she said with a hint of agitation.

"No, I'm sorry," he said, lightening up. "It's just that...I've decided to let all the past go. I just want to move forward from now on. The past can't be resolved."

"The past can't be resolved," Zoey repeated, as if considering the idea.

"I mean, there's nothing I can do to change it now," he clarified.

"I get it," she claimed, the words coming out her mouth contending with a yawn.

"You should get back to sleep. I'll keep watch," he reassured her.

"Thank you," she said with a stroke of his arm. "I'm sorry I freaked out on you. You did the right thing," she added. She didn't want him to feel guilty for the way he disposed of Hutch's body.

They shared a look that expressed a lifetime's worth of adversity, each of them nodding a confirmation of understanding.

SEATON ROGERS

Day 22

5:33am

Age: 33
Occupation: Screenwriter
Home: Utah
Status: Single

Seaton Rogers woke to the sound of chopping wood. Frigid air nipped at his nose in the dim, predawn morning. His steamy breath huffed and rose. "You gotta be kidding me," he mumbled as if a camera was watching. Lifting his head, he could see the dark silhouette of Wes Wood on the other side of the fire, splitting a thin log with an axe.

Seaton pulled the sleeping bag up over his head. There was no way he was getting up that early, whatever time it was. For a moment, he considered the possibility that he had slept through the whole day and it was now dusk rather than dawn.

No, that couldn't be. Wes wouldn't have let him sleep all day. It didn't really matter. Either way, he wasn't ready to rise. His eyelids slumped shut, back into sleep where nothing was asked of him.

His eyes cracked open what seemed like a few seconds later. The sun was up, casting shadows through the tall trees. The fire was roaring outside, a slight breeze blowing warm air into the narrow temporary shelter. It was still too early to get up and too warm and cozy to leave his cocoon. Seaton cleared his throat and shifted onto his side, careful not to let an ounce of warmth escape.

Wes's head appeared sideways in the opening to the shelter. "Finally wakin' up, huh? We got plenty'a work waitin' fer us," he rattled off, fast and incoherent. Even if Seaton had been awake and alert he would have had a hard time understanding.

"What time is it?" Seaton croaked, instantly regretting he

hadn't had the sense to pretend to still be asleep.

"Time? I ain't got no watch. It's time to git up. Git up and git along little doggy," Wes twanged like only a morning person could and then his head disappeared.

Reality seeped into Seaton's sleepy head—the island, the killer, Zoey and Ezra. There was so much work to do and their lives depended on it. But, the warmth begged him to stay. The fatigue whispered in his ear, telling him to surrender. Just one more hour. Twenty minutes. Ten minutes, like hitting the snooze button. It was too cold out there. Too wet with morning dew. Too harsh. For the first time, all he wanted was to go home.

Wes reappeared in the opening, squatting. "Hey!" he barked, snapping his fingers like he was commanding a dog. He tried to pull the sleeping bag off but Seaton was wrapped tight as a burrito.

"All right. I'm coming out. Is there any coffee? Seaton asked. "I'm going to need some."

"I'll git some goin'," Wes promised. "Y'all come on, now."

It was like tearing off a bandage—a warm, comforting bandage. Seaton unzipped and threw the flap of the sleeping bag off him. The cold rushed in like it had been waiting for the opportunity. He crawled out of the shelter on his hands and knees, the cold damp grass announcing itself through his pants and gloves. A change of clothes would be nice. Twenty-two days without a shower and counting.

He had slept in his boots, unwilling to be zipped into the sleeping bag all night with smelly socks exposed. There was still one clean pair left and it was just what he needed for a little jolt of freshness. Sitting by the fire, he pulled one boot and sock off. His feet ached through the cold numbness somehow. The new, dry, woolen sock went on like a hug, his head swimming in a comfort his feet hadn't felt in a long time. When the second sock was on, he wished he had brought ten more pairs.

"I hope y'all ain't aimin' to set there all day. We's got work to do," Wes intruded.

"I ain't gonna set here all day. I know *we's* got work to do," Seaton mocked, mimicking his partner. Maybe speaking Wes's language would help. The look he got from the farmer suggested it wasn't well received. He dropped the phony accent. "I just need a few minutes to wake up." So much for letting his boots dry by the fire. He put them back on, making his socks feel dirty upon contact. "So, what's the plan?" he asked.

"Plan?" Wes replied as if he had no idea what Seaton was talking about.

Seaton's head fell forward. This was going to be like pulling teeth. "Yes, the plan. What's the plan? We need a plan, right?" he snapped. He may have had more patience if it wasn't so early or if Wes wasn't so irritating.

"I ain't got no plans. We gotta build a camp, first," Wes replied.

"Well, then, that's part of the plan, isn't it?"

"I reckon," Wes conceded, setting the coffee pot on a rock in the fire. "What's yall's plan?"

Seaton cringed. He hated being referred to as *y'all*. "What's my plan? Is that what you're asking me?" he spat. If Wes was going to be difficult to hold a conversation with, Seaton could be just as difficult. The morning did that to him.

Wes nodded, confused by the hostility. "Y'all ain't a mornin' person," he said with a laugh as if he just figured it out.

"No, I'm not. Not even on a good day and this is nowhere close to qualifying as a good day," Seaton grumbled. He rubbed his eyes with gloved hands and dragged them down his face, trying to massage some life into himself. "I'll be okay after a little coffee and a little time to myself," he promised. "As far as the plan, I've got a few ideas. We have to scout out the area, first. Get familiar with the lay of the land. We can set up a trip wire and traps to alert us of intruders. Any animal trails or paths of least resistance should be rigged with spike traps. If the killer spots the trip wire and attempts to step over it, his foot will come right down in a little ditch with wooden spikes, hopefully crippling him."

"That sounds like a lot of work, Crabby. Y'all up to it?"

"I'm not done. We should make a couple of atlatls and a stockpile of spears."

"A what ladle?"

"Atlatl. I'll show you. It's basically a spear-thrower," Seaton explained, dumbing it down as far as he could. He mimed a throwing motion with one arm drawn back, flinging forward.

"I don't recommend wastin' time on your high tech little gadgets..." Wes started.

Seaton sighed in frustration. Wes's voice grated on him like a chainsaw on a chalkboard. "It's not high tech. It's *old* tech. Humans have been using atlatls for centuries, er...actually, probably longer than that. It increases your leverage which in turn increases the velocity of..." He ceased his futile attempt to explain in detail in favor of a simpler explanation. "With an atlatl, you can throw a spear harder and farther. Just trust me on this."

"It ain't about trust. It's about time..."

"It won't take me long. And, while I'm working on ways to defend ourselves, you can go ahead and work on whatever it is you think needs to get done. Deal?"

Wes scratched his head through his hat, staring down at the ground as if Seaton's words weren't sinking in. He took the hat off, brushed his receding hair around with his fingers and returned the hat, readjusting it nervously. Finally he conceded. "I reckon y'all do what y'all gotta do and I'll do what I gotta do."

Seaton stared at him for a beat. What was this guy's problem? There was a distinct possibility Seaton would have fared better on his own, but he was stuck—unless he wandered off into the woods and disappeared, but that wasn't his style. He had suffered through the company of much worse than the likes of Wes Wood.

"Great. I'm glad we could reach an understanding," Seaton said. "I can work on my projects while I wait for the coffee." Hearing his own tone of voice, he reminded himself to bring it down a notch and not talk down to Wes.

10:10am

Seaton Rogers sat by the fire with the materials he intended to use to make an atlatl. He set up a camera to capture the process. "Okay, so, we're out here in the woods and there are predators on the loose. Not just your typical garden variety bears and wolves, but an honest to goodness freak of nature. The people who've seen it are either dead or describe it as half-human and intelligent," he explained as an introduction on the new memory card. He wanted each recording to have an explanation of what was going on in case something happened to him and only one recording was found in the future.

"Now, we've got two bows and a few arrows and that's something, but we need more weapons. As for the knives and axes we have, using them involves getting a little too up close and personal for my taste. I don't want to be within reach of this thing. We've got some bear spray to incapacitate it, which I would use before getting close even to use a knife or axe."

Wes dropped a long log off his shoulder onto the ground nearby, apparently trying to make a scene of it. Short of breath, he came to investigate Seaton's progress. With his hands on his hips he huffed, "Y'all done with this shit yet?"

"It's not shit and I'm not done yet," Seaton replied, although he was close to finished.

"Ya know, the game's over. No don't gotta be filmin' this shit no more," Wes griped. "You should be helpin' me with the shelter."

Seaton ignored the comment and continued. "While my...," he said, clearing his throat, searching for the most tactful description, "...*companion* is busy building us a fortress, I'm working on the basics of defense and making an atlatl. I've made them before and used them for hunting with a great deal of success. When you're out in the wild without a gun, you have to make use of what you have. In the forest, that means sticks and stones, feathers and bones."

Seaton held up the atlatl for Wes's sake as well as the camera. "This is nothing more than a stick, stripped and, as you can see, I carved out this little spur at the end." He tapped the spur with his finger. "This was a twig branching out and I shaved it down. My spear or dart is a little over five feet long," he continued, holding up the spear to show the camera. "One end is pointy and, on the other end, I'm going to carve out a divot where the spur from my atlatl will fit."

He used a knife to carve out the divot but explained that he had made atlatls in the past by the most primitive means possible—using only a sharpened stone instead of a knife. When he was done, he demonstrated how the parts fit together.

"Now, the atlatl is an extension of my arm," he said, standing and bending his elbow to hold the contraption over his shoulder. "This creates greater leverage which some people, not me probably, but some people claim they've reached throwing speeds of up to one hundred miles per hour. I doubt I can get up to that speed, but it still gives me a significant advantage." He hurled the spear off camera more for the benefit of his skeptical companion.

Impressed with the distance as well as the velocity, Wes still wasn't convinced. "Not too shabby there. But what'd you ever kill with one of them, rabbits and skunks?"

"It's actually better for bigger animals that can't dart away quickly. I've bagged deer, elk and, once, a two hundred pound caribou. You could kill a freaking moose with an atlatl, but that's pretty hardcore. Either way, it's more than adequate for killing a human or human-like creature. I hope." Seaton looked at Wes's suddenly envious eyes. "You want to try?"

"Heck yeah!" the Mississippi farmer exclaimed, excited to try a new hunting tool.

Seaton was happy to coach him and the two bonded over target practice. No matter what their cultural and geographical differences may have been back in the real world, they still had one thing in common—survival.

Chapter 25

Day 22

11:30am

    Zoey Price and Ezra Greer floated slowly down a shallow portion of the river. Reflections of the sun glistened off the surface ahead, but the temperature remained steadily low. Zoey watched the varying colors of rocks ease by under the crystal clear water. Mesmerizing. She needed the respite and she let it consume her. This is what life was all about—peace, harmony, nature, clarity.

    There was something about being in the wild, with only yourself to rely on. She couldn't call 911 for help. There was no point in screaming or crying. She couldn't run to a neighbor's house for help. She couldn't depend on strangers like Ezra, Seaton and Wes to protect her. She didn't need to. She wasn't the little astrology girl checking her horoscope every day and shelling out money to psychics to lie to her. Not anymore. Zoey had been through more than any of the contestants had in the past twenty-two days—an awakening of sorts, and a rather rude one at that. But, she needed it. She knew that now. It had given her a new strength she had never even sought before. She never knew existed.

    The river widened and lost depth. The obstacle course of rocks protruding from the water ahead made it obvious they couldn't float through. It was time to pull the raft out of the water again, the third time that day. They had spent more time pulling the raft on land, carving paths through the woods than they had spent on the water.

    Ezra threw the paddle ashore in frustration. "This is stupid. We could cover more ground on foot," he said, his bare feet in the ice cold water.

    He pulled the raft toward shore with Zoey still sitting on it. She moved to get up, but he wouldn't let her. "No point in both of us getting our feet wet."

Ezra took his time on the slippery rocks. The water was threatening to freeze his feet, but a fall would be a total disaster. At the very least, they'd have to stop and make a fire to get dry. Every step had to be considered and calculated if they wanted a chance of surviving.

"If we can find a clear stretch of deeper water..." Zoey began as she stepped onto land with one foot and unloaded their supplies. She didn't need to finish the sentence. A stretch of deeper water would take them farther.

Ezra pulled the raft out of the water with a single heave powered by frustration. The rolled up cuffs of his pants were wet with river water.

Zoey called him over to sit on the trunk of a downed tree and tended to his frozen feet, drying them with a spare shirt from his backpack and massaging some warmth into them. "Do you have another pair of pants? These just keep getting wetter."

A rustling behind them gave both their hearts a jolt. Ezra sprang to his feet and lunged for his bow. Whatever was walking around them sounded heavy and difficult to flee from without any shoes on.

Zoey held up an open palm to stop him. "Sh." She inched toward the noise, ducking her head to see under branches. The sound was steady with intermittent twig-snapping—no attempt at stealth. It was getting closer, but still far enough away to not discover her.

She bobbed and weaved, trying to increase visibility. She let out the breath she had been holding in, hand on her chest to still her pounding heart. Two small does rummaged around with their noses in the leaf litter, looking for tasty morsels. They stopped and stared at Zoey from several yards away, ears at attention as their jaws chewed laterally. The life and innocence brought a smile to her face.

Ezra snuck up behind her, arrow ready to fire.

"What are you doing?" she demanded, somehow shocked he would pounce on the opportunity to bag some protein. Her voice was enough to send the deer running.

Ezra sighed, shaking his head. "Good job. You scared them away."

"So what? We don't have time to shoot and skin a deer and,

even if we did, there's no way we're carrying a hundred pounds of deer meat with us," Zoey pointed out.

Ezra bowed his head. "You're right," he said, looking down at his cold, bare feet.

The radio on his hip crackled to life. "Zoey? Ezra?" It was Seaton Rogers.

Ezra turned up the volume a notch before answering. "Please tell me you're not calling with a problem. Over."

"Not really. I'm calling to avoid a problem. Just wanted to let you know we're working on some traps. When you reach the bend in the river, radio to us to come get you. Over."

"How will we know it's the right bend? Over."

"We're planting a flag. It'll be on your left side. You can't miss it," Seaton explained. "Over."

On the left side. That meant they'd have to cross to the other side of the river. Their decision was made. The debate over going by land or water was moot. They needed at least one more stint on the river.

"Roger that," Ezra sighed. "We'll check in later when we get back on the water. Over and out."

WES WOOD

Day 22

4:52pm

Age: 57
Occupation: Farmer
Home: Mississippi
Status: Divorced, 8 children

"Welcome to Fort River Bend," Wes Wood hollered to the camera, arms spread open to his sides in a triumphant display.

The "fort" was far from complete, but given Seaton's habit of naming everything, he had chosen a name for it and Wes loved it. The fort didn't even have any walls yet. All they had managed to construct was a series of stilts upon which they planned to build the fort, ten feet off the ground, large enough for four people. They knew they wouldn't have much luck hiding on the ground so, they opted to make themselves hard to reach. The killer would have to climb to get to them and, thus, leave himself vulnerable to attack.

Seaton had made a stockpile of spears to use with the atlatl. Wes made a ladder they could use for accessing the fort. In the meantime, he planned to use it to build the fort while Seaton was off setting a perimeter trap and alert system.

"This here's Colonel Wes Wood's Last Stand," Wes continued to joke. Acknowledging the severity of the situation just wasn't his style. There was no point in worrying, no point in showing any weakness. You live and you die—plain and simple. He didn't waste time regretting decisions or wishing he had chosen a different path. It was all part of god's plan in Wes's mind and he expected god to help him defeat the abomination—the creature, the critter, the monster. He had a hundred names for it, but it all amounted to the evil created by man's manipulation of god's good Earth.

"Y'all can see up yonder," Wes said, pointing to the cross he had already mounted to the base of the fort for good luck. "We's got god on are side. Ain't nobody gonna mess with us."

He stretched to his tippy-toes to kiss the simple cross made of two twigs tied with cordage. It gave him confidence and a sense of power. He continued working into the night, as did Seaton.

"We're going to have to set up camp for the night," the radio squawked. It was Ezra, exhaustion in his voice. "We'll be back on the river first thing in the morning. Over."

Wes listened as Seaton responded. "Roger that. We'll be looking out for you tomorrow. Good luck. Stay safe. Over and out."

Day 22 passed without another death.

Chapter 26

Day 23

3:03pm

Zoey Price and Ezra Greer drifted down the lazy river all day. The going was slow, but at least, they spent the majority of the time on the water without any obstacles. The river narrowed making it deep enough to not have to worry about running aground. Now the danger shifted to the possibility of falling in. They opted to use the down time to sit still and fish rather than paddle.

Ezra's makeshift fishing pole lunged. He pulled in the line. "I got another one," he announced, the fishing line dancing around. The small triumph almost brought a smile to his face. He yanked a fourteen inch trout out of the river, onto the raft. It flopped around violently trying to escape before Ezra pinned it down. He pulled the trout off the hook and strung it through its gills using paracord, together with the first two fish. That made three—a veritable feast. "One more and we'll each have a fish for dinner if we find Seaton and Wes," he bragged.

"And when do you think that might be? We've been on this river forever," Zoey barked, a bit frustrated and testy.

"Any minute now. Any minute now," Ezra promised, more focused on getting his line back in the water. He baited the hook with another worm he had dug up that morning and tossed it back in the river.

"You've been saying that for two days," Zoey reminded him.

He gave her a what-do-you-expect look. "I get it—you're cold, tired and hungry, but don't forget, I know as much as you do. If you want to get there faster, start paddling. I'm going to keep fishing, if that's okay with you."

Zoey pulled her line in and took Ezra's advice. She needed to straighten the raft out anyway. "I'm sorry. I've been on the move since my camp burned down. Feels like forever. I just want to stay in one place for a few days. I haven't felt safe in a long time."

"I hate to burst your bubble, kiddo, but I don't know that it's going to be any safer with Seaton and Wes."

"Thanks. That makes me feel better," Zoey spat, her voice thick with sarcasm.

"Yeah, well, reality is a cruel bitch," he began, but he didn't have the heart to continue. Zoey had been through enough already. He chose his next words carefully. "We might not be a hundred percent safe, but we'll be much better off all together. Safety in numbers, right?"

"Do you think that thing is following us?" she asked, checking the river bank behind them for the millionth time.

"I doubt it. There's been no sign of him. But, that could mean…" Ezra trailed off, regretting his words as soon as they left his mouth. His first instinct was always to be honest. He couldn't help it. Sugar coating took too much effort and lying in a survival situation could put lives at risk.

Zoey stopped paddling and twisted around to look at him. "That could mean what?"

He sighed, but went on to explain, "You said the killer is intelligent and slightly injured."

"So?" Zoey demanded he continue.

"So, think about it. What would you do? He saw you take off on a raft on this particular river. If it were me and I was determined to kill us and I had access to a boat…"

Zoey cut him off, finishing his thought process as she figured out where he was going. "You'd take the boat to the end of the river and follow it inland until you found me and the raft," she said.

"It *is* a one-way street," Ezra added.

"So, we could be paddling right into his hands," Zoey surmised.

"Possibly. On the plus side, we could be luring him into our trap, provided he doesn't know about Seaton and Wes."

Zoey turned back around and started paddling hard. "What the hell?" she shouted. "We should have been paddling the whole time. We need to get to them before the killer does." She continued, double-time into a right turn in the river. The water sped up as well, but she kept paddling frantically.

"Calm down. Expending all your energy is not going to do anybody any good," Ezra chided her.

Up ahead, the water was rough and riddled with boulders. She laid the paddle across her lap and let out her frustration in a long, bellowing scream.

"Don't freak out on me, Zoey," Ezra begged. "We're going to be fine."

She didn't respond.

"Zoey? Look at me," he said, calmly.

She took a deep breath and turned around.

"We're going to be…"

"Is that you?" the radio interrupted.

Their eyes widened at the same time, both realizing it was Seaton Rogers—and he must be close. Unfortunately, the distraction took their attention away from the maze of rocks they were heading into. Ezra tried to warn Zoey, but it was too late. The bottom of the raft scraped a hidden boulder near the surface, throwing the raft off kilter, redirecting it toward a rocky gauntlet.

"Hold on," Ezra yelled, but there was nothing to hold on to. The raft rocked back and forth, pushing them around.

Zoey tried to paddle her way out of the white rushing water, but the raft slammed into a boulder, bounced off another boulder and threw her into the river. Half their equipment followed her.

Ezra caught himself on a length of paracord used to tie the tarp to the raft and grabbed the steering stick, saving it from ending up in the river. "Zoey," he shouted, but she was still under water. Ice cold, fast-moving water.

He used the stick to stop the raft before slamming into another series of rocks. Zoey's head popped up behind him for a moment before going back under, caught up in a current taking her away from the stalled raft. Ezra pushed off and tried to catch up with her. A scream rang out every time her head breached the surface.

Seaton's voice squawked over the radio, asking questions which would have to be ignored. Ezra had his hands full trying to keep himself out of the water and the raft in one piece. He zigzagged through the rocky maze using the long stick to push off boulder after boulder like a pinball.

The obstacle course was short, ending as abruptly as it began, but it was only one danger removed. Zoey was too cold to swim effectively. Her arms flailed in a distressed attempt to get to shore. Ezra tried to push off the bottom of the river to catch up to her, but the water was too deep. The paddle was lost, floating out of reach along with the tarp Zoey had been using for a backpack. He crept to the edge of the raft to paddle with his hands. With the raft off balance, he sunk the corner a few inches, enough to get his legs soaked. Worst of all, he wasn't making any progress.

Zoey didn't have much time before she drowned or hypothermia set in and Ezra knew it. He unzipped his coat and took it off, along with his boots. Clutching a length of cordage, he jumped into the river, the cold water knocking the wind out of him. He swam like a frog, pulling the raft behind him.

Zoey stopped her thrashing. Her head floated just above the surface, her eyes wide and fixed in shock. She disappeared around another bend, Ezra increasing his speed in pursuit. When he rounded the corner, she was gone. He called out for her and kept moving forward, but his swimming strokes were stifled by the cold and he began to sink.

His head going under water in such frigid conditions was like injecting ice water into his ears. It entered his nose and mouth, causing a full-cranium brain-freeze. When he tried to resurface, his head banged off the bottom of the raft, like being trapped under ice. He felt around for an unimpeded area, letting out the shallow breath he had taken before going under. The raft ran him over and spun around. Yanked by the paracord, Ezra refused to let go. He thrust his head above water and took a wheezing breath in, throwing his arms onto the raft to keep him from going back under.

His eyes seared with pain, but they didn't deceive him—a strip of red cloth waved in the wind atop a crude flagpole on his left. His kicking feet drifted down until they touched bottom. Up ahead, Seaton Rogers was in the river up to his waist, dragging Zoey to shore. She didn't appear to be assisting, her head slumped forward motionless.

Ezra rushed to their aid, grabbing her by the legs to carry her to shore. "Zoey? Talk to me," he rasped before a coughing fit struck him.

"Put her down, put her down," Seaton yelled as soon as they were on dry land.

They set her down on the grassy river bank and Seaton

attempted a resuscitation while Ezra coughed his frozen lungs out. Seaton took off his coat and covered her wet torso before checking for a pulse. It was hard to find and it was weak, but it was there, accompanied by shallow breaths which were hard to distinguish as her body began to shiver.

Seaton hollered over the radio, "Wes! Make sure the fire is roaring. Zoey and Ezra fell in the river." His report wasn't exactly accurate but the details weren't important. "She's breathing," he said to Ezra who was finally getting his coughing under control. "Can you walk?"

"I think so," Ezra replied, his hands on his hips as he tried to regulate his breathing.

Seaton patted Zoey on the cheek. "You're going to be okay, Zoey. We're going to warm you up," he reassured, a jolt of adrenaline hitting him as she opened her eyes a crack.

With Ezra's assistance, they threw her over Seaton's shoulder, covered her with his coat, and hurried to camp. Ezra peeled off layers of wet clothing on the way. By the time they got there, Wes had two fires blazing along with blankets, sleeping bags, and dry clothes ready.

"Set her down right here," Wes directed, motioning toward the space between the two fires.

"We need to get her clothes off," Seaton said, laying her down on the sleeping bag, but the three men hesitated. The idea of stripping a semi-conscious young woman's clothes off in the middle of the woods seemed wrong. They all looked at each other with faces that said, "Go ahead, *you* do it."

The standoff only lasted a moment before Seaton jumped into action. One of her socks had already fallen off and the other was half off. He tugged it the rest of the way, tossed it to Wes and went for the rest of her clothes. Ezra was busy taking the rest of his own clothes off. Wes collected them all and set to the task of hanging a paracord clothesline.

Seaton took off his shirt, wet with transfer from carrying Zoey. He redressed her in some of his own dirty clothes. "Sorry these smell so bad," he apologized, sitting her up and pulling a hoodie over her.

She made a grossed out face but remained sitting up under her own power.

"Hey, that's good. See? It's like smelling salts," he joked, his ribs visible through his skin like a xylophone on his emaciated body. Wes threw him a sweater to wear which was about four sizes too big. They were all huddled together, warmed from both sides by the fires when the radio came to life.

A woman called out in distress, her message muffled between the tangle of shivering bodies. Seaton and Wes shared a look of confusion. Every living person on Isolation Island was accounted for, so they thought.

The chatter ended before Wes could get the radio out. He held it up to his mouth, hesitating for a moment. Seaton gave him the nod to go ahead. "This here's Wes Wood. Please repeat your transition," he said erroneously. "Who is this? Over."

The voice, weak and distant, condensed by the radio's speaker, replied. "This is Stephanie. Stephanie Hamilton. I just saw a boat pass by."

STEPHANIE HAMILTON

Day 23

2:29pm

Age: 29
Occupation: Artist
Home: Colorado
Status: Single

Stephanie Hamilton scoured the shoreline, plucking the last mussels and limpets she could find from the crevices between rocks. Each dove through the little bit of saltwater she had scooped into the pot and hit the bottom with a ping. She had counted only six pings. This easy resource was running low, but it was better than nothing. She would trade them all for a trip back home, if she could.

Stepping out into the open on the shoreline gave her anxiety. She had been listening to the radio transmissions, monitoring the progress of the killer as told by the last remaining contestants. So many people had died, she told herself, because they didn't hide. In her mind, hers was the only strategy with a chance of survival. Even so, she didn't feel safe in her little corner of the island, closed in by the towering cliffs and impassable beach. If she had to run, she wouldn't be able to run far.

Hopefully, it wouldn't come to that. If she stayed out of sight, stayed away from the others, she was convinced she could go undetected. Still, she was drawn to the shoreline for food and the off chance of spotting a ship on the horizon. The slim pickings urged her to get back to her new camp and find a more significant food source elsewhere from now on.

As Stephanie turned to leave, she heard the low hum of the Medline's engine, barely audible. She froze. Her eyes widened. Was it real or was she just imagining it? Perhaps her ears were playing tricks on her. The sound was coming from the west, steady and getting louder. She ran for cover, hiding behind a twisted tree hanging over the beach for its place in the sun. The cliff jutting out into the ocean nearby further obscured the view for anyone coming from the west by boat. She ducked down, peeking out as the engine noise grew louder. Part of her wanted to run out into the open, waving her arms to flag down the approaching vessel. If it wasn't a friendly face at the wheel, she could catch the killer off guard and fight, or so she fantasized briefly. It was far too risky.

The Medline came into view sooner than she expected along with a wall of engine noise, the bow skipping and splashing through the waves beyond their breaking point. The creature stood at the controls bundled up with stolen clothes. He could have passed for human at that distance except for his exposed head which seemed to be covered in dark green scaly armor which turned iridescent with the sun's reflection.

The creature turned its head as if looking directly at Stephanie. She resisted the reflex to cower. If it hadn't spotted her already, any movement could draw attention. She stopped breathing, staring the creature down as the boat sped past. Did it see her? Did it have extra senses which could detect her? Maybe it could simply smell her. It wouldn't be difficult after twenty-three days without a shower.

The Medline continued forward, the creature returning its focus to the water ahead. When it was finally out of sight, it struck her—the fire! She scooped more water into her pot, losing a couple of mussels in the process and ran inland to her camp. Half the water spilled on the way as she sprinted back, hoping the smoke from the fire hadn't already alerted the creature.

Her camp was nothing more than a cave and a fire which, much to her relief, had petered out to a smoldering pile of ash. Perfect. It wasn't enough smoke to give away her position and there were plenty of live embers to rekindle it easily. She put the pot down, spilling more seawater and bent over with her hands on her hips, trying to catch her breath.

The camp was constructed with a quick exit in mind. Her supplies were either packed and ready to go or else hidden. She always had a pot of seawater handy to put out the fire and a five-foot tall bush plucked from its home was standing by to hide the fire pit once extinguished. If all routes of escape were blocked, she had one last place to hide. In a deep corner of the cave, she had set up a tiny panic room she could crawl into and barricade the entrance with driftwood. She hoped she wouldn't have to use any of it.

She had been doing what she felt she needed to do to survive on her own, but now she faced a moral dilemma. Looking out for yourself was one thing, but having spotted the killer and the direction the creature was travelling, withholding the information could be putting lives in danger. She wasn't willing to do that. It was a quick decision.

Stephanie pulled out the radio and pressed the talk button. "I just spotted the creature traveling east on the Medline not far from the northeast shore," she reported. "If anyone can hear this, beware. Please reply. Over." As soon as the words left her mouth she cringed, ready to face the possible wrath of the other contestants angry with her decision to fake her own suicide.

"This here's Wes Wood. Please repeat your transition. Who is this? Over."

"This is Stephanie. Stephanie Hamilton. I just saw a boat pass by." She braced for wrath again, but was met with a moment of silence first.

"We thought you was dead," Wes replied, jovial. "Where you been at? Over," the southern farmer asked.

"I'm not sharing that information over the radio. I was near the northeast corner of the island when I spotted it. That's all you need to know. Over."

"It's all right. The killer don't understand us," Wes replied. "Over."

"Right. So you think. I've been listening. Look, that thing just passed by on the Medline. I'm just trying to warn you. Over."

"You let us think you was dead all this time and now you callin' tellin'..." Wes began to complain, but he was cut off.

Seaton's voice took over. "Stephanie, this is Seaton Rogers. Did it see you?"

"I don't think so. It looked in my direction for a moment but I was well hidden. It didn't slow down or change course. Unless it has some kind of extra senses, I don't think it knew I was there. Over," she reported, adding as much detail as she could think of.

"Good. Good. I think I know where it's headed. Are you

okay?" Seaton asked.

"I'm still alive, obviously. I'm cornered on this section of the island and I'm running out of food sources, but I'm getting by. I'm sorry for making you all think I was dead. I have no way to get to you anyway. Over." Stephanie replied, not sure what else to say.

"It's okay. As long as you're not in danger, keep doing what you're doing. Let us know if you run into trouble. We'll come get you after we deal with this creature. Over," Seaton instructed.

"I'm surrounded by water and cliffs. Coming to get me will be difficult. Over," Stephanie explained.

Seaton replied, "With any luck, we'll have control of the Medline by the time this is all over. Sit tight and keep us updated if anything goes wrong. Over and out."

Stephanie choked up a bit, the reality of a surreal situation creeping in. "Good luck guys," she offered, not sure if she'd ever hear from them again. Not sure if they'd live another day. "Over and out."

Chapter 27

Day 24

9:10am

Zoey Price woke to the sound of construction seeping into her dreams. Someone was hammering a nail into a wooden box which she knew by the magic of dreams was meant to be her coffin.

In reality, the hammering was Wes Wood, working on the fort. It was coming along nicely and getting bigger, enough to accommodate all four survivors. Ezra was off hunting for food while Seaton worked on the early warning security alarm and various traps, focusing on the area of land downriver, now that they knew which direction the killer was coming from. He hoped to set enough traps to kill the creature or, at least, slow it down before it got close enough to attack their little tribe.

Zoey realized she was dreaming when she saw the hammer pounding without a hand to swing it. She eased herself out of the dream, opening her eyes and blinking her way out of the haze. It was too bright, not for her eyes to handle but to still be asleep. She sat up and found herself surrounded by empty sleeping bags and full daylight seeping into the temporary shelter. An involuntary sigh escaped her mouth. How long had everyone else been working while she'd been asleep?

She crawled out of the shelter to find Wes ready to greet her as if he had been anxiously waiting while he worked.

"Mornin' Princess," Wes twanged with his heavy southern drawl.

"Don't call me that," Zoey snapped, stabbing him with her eyes.

"I just call it like I see it," Wes countered. "Y'all been sleepin' while we been workin' to keep Princess Zoey safe."

Ezra and Seaton returned just in time to referee. Seaton wore his waders, saving his hiking boots for Zoey. Ezra and Zoey had both lost their shoes in the river so, they were forced to make do with borrowed footwear. With a second pair of socks on his feet, Ezra fit into Wes's tall, waterproof rubber boots.

"Well, someone should have woken me up. I nearly died yesterday, so excuse me if I'm a little tired," she barked, catching the sound of her own voice by the end—irritated, bitter, and unappreciative. After all, they had been the ones who saved her life. Ezra risked his own life in the process. Still, she wanted to stop the Princess comments before they went any further. No one had the right to claim she was anything but a badass after everything she had survived so far.

She dragged her hands over her face in a sobering gesture and shifted her tone. "I'm sorry. I just...I want to thank you all for what you did yesterday. You saved my life and I appreciate it. That being said, I don't want to be treated any differently around here. I don't want any special treatment. I'm here to contribute. I'm here to help us all survive. So, let's focus our energy on killing this horrible creature and don't worry about me. I can take care of myself. From here on out, I don't want anyone risking their life for me. We're all equal here."

The reactions from her tribemates weren't convincing, but they all agreed without objection.

"Oh, and I'm telling you right now," she added. "If anyone calls me Princess or Sweetheart or any other belittling, sexist name, I'm going to punch you in the balls. Got it?" Although she was serious, she couldn't help cracking an endearing smile.

The warning was taken in the spirit it was given. They were a tribe now—a family, whether they liked it or not. Brothers and sisters were bound to outbursts and juvenile threats. No one took it personally.

Seaton tried to help break the last bit of tension with his own brand of comedy. In a halfway decent southern accent he teased, "Oo, I love it when you git that fire in yer eye." He followed it up with a playful nudge with his elbow.

Zoey couldn't help laughing. She checked him, pushing into his thin frame with her shoulder. "Oh, you too? I would have expected that from Wes, but..."

Wes chimed in, "Me? I ain't gonna mess with y'all no more, Prin...uh, Zoey...Miss Price." He removed his hat in a sign of chivalry and bowed in her direction.

Seaton pointed to his hiking boots next to the fire. "Try those on Zoey. They'll probably be way too big, but that's all we've got." They were, indeed, like wearing boats on her petite feet, but she was thankful to have anything.

Through all the chatter, no one had noticed Ezra carrying a kill. He raised a rabbit carcass by its ears. "Now that that's settled, who wants breakfast?" he asked and they all cheered.

Even a tiny triumph was enough to bring a fleeting moment of elation after twenty-four days in the wilderness, being hunted. The smell of the rabbit meat cooking—the promise of protein on the way—gave them all a boost of energy, even the former vegetarian. Except for meals and bathroom breaks, there was no downtime for anyone the rest of the day. They worked together toward one common goal—survival.

5:21pm

Wandering around away from camp was now dangerous for everyone. Although Seaton had walked them through all the traps he had set, there was still the risk of failing to recognize a trapped area and ending up impaled on sharp sticks.

Zoey, Seaton, and Ezra stayed close to Fort River Bend, collecting wood to make into spears. They were building several arsenals, spaced out, in and around camp. Ezra had taken the lead military role after much objection from Wes. None of the survivalists had any military experience, but Ezra was deemed to be the most capable of making a plan of attack and defense.

Several locations were selected for attack, other locations were selected as fallback positions and two areas across the river were stocked with extra weapons in the event of a total retreat. They stocked the latter with food and supplies as well. Unwilling to fight to the death, they decided against an all-or-nothing stand, with the exception of Wes Wood. He was in favor of an all-out victory or death attack.

"Where's Wes?" Ezra asked, noticing the extended absence of the Mississippi farmer.

"I think he's gathering firewood," Zoey answered, but her

voice betrayed the fact she was guessing.

"He's probably trying to track down the killer on his own," Seaton interjected, only half-joking.

"Would he really do that?" Ezra asked, unfamiliar with Wes.

Seaton hesitated. He looked like he was going to say no, quickly dismissing the question, but he paused to think, taking it seriously. In the end, he waved the question away with his hand, singing, "Nah," as if it would be too ridiculous. It sounded like he was struggling to convince himself. He wagged his head back and forth as if reconsidering.

Ezra watched and waited, furrowing his eyebrows.

"He can't be that stupid," Seaton finally decided, but he continued to make faces suggesting he was debating with himself.

"Maybe you should check on him with the radio," Zoey suggested, looking at Seaton, assuming he was closer to Wes having spent more time with him than Ezra and herself.

"Maybe *you* should check in with him on the radio," Seaton returned. "I can't understand a word he's saying half the time and I don't really care what he's up to." He acted overly-absorbed in the task of hard-firing a spear point all of a sudden.

Before the debate could go any further, the right side alarm went off. Cans filled with pebbles rattled against each other. Seaton had rigged up two alarm systems to approximate the location of the disturbance. Something or someone had tripped the fishing line or triggered a trap. The rattling cans made the survivalists' hearts jump. They looked at each other for reactions and instructions.

"If we're lucky, it's just an animal," Seaton offered.

Ezra grabbed a radio and called out to Wes to warn him an alarm was going off while they all scrambled to take up arms.

WES WOOD

Day 24

5:33pm

Age: 57
Occupation: Farmer
Home: Mississippi
Status: Divorced, 8 children

Wes Wood explored the area east of camp, fueled by over-confidence and a desire to be the hero. He knew, or thought he knew, the rumors they were throwing around back at camp about him. It was his assumption that everyone in the world knew he had once been suspected of being a serial killer. He almost enjoyed the notoriety and the fear that came along with it, which he misinterpreted as respect. But, this wasn't the place for any of it. The other three survivalists could easily kill him rather than risk camping with a suspected serial killer. They'd be less likely to banish him if he killed the creature and saved the day. Heroes don't get banished.

If they also managed to get off the island, he'd be the one to grab the spotlight—interviews, book deals, movies. He'd be an international hero, not only for saving lives but for being the only man to slay an unknown creature. It'd be like capturing Bigfoot. This was a once-in-a-lifetime opportunity to Wes. His mind wandered, daydreaming about what actor would play him in the movie. Maybe Clint Eastwood was the wrong choice. Could Sylvester Stallone pull off a southern accent? Wes had fancied himself a southern Rambo for quite some time. Perhaps sleep deprivation had something to do with it.

When the call came in, Wes's face lit up. He had been bragging to the camera about his fearless nature and about how he hoped to find the killer and save everyone's lives.

"Come in, Wes. This is home base. The right side alarm just

went off. Where are you? Over," the radio crackled.

A little twitch in the corner of his fake smile threatened to divulge his true fear. Could the killer have found them so quickly? The nearest beach was a two-day hike away. Perhaps the creature had no need for sleep.

"Y'all think it's him?" Wes asked, spitting on the ground at the end of the question.

"Whatever it is, we need to check it out," Ezra returned. "Where are you right now?"

"I ain't far from the right side traps. I'll check it out. Over."

"Be careful. We're on our way."

Wes let the camera mounted on his head continue to roll. He wanted to capture every moment of the monumental battle he imagined was about to take place. It crossed his mind that he might actually be filming his own death, but he didn't let that stop him. All the glory he imagined he'd receive was worth risking his life for.

He scurried through the forest, ducking behind trees and crouching behind bushes, hoping to get the drop on the killer. Assuming the creature was following the river, Wes doubled back to the line of traps and tripwires near the water. A plan formed in his head along the way. If he found the creature killed by a trap, he'd set it free and stage the scene to take credit for the kill. Some creative video editing would also be necessary.

Wes reached the river and followed it to the first trap. A large distinctive boulder marked the spot where the line of traps began. He followed it away from the water. None of them appeared to be disturbed. The tripwire for the alarm was intact and taut. A false alarm? He doubled back to the river on the other side of the line, looking for any indication of a trail left by the creature. All he found were hoof prints and paw prints—deer, wolf, bear, possibly even a boar. They were all hardened into the ground. Although he wasn't really sure what the creature's footprints would look like, there was no sign of anything walking on two legs except for his own boots and prints he was sure belonged to Seaton.

He continued to film anyway, putting up a fearless façade for the camera the more it became evident he wasn't in any real danger.

"Welp, there ain't nothin' out here," he said, still holding his bow at the ready as he stood from a crouching position over a set of paw prints. "I reckon it ain't nothin' but a false alarm. The kid probably rigged it up wrong." The "kid" he was referring to was Seaton Rogers.

The camera whipped around with his head and they both spotted something floating in the river, caught in a corner created by the boulder that marked the trap line. He rushed over to investigate. The raft, still wrapped in the blue tarp, bobbed up and down in the water, trying to get past the boulder. It hadn't been there when Seaton was setting the traps, unless he overlooked it, which wasn't likely. Perhaps, it was a trap itself.

"Well, looky there. How 'bout that?" Wes exclaimed, approaching without caution.

All the supplies the raft had once carried were gone except for Ezra's backpack. Wes pulled it and the raft ashore.

"Never know when a raft might come in handy," he explained to the camera.

No sooner did he get the raft ashore than a noise startled him. Something was running through the woods and fast, scrambling with a purpose. It was coming toward him. He readied an arrow, sidestepping away from the river in case he had to make a quick getaway.

Two deer emerged from the brush, bouncing and leaping at full speed. One was coming right at Wes but changed direction when he let the arrow fly. It glanced off a tree and redirected into the river as both deer bounded into the shallow water to cross. He ran closer and took aim with another arrow, debating whether he should risk losing it, too. The lure of meat made him pull the arrow back, but the deer were gone in an instant and he was now contending with the pack of wolves that had been chasing the deer.

They came running out of the woods behind him in a hunting formation. With the deer out of sight, the dogs changed their target without hesitation. Two of them charged Wes while three moved to flank him on either side, removing the water and the raft as an escape route.

Wes aimed and released the arrow, hitting one of the charging canines in the hind quarters, but the pack was coming too fast and he only had one arrow left. He turned and ran, hoping to lead the wolves into the traps, screaming, "No. Get away. Heeeelp." But, his comrades were not within earshot.

He dropped the useless bow, switching to a double-fisted defense, a hunting knife in one hand and a canister of bear spray in the other as the wolves closed. He hopped over the alarm wire, landing with one foot in a spike trap. The sharpened wooden stakes pierced right through his boot and foot as they were designed to do. Another scream rang out through the forest as he pulled his foot free.

The injury didn't slow him down as he ran for his life into the forest, hoping to climb a tree or put some obstacles in between himself and the attacking dogs. Feeling the wolves right on his heels he spun around to retreat backward and let out a stream of bear spray, sweeping from right to left in hopes of hitting as many of them as possible. It slowed down two of the five wolves. The one with the arrow in its backside fell back and collapsed. The rest charged on, surrounding him.

Wes let out another burst of spray, hitting the closest wolf in the face, but another got hold of his arm, sinking its teeth into muscle, clamping down on bone. The panicked survivalist tried to pull free of the predator's grip but the animal dragged him down, knocking the camera off his head. The rest of the pack joined in on the attack as the camera captured the frenzy of snarling teeth and growls. The alpha male went right for Wes's throat, piercing his jugular, sending dark red blood exploding into the wolves' fur and onto the camera lens.

Wes's last blood-gurgling screams were recorded on the same memory card he had hoped to capture his heroic, life-saving victory over the killer. It was not to be. Another reminder that there were plenty of other things to worry about in the wild.

Chapter 28

Day 24

5:55pm

Seaton Rogers, Zoey Price, and Ezra Greer trudged through the forest armed with their primitive weapons. Each carried a spear. Ezra had the last bow and the few remaining arrows. Seaton had the atlatl and throwing spears. Zoey had the last can of bear spray. They marched along, single-file into uncertainty.

Wes wasn't responding to their repeated calls over the radio. They were expecting the worst, but the worst could mean a variety of dangers in the wild.

Ezra led the dwindling tribe, scolding anyone who violated the no-talking rule he had invoked. The gray, overcast sky darkened the forest prematurely, but there was still enough daylight to navigate, find Wes and return to camp, provided they didn't run into any problems.

Seaton brought them to a halt. "Hold up, hold up. We're at the trap line," he said, spotting a piece of rope from one of the hammocks tied around the trunk of a tree which marked the spot.

"I see it," Ezra confirmed.

"Maybe I should take the lead," Seaton suggested. "I know where all the traps are."

Ezra didn't object, stepping out of the way for Seaton to lead them along the trap line. They employed the same tactic as Wes—following the trap line to see if any had been triggered to narrow their search. The line took them all the way to the river where the raft first caught their attention. On their way to examine the raft and backpack, they found the small hole and bloody stakes Wes had stepped into.

Seaton crouched near the trap. Bits of flesh clung to the sharpened sticks, but it didn't explain what triggered the alarm and the flesh was unidentifiable. He looked up at Ezra and Zoey for input, but they were looking past him at the trail of blood. Ezra brought it to Seaton's attention with a point of a finger.

"What the hell?" Seaton mumbled, standing up.

The raft, the blood leading away from camp—it didn't fill them with confidence.

Zoey attempted to explain. "Someone found the raft and pulled it out of the river and someone stepped in the trap. Was it Wes? Or was it the monster?"

No one had the heart to speculate. They followed the blood trail back into the woods to investigate, weapons ready to defend themselves. The gruesome scene revealed itself from behind a wall of brush. The wolf injured by Wes's arrow was sprawled on the ground close by, bleeding and breathing its last shallow breaths. Up ahead in the distance the rest of the pack was chewing on bloody bones, tearing off bits of Wes's meat. The mangled carcass of the Mississippi farmer was unrecognizable, except for the beard-covered face with its lifeless eyes staring into oblivion.

Zoey turned away with a muffled whimper as they took up hiding places and watched. The alpha male licked its bloodied chops, its ratty fur bathed in crimson. The scattered, torn pieces of cloth strewn about were unmistakable, along with the Isolation Island-issued camera and fluorescent yellow radio. The wolves seemed unaware they were being watched or they didn't care.

"We need to get that radio," Seaton whispered. It was the last one left besides the one they carried.

"Don't worry. They're not going to eat the radio," Ezra whispered back. "We'll get it when they're finished."

They weren't the only ones waiting for their turn. Crows were gathered and perched in the trees around the carcass, eager to swoop in and scavenge their share of the kill. The sound of cracking bones in the wolves' jaws excited them all the more. One brave bird dove in, pecked a few pieces from the torso and quickly escaped with a beak-full of meat. The wolves ignored it.

"What's the plan?" Seaton whispered to Ezra. "We might be able to pick off a couple of them, but the others will surely attack."

Ezra pursed his lips, struggling with the decision. He shook his head. "It's too risky. We're outnumbered," he said, as if one or two two-hundred-pound wolves wasn't risky enough. "Let's leave carefully, one at a time, go back to the river, and get the backpack."

Seaton nodded in agreement and turned to Zoey who was on her knees rocking back and forth with tears streaming down her face. "Zoey," he called out in a whisper and waved her to retreat.

She stood carefully and chose her steps wisely, creeping away without making a sound. Ezra and Seaton fixed their eyes on the wolves, waiting for a reaction but the dogs were focused on their meal.

Seaton backed away next while Ezra stood guard. The three survivalists snuck away quietly, dodging another bullet. With daylight slipping away, they retrieved the backpack and returned to camp, somber and disheartened.

They'd have to sleep in shifts for another night, leaving someone to stand guard against the wolves, bears, moose, the killer and any other unwelcome guests. It was going to be another long night with one less body generating heat to keep the tribe warm.

ZOEY PRICE

Day 25

10:10am

Age: 24
Occupation: Dance Instructor
Home: Montana
Status: Single

Zoey Price brought a camera along to document the carnage from the previous day's loss. The men wanted to leave her to stand watch at the camp, but she had refused, opting to stay with the pack. Safety in numbers.

The general consensus was to keep filming as much as they could without taking any unnecessary risks. Part of the decision stemmed from a mutual hope they'd be rescued. If the time came, they wanted proof of what took place on Isolation Island. Even with video and corroborating stories, they knew they'd have a hard time getting people to believe them. They didn't even have a blurry "Bigfoot" picture of the creature yet.

Their first stop was the raft, to make sure it was still there. It was as they left it, undisturbed. From there they followed the blood trail back to where Wes met his ultimate demise. There wasn't much left. The wolf Wes had killed was gone. All that remained of the Mississippi farmer was a few bones and body parts. Feeding crows scattered as the trio approached, but the rats were braver, continuing to nibble among the flies and insects that had gathered for the free feast.

Zoey handed the camera to Seaton. The gruesome sight made her stomach heave. She knelt near a tree, trying to settle herself but ready for her breakfast to make a return.

Ezra collected the last of Wes's possessions—the radio, the bow, one arrow and a wedding ring, even though he had been divorced. The radio had been left on and it was almost out of juice.

Ezra tested it out, calling Zoey's radio for a sound check.

Zoey lifted the radio to respond but was interrupted by a distant crack coming from the woods behind them, back toward camp. She sprang to her feet. The crack was followed by rattling leaves and branches and then a dull thump. They all turned in the direction of the noise, waiting for more, but the forest had gone silent again. They shared a look of confusion.

"What the hell was that?" Zoey whispered. She took the camera from Seaton and used it to zoom in on the area the sound seemed to come from, but it was too far and deep behind a wall of green.

"It was probably just a tree branch falling," Seaton guessed.

They stared into the woods, motionless. A rattle above them interrupted the silence. The hungry crows waiting to resume feeding jockeyed for position.

"Let's hope that's all it was," said Ezra. "Come on, let's keep moving."

They followed the trap line to the animal trail that marked the center between both lengths of the river. The traps remained set and the hidden trip wire looked undisturbed, but down the path toward camp, something was missing. They all seemed to notice at the same time, stopping them in their tracks. A light drizzle had begun, pelting the leaves and forest floor, masking any other sounds.

"Where's the lookout tower?" Zoey asked, a hint of fear in her voice.

The tower that once peeked just above the brush off to the left of the trail wasn't visible. Ezra searched the ground for tracks or footprints. Aside from a wolf's paw print in the dirt, nothing else jumped out at him.

"We have to check it out. I'll go around this way," Ezra said, pointing to the right flank. "You two circle around the other side. Keep your distance until I move in to inspect and cover me. Something's not right about this."

Zoey zoomed in on his worried face for a moment before he snuck off the trail, then turned to Seaton. He had the same look on his face, only less hidden as a result of his softer, patchy facial hair.

"Come on," Seaton said, leading the way.

Zoey followed a few feet behind, the camera in one hand, bear spray in the other. As they circled the area, the wreckage of the lookout tower came into view. It had collapsed. Ezra beat them to it, examining the posts left in the ground which once anchored the structure. Seaton kept a vigilant eye on their surroundings as Zoey closed in with the camera. The two back posts had snapped under the weight of the tower. Ezra crouched near one of the front posts, running his hand over a sheer cut. It was evident both front posts had been chopped with an axe.

Ezra looked up at the camera, a huff of vapor escaping his mouth with a sigh. "This was no accident," he said. "You better put the camera away."

Chapter 29

Day 25

10:37am

"This can't be what made that noise," Ezra said.

"Then when did it happen?" Zoey asked.

It was a frightening question no one wanted to answer with speculation, but they knew the tower must have been brought down much earlier, before they were within earshot. They surely would have heard the chopping and the collapse, or spotted whoever was responsible. They had to assume it was the work of the killer.

"We better get back to camp," Ezra decided.

"Back to camp? Are you crazy? It could be waiting for us," Zoey objected. She paced around in a circle, wringing her gloved hands on the brink of panic.

"Then what do you suggest we do?" Ezra demanded, frustration hitting him hard. "All our supplies are there, the extra weapons, the retreat routes. Our whole plan hinges on using the fort for protection. We can't keep running away. Fleeing into the forest with no supplies, we'd be as good as dead anyway."

"I've survived on my own with no equipment. I can do it again. Seaton, you're the tie-breaker. What do you think?" Zoey asked.

Seaton seemed to be somewhere else, nose in the air, scrutinizing eyes. "I think I smell smoke," he said. "Do you smell that?"

Zoey inhaled deep and steady and nodded her head. "Yeah, I smell it too. Where's it coming from?"

"It's probably our own campfire," Ezra suggested.

"From this far away?" Seaton challenged, walking off to get a look at the sky beyond the tree canopy above them. A cluster of pine trees with their narrow, pointy tops gave him a clearer view.

The gray sky was still spitting raindrops, but a billowing cloud of black smoke cover the sky.

"Son of a bitch," Seaton exclaimed. "It looks like it's coming from camp."

Without a second thought, he took off running toward the smoke. Zoey and Ezra had little choice but to follow.

As they neared their camp, the smoke was more prominent, floating through the forest, thick and heavy. A streak of flames reached up into the trees in the distance. Fort River Bend was on fire. The wooden structure meant to be a safe-area was engulfed in flames, singeing the tree branches above it and spreading across the ground below. The tribe gave it a wide berth as they hurried by to check on the shelter and salvage anything they could.

It was too late. The shelter was melted and burning. The supplies were out of reach in the ball of fire. They stopped on an unaffected patch of grass between the fort and the shelter. There was nothing they could do. The last of their food, the cameras and all the footage they had recorded over the past twenty-five days was gone, along with the rest of the supplies and weapons.

"This was deliberate," Ezra insisted.

They were standing on the proof. If their campfire had gotten out of hand, it would have burned the shelter, but it couldn't jump fifty feet to the raised fort on its own.

"We gotta get out of here," Seaton shouted over the roar of the growing inferno. It was spreading quickly, threatening to cut them off from any escape route.

"And go where?" Zoey demanded, desperation in her voice.

"Back to the raft," Ezra decided, his head darting around, watching out for an attack by the killer.

"What about the weapons stashed across the river?" Seaton asked, but Ezra was already on the move, leading them out before the fire could cut off the route. Zoey was right on his heels, leaving Seaton with little time to make a unilateral decision. He looked in the direction of the retreat route, but something told him not to go for it. He still had his backpack rigged to hold the atlatl and throwing spears on his back along with a bow and the last of the arrows. It was better than nothing. Other than a hunting knife and the spear he carried in his hand, the weapons they had worked so hard to accumulate were lost.

Seaton ran to catch up to Zoey and Ezra, leaping over a

decaying downed tree as they disappeared into the thick forest. The lack of a cleared trail slowed them down. Seaton lagged behind, his coat caught on a branch. The rattling of leaves above them sent his eyes skyward.

The creature, stripped down to only a pair of forest camo pants, dropped down from high up the tree in front of Seaton, hitting the ground with little effort or consequence. Before Seaton could yell out a warning, it grabbed Zoey by her back ankle as she stepped through the brush. She hit the ground with a shriek, squirming in an attempt to get lose. The creature grabbed her other ankle, spun around and swung her body at Seaton, causing him to jump back out of the way. Zoey's body missed him, but the creature followed through, smashing her against a tree trunk. The crack of her spine accompanied the shattering crush of plastic from the camera in her pocket. Her body twisted in an unnatural angle, killing her instantly.

Ezra spun around behind the killer and readied an arrow, but hesitated. If he missed, he risked hitting Seaton who was now rushing at the creature, clutching a spear. The creature grabbed the spear by the shaft sidestepping out of the way like a matador and flung Seaton into Ezra, knocking them both down and sending the arrow flying off to the side.

The creature let out a high-pitched, ear-piercing roar like an angry dinosaur. Three-inch claws projected from its fingers, appearing like switchblades. Seaton rolled off Ezra to find the spear stuck in Ezra's shoulder. Ezra pulled it out with a groan.

The creature closed in on the squirming men, its black eyes unblinking, baring its teeth with a slow, guttural growl. The sight was enough to scare them to death. The killer was covered in scales over its head and face, down its neck in a V-shape to its torso. Leathery skin filled in the blanks. Its hands and forearms were covered in similar dark green scales, like armor gloves. There was no hair to suggest it was a mammal but it had human-like skin, human-shaped ears, opposable thumbs and an upright, two-legged stance—a twisted hybrid of man and reptile, possibly born in the lab it still sheltered in.

Seaton pounced, landing his hunting knife in the creature's abdomen, below the line of scales. It lashed out, shrieking in protest, sinking its claws into Seaton's back, piercing through the backpack and clothing. Ezra jabbed the spear at the creature's eyes, narrowly missing as it leapt backward, black blood spurting from the wound Seaton had inflicted.

Ezra approached the creature with caution, the blackened spear point ready to run through the abomination. "Get an arrow ready," he instructed Seaton.

He did as he was told, moving slowly as the creature held a scaly hand to its wound. Ezra crept closer as Seaton pulled back an arrow and let it fly. The creature jumped up the tree to its left. The arrow caught it in the side of its thigh, but it was ten feet up the tree trunk, using its clawed hands and feet to scurry higher.

Seaton launched another arrow that ricocheted off a branch, missing its target and almost landing on Ezra as he ran to Zoey's side to see if anything could be done for her.

The killer was twenty-five feet up the tree in an instant, black blood dripping down the trunk and branches. It leapt to an adjacent tree with the grace and expertise of a squirrel. It flung itself from tree to tree like a monkey on the run.

Ezra pulled a glove off with his teeth and checked Zoey's jugular for a pulse but it was gone. She wasn't breathing and her eyes were fixed in the same look of terror she had when the creature had gotten a hold of her.

"She's gone," Ezra announced. He took her knife and bear spray. Checking her coat pocket, he found the broken shards of the smashed camera.

"We can't let it get away," Seaton said between labored breaths, his heartrate breaking a personal record. He handed over the last two arrows, pulled the atlatl out, and they gave chase.

The creature had a head start, but the rate of rattling leaves and crackling tree branches suggested its injuries were slowing it down. The fire behind the survivors was spreading, following their progress through the forest at a snail's pace, but smoke blowing in the wind soon became irritating to their lungs and threatened to give the killer sufficient cover to disappear. They couldn't let that happen. Ezra led the way, his right shoulder slumped from the spear wound, but it hadn't penetrated far enough to stop him. He kept pressure on it with one hand, hoping to stem the bleeding.

Even though the creature was injured, Seaton and Ezra, injured themselves, couldn't keep up with its pace, but they kept moving, determined to have their revenge. Seaton's back seared with pain from the holes and cuts made by the killer's claws.

Up ahead, the creature was slowing and descending gradually. Before they could catch up, its body dropped out of sight, flashing by through the branches. A dull thump suggested it had hit the ground.

"It's down," Ezra announced, exasperated. He was right.

When they came up on it, they found it flat on its back, motionless. The arrow stuck in its thigh was broken off close to the skin. Nonetheless, they approached with caution, spears ready to stab.

Ezra wasn't taking any chances. He raised his spear over his head with both arms, his injured shoulder protesting with stabbing pain. As he came thrusting down, aimed at where he hoped the creature's heart would be, it lifted its uninjured leg in defense, hitting Ezra square in the chest, the short claws on its feet tearing into his skin as it sent him backward.

Seaton hurled his spear at the creature as it stood up, but it bounced off the scaly armor on its chest. Behind the struggle, a steady, easterly wind was whipping speed into the forest fire as it devoured everything in its path. For the first time on Isolation Island, Seaton hoped the drizzle would turn into a pouring rain that might have a chance at keeping the fire from spreading too fast, but it was not to be. The inferno was making up ground as they fought for their lives. The creature picked itself up and crouched in an aggressive stance.

Ezra looked back at the wall of flames closing in on them. "Forget it," he shouted to Seaton. "Let's get to the raft and get out of here."

The creature didn't give them the option. It pounced on Seaton, pinning him to the ground. Seaton screamed his lungs out trying to keep the creature's head and teeth away as it pressed forward, mouth wide open.

Ezra lunged with his spear, stabbing the creature in its left eye. It yanked its head back, reacting before the weapon could penetrate any further. It pulled the spear out of Ezra's hands and turned it on him as it got to its feet, straddling Seaton.

With a head full of steam, Seaton kicked up at the creature's crotch as hard as he could, hoping there were tender genitals to strike. He hit a hard, flat emptiness without so much as causing a reaction. It had its one remaining good eye set on Ezra and thrust the spear forward.

The tip fell short of contact, but drew the creature close enough for Ezra to zap it in both eyes with the bear spray. The resulting cry of pain was unearthly. Seaton let out his own objection, feeling the burn as some of the mist rained down on his skin as well. He got to his feet, rubbing his face as he put some distance between himself and the creature.

The scaly monster was stunned and blinded, staggering backward with enough wounds to kill a weaker animal. It swung its arms and claws in blind defense, roaring out in pain.

Seaton readied his atlatl with a throwing spear and cocked it back. "Get out of the way," he ordered Ezra as he moved in for the kill.

With the moving target staggering, Seaton launched the spear with all his might. It struck center mass, right through the creature's chest, penetrating the scaly armor, protruding out its back like a skewer. But, it didn't bring the monster down. The creature pulled the spear back out of its chest and spun it around to use as a weapon.

Seaton remained steadfast. He launched another spear and another and still another in quick succession, all three striking with precision in a cluster around the first wound, knocking the creature down. Its back arched awkwardly, the tips of the spears preventing it from lying flat. Black blood shot from the wounds and oozed from the corners of its open mouth, spurting like a volcano with each cough of its last labored breaths.

The survivors weren't done. They were leaving nothing to chance. They each hovered over the monster stabbing it in the chest with their spears until they were sure it was dead. Its body twitched like a snake with its head cut off.

"Okay, I think it's dead," Seaton finally said, realizing they were now damaging evidence and a rare specimen.

"Doesn't hurt to be sure. There's no telling what this thing is capable of," Ezra replied, pulling his knife out for one last measure as the creature's arms and legs continued to switch.

Seaton stopped him, pointing at the fire they couldn't ignore any longer. "Forget it. It's dead. We gotta get out of here."

Ezra ignored him, stabbing his knife into the creature's neck, sawing across through tough, scaly skin. The head twitched forward as if on autopilot, biting down on Ezra's arm. The needle-like fangs between the larger teeth injected him with a dose of venom and let go. The stricken man fell backward, cursing, unaware the creature possessed a venomous bite. No one had told them about Kimmie Arden's encounter.

"Shit. It's not dead," Ezra spat, stabbing frantically again. He didn't stop until the chest was Swiss cheese, assuming the heart and lungs had to be somewhere in the vicinity.

"That's enough. It's dead," Seaton said, lightly kicking the now completely limp body. He was more concerned with the approaching fire. "Are you okay?"

"I'm fine," he insisted. "Come on, let's get this thing to the raft," he added, lifting the creature by its arms, careful to avoid the mouth and the sharp claws still protruding from the fingers.

"What? Why?"

"You want it to get burnt up in the fire? It's the only proof we have that it existed. Now come on, we're running out of time."

Seaton didn't argue. He grabbed the creature under the knees and they toted him through the forest as the smoke thickened in the wind. They weren't far from the raft, but Ezra, bleeding and full of venom went down to one knee, halting their progress.

Seaton dropped his end and tried to tend to his partner. "See? You're not okay. We gotta stop the bleeding at least."

"There's mo twime," Ezra slurred, getting back to his feet by sheer willpower. "Con'on."

Seaton complied and they made it another twenty or thirty feet before Ezra collapsed again, speaking unintelligible gibberish that only managed to convey the confusion and discomfort he was experiencing.

Seaton dropped the creature's legs and pulled Ezra to his feet in the face of slurred objections. "Come on buddy. Let's get you out of here." He threw Ezra's good arm over his shoulder and crutched him off to the raft which was closer than he had anticipated. He laid the dying man on the raft and began pulling it into the river.

"Wait! Don't leaf wivvout the fing," Ezra croaked.

Seaton looked up at the wall of flames spreading their way. It was closing in and things were heating up, but he might still have enough time. He left Ezra by the river's edge and ran back to retrieve the monster. Hurrying to where he thought they had abandoned it, fear struck his heart when he saw the empty matted grass where he had dragged Ezra from.

"Oh, no. You gotta be kidding me," he said in a state of instant panic. He grabbed his hat, pulling it down tighter and looked up, spotting the creature's foot jutting out from behind a tree in the distance. Relief washed over him, but he approached with caution, making sure it was still dead.

The body looked somehow worse than before. Deader, if such a thing were possible. He grabbed it by the ankles and dragged it to the river where he found Ezra quiet and still.

"Ezra," he shouted, hurrying to his side. He knelt next to him, propping the injured man's head on his lap. "Come on buddy. Stay with me." He checked for a pulse. It was weak, almost undetectable but it was there.

Ezra cracked his eyes open and let out a weak moan. "Leave me here."

Seaton ignored the request. He dragged the creature onto the raft beside Ezra and shoved it into the river, hopping on before the current swept them away.

SEATON ROGERS

Day 25

11:58am

Age: 33
Occupation: Screenwriter
Home: Utah
Status: Single

Seaton Rogers floated down the river without a paddle or anything to guide the raft, steady rain pelting him. The river was calm and lazy, getting deeper and narrower. He checked Ezra's pulse again. It was gone. Seaton had no medical training but attempted CPR anyway. He knelt over Ezra's fading body, administering chest compressions—how many? He wasn't quite sure, but settled on twenty, a number he thought was more than required but actually less than recommended.

"Come on, Ezra. Stay with me," he urged, rainwater streaking down his face as his hat became saturated.

After twenty compressions, he pulled his wet hat off his head and gave Ezra two breaths of air. Twenty more compressions. He continued to alternate for what seemed like an eternity, all the while keeping one eye on the killer's body.

The adrenaline Seaton had been running on was wearing off. His hands began to tremble. The raft bobbed up and down, disrupted by the chest compressions which were getting weaker and shallower as Seaton's energy drained and the cold penetrated to his bones.

One more cycle. Two breaths and twenty compressions. If he didn't elicit a response he'd have to give up before he collapsed. He administered the final breaths. Moving on to compressions, his lips tingled and burned like he had been kissing a puddle of hot sauce. He rubbed the sensation away with the wet gloves he was wearing. His lips began to chap and blister. Ezra's lips were doing the same, but the effect wasn't localized. The rest of his face seemed to be melting.

Seaton removed one of Ezra's gloves and found a hand that looked like it had been roasted over a fire or burned by acid. There was no resuscitating him. Panicked by the reaction, Seaton acted fast, guided by reflex. He emptied the dead man's pockets and, careful not to touch the skin, he flipped the body off the raft into the river. It sunk like a bag of stones.

Ezra Greer, the widower, the father, the falsely accused, the great survivalist, was gone, succumbing to the lethal venom coursing through his veins. The monster had claimed one more victim, even after its own death.

Seaton collapsed, lying flat on the cold wet tarp wrapped around the raft. He didn't know if he would be the final victim of the mysterious creature after touching Ezra's affected skin. Could the venom transfer in such a way? Only time would tell. The irony hit his weary mind—time is supposed to heal all wounds.

He lifted the radio to his mouth and called out, hoping Stephanie was listening. There was no response.

"Stephanie, if you can hear me, please respond. I'm the only one left. I've killed the monster. Over," he tried, providing more information.

"Are you sure?" Stephanie responded.

Just hearing another person's voice and knowing he wasn't alone brought him a great deal of comfort for the first time in his life. "I'm pretty sure. I've got the body with me and it hasn't moved in about twenty minutes," he reported, his words slow and weak. "I'm on the river, headed to the sea. Where are you? I need help. I'm injured and I'm freezing."

"Did anyone else make it?"

He choked back the urge to break down. "No." It was all he could muster.

"I'm in a cave on the northeast corner of the island. My territory is surrounded by water on three sides and a giant cliff on the other. I've got no way to get to you. Over."

It wasn't what Seaton wanted to hear, but he knew he couldn't expect anything more. She couldn't exactly hop into an ambulance and race across the island to save him.

"Do you still have a first aid kit?" he asked, fishing for any shred of hope he could find.

"Yes."

"Take the first aid kit and follow the shore. I'll try to get to you somehow. Do you copy?"

"Yes, but how are you going to get to me? You're going to have to cross the water one way or another. Over."

She made a valid point, but Seaton's mind was running on pure desperation and wishful thinking.

"Maybe I can find where the killer left the Medline. If not, Wes Wood told me where to find a boat he made. Worse comes to worst, I'll try using the raft I'm on now. Over."

"That sounds very risky, Seaton. Maybe there's another way. I can try to come to you somehow," Stephanie suggested. "Over."

"That'll take too long. I've got no supplies. I can't even start a fire. I'm wet and cold and exhausted. If I don't bleed to death, I'll freeze to death. Keep the radio on. I'll contact you when I reach the ocean and assess the situation. Over."

"Okay. I'll be waiting. Please be careful, Seaton. And, good luck. Over and out."

Seaton clipped the radio to his beltline and gave the creature a nudge with his boot. It was still dead.

4:19pm

Despite Seaton's fear, the river was gentle on him, carrying him and his cargo toward the ocean. He wasn't sure how long it had taken, curled up in a ball in the rain, trying to keep from shivering to death, but when he saw the open water spreading out like a misty mirage in front of him, he wondered if it was real or if he had died and entered some disturbing purgatory.

Much to his surprise, in answer to his repeated wishes over the past few hours, the Medline appeared anchored near shore, up the rocky beach. Tears flooded his eyes. Until that moment, he had refused to believe he was doomed if he couldn't find the boat, but deep down, he knew it was true. Thankfully, he didn't have to find out. He plunged his freezing hands into the icy water, paddling slowly but surely toward land. He didn't want the river to spit him out into the ocean.

He guided the raft into a bank of boulders on the edge of land and hopped off. His tired, stiffened muscles had a hard time pulling the raft out of the water, but fueled by hope and optimism, he managed.

No matter how exhausted he was, after making it so far, he refused to abandon the only proof he had of the true nature of what had happened to the contestants on Isolation Island. He dismantled the raft, wrapping the monster in the tarp and using the cordage to drag the body to the Medline. His feet plunged into the ice cold salt water, slipping on sharp rocks as he reached out a hand to touch the boat. It was there. It was real. It was manmade, a reminder there was a whole civilization thousands of miles away waiting for his return; waiting for his remarkable story.

He climbed aboard the Medline with cordage in hand to pull the killer's body after him. It took all his remaining strength. As soon as the body was settled on the floor, his stomach began to growl as if it had been waiting for the proper time to remind him he hadn't eaten since early that morning. He pulled up anchor, sat down under the canopy, out of the rain, and started the engine. The sound was pure music to his ears. He radioed Stephanie to report his status. If he could make it to her cave, he might have a chance of survival.

Chapter 30

Day 25

5:22pm

Seaton Rogers made landfall, accelerating the Medline up on the sandy beach Stephanie had guided him to. The beaching of the boat wasn't intentional but it was done and undoing it wasn't the priority.

Stephanie rushed over, wrapped in a tarp to keep her clothes dry underneath. She motioned for Seaton to hop off the boat. "Come on. We have to get you out of those wet clothes," she said, the rain still coming down steadily.

Seaton wobbled on his feet. The waves lapping the back end of the boat knocking him off balance. He disregarded Stephanie's instructions and pulled the monster's body over the edge.

"Lookout," he warned, flipping the body onto the beach as soon as she was clear. He jumped down, his legs folding like an accordion upon impact.

Stephanie helped him up, ignoring the wrapped body. It was the first time they had come face to face. Even though he was half dead, he couldn't help noticing her warm, inviting facial features penetrating through the dirt and ash on her face. It was a mild relief, but looks could be deceiving.

Seaton dragged the body away from the reach of the ocean. Stephanie followed, urging him to take it easy and get out of the wet clothes.

"I've got some dry clothes for you wrapped in a tarp. You can use my rain gear, too. It's going to be a little short," she said, sizing up his body. "But it'll do." He was about seven inches taller than her, but his string bean physique made sharing her clothes somewhat doable. "Wow. Were you always this skinny?" she asked, pulling his wet coat off like a mother undressing a child who came in from playing in the snow.

She had a fire waiting for him and walked him over to it. The warmth hit him like a soft embrace, the flickering flames of life mesmerizing him. He had just been running from one fire and now saved by another. He let Stephanie continue. His weakened body jerked around as she peeled off layer after layer of wet, dirty clothes. The holes and tears in the ones coming off his back didn't escape her attention. She held up his sweater, looking through the large holes.

The last layer, a smelly old t-shirt held onto the wounds on his back. She spun him around to examine the resistance and found the scratches inflicted by the creature peeking through the shredded, blood-soaked shirt. She pulled it off gently. He was too cold and tired to object or acknowledge the pain.

"Did that thing do this?" she asked.

"Yeah," Seaton replied. "But, wait till you see what *I* did to *it*," he quipped with a nod and a smirk.

Suddenly, he was aware of the fact he was standing almost naked in front of a woman he had just met, stripped down to only his boxer shorts. She didn't seem to care, spinning him back around, reaching to pull the boxers off. He pulled away guarding himself.

"Hold on there," he said, almost backing into the fire.

"My goodness, when was the last time you ate," she exclaimed, seeing the ribs protruding through his skin. "Come on, off with the underwear. This is no time to be shy. We have to get you into some dry clothes, warm you up and get some food in you."

He turned away and followed her orders while she unpacked some dry clothes from the tarp full of supplies. He stood bare-assed for a moment, his skin and bones shivering near the fire. She tossed him a pair of long underwear with pink flowers on them.

He pulled them on, the cuffs gripping his calves a few inches below the knee. She threw a pair of sweatpants at him next, same size. She had a pair of long socks he could use to cover his feet and pull up over the bottoms of the sweatpants, giving him a poor man's golfing knickers look. A blanket flew through the air next, landing on his head.

"Sit down and cover up your front with that," she instructed, opening the first aid kit as she approached him.

"Thank you."

She draped his front with a tarp to keep out the rain. Once the blood on his back was mopped up with gauze, it became apparent the wounds weren't as bad as they first looked. She used a small bottle of hydrogen peroxide to disinfect the wounds and patched them with antibiotic ointment and gauze. He did his best to mask the pain it caused him, choosing a brave face over the risk of looking like a wuss. Heroes don't cry in pain.

He *was* the hero. He had slayed the proverbial dragon, but they literally weren't out of the woods yet. They were stranded on a deserted island with limited supplies and no realistic way to leave.

Stephanie pulled the pot of coffee from the fire and poured him a cup. She had thought of everything to make him more comfortable and nurse him back to health and it didn't go unnoticed or unappreciated.

Seaton sipped the unsweetened brew, enjoying its warm trickle down to his stomach with every swallow.

"Did you bring the cameras?" he asked, hoping she had complied with the request he had made from the Medline.

"Yes sir, right here," she replied, pulling the handheld from her backpack to prove it.

"Good. We'll be losing light soon. Let's get this monster on the record."

"Let's do it. I'm dying to see this thing."

Seaton attempted to untie the cordage binding the killer's body but his hands started trembling as he stepped away from the fire. Stephanie took over.

"Here, let me do it," she insisted. "You stay close to the fire."

"Give me your knife." He held out his hand, eyes on the package. "Just in case," he added, glancing at her face.

She handed it over and he stood ready to attack as she untied the knots and slowly peeled the tarp back. The creature's uninjured eye was the same in death as it was in life, deep and dark like a shark's eye.

"Stay clear of its head," Seaton warned. "The bastard bit Ezra after it was dead. Some neurological reflex."

"That's how Ezra died?" she asked.

He nodded in reply and she readied the camera.

"This is it," she narrated, sweeping the camera slowly around the details of the monster. "This is the creature that has made our life a living hell on Isolation Island. This the animal that killed everyone else."

She zoomed in on the face, the scales on its chest and arms, down past the torn pants it was still wearing, to the claws on its feet. She lifted the arms out to the side to continue the visual examination. Under its right arm she found the number 23 tattooed on the human-like skin below the hairless armpit.

"Did you see this?" She motioned for Seaton to see for himself.

He furrowed his brow. The evidence this creature had ties to normal humans did not compute. They checked under the other arm. They documented a series of Korean symbols along with some Russian letters tattooed on that side. Neither of them knew what they meant. They flipped the creature over and checked for more but they didn't find any. It was enough to suggest the creature had been engineered by man or at least had enough previous contact with humans to be marked.

"Okay," Stephanie said, holding the camera steady with both hands. "Now for the money shot. Take its pants off and let's get a look at its junk," she said, trying to lighten the mood. Although many people had died, they should both be happy to be alive and enjoy the victory.

Seaton couldn't help cracking a smile as he followed her instructions. His lips quivered back to a frown when he flipped the creature over and the menacing teeth were within striking distance. He wasn't convinced they were safe, despite the fact the creature hadn't moved since biting Ezra and its throat had been slit.

He yanked the pants off to find nothing but a patch of scaly armor where they expected its reproductive organs to be. "Okay. That's weird," he commented.

"It's no weirder than the rest of it," Stephanie said, getting a close up of the area.

The backside wasn't any more remarkable. They found a standard human butt—two cheeks and a hole.

"Should we give it a name?" Stephanie asked, doubling back on small details with the camera for the sake of being thorough.

"You mean like, Frederick or…"

"No. I mean like Bigfoot or the Chupacabra," Stephanie

elaborated.

"How about the Abominable Asshole?" he joked.

"Or something scientific," she suggested. "Like, Abominabus Assholus."

Seaton looked the creature up and down trying to define it. All he saw was a monster, an abomination, a creature that shouldn't exist, a savage killer. "It doesn't deserve a name," he decided, turning away back to the fire.

"What are we going to do with it? Bury it?"

"I haven't decided yet. We'll bring it back to your camp for the time being.

11:58pm

The killer attacked Seaton in his dreams. The faces of the dead flashing in his mind as the monster took their lives with snarling teeth and razor sharp claws. He woke up screaming, arms flailing in defense of the invisible attacker within his nightmare.

Stephanie jolted out of her slumber, curled up next to him and grabbed his arms. "Seaton! Stop! You're dreaming. You're okay," she repeated, trying to subdue him with an embrace, pinning his arms against his body.

His eyes opened to the flickering light of the fire, distant ocean waves erasing the screams from within the nightmare. He wasn't convinced it was only a dream. He wasn't convinced they were safe.

"Are you cold?" Stephanie asked. "You're trembling."

He turned to look at the tarp-wrapped body of the monster which had tormented him in his dreams and in real life. "It's not dead," he insisted. "It's waiting to kill us while we sleep."

"We've been asleep for a few hours, Sweetie. If it was waiting to kill us, it would have done it already." She looked up at him, turning his head toward her with her hand. "It's dead. It's not coming back."

"We have to get rid of it," he decided.

"Get rid of it? How?"

"We'll wrap it back up in the tarp so birds won't get to it, stick it on a raft and float it out to sea. We can use the boat Wes built. We add a message in a bottle, an SOS with our GPS coordinates. No matter where the boat floats to, with the creature aboard, someone will definitely investigate. It might be our only chance at getting rescued."

"That's like a one in a bazillion shot."

"If you have a better idea, I'd love to hear it."

"I was kind of thinking we'd use the Medline to get the hell off this cursed island," she said.

Seaton shook his head. "We can't travel across the Pacific in that thing. There isn't much fuel left. Even on a full tank, how far do you think we could get? And then what? We'd just float around the north Pacific. No thank you. We can use the last of the fuel for traveling around the island or fishing or we can save it for an emergency."

"You're right. And, we can't keep this decomposing body here. We can send it out to sea tomorrow. But, right now, you need to get some sleep. You should see the wild look in your eyes. I'm worried about you."

Seaton agreed but insisted on wrapping the creature in the tarp again and binding it with cordage, still unconvinced it wasn't going to come back to life and eat them in their sleep. Stephanie humored him.

STEPHANIE HAMILTON

Day 26

4:09pm

Age: 29
Occupation: Artist
Home: Colorado
Status: Single

Using her own blood, Stephanie Hamilton wrote an SOS message on the backside of the parchment which bared the treasure clues.

SOS
STRANDED
TWO SURVIVORS
SEATON THEODORE ROGERS
HANKSVILLE, UTAH
STEPHANIE PEACHES HAMILTON
SILVERTON, COLORADO

She squeezed more blood from multiple sites to pen the GPS coordinates of their exact location. Seaton had begged her to let him do it, but she insisted she be the one to do it, using the fact that she was the island's official artist. He countered that he was the island's official writer and a playful debate ensued over whether the job was a work of art or literature. Stephanie won the argument when she pointed out he had lost enough blood already.

Seaton furrowed his eyebrows, squinting at the finished distress letter. "Your middle name is Peaches?" he asked, pretending to stifle an artificial laugh.

"Yeah. Stephanie Peaches Hamilton. You wanna make something out of it," she said in a mock tough-guy voice, pretending to threaten him with her dukes. "What's wrong with

Peaches?" she smiled. "Everybody likes peaches, *Theodore*."

"Okay, okay," he conceded, signaling a desire for a ceasefire.

"Teddy," she continued to tease. "Teddy Bear. You're the skinniest Teddy Bear I've ever seen. We must to fatten you up." The latter she turned out in a harsh, generic European accent.

"All right, all right. Peaches is kind of cute. I like it on you. I'm just worried if anyone finds the note they might confuse you with all the *other* Stephanie Peaches Hamiltons out there."

She ignored the jab. "It'll be fine. Let's get this over with," she encouraged.

They loaded the killer's body into Wes Wood's crude boat. They had used the Medline to bring it to Stephanie's peninsula and reinforced the frame with extra wood, but it was still going to have a hard time surviving the Pacific Ocean. Anything they could have built would have had a hard time. They knew there was little chance of success, but even a one percent chance was better than nothing. The afternoon's ceremony was more for closure than anything else. Stephanie went along with it because she knew Seaton needed it to regain his sanity. The paranoia he experienced over thinking the creature might come back to life any minute would have torn him apart eventually. If it was floating in the ocean somewhere, it couldn't hurt them on the island.

They did keep one piece of the monster. A sliver of "forensic evidence" as they called it. Since the head had been halfway chopped off by Ezra's knife, Seaton finished the job. They had buried the head to keep as proof the videos weren't a hoax in case the body disappeared in the ocean. The rest of the headless body was wrapped in a tarp (trimmed down to only what was essential to cover the creature) and ready to set adrift.

Stephanie captured the moment on video. They placed the SOS message in the big glass bottle, tossed it in the boat and shoved it off. The tide pulled it out over the calm waves without capsizing it. Soon it would become a tiny dot in the watery desert called the Pacific Ocean.

Seaton and Stephanie had the entire island to themselves now.

Their spirits were up, perhaps only high on the triumph of defeating the killer. But, the reality of survival in the wilderness would soon even them out again. Only one of the dangers had been removed and new ones were coming. Winter wasn't far off and, although they had food, they were losing weight, withering away slowly. Winter would pose a new set of challenges. Without carbohydrates, their bodies would continue to breakdown muscle instead of fat. Sources of vitamin C were in short supply and would disappear over the coming weeks. Scurvy was a real and agonizing possibility.

Isolation Island had been meant to be an endurance survival competition, but it was also supposed to be a TV show. If the survivalists stayed too long, it'd make for boring TV. The harsh winter was meant to up the ante and force an end to the competition, the last hardcore survivalist taking victory and the million-dollar prize.

Seaton and Stephanie knew winter was meant to be the end. Deep down, they felt the nagging voices reminding them they'd have to endure the impossible. It was no joke, but for now, they were content, basking in victory, spitting in the face of the unknown, prepared to fight anything that tried to stop them.

They each held up a big middle finger directed at the creature as it floated away from *their* island, *their* home.

Chapter 31

Day 39

4:20pm

By Day 39, a little island romance was brewing. They were quickly finding they had a lot in common and they enjoyed each other's company. They joked that because they were both introverts, they'd end up living on opposite sides of the island, but the truth was, they liked each other. Whether it was the circumstances they overcame to get to Day 39 or the last man and woman on the planet feeling, a bond was forming which could only be beneficial to their survival. Parts of them wanted to jump all over each other and go wild, but there was no need to rush. There was all the time in the world.

Using the Medline, they had located several camps and belongings they planned to use to create a memorial for the contestants whose bodies and bones would forever remain scattered throughout Isolation Island. They had collected some additional supplies from the fallen survivalists, too, and they moved everything to Seaton's original camp in the southeast corner of the island. Things were looking up.

Seaton and Stephanie hadn't gotten past the celebratory phase yet. Survivor's guilt hadn't gotten a hold of them yet. They fluctuated between the grief attached to all the deaths of their fellow survivalists and being thankful—not just that they themselves were alive, but that anyone at all had survived to someday tell the world what had happened on the tiny, unknown island in the frigid Pacific Ocean.

Stephanie made a point to be chipper and positive, hoping to prevent PTSD from grabbing Seaton by the brain. They spent day 39, an unseasonably warm day, on the sandy beach they called Daytona Beach because of its proximity to Seaton's original camp which was situated on a Florida-shaped peninsula.

Seaton sat on a blanket on the sand enjoying a cup of

dandelion tea made from the last of the little yellow flowers they'd see until spring, should they survive the winter. Using the video camera, he watched clips Stephanie had filmed the first two weeks after insertion.

Stephanie knelt down next to him, her hands behind her back concealing a surprise. "You know what today is?" she asked.

"Another day closer to winter?" Seaton replied, not meaning to sound as negative as it came out, but it was true.

"It's Day 39," she perked up an extra notch with a smile. "You know what that means?"

Seaton smiled, he knew what it meant. "If we were on Survivor, we'd be done today." A favorite pastime of theirs involved going through each Survivor season with a fine toothed comb, analyzing each player's behavior and strategy. "But, we would have had to deal with like twenty other people. That would have been impossible," he joked, pretending to prefer dealing with a vicious mutant killer over being forced to socialize.

"Ding, ding, ding, ding. Bingo. Give the man a prize," Stephanie rang out. From behind her back, she pulled a homemade, (or island-made) ukulele. It was raw and primitive, like it had been stolen from the set of The Flintstones, with fishing line for strings, but it was a thoughtful gift.

"Oh my god. You made this?" Seaton delighted.

"Do you like it?"

"I love it," he admitted, giving it a hug before trying to tune it with the wooden pegs that were going to need some extra work.

"Sorry it's not a guitar. I ran out of room for the strings. You only have four," she explained.

"That's okay. A ukulele is more fitting for island life. Maybe we can make some fake palm trees and grass skirts so we can feel like we're in Hawaii." He gave her a hug and a peck on the cheek. "Thank you so much."

Stephanie wrinkled her nose with a playful smile and wiggled her way under the ukulele, into his arms, turning to face the ocean. "Hawaii? Really? That's your go-to tropical destination?"

"What's wrong with Hawaii?" he asked, strumming the still out of tune instrument in front of her crossed arms.

"Too crowded," she replied, resting the back of her head on his chest.

"Well, you have a point there. Where do you want to go when we get out of here?" he asked. They had made a pact not to use ifs while talking about leaving Isolation Island. They *were* going to leave, someday. They made their own entertainment out of planning their future off the island—interviews, book deals, Stephanie's art would be priceless, Seaton would write the screenplay in a blitz of fame and fortune, they dreamed. Then, they'd take the money and buy their own island in the Caribbean and disappear forever.

To their left were the three bundles of firewood waiting to be lit to signal for rescue to passing ships or aircraft. In front of them, a small fire kept them warm because "unseasonable warmth" on Isolation Island only meant a high in the 50s.

"We can move to Coxen Hole," Stephanie replied, the chuckle in her voice suggesting she was making up the provocative name.

"Cocks in hole?" Seaton laughed. "That's a real place?"

"Coxen Hole," she repeated and spelled it out for him. "It's on an island called Roatan in Honduras."

He couldn't help laughing again. "Seriously? I've heard of Roatan but Coxen Hole? That sounds like it can't be real. Although it does sound like a fun place."

"Oh, it's lots of fun. We definitely have to try it," she flirted. "What were you planning to do tonight?"

"I was going to work on the chess set." He had been working on it for days, carving out a new piece every day.

"When are you going to teach me to play?"

"When I've got the set complete. Don't worry. There'll be plenty of time. Or maybe, I'll write you a song tonight with my jiffy new ukulele."

"Jiffy?"

"Yeah. Jiffy. It means…"

Both their faces reacted at the same time, eyes bulging as if they'd pop right out of their heads. Their ears seemed to tingle with the faint sound in the distance. They held their breath in unison, afraid to say a word lest it hinder their ability to tell if the sound was getting louder or not, whether it was coming or going or passing by. The deep whirring pulsated louder, sweeping across the sky, bouncing off the ocean surface.

They looked up and started screaming, the sound now obvious

and unmistakable. Seaton took a burning stick from the fire and hurried to light the signal fires, the wind fighting him in a stubborn attempt to make things difficult.

The helicopter appeared in a flash, sweeping out from above the treetops, turning in their direction. Stephanie and Seaton jumped up and down, waving and yelling for help. The giant SOS sign they had laid out with rocks on the beach was enough to get the pilot to land.

A rescue crew poured out as soon as they touched down, swarming on the survivors. One of them attempted to shout questions over the roar of the chopper, but he couldn't be heard entirely except for, "Is there anyone else with you?"

Seaton shouted NO and shook his head. Sand seared into their skin, whipping up from the beach, caught in the chopper's whirlwind.

The rescuers whisked away the couple, into the helicopter, taking off as quickly as they had arrived. Their priority was making sure the survivors were safe, not the story they had to tell. There would be time for that later. They'd make several trips to retrieve remains and lost video footage over the next few days.

A paramedic checked out Stephanie and Seaton in the helicopter—vital signs, injuries, mental status. It was obvious they were suffering from malnutrition.

It all happened too fast. One minute they were stranded, the next Stephanie was looking out the window of the recue chopper, watching the island pass by underneath them—so peaceful and innocent. Trees blanketed the amoeba-like body of land. She couldn't even see the old, abandoned lab. She smiled watching the island getting smaller as they sped away over the ocean.

Seaton leaned in toward the pilot to holler above the stifling sound of the chopper. "Did you find the creature?"

The pilot turned to check Seaton's facial expression. Seeing the castaway wasn't joking, he asked, "What creature?"

Seaton waved him off. He'd have to explain the whole ordeal later under less noisy conditions. He reached out to hold Stephanie's hand and they shared the look they had been dying to experience—they were saved. They were going home.

Seaton looked out the window at the ocean, the rescue ship in sight. The blackened remains of the Mothership passed beneath them. Rescuers collected piles of barely recognizable human body parts on deck.

Seaton clutched the camera, hoping the video evidence would be enough to convince the world of the strange face of death he and Stephanie and all their fallen comrades had encountered on Isolation Island.

THE END

Also by Johnny Moscato:

BLOBS

The Project

Jimmy Darwin

The Project 2

Printed in Great Britain
by Amazon